W9-BWM-958

THE TASTE OF
SUGAR

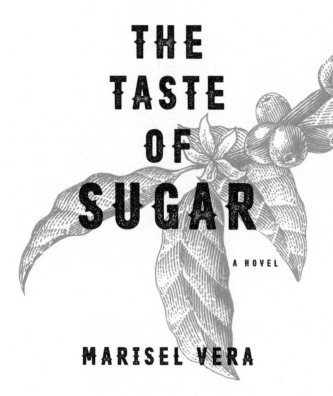

THE
TASTE
OF
SUGAR

A NOVEL

MARISEL VERA

LIVERIGHT PUBLISHING CORPORATION

A Division of W. W. Norton & Company

Independent Publishers Since 1923

This is a work of fiction. All incidents and dialogue, and all characters with the exception of some well-known historical and public figures, are products of the author's imagination and are not to be construed as real. Where real-life historical or public figures appear, the situations, incidents, and dialogues concerning those persons are entirely fictional and are not intended to depict actual events or to change the entirely fictional nature of the work. In all other respects, any resemblance to persons living or dead is entirely coincidental.

For information about permission to reproduce selections from this book, write to Permissions, Liveright Publishing Corporation, a division of W. W. Norton & Company, Inc., 500 Fifth Avenue, New York, NY 10110

For information about special discounts for bulk purchases, please contact W. W. Norton Special Sales at specialsales@wwnorton.com or 800-233-4830

Manufacturing by Lake Book Manufacturing
Book design by Chris Welch
Production manager: Beth Steidle

Library of Congress Cataloging-in-Publication Data

Names: Vera, Marisel, author.
Title: The taste of sugar : a novel / Marisel Vera.
Description: First Edition. | New York, NY : Liveright Publishing Corporation, [2020] | Includes bibliographical references.
Identifiers: LCCN 2019056388 | ISBN 9781631497735 (hardcover) | ISBN 9781631497742 (epub)
Subjects: GSAFD: Love stories.
Classification: LCC PS3622.E7 T37 2020 | DDC 813/.6—dc23
LC record available at https://lccn.loc.gov/2019056388

Liveright Publishing Corporation, 500 Fifth Avenue, New York, N.Y. 10110
www.wwnorton.com

W. W. Norton & Company Ltd., 15 Carlisle Street, London W1D 3BS

1 2 3 4 5 6 7 8 9 0

For my husband and our children.

In memory of our ancestors.

INDEX OF CHARACTERS

Juan Cortés *m.* Margarita Fernández

Claudina

Ysabel Cortés *m.* Alegro Villanueva

Eusemia Villanueva

Raulito Villanueva

Luis Manuel Vega

Raúl Vega *m.* Angelina Maldonado ~ Inés Quiñónes

Luisito Vega

Teodoro Sánchez *m.* Prudencia Ortiz

Elena Sánchez de Rojas

Vicente Vega *m.* Valentina Sánchez

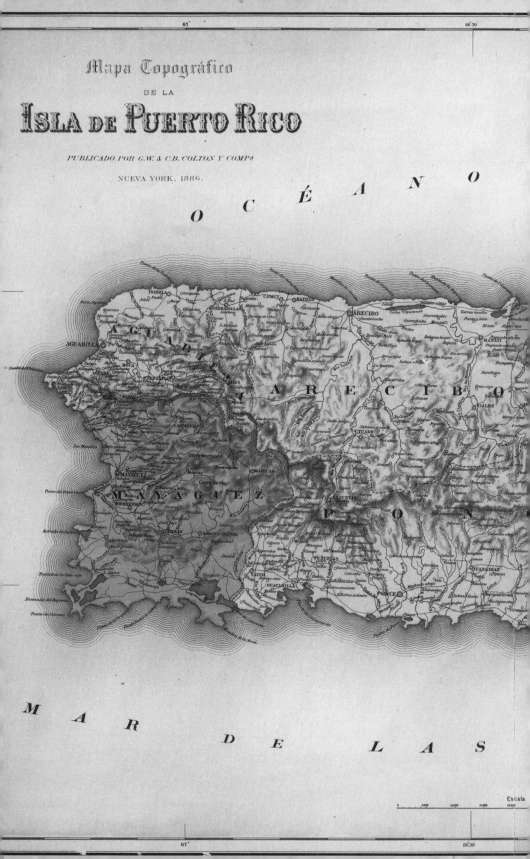

Mapa Topográfico

DE LA

ISLA DE PUERTO RICO

PUBLICADO POR G.W. & C.B. COLTON Y COMPª

NUEVA YORK, 1886.

O C É A N O

M A R   D E   L A S

Escala

A T L A N T I C O

S. JUAN DE PUERTO RICO

B A Y A M O N

ISLA DE VIEQUE

A N T I L L A S

Signos convencionales

Límite de departamento
Cabecera de departamento
Cabecera de término jurisdiccional
Barrio

250.000.

10.000 Metros

THE TASTE OF
SUGAR

ONCE UPON A TIME ON THE ISLAND OF PUERTO RICO

I n 1825, on the journey to Utuado to buy land, Vicente's grandfather, Don Luis Manuel Vega, saw what he thought were piles of rubbish along the side of the road. But as his carriage drew nearer, the rubbish became rows of people—men, women, and children—passed out in a faint. When he stopped for supplies with his black slave Benedicto, Luis Manuel Vega learned that these poor souls were among los hambrientos, the starving, who had left the villages and countryside for the city of Ponce to beg for bread. Luis Manuel Vega felt sorry for the hungry people, but quickly turned his attention to the variety of goods at the market; it seemed everything was sold en la plaza, including black slaves punished for rebellion or disobedience with iron collars shackled around their necks. When his master's back was turned, Benedicto and the other enslaved men nodded to each other. As they continued their journey, Luis Manuel Vega thought it prudent to remind Benedicto of how fortunate he was to have a kind master who would never think of putting him in manacles.

Luis Manuel Vega, father of Raúl Vega, grandfather of Vicente, had little knowledge of the reality of coffee farming. As a former merchant, he had been drawn to his new vocation by his coffee addiction and what he imagined would be an easy life such as that of a hacendado he had once known. The man had owned a large coffee hacienda and had spent his life in idleness because he had many slaves. But Luis Manuel Vega had only the young Benedicto, whom he had bought from a hacendado with a coffee plantation in Peñuelas. Benedicto turned out to be a good investment for Vicente's grandfather because he knew how to prepare virgin land for planting shade trees like the banana and guava trees necessary to protect the coffee bushes. (Luis Manuel Vega supervised while Benedicto and some peones cleared the grass and weeds with machetes.) He taught Luis Manuel Vega, and later his son Raúl, who would become Vicente's father, everything he knew about growing coffee: like how to drop the seeds in holes deep as a man's hand, seeds that would take five years to bear good fruit. (Luis Manuel Vega was too cheap to buy the coffee shrubs that would flower within months, and his son Raúl too poor.)

Benedicto didn't know that while many workers would be needed during la cosecha de café—the laborious coffee-cherry picking harvest— few workers in those early years were to be found among the meager population of Utuado. He didn't know about the heavy expense of hiring oxen and experienced oxen drivers to transport coffee berries to the merchants from a mountainous region with poor or nonexistent roads. He didn't know that during the rainy season, teams of oxen got stuck in the muddy trails. He didn't know about the bandits who robbed and even killed the oxen drivers. Worse, Benedicto didn't understand the complex system of coffee financing—the never-ending borrowing to meet expenses and subsequent mortgaging of the land, or the fact that the coffee market was at the mercy of foreign manipulation of coffee prices and import/export duties.

On his eightieth birthday, years after Benedicto had died from overwork, as Luis Manuel Vega drank a cup of café negro made from his own coffee beans, his heart ceased to beat and his son Raúl Vega found himself owner of a coffee plantation that belonged more to the island's Spanish businessmen than to him. But even with the labor of his two sons, Vicente and Luisito, Raúl Vega was forced to sell all the land except for a hundred cuerdas, which he proceeded to mortgage as necessary. As the years passed, when the coffee harvests were good and prices high, Vicente's father paid off his debts, and when the harvests weren't as good and coffee prices sank, he went to the merchants for credit. Such was the life of a small coffee farmer.

PART ONE

PUERTO RICO

CHAPTER ONE

THERE ONCE WAS A PROMINENT FAMILY

Years before Vicente's grandfather migrated to Utuado, la familia Cortés was a prominent landowning family. Like so many of the pioneer families, los Cortéses were analfabetos—they couldn't read or write or do simple arithmetic, and were easily swindled by ladrones, the merchants and government officials who could.

When Juan Cortés and Margarita Fernández married in 1839, they had modest hopes—such as that they could send their children to bed with bellies full of rice and beans and maybe bacalao, and live in a decent house of their own where the cold rain from a good aguacero didn't startle them awake. But Juan Cortés was forced to work as an agregado for Luis Manuel Vega, on land that had once belonged to his ancestors.

Now a tenant farmer, Juan Cortés was lent a parcel of land where he built his home, a bohío of coconut palms. Juan Cortés planted corn and tomatoes and root vegetables like ñame and malanga and batata. He raised a goat so his children could have milk. As agreed upon, he turned over to Luis Manuel Vega half of his crops and a quantity of goat milk.

Juan Cortés, whose destiny was to become the great-grandfather of Vicente's half brother Raulito, managed most days to feed his family— six children in ten years—some kind of meal, even if only batatas that his wife boiled in salted water. His children, like many others in the countryside, were naked until they were seven or eight years old. Twice yearly, Juan Cortés was taxed on a third of a half year's expected earnings. As the cost of basic necessities such as a pair of pants, a cooking pot, kerosene, sank Don Juan Cortés and Doña Margarita Fernández deeper into debt, the honorific *don* y *doña* titles were used only in reference to what la familia Cortés had once been.

Don Juan Cortés learned over the years to be grateful to have something to eat and a mat of dry straw to lay his head. Now the entire Cortés family woke at dawn. On good days, they drank their breakfast of café puya, black coffee without milk or sugar, and worked until the sun eased back into the earth. When their first daughter, Jesenia, died, Juan Cortés recalled a particular day when they had picked coffee in the rain. The little girl had cried as the cold raindrops fell on her skin, and he'd turned away.

Everything changed for la familia Cortés in 1849 because of "la falta de brazos," the scarcity of workers. Puerto Rico's new Spanish governor, the soon-to-be-despised Juan de la Pezuela, under the pretext of maintaining civil order, decreed that all free males from sixteen to sixty who owned less than four cuerdas of land, and had no other means of support, register as jornaleros. Dayworkers. It was illegal for landowners like Vicente's grandfather to have agregados or sharecroppers. Now, instead of continuing as a tenant farmer, Juan Cortés was obligated to work a year at a time for a landowner under penalty of prison. He was paid una miseria. Jornaleros like Juan Cortés were required to work where they were assigned, often far from where they lived. Barefoot men carried the poles and the plant fiber walls of their bohíos from one place to the other with their families in tow.

When Juan Cortés registered as a jornalero, he insisted that his name be written down as *Don Juan Cortés*. It was true that he was little better than a slave, but he was still proud that he had come from buena familia. At any given time, the authorities could ask Juan Cortés to produce la libreta, the notebook he was required to carry that detailed his physical characteristics, his name, place of residence, debts, terms of current employment, specified hours of work, and in which his employers praised or condemned his labor—a libreta that he couldn't read. Juan Cortés was paid with vales, tickets or scraps of scrip, which could be redeemed only at the plantation store for goods at exorbitant prices.

Once a month Juan Cortés reported to the mayor with la libreta to prove that he'd worked the required number of days. Employers could add a complaint in the notebook for any reason—el jornalero had taken sick or broken the blade of the employer's machete, or worked too slow or talked too much, and so on. After a third complaint, el jornalero would be sentenced to the penitentiary. No one sentenced to the chain gang at La Puntilla de San Juan had ever been seen again—like a vecino of Juan Cortés, his neighbor Ismael Pagán, the father of eight children.

The wife of Juan Cortés, Doña Margarita Fernández, and four of their six children died only a few years after the inception of la libreta from illnesses he could not name. He knew only that they'd been hungry and without proper clothing, and that they'd slept on the ground in a hut made of straw susceptible to wind and rain. His wife had cooked their daily meal of plantains or sweet potatoes or sometimes beans in an iron kettle over a fogón, a makeshift stove of sticks and stones. Smoke stained the walls and the ceiling, where spiders the size of a woman's palm made their home between the plaited leaves. Juan Cortés had kept vigil with his children upon his beloved's death. Days before, she had turned forty. People in the old days had lived much longer than forty years; why, his grandmother had lived to be ninety! When they first married, Margarita Fernández's face had been so full and round that dimples flashed in her cheeks when she smiled. Juan Cortés hadn't seen those dimples in years.

The day after Doña Margarita Fernández died, pallbearers carried her in a plain wood box down the mountain to the church graveyard in town. Juan Cortés followed the coffin. He hoped that he could persuade the priest to consent to say a prayer, although he didn't know how he could pay him. His wife would have wanted it.

The next day, the hacendado registered his absence from work en la libreta.

"I wrote that you missed a day of work." El hacendado was descended from merchants in Catalonia, and he prided himself on his scrupulous honesty. He made a point of explaining his notes to his illiterate jornaleros como Juan Cortés.

"Enterré a mi mujer ayer," Juan Cortés said.

"Yes, it's too bad about your wife, but my business is coffee." El hacendado scribbled in the notebook.

Juan Cortés raised his hand to strike him. But what would become of his children if he were sent to prison at La Puntilla de San Juan? A poor man, a father of motherless children, could not afford to give a hacendado una bofetada even if el cabrón deserved it. He dropped his hand to his side.

When Ysabel and Claudina, the only two children of Juan Cortés and Margarita Fernández to survive to adulthood, fell in love, Juan Cortés gave them fatherly advice.

"No te juntes con los prietos," Juan Cortés told Ysabel. "He is black and we are descended from familia blanca."

To his daughter Claudina, "Ese hombre loves the card games more than he loves you."

Though his daughters listened with respeto, they both chose to go off with their lovers. Juan Cortés was partly mollified to learn that when Ysabel's husband, Alegro Villanueva, had registered as a jornalero at the mayor's office, he had declared himself hijo de padre blanco.

It didn't matter to Ysabel Cortés whether her bridegroom's father was white or not because she had married Alegro Villanueva for love. She wanted to gaze forever into his eyes that were the brown of a coconut husk. Her fingertips brushed the softness of his hair that her father derided as grifo or pelo malo, but that she called pelo bueno because it was good hair the way Alegro Villanueva was a good man.

Alegro Villanueva had a slave for a mother and un hijo de la gran puta for a father, who had sold his son to pay off family debts. Alegro Villanueva's master in Ponce had a deathbed revelation, involving an angel and a goat, that in 1863, a decade before slavery was abolished throughout the island, somehow led to Alegro Villanueva's freedom. Alegro Villanueva didn't stay long enough to hear his master's reasoning; he fled up to Utuado, where he worked from dawn to dusk and slept on a pallet of straw. In some ways, he found the life of a jornalero similar to his life as a slave. La gente needed permission for everything from the Spanish authorities—even a fiesta or dance required a license and a fee, dinero that nobody had; they were even charged a few centavos to sing un aguinaldo, which was always sung at Christmastime. So many laws to break a person's spirit, so many laws that had to be broken.

When Alegro Villanueva and Ysabel Cortés got together, they didn't wish for anything, as Ysabel's parents had on their wedding day. Ysabel Cortés had witnessed how wishes turned out for her parents; and Alegro Villanueva already had his wish granted—he was a free man, at least as free as a jornalero was permitted to be. Alegro Villanueva took on credit from the plantation's tienda de raya a few essentials like a roll of cloth for a hammock, candles, a pot, but not plates. They were lovers; they could eat from the same pot. There was much food for sale: rice, sugar, bacalao, lard, beans. Alegro Villanueva couldn't afford rice at four centavos a pound, or American lard at twenty-four centavos a pound. They would have to be satisfied with plantains and bananas. Bacalao and rice and beans were only for when times were good, and they were never good, especially for jornaleros in 1863. In seven years, Alegro Villanueva and Ysabel Cortés had five children who were always hungry. When Alegro Villanueva grew malanga, a root vegetable, on a tiny plot of land that didn't belong to him, he told his wife, "Hay que vivir por la izquierda aquí en Puerto Rico pero sin perjudicarse." When Ysabel worried that if he were caught, he'd be sent to the penitentiary, he agreed that it was a risk. But shouldn't a father do what was necessary so that his children wouldn't starve?

Years before, Alegro Villanueva had eaten arroz con gandules with eggs in his late master's house. When he told his wife, who had never eaten arroz con gandules or even an egg, it sounded like a fairy tale. Alegro Villanueva would tell the story to his family often throughout the years as if the dish could fill their empty bellies. Sometimes he would embellish the tale. Golden eggs had smiled at him on top of the fluffy rice seasoned with chunks of pork like treasures and studded with so many freshly picked gandules that it had been impossible to count them; the delicate fragrance of the rice had lingered in his mouth for days. But one night Ysabel Cortés yelled at him not to utter another word of that maldita meal! Not unless he wanted her to slit his throat with his own machete. She had never before raised her voice to him. He looked at her as if she had el demonio inside her. He took the children with him when he went to ask at the other bohíos if anyone knew of a spell that would cast off his wife's demon.

Alegro Villanueva was known all over the mountain because he was one of a handful of black men, and when people spoke of him, they said, Alegro Villanueva was un negrito pero buena gente. Alegro Villanueva filled the basket strapped around his neck six, seven, and sometimes even eight times a day. He could strip a branch of coffee cherries without ever breaking the branches. After all the ripe berries were picked came el raspe, so called because it was like scraping the bottom of the pot for grains of rice. The pickers scoured the trees for green or pink berries concealed among the leaves.

In the early years of their marriage—although neither Alegro Villanueva nor Ysabel Cortés knew it—the American Civil War ended and Puerto Rico's exports like sugar and coffee were no longer needed. Men like Vicente's grandfather, Don Luis Manuel Vega, lost to their creditors much of their land, which they had mortgaged on expectation that they would recoup their expenditures for supplies and labor. In 1873, only months before both slavery and la libreta system were abolished on the island of Puerto Rico, Alegro Villanueva was sentenced to La Puntilla de San Juan for picking pomarrosas in someone's orchard. His wife Ysabel Cortés cried out in mourning. Later everyone would wonder how she had known that her husband would soon be dead. La Guardia Civil took Alegro Villanueva away at gunpoint. She ran after him, pulling at his clothes until the policemen pointed their guns at her, shouting ¡Alto! Alegro Villanueva begged his wife to return to their children, and she fell to the ground in a faint.

Alegro Villanueva's body was discovered sprawled alongside the dirt road near the town of Adjuntas. A pair of jornaleros dumped him in a ravine. Better for him to wash down into the river and out to the sea than to let the vultures feed off him, wasn't that so? The men hoped that they had done right. Ysabel Cortés would learn that Alegro Villanueva had been shot while trying to escape.

Ysabel Cortés and her two surviving children, Angelito y Eusemia, went to work for the coffee farmer Don Raúl Vega, Vicente's father. They lived the life of serfs, what Juan Cortés called la vida de perro.

Ten-year-old Eusemia was already an experienced coffee picker. Her first memory was of a red berry in the palm of her hand. When she was three years old, her mother sat her under the coffee branches and showed her how to harvest. Ysabel Cortés smacked her tiny hand when she plucked the green ones, and it didn't take her long to learn to only pick the red. When she popped a berry in her mouth, her mother squeezed her jaw until she spit it out. Eusemia didn't do that again, either.

The coffee pickers were at the mercy of insects like the plumillas, which resembled white caterpillars and dropped from the shade of the guava trees. Tiny fire ants called aballardes left red welts from their merciless attacks. When Alegro Villaneuva was still alive, he'd search in the dark for the aloe vera plant when his daughter suffered terribly from insect bites. Ysabel Cortés sliced the leaf and scooped out the pulp to smooth over the little girl's sores.

With the exception of Angelito, her younger brother, all of Eusemia's siblings died in childhood from illnesses like smallpox or tuberculosis, or from la pobreza, because poverty was a disease, too. Eusemia thought the ache in her belly was a monster grumbling about the plátano she fed it or the few beans that were her daily meal. She imagined it growing as she grew, stretching along her torso, tapping against it, clamoring to be fed. She tried appeasing it by eating dirt, but that only made her vomit. She searched the ground for half-eaten fruit like quenepas discarded by birds. Still, the monster wasn't satisfied. Its growls often kept her awake at night. The monster became a steady companion, accompanying her when she picked coffee or went to the stream to fetch water; the old tin that years ago had been filled with imported oil pressed against her stomach, the coldness shocking the monster into momentary stillness. On the rare occasions that she went a whole day without feeling the monster's rumbling, Eusemia pinched her stomach to awaken it.

At six, she was given the shirt of one of her dead cousins. The sensation of the threadbare fabric on the little girl's skin was a blessing and a curse because it protected her from insects, rain, and sun, but the weight of the cloth pressed heavy against her bloated belly.

When Vicente Vega came to know Eusemia, the granddaughter of Juan Cortés, she would never tell him that her grandfather had called her his beloved negrita. Although Juan Cortés lamented the blackness of his granddaughter's skin, while he was alive, no man dared to approach her with bad intentions. Juan Cortés had once said that at least el patrono Raúl Vega paid his workers in bananas and plantains instead of paper scraps. But Juan Cortés added that was only because Raúl Vega didn't own a plantation store.

In 1880, Eusemia was thirteen, her father had been dead seven years, and her grandfather only months. Raúl Vega called down to her from the height of his horse.

"Muchacha," Raúl Vega said, "what do they call you?"

Eusemia stared into the basket of coffee berries she had just picked. Her mother spoke for her.

"She is Eusemia Villanueva Cortés," she said. "Soy la mamá, Ysabel Cortés."

Raúl Vega looked first at the white mother and then at the black daughter. "Your daughter must be deaf and dumb," he said.

"She doesn't talk much," Ysabel Cortés said.

"That's good." Raúl Vega rode off on his horse.

Ysabel Cortés didn't need to explain why el patrono's interest in Eusemia must be welcomed. Not when she and her daughter lived in a house of straw and ate only a plantain or a sweet potato for their daily meal. They ate the plantain while it was still green because they were too hungry to wait for it to ripen, and sometimes they ate it raw because they couldn't muster the strength to cook it. If el patrono favored Eusemia, it would be good for both of them.

Vicente's father, Raúl Vega, came for Eusemia during el tiempo muerto—the dead season—when mother and daughter spent their days like all the other unemployed and hungry jíbaros, scrounging for something to eat. They came out of their bohío at the sound of the horse.

"Me la llevo," Raúl Vega said.

Ysabel Cortés nodded.

Raúl Vega scooped up the girl, lifting her onto his horse.

Eusemia turned to look at her mother.

"No te muevas." His grip was firm around her waist.

Eusemia stayed still, as he commanded; her mother watched until she couldn't see them anymore.

That first time, Eusemia feared that the horse would bite her and she would fall. In the period of months since he had first spoken to her mother, Raúl Vega had ascertained everything he needed to know about Eusemia: her father was dead, her grandfather was dead, her brother, gone off no one knew where, and she had no lovers.

He rode the horse up the mountain and stopped at a bohío. He dismounted and tied his horse to a tree. His large hands gripped her beneath her armpits, then he dropped her on the ground like a sack of coffee beans. He removed the plaited palm door of the bohío so that she could enter.

The hut appeared to be like that of any peón's—with a plant fiber roof and straw walls—but Eusemia saw that it was in better condition than the one she lived in with her mother. Sacks of coffee beans were stacked against the walls. She was surprised that there was a table and a bench and a second room with a cot. On the table were an empty coffeepot and tin cups. There was a kettle next to a fogón. She wondered if someone lived there.

When el patrono entered the shack, his body blocked the sun. Eusemia kept her gaze on the saddlebag he dropped on the uneven planks of the floor. She heard the rustle of clothes and was startled by the thud of his boots. He led her to the cot. Eusemia bit her lip to keep from crying. She hoped it would be quick and that there was food in the saddlebag. She imagined pulling out a tin of coffee. Another tin of crackers. Then sugar and apples, one for her, one for her mother. Maybe there would be a jar of honey like the one her father had once received for a day's pay. Bread. Cans of food that she had seen in the tienda de raya. She wouldn't eat too much so that she could take food back to her mother. After Ysabel ate, she would heat water in the kettle on the fogón. She would dip a rag into the warm water and wash Eusemia, gently.

When Eusemia became pregnant, she was still thirteen; her mother Ysabel Cortés helped deliver the baby, whom they named Raulito after el patrono Raúl Vega. They sent word of the boy's birth and asked el patrono to send food. One of his peones brought root vegetables like ñame and yaútia and yuca and also salted codfish, bacalao, which they'd never dreamed they would ever be so fortunate to eat. There was even coffee and sugar. Eggs! Her mother Ysabel Cortés cried when she saw the eggs. El peón told them that the food came from Doña Angelina, the patrono's wife.

CHAPTER TWO

FRENCH MADEMOISELLES CIRCA 1889

Before Valentina Sánchez met Vicente Vega, she was just a girl wishing for romance and adventure like in the French novels she loved. Her best friend, the wealthy Dalia, was to marry the Spanish caballero she'd met in Paris on a visit to a new exhibit called the Eiffel Tower. (At night it was lit by gaslight! It reached the clouds, Valentina!) Valentina feared that the closest she would ever get to the Eiffel Tower was the drawing Dalia had sketched on the back of a missal.

In the tiny bedroom of her parents' small house in Ponce, Valentina woke to the woodpecker's tap on a tree, to the footsteps of the tradespeople walking to la plaza to sell their wares. The slant of morning sun sneaked in through the shuttered windows and caught her in the mosquito netting draped over her bed.

Mamá told her daughters not to complain because there were no trips abroad or fans of peacock feathers. Valentina and her sister Elena had food to eat, didn't they? They slept in beds with mosquito netting and not in doorways, didn't they? Did they notice the mother and her naked children sleeping on the steps of the alcaldía? Not even the mayor would help them; he said that he couldn't because tax money went first to Spain, and then there was the town's sanitation, and on top of that, he had to pay the salaries of administrators, and then—bueno, always something. Listen to me, muchachas, count your blessings like raindrops.

Valentina's hometown of Ponce was a city of the very rich and the very poor, including many former slaves; mostly, the poor worked for the rich in their grand houses. But there was also a tiny middle class to which Valentina's family belonged, mainly due to the family connections on her mother's side, something that Mamá reminded her husband as often as she deemed necessary.

Mamá was always economizando. She made do with a single servant, and a woman came just once a week to scrub the floors while she stood over her, supervising. Valentina's mother went daily to the market, cooked most of the meals, and mended the family's clothing with her daughters' help. La lavandera Claudia la negra came with her children to collect the family's dirty laundry; the littlest child of four years carried a bundle of towels on her head with the care of an experienced laundress. Valentina had once heard her mother say that she didn't know how one person could eat, let alone feed a family, on the earnings of a laundress.

Everywhere they saw the indignities and tragedies that came from lack of money. When the girls accompanied their mother to the cemetery to say prayers at the graves of dead relatives, they often saw silent funeral processions of barefoot men carrying a plain three-sided wood box balanced on long poles like a crude hammock, a black cloth thrown over the cadaver. The gravediggers would flip the coffin over a newly empty grave and dump the pauper's body—headfirst. Beyond the marble mausoleums decorated with exquisite French porcelain roses, Elena led Valentina to an area surrounded by a wall of stone. Valentina, see over there? That's for los pobres. It's la huesera, the boneyard, where the skeletons are tossed to make room for more muertos.

When Elena, two years older, married a tax collector transplanted from the capital of San Juan, Valentina was determined that she would be the romantic heroine in her own adventure—just like the mademoiselles in the French novelas Dalia passed on to her when she was finished. No dull tax collector for her. She dreamed of being a fine lady with many servants in a place far away from Puerto Rico. Un país where everyone was rich and had plenty to eat, and where there wouldn't be barefoot mendigos with their knapsacks hooked on branches slung over their shoulders, and barrigones, small children with the bellies of pregnant women. Or where she'd never have to witness again the horror of a man or woman with grotesquely swollen legs or ankles, limping down the street.

The evening that Valentina jeopardized her family's honor, her father, with his usual hesitation, entered his daughter's virginal chamber to hurry her along. It was their first attendance at a society wedding—and they'd been invited because of Valentina's schoolgirl friendship with Dalia. Papá found Valentina dressed only in her corset and frilly pantaloons. His words of reprimand about her tardiness caught in his throat. His daughter, who only a few years before had resembled a ten-year-old boy, now possessed breasts, the likes of which he'd seen in the French postcards that arrived wrapped in discreet brown paper at his job at the pharmacy. He had first discovered the postcards of naked women in his brother-in-law's account book, and he had since ordered them whenever he managed to save the money. He kept the postcards locked away in his own private drawer. When his brother-in-law left for the evening and Papá had secured the door after the last customer, he'd fan out his favorites on the medicine counter. But it was one thing to lust after the breasts of a mademoiselle in a French postcard, and quite another to be exposed to your daughter's bosom.

"Prudencia, is that really necessary?" He pulled at his collar.

"It's practically required." His wife adjusted their daughter's corset.

"Mujer, what are you doing?" He waved in the general direction of Valentina.

Prudencia dabbed Valentina's breasts with white powder, so that they took on a translucent quality like a string of pearls.

"Don't you remember? I bought it at the pharmacy." Prudencia inspected the puff of feathers tinged with powder. "It's French. To make Valentina's breasts very white."

"And smell like strawberries," Valentina said. "Can't you smell the strawberries, Papá?"

Prudencia brought the feathers to her nose. "It does smell like strawberries! But the box said roses."

Teodoro tugged at his collar with both hands. "Strawberries! Roses!

I should hope that no man would get close enough to your—your womanly attributes—to smell them!"

"Let me be in charge of our daughter's bosom."

Teodoro removed his collar. "Why is it necessary for Valentina to flaunt herself?"

"How else is she to catch a husband?" Prudencia said. "Go away, Teodoro."

"No te preocupes, Papá." Valentina embraced her father, the pillowy softness of her bosom pressed against his chest.

He brushed the white powder from his suit and fled his daughter's bedroom.

Mamá returned to preparing her daughter for exhibition. Valentina and her mother had labored over her gown for weeks. They had sewn the dress on the English sewing machine with the hand crank, a hand-me-down from the wife of Mamá's brother, the pharmacist. They embroidered the white cloth with silver thread; when Mamá's fingers tired, Valentina took over. Mamá proclaimed that none of Dalia's Parisian frocks could be more beautiful.

After she helped Valentina step into her gown, Mamá attended to the various accouterments of her daughter's dress; she brushed scented oil through Valentina's glossy black hair and pinned Elena's lace mantilla in the style of a Spanish señorita with the ivory combs borrowed from the pharmacy's display counter. Valentina had lapsed into one of her favorite daydreams, that of two dashing caballeros fighting a duel for the pleasure of carrying her off to Madrid or, better yet, Paris.

When you flaunt your bosom, smile like a little girl, because otherwise Juan Moscoso will think you a flirt; worse, so will his mother, it's important to have his mother's good opinion because Juan Moscoso wants to marry you; don't frown, you'll get those deep ridges between your eyes that will never go away, trust me, they won't; think of your father's sister, the spinster, your Tía Evangelina la solterona. Do you want to be like Tía Evangelina la solterona? No husband, no children, no home of her own, ridges between her eyes? There is nothing else for a woman, not in Puerto Rico, not en España, not even in your precious Paris. I'm sure nowhere in the world, so don't be too full of yourself, Valentina. Tía Evangelina la solterona was once pretty like you, but now she is a middle-aged lady still in the home of her parents, and any day now los ancianos will die, and where will she go? We might have to take her in or else she'll have to roam the streets like a mendiga, hand outstretched like any beggar; if you don't want to die a solterona, be sure to smile at Juan Moscoso, but don't show all your teeth or he will think you a tonta; take care around the mother of Juan Moscoso because it is always much worse for the man's mother to think you a fool than for the man. Drop your handkerchief just so in front of Juan Moscoso, watch . . . watch . . . bend like this, the lace must slip from the fingertips just so. It must be done exactly this way because you are a proper señorita; bend a little more—now, you do it, yes, like that, exactly; you must do as I instructed so that Juan Moscoso can want your breasts like a thirsty man wants oranges; why do you think that the good Lord gave you such beauties, we can get a peona to nurse your babies, you're not a jíbara; no, Juan Moscoso isn't too old; he is forty, fifty years old, you are seventeen, you are perfect for each other, he will be like your second father; he is not handsome, it is true, but Juan Moscoso comes from a family with money, what girl in your circumstances could ask for more; we sent you to the nuns to learn that which is most necessary for a wife, to obey her husband; you will never read French novelas again once you are married because you will be too occupied with your new husband and his mother; take heart, Juan Moscoso may not bother you too much since he is of a certain age, especially once you give him a son; when you are married, let Juan Moscoso do what he pleases whenever he likes, it is a wife's duty, it doesn't matter if you don't like it, because God said so; ask the priest if you're so doubtful, he gets his instructions directly from the Son of God; remember that you are only a girl, your soul will be snatched away by the devil if you disobey the Son of God; by now you should know that one is born lucky or one isn't, the moment you are born your destiny is written in the stars, and yours didn't say Paris; go ask the curandera to make up a spell to change your destiny, if you want to get mixed up en brujería y cosas malas; happy, what do you mean you won't be happy? Who is happy?

Valentina had been obligated to dance the first dances, a waltz and a polka, with the decrepit Juan Moscoso. Twice, Juan Moscoso spun Valentina into the other dancers. Valentina stared up at the Baccarat crystal chandelier festooned with orchids for the occasion. The few times she'd been invited to Dalia's home, she had been awed that such a beautiful thing had come from that magical place, France. She doubted that she would ever see the chandelier again. When Rudolfo Vargas (Dalia's cousin, whom Valentina had known all her life) requested a dance, she flew into his arms like a freed bird.

"Felicidades on the munificence of your bosom." Rudolfo glanced down with discretion.

"You once thought them pancitos," Valentina said.

"Because they were soft like bread rolls," Rudolfo said.

They laughed loud enough to draw the attention of her mother and the lady chaperones, las damas sitting in a row of gilded chairs.

Rudolfo had grown into the kind of man that mothers wished their daughters would never meet—at least not until they were their husbands' responsibility.

"I've often dreamt about that time in the garden, except that in my dreams you always look like you do tonight," Rudolfo said.

That time when they were still children, Valentina had wandered away from Dalia and sneaked into the grand garden with Rudolfo. A strand of her waist-length hair caught on a branch, and Rudolfo reached out to loosen it.

They'd ducked behind a tree, where Rudolfo had considered Valentina's girlish breasts the way her mother considered the family's daily bread.

"They're small," Rudolfo said.

"Maybe they'll grow." Valentina looked down at her chest.

"Maybe," he said, the way Valentina's mother would say to the peddler, Are you sure el pan was baked today? It doesn't look very fresh.

"Touch them," Valentina said.

Rudolfo patted them.

"They're not pancitos." She took his hand. "Like this."

"Pull up your skirt, Valentina," Rudolfo said.

"Pull down your pants first," Valentina said.

He cradled his penis in his palm.

"It's kind of small," Valentina said.

"Touch it."

She patted it.

"Like this."

It sprang like a snake in her hand.

"Would you like to lick it?"

"That dirty thing?" Valentina had run away, her giggles rising over the crowns of the trees.

The scalloped edges of the mantilla's delicate lace framed Valentina's face, a bit of it coming to a point between her brows and drawing attention to her dark eyes. She tried to hypnotize Rudolfo with her wide-eyed gaze. Maybe he would rescue her from her fate with Juan Moscoso.

"Let's walk in the garden," Rudolfo said.

"I'd rather go to Spain with you," she said.

"It's all been planned by the family, the people I am to meet, the places I must see," Rudolfo said. "Spain, Italy, France."

"I could go with you if we were married," Valentina said. "To Spain, Italy, France."

"If only you could," Rudolfo said. "But don't worry, we'll get married the moment I return."

"Why not marry me now? We needn't wait." Mamá would say that she would be a tonta to wait for Rudolfo, who already had a reputation among the ladies as a picaflor. And why not? He was young, from buena familia, and could charm a coquí from forgetting its nightly chant.

He laughed; Mamá clacked her fan in warning.

"You're still so impulsive," Rudolfo said. "Four years will go by fast."

"For you." How dare he laugh at her!

Rudolfo whispered in her ear, "Will you wait for me?"

But Valentina knew how their story would end. After their parting, proof of his honorable intentions would arrive on every Spanish ship that came to port. He would write in detail about what he had seen and the people he had met and how he could not wait for them to become husband and wife. Soon Rudolfo's infrequent letters would prove that his affection had faded, until there were no more letters and she would have to accept that his destiny was in Europe, while hers was not.

"Let's go into the garden," Rudolfo said. "Let's make a memory to last four years."

He was so confident that she would agree to such madness.

Annoyed, Valentina glanced around the room; her gaze fell on Vicente for the first time.

"Who is that with Dalia?"

"Nadie," Rudolfo said. "Some third or fourth cousin. His father is a coffee farmer."

"A coffee farmer." Valentina repeated it with a slight sneer in the way of townspeople when they talked about country folk. Still, the stranger was nice looking. In one French romance she had particularly liked, the handsome farmer murmured *chérie, chérie* as he made love to the French mademoiselle in a field of lavender. Valentina had spent many a satisfying hour lying with a handsome farmer on a bed of purple flowers.

"We'll go over the first bridge, past the marble fountain with the bathing Greek goddesses, by the giant coconut palms," Rudolfo said. "No one will find us there."

How dare he continue to make such inappropriate propositions! Valentina noticed the farmer cousin looking at her. The waltz ended and Rudolfo reached for her hand to lead her into the garden. Every Spanish lady had a fan tied by a ribbon to her wrist, and Valentina flicked hers open with a loud clack.

"I must decline your kind invitation, caballero, pero *merci*." Valentina peered at Rudolfo over the silver-painted parchment paper. "Bon voyage, Rudolfo, and when you're in Paris, please say *bonjour* for me."

Dalia's third or fourth cousin wasn't as tall as Rudolfo, but he was tall enough. Rudolfo was the better dancer, renowned for his skill at the popular European dances, el vals y la polca. When Valentina and the farmer waltzed past las damas, the mothers and grandmothers and maiden aunts, the furious flick of her mother's fan warned her to take care.

Her partner didn't speak for several minutes and Valentina bemoaned her bad luck—first the humiliating dances with the old man Juan Moscoso, then the disappointing ones with Rudolfo, and now this mute farmer!

"Strawberries," the farmer said.

"What?" If only he wouldn't mumble, if only he would *speak up!*

The farmer said, "Did anyone ever tell you that your eyes shine like roasted coffee beans?"

They meant only to look up at the stars from the veranda, but the scent of orchids lured them into the garden and soon they were enveloped by coconut palms. Las damas de noches opened their white petals for the moon, and the moon mistook the silver embroidery on Valentina's dress for stars. The owl called out to its mate over the chanting of the coquís. Their hands met as they walked deeper into the garden. The rustle of Valentina's skirt was the sound of the breeze when it skips over leaves.

Valentina held onto the lapels of his jacket when they kissed under a coconut palm. She learned that she liked kissing.

"Vicente Vega, a la orden," he said.

"My name is Valentina, I'm almost eighteen," she said. "How old are you?

"Twenty-one," he said.

"Do you have a mujer?" Maybe he'd left a woman in the countryside.

"No," he said. "Do you have a husband?"

"Un viejito wants to marry me," Valentina said.

"An old man? That would be a crime," he said.

"You're not from Ponce."

"I live in Utuado. We're coffee farmers," Vicente said. "We grow the best coffee in the world."

"*You* do?"

He laughed. "Not just me. Us. My father. Puerto Rico. Europe buys most of it."

"France buys your coffee?" Valentina imagined a fleet of ships filled with coffee beans, its course set for Paris.

"Claro," he said.

"Do you have a big coffee plantation? I think Dalia and her family have often spent the summer at your hacienda," Valentina said.

"We don't have a coffee plantation or hacienda," he said. "Nothing so grand."

"Oh, that's too bad." Maybe his kisses weren't as sweet as she'd first thought.

"The farmer's life isn't an easy one—coffee prices go up and coffee prices go down but my father says that right now coffee's up," Vicente said. "My father taught my brother and me everything we know about coffee. He learned from my grandfather."

"But why aren't you rich, then?" For the first time in her life, Valentina was interested in coffee and not just drinking it.

"Maybe I will be one day when I have my own farm," Vicente said. "But tonight I'm just one of Dalia's poor cousins."

"Your people are poor?" Valentina thought of the mendigos and los hambrientos who begged for food in the street and around Ponce's Plaza Las Delicias.

"Somos gente regular," Vicente said. "People doing the best we can, like everyone else."

"Dalia's family has a lot of money," Valentina said.

"If I had my own coffee farm and a beautiful wife like you, I'd be satisfied," Vicente said. "I wouldn't need to be rich."

"You wouldn't?" She smiled because he thought her beautiful.

"¡Valentina! ¡Valentina!"

"That's my mother!"

Vicente offered her his arm.

"I'd better go alone," Valentina said.

He bowed, then disappeared into the coconut palms.

Later, when Elena asked Valentina why she would go into the garden with a strange man and risk her reputation and that of her family, Valentina told her how much she enjoyed the farmer's kisses. Of course, she'd pitied the good-looking farmer who would never be rich. Maybe she'd think about him toiling en la finca when she sipped coffee in a Parisian café.

CHAPTER THREE

BOYHOOD CIRCA 1880

Sometimes in whispers, Vicente and his brother Luisito called their father Raúl Vega "el General." His father's temper was infamous throughout the countryside; he often overheard people say that Raúl Vega tenía mal genio o un carácter fuerte. So whenever el General inflicted scorn that scarred their skin like the slash of the whip, his older brother's eyes bore into his: *Say nothing!*

Raúl Vega had taught his sons that the way to know coffee was with your hands and your feet. When Vicente and Luisito were children, their father had set them under a bush to pick coffee berries. Vicente hadn't dared to complain about the mosquitoes and other insects that flew into his eyes and stuffed themselves up his nose. Evil branches scratched his face and tried to thwart his picking.

He dreamt of trees. When a tree asked if he were a bird, Vicente observed the ghostliness of the moon, free to come and go as it pleased. Vicente whispered: I am the Moon Bird. The tree whispered cuentos that the birds had brought back from other lands, tales of riches and pirates and oceans longer than days. A tree complained about the owl that kept it awake each night. Why didn't it fly down the mountain and bother those trees? The coffee trees wished that their taller cousins, the banana and plantain and guava trees, wouldn't hog all the sunlight, because they too wanted to bask in the sun. There was the eagle that perched on the crown of a tree with such delicacy; the swish of its massive wings as it flew away woke Vicente from his dream.

Even Raúl Vega admitted that Vicente had the gift. Vicente's fingers need only touch the coffee berry for it to drop into his palm. He didn't mind that the berries didn't ripen all at once, and that the trees must be picked over again and again throughout the harvest. He told the trees: Your berries will be washed and dried and roasted to make coffee so delicious that it is a drink for the gods. Mere mortals will pay for it in gold and silver. Your berries will become coffee beans that will be transported in ships to faraway places I could never hope to see in this life or the next. Your berries will be transformed into coffee that will be served in the palaces of the most important people in the world—the kings and queens and popes. Your coffee will kiss the lips of the most beautiful señoritas and be served in cafés to idle people who will linger over tiny cups, bewitched. There are people in the world who could never live a day without you.

Vicente never shared with others his conversations with the coffee trees, but it wasn't because he thought his brother Luisito would laugh at him, or that his father might question his sanity; it was because it was between him and the trees. The trees liked the murmur of his voice, his words wrapped around their leaves as gentle as the nightly fog. When he ate dinner, his thoughts were of the red coffee cherry nestled in the green leaves, not the rice and beans and malanga, and not even when they had pollo fricasé, his favorite. He was back en la finca, his gaze on the banana and plantain and guava shade trees, blessing their huge green fronds. When he examined the coffee cherries, he held his breath, exhaling only when he saw that they were healthy, that the lack of rain hadn't dried the berries, or that too much rain hadn't stripped the branches bare. When the green berries ripened, they would glisten on his palm like rubies.

When he was a young boy, an eagle swooped down and tried to carry him off. Vicente was perched in a coffee tree, the basket full of berries strapped to his waist. The bird clutched his shirt in its yellow claws, and its great wings flapped like the sound of wind. The shirt tore. The strap snapped. Berries fell to the ground like hard rain. He tumbled down.

"Wake up!" His father stood over Vicente, who had fallen out of bed. "We have to go see about a pig."

Dawn had yet to arrive when Vicente and his brother Luisito followed their father to la sala, where he took down the machete from the wall. The boys' mother, Angelina, hated to see el machete hang beside the thick coil of rope as in any jíbaro home, but her husband insisted that it was the custom of the country to have tools near at hand. Vicente and Luisito stumbled behind their father in the fog. Cerro Morales, the mountain on which they lived, was colossal and forbidding; the boys, less sure-footed than their father, grasped at branches and vines along the way; they feared their father's wrath more than the edge of the cliff.

The rooster announced them as they entered the batey of Sevilla's house. A door opened and light came from a kerosene lamp.

"Sevilla, I warned you."

Vicente shivered at his father's words.

"Raúl Vega? Is that you?" Sevilla held up the lantern. "What do you mean coming to a man's house like a thief?"

"I told you to repair your pigpen," Vicente's father said. "I grow vegetables to feed my family, not your pigs."

"You can't blame the pigs because your vegetables are so tasty," Sevilla said.

Vicente wished that Sevilla wouldn't laugh.

The boys ran after their father; they heard the grunts of Sevilla's pigs over the clamor of the tree frogs. Glimmers of morning sun streaked through the mist toward the vegetable patch where Raúl Vega had planted two different varieties of beans along with yuca and calabasa, tomatoes, and corn. The boys chased the pigs away, but Raúl Vega caught one and pinned it between his knees. His machete flashed silver as he slit the pig's throat. Vicente saw the animal's startled expression.

What did I do that was so wrong? I'm a pig!

Raúl Vega and Luisito carried the hog back to Sevilla's finca. Vicente hurried after them, and when his shirt caught on a branch, he stifled a scream. He'd thought a spirit had grabbed him; people said that spirits wandered the countryside in the dark; Luisito would tease him for being such a miedoso. Vicente stepped over the pig's blood that dripped on the ground; he couldn't see the blood, but he knew it was there. He hoped that Sevilla wouldn't shoot them. Pigs were for market or for special occasions like Christmas. Vicente loved the smell of pig cooking on a spit, a fragrance so delicious that it tantalized everyone who smelled it roasting from dawn until night, its skin toasting until it deepened to the dulce de leche color of caramelos. Only then would it be ready, only then would the skin crunch in one's mouth and the succulent meat glide down one's throat. His mother would share the lechón with the poor jíbaros who never had enough to eat, even at Christmastime, peones lured by the scent of roasting pig. The pig's tail and nose, prized delicacies, were always saved for the old or the pregnant.

When they arrived at Sevilla's house, Vicente's father and brother dropped the pig on the ground with a thud that woke the whole mountain. The rooster and the chickens tiptoed on dainty feet to peck at the carcass. The boys followed their father back through the mountain; their footsteps vanished behind them in the fog. Vicente feared a bullet in his back; not until they arrived home did he breathe a sigh of relief.

Vicente's mother stood at the window; she turned to look at her husband's blood-splattered clothes. As long as Vicente could remember, his mother had stared at the horizon for hours. Often he had to call her name several times before she came back from wherever she'd been. Oh, it's you, Vicente, she'd say.

A few nights after the pig tragedy, Raúl Vega was walking in the fog that shrouded Cerro Morales on his way to visit a woman. He had grown up on the mountain and knew well the slopes and ravines, as did Sevilla and his brothers. Sevilla left his knife inside the stomach of that maricón Raúl Vega. Before he lost consciousness, Vicente's father thought: *I'm going to die because of a fucking pig!* A jíbaro, his horse loaded with plantains for market, found Raúl Vega before he bled to death. The man held the knife steady in Raúl Vega's stomach all the way to the town of

Utuado, where there was a doctor at the mental asylum. The knife saved Raúl Vega's life and sent Sevilla to jail.

The months when Raúl Vega was forced to convalesce at home were the longest of Vicente's life. Once Vicente thought he heard laughter when his mother was in the bedroom, but how could that be? Each night when the boys were called to report on their labor, Vicente folded his hands behind his back to hide their trembling.

CHAPTER FOUR

HOW ANGELINA WAS SAVED

One day when Vicente was still a boy, Angelina woke to the rooster's crow and went to the river to drown herself. She stopped to disengage the hem of her nightgown when it caught on a branch. Only when she stepped on a twig did she realize that she was awake. Her bare feet were cold and wet with dew, but what of it? She reached the river where the laundress Destina washed the laundry and bedding. Her husband bathed here every night, but Angelina was of the class of woman for whom it was not proper. Angelina stepped forward and gasped at the water's coldness. She had never learned to swim, but she felt a sense of peace. When next she opened her eyes, she was on the riverbank.

"What's wrong with you? Are you crazy?" Raúl Vega shook her.

"Don't save me next time," Angelina said.

"I won't," Raúl Vega said.

Angelina spent her days in loneliness and drudgery. They didn't have money to spare for her to visit her family, who lived only a few towns away; the roads were poor and would require a special carriage.

When los hambrientos—so underfed that they resembled stick people—came to their door to beg for food, she bit back her complaints. She gave what could be spared and granted permission for the hungry people to pluck grapefruit and oranges from their citrus trees. Some days she gave away her own meal and pretended that she had already eaten when she sat down with her husband and sons. There were evenings when she was alone at the table after dinner and smoked a cigar, filling her lungs with smoke as if it were her last breath.

There was a time when Angelina blamed her discontent on her husband because he had never loved her, but then she hadn't loved him, either. It had been a simple matter of need: he for a wife and she for a husband. Angelina's family gave some money for her marriage and it had saved the farm. But there were taxes and expenditures and always creditors. Every coffee farmer with a little education knew that the coffee harvest was at the mercy of the gods and the coffee market. Luckily, los peones who helped during the harvest could be paid in plátanos and bananas.

Angelina employed a single servant, Gloria, whose hands had not been created for handiwork, but rather to pound the giant pestle in the mortar carved from the trunk of an old tree, pound pound pound until the coffee beans were crushed into brown sand. Pound pound pound until Angelina wanted to scream and bang her head against the kitchen table. She restrained herself because she doubted that it would bring any relief, only a cracked head. Also she didn't want to scare Gloria, who worked for room and board instead of wages, because, like most small coffee farmers, they had little hard cash.

No one could say that Angelina wasn't a proper mother. As was the custom, upon the birth of each of her sons, she sent the baby off to live with a wet nurse, one of Raúl Vega's peonas who had also recently given birth. Angelina preferred a nursing mother whose child had died and she lamented that she wasn't so fortunate to find such a woman for baby Vicente. She insisted that the peona send her own baby away while she nursed Angelina's son. She felt entitled in her demand because Raúl Vega provided rice and plátanos for the entire family. Angelina visited her child monthly to ensure his well-being, despite the steep climb up the mountain; the poorer the family, the higher up they lived. Other women of Angelina's class had been known to leave a child in the care of a wet nurse without ever visiting for an entire year or even two, but she reclaimed her son upon the boy's first birthday. It wasn't uncommon for a woman to feel as if the child she was nursing were her own. When Angelina went for her firstborn Luisito, she and la peona were in a tug-of-war, with Angelina's baby in the middle. Everybody screaming—

Angelina, Luisito, la mujer who was nursing. The woman's husband had come running, demanding that his mujer release the baby and begging la doña's perdón. When it was time to retrieve Vicente, Angelina hadn't forgotten the scene with Luisito, and Raúl Vega came along to extract the baby from the wet nurse's arms.

Evenings for Angelina were the worst, especially when she sat at the table, the candle burning down to the saucer, the dirty dishes from dinner in front of her, Gloria hurrying to remove them, chiding Angelina like any mother for leaving food on her plate, for sitting in the dark as if she were awaiting a visitation from los espíritus. Why was she moping? She had no reason to mope when life was so much better for her than so many others como los hambrientos, wouldn't she agree, Doña Angelina? So what if her husband was a mujeriego, always a different woman, that's how Papá Dios made los hombres. They probably couldn't help themselves, and anyway, lots of mujeres had problems like that; it wasn't a curse, just la vida. Or so she thought, since she'd never been lucky or unlucky enough to have a husband herself, but from what she'd seen in her fifty years or so of living, she wasn't sure how long, because her mother couldn't remember quando nacieron los bebés, she had so many, and nobody bothered to write it down, claro, nadie podía escribir, what was she trying to say? That, from what she observed, it was better to keep your mouth shut and go about your cosas like la señora did, sí señora, calladita, not a word, la vida tranquila es más importante que los amores. (Gloria pointed to herself. She had a calm life.) So count your bendiciones, señora, starting with your health, and then this house, and your sons. Are you finished with that cigar?

Angelina handed her the stub; Gloria drew it to her lips and smoked it.

One morning, Angelina was drinking coffee when a peón came to the door to ask for Don Raúl.

"Don Raúl ordered me to go to la casita." El peón pointed up la montaña. "Did el don have special instructions?"

"My husband has a house up the mountain?" Angelina's gaze followed his finger.

The jíbaro looked at the straw hat in his hands. Que metida de pata he would tell his wife that night. The trouble he'd caused to Don Raúl and maybe to himself with his big mouth!

Angelina stared at the bohío. This was where Raúl had his assignations? No, no podía ser. After all the years of Raúl's pocas vergüenzas, his many affairs that she had heard about from Gloria, who heard all about it from la lavandera or one of the peones or fulano or fulana, and thought it her duty to tell her. Angelina didn't care, but she couldn't help but be curious to see where Raúl conducted his assignations. Bejuco vines secured the palm frond roof to a frame of poles. Because it was day, the hut's door had been removed and propped against a wall; at night, it would be set in place and fastened with vines or rope. El peón waited outside en el batey, while Angelina entered como la ama de casa, as if it were her own house, because, in a way, it was. She was careful where she stepped on the uneven wood plank floor, not the usual dirt floor of a bohío. Light came from the doorway; there was no window. A bird with a long beak flew inside and took a turn around the hut.

El fogón sat on top of the crude wood table. There was a bench instead of chairs. Two cups, a coffeepot, and a cracked blue pitcher stood empty. A tin gallon with *Aceite de Italia* embossed on the label was filled with water. Angelina lifted it by the wood handle nailed to the top and poured a cup. Kitchen and eating utensils hung from the ceiling on long strips of emajagua vines. Sacks of coffee beans leaned against the straw walls. Angelina carried her water to the second room, which held a cot and a small clothes trunk. More sacks of coffee beans. She shook her head. Ay, Raúl, still so practical, even in your love nest. She had her hand on the trunk when a young blonde entered, her arms full of flowers. The blooms splashed red and pink and yellow on the faded blue of her dress.

"You must be Doña Angelina," the woman said.

"Mujer de Raúl Vega." Angelina came into the front room. "And you are?"

"I'm Inés Quiñónes." She set the flowers on the table. "It won't take me long to finish here."

Angelina heard the lisp in the woman's Spanish like that of a Spaniard.

"Doña, con permiso, but Don Raúl's orders?" the peón called out from the doorway.

"Don Raúl wanted you to help me with my trunk." Inés arranged the flowers in the pitcher.

"¿Por qué te vas?" Angelina looked at the pretty woman over the rim of the cup.

"Your husband told me to leave."

"Another woman?" Angelina drank water.

Inés shrugged.

"Have you family?" Angelina noted the woman's worn dress.

"I'm that most tragic of women. Una viuda," Inés said. "No children."

"You're a widow?" Angelina frowned. "And your mother, your father?"

"No mother, no father," Inés said.

"Where will you go? A woman alone." Angelina set the cup on the table.

"Maybe someone in town—"

El peón cleared his throat. "Doña Angelina, the day is passing and Don Raúl—"

The bird flew out.

Angelina beckoned. "Take the trunk to my house."

"Your house!" El peón's hat slipped from his fingers. "Don Raúl's orders—"

"Your house!" Flowers slipped from Inés's fingers onto the table. "Doña, perhaps you should think it over."

"Don't worry about Raúl," Angelina said.

"Él se enojará. His temper—"

The women exchanged glances.

"You haven't anywhere to stay," Angelina said.

"Perhaps I should apologize about your husband and—" Inés fumbled with the flowers.

"No te preocupes," Angelina said. "My heart isn't broken."

Sometime later, she would confess to Inés that on that day, she'd thanked God for her husband's pocas vergüenzas.

CHAPTER FIVE

ONCE UPON A TIME

O nly through the grace of God, and only because the groom was making a toast, had Valentina's absence gone unnoticed by her father. Mamá, of course, scolded her again the next day. Valentina, are you paying attention, señorita? She should fall to her knees and thank Papá Dios that no one noticed that she went off with a man! A stranger! Some fulano de tal! For shame! Yes, the stranger was guapo, but what was a good-looking man without money? A woman soon tired of a man without money. She had heard that he was only a farmer and lived on a mountain. Somebody had said there was something funny about the father—or was it the mother? It didn't matter. Who wanted to live on a little farm anyway, especially up on a mountain, when they could live in Ponce? ¡Ponce es Ponce! If the mother of Juan Moscoso— Valentina, how could you!

Never in his life did Valentina's father imagine speaking to his daughter on a subject of such delicacy—especially in the girl's bedroom.

"Papá, the bread man is here." Valentina looked out the window.

Together, they watched Valentina's mother select a loaf from the enormous straw basket balanced on the bread man's head.

"I've never seen a single loaf fall in all my years," Papá said.

"If the milkman comes soon, you'll have café con leche with your bread," Valentina said.

"There is nothing better for desayuno than pan con mantequilla y café con leche," Papá said. "Don't you think so, Valentina?"

Valentina smiled at her father and he wondered why he didn't stop to appreciate her sweetness more often, maybe he should see if he could bring home some chocolates from the pharmacy, claro, his wife would complain about the expense—his wife!

"Hija, your mother wished me to say—" Teodoro looked around for a chair, but his daughter was sitting on the only chair. There was the bed—no, not the bed!

"There are certain—ah, certain—things—a señorita—her future husband expects—" His gaze caught sight of a lace pillow. Where had he seen that before? Until last evening, he hadn't been in his daughter's room in years. Lace. Pillow. Bed. A pillow tied with a blue ribbon. Ay, Brigitte from his French postcards. A smile came to his lips. Sweet Brigitte with a ribbon in her hair—a white bedspread—little Mademoiselle Brigitte grasped the pillow between her legs in such a way that a man wanted to . . . A father had no place in a daughter's bedroom!

"I never realized how tall coconut palms grow." Valentina brought an orchid to her lips.

"What?" He took a handkerchief from his sleeve and wiped his forehead.

"Coconut palms," Valentina said. "They're tall."

"Sí, sí, coconut palms are tall." He wiped his palms. "They grow up to a hundred feet high. Did you know that coconuts kill half a dozen people each year? They fall and knock people on the head. Never stand under a coconut tree, Valentina."

Papá mused for a moment about a boy he'd known whose head had been bashed in by a coconut. He removed his eyeglasses and polished the lenses. His eyeglasses slipped from his fingers. He got on his knees, ah, there they were; he brought the eyeglasses up to his face. His gaze fell on the white bedspread. Damn his wife!

Then it was her sister's turn.

"Look, Elena, the milkman."

Elena joined her sister at the window.

They watched the servant bring out empty milk jugs. The milkman tied his cow to a post and then urged its calves to suckle its teats; once the milk began to flow, the milkman pushed the calves away and proceeded to fill the jugs. The bleating of the hungry calves summoned more customers.

"Poor little babies," Valentina said. "They're starving."

Elena pointed to the flower in her sister's hand. "The *Brassavola nodosa*. The Lady of the Night orchid."

Valentina kissed the petals; she breathed stars and moonlight.

"Mamá sent me to lecture you because you vanished into the night with a strange man."

"He was a stranger," Valentina said. "Not strange."

"You shouldn't have taken such a risk." Elena sat down on the bed. "All those high-class snooty bochincheras en la boda. Esa mujeres son las más chismosas. This very moment, the whole town of Ponce could be tearing the family apart while the bread man makes his deliveries."

"Elena, I won't be going to Spain with Rudolfo." Valentina tucked the orchid inside a box of hair ribbons.

"Of course not, tontita," Elena said. "Eso era una locura."

Valentina sat on the bed beside her sister. "I don't think it was a crazy idea."

"No?"

"Quizás un poquito." Valentina raised two fingers an inch apart.

The sisters laughed.

"What about the stranger?"

"No money." Valentina picked up the white pillow; her fingers toyed with the blue ribbon.

"Life is terrible without money," Elena said. "Trust me, you don't want the problems that come when you don't have enough money."

"I know, all the beggars—"

"Ernesto and I can hardly pay our bills and he has a government job," Elena said.

"I will just have to be a solterona like Tía Evangelina. It won't be so bad. I'll take care of our parents, and when they die, I'll come live with you and Ernesto and your children."

"Tontita." Elena poked her sister in the ribs; Valentina slapped at her hand.

"Mamá said to convince you to marry Juan Moscoso."

"It would be like marrying our grandfather."

"Think of his advanced age as a good thing," Elena said. "You'll have nice things and won't ever have to worry about how to pay your bills."

"But he's so ugly, Elena."

"He *is* ugly. Mala suerte."

"Bad luck for him or for me?"

"Both."

Valentina tapped her sister on the head with the pillow.

Elena took the pillow away and sat on it.

"This farmer, did I say he was a farmer—don't look at me like that, Elena—farmers are necessary for coffee and things like that—anyway, he told me that my eyes are like coffee beans."

Elena giggled.

"Why are you laughing! My eyes could be coffee beans."

"Small and hard?"

Valentina laughed. "Tontita, it was something pretty!"

"Can you see yourself as the wife of a coffee farmer? Cut off from civilization up on some mountain with nothing to do except milk cows?"

"I know, but the stranger's arms were so strong—I felt—when he held me—it felt—" Valentina reached for her sister's hand.

Elena pulled her hand away. "He embraced you?"

"No te preocupes, we were deep into the garden by the coconut palms. Nobody saw us."

"Too bad a coconut didn't fall on your head and knock some sense into you."

"Don't be like that, Elena."

"If somebody saw you—"

"Nobody saw us—"

"It's not only your reputation but also that of nuestros padres and Ernesto's and mine and our children's—"

"Perdóname, Elena, por favor." Valentina reached for her sister's hand again.

Elena let her hold it. "Start at the beginning, don't leave anything out."

CHAPTER SIX

STRAWBERRY GIRL

T ell us all about the wedding, the women of the family demanded of Vicente when he returned home. They sat together on the veranda as Vicente wove banana leaves into an aparejo saddle to sell in town. Vicente told las damas about the coconut flan that trembled under a thick layer of caramel sauce (he ate two servings), about the bubbles that had almost choked him when he gulped down his first glass of champagne (the bridegroom had cases of champagne brought specially from France), and about the tiny cups of black coffee, coffee so strong that the taste lingered on the tongue like tobacco.

"And the bride, your cousin? I'm sure she was beautiful." Inés looked up from the lace she was weaving.

"She is Vicente's second cousin." Angelina was smoking one of her little cigars. "Maybe third."

"Second cousin, third cousin. Nobody cares, Angelina," Inés said. "The dress, tell us about the dress."

"My cousin? Yes, I think she was beautiful. Yes, I'm sure she must have been," Vicente said. "I really don't remember."

Inés laughed. "You don't remember the bride? Your own cousin?"

"His third cousin, twice removed, I think," Angelina said.

"You're right, Angelina, third cousin, twice removed," Inés said. "Did you dance with lots of pretty girls? Maybe one particular pretty girl?"

Vicente continued to interlace the leaves into the aparejo that was the jíbaro's saddle; he and his brother Luisito had learned the skill from their father. Now his fingers fumbled and he saw that he would have to redo a section of the large leaves.

"I danced with lots of girls," Vicente said. "Nobody special."

"That's good," his mother said. "You're much too young to fall in love."

"You fall in love when you fall in love," Inés said. "Nothing can stop it."

Angelina smiled at Inés. "I think I meant that Vicente is too young to marry. He'd have to wait a few years."

"Last year when your brother Luisito married, he was twenty-five." Inés checked her handiwork. "That's the custom, isn't it, Angelina?"

"A son works for his father until he is at least twenty-five years old." Angelina tapped her son's arm. "That's the only way the family farm can survive."

"That's four whole years," Vicente said. "What girl would wait four years?"

"Are you thinking of someone, Vicente?" Angelina's tobacco-stained fingers held her cigar halfway to her lips.

"Nadie, Mamá," he said.

When he sat en el balcón with las damas, he noticed for the first time that his company was unnecessary; Angelina and Inés were content with or without him. Vicente even envied his parents the few daily words they spoke to each other at dinner. During the day, Vicente liked the solitude of picking coffee berries; he appreciated the repetitive movement that required only his body and did not task his mind. The sweet scent of the guava trees, the birds flying together in the sky, and especially the red coffee berry clustered in the bright green leaves of the coffee tree filled him with a wistfulness he didn't understand. At night, when his father was out engaging in his nocturnal pursuits, and the house and its inhabitants—Angelina, Inés, Gloria the servant—settled into peaceful slumber, Vicente took to roaming Cerro Morales, restless as the spirits.

Some weeks after Dalia's wedding, Vicente and his father rode to town, their horses loaded with sacks of coffee beans. While Raúl Vega haggled with the creditors, Vicente sold for a few dollars the aparejo he had made and exchanged his mother's list of provisions at the general store for a letter, his name written in an elegant hand. He looked at the unfamiliar handwriting. He felt the weight of the envelope in his palm. Never before had he received a letter. He liked the way his name looked, *Vicente Vega*, black ink against the white paper. Who would write to him? It had to be the girl. He sniffed the envelope. Did it smell like strawberries? He looked about him to see if anyone had noticed that he had received something so special. The clerk looked at him with curiosity, men usually didn't sniff envelopes; Vicente tucked the letter in his satchel.

"It must be a letter from my cousin in Paris on her honeymoon," Vicente said, as if to defend the letter.

The clerk packed the provisions—a box of small cigars, candles, matches, soap, a tin of Danish butter, a can of aceite de oliva from España, two pounds of flour, one pound of sugar, five pounds of bacalao, a small box of embroidery thread—into the saddlebags; Paris meant nothing to him.

Vicente pretended interest in the arroz del país that filled wooden boxes and was sold by weight.

The clerk looked at the paper. "I forgot the rice."

"Better pack it up," Vicente said.

Vicente's father arrived to settle his account.

"I got a letter." Vicente flashed the envelope. "Remember that wedding in Ponce?"

"No time for foolishness," Raúl Vega said. "Take the saddlebags out to the horses."

Vicente didn't have to worry that his father might mention the letter to Angelina; doing so would require more than their daily allotment of words.

The letter:

> *Dear Señor Vicente Vega,*
>
> *As the older sister of Valentina Sánchez, my mother has asked me to write to you and impress upon you that even the merest hint of impropriety*

may ruin a señorita's reputation and her family's good name. I'm sure as
an honorable man, you wouldn't wish ill on my beloved sister.
    Sincerely,
    Señora Elena Sánchez de Rojas

Vicente paced el balcón like a caged animal. Angelina and Inés tried
to ease his distress. Have more coffee, Vicente. Maybe you need to eat
something. Or take a nap. Or visit your brother. Maybe you need to go
to town and do the things young men must do. What is it, muchacho?
Tell us, tell us.

"I'm going crazy," Vicente said to his mother.

"Inés and I have noticed that you've been moody," Angelina said.

"Moody?" Vicente laughed—if his mother only knew.

"Is it a woman?"

"I think I need a wife."

"Banish that thought!"

"Mamá, I can't stop thinking about a strawberry girl I met at my cousin's wedding and—"

"A strawberry girl! How can a girl be a strawberry? Maybe you got too
much sun—"

"No, Mamá, she's not—forget the strawberry part—this muchacha at
my cousin's wedding—"

"There are women for problems like yours," Angelina said. "Your
father has never had any difficulty finding them."

Vicente stared at his mother. What about Inés? She had once been his
father's querida. In a rash moment, he packed a clean shirt in his saddlebag
and kissed his mother goodbye. He had to pry her fingers from his arms.

"Tell Papá that I've gone to Ponce," he said.

"Vicente, think it over," Angelina said. "Your father won't like it."

He left with Elena's letter in his pocket.

·

Except for the few dollars he had saved from selling his aparejos, Vicente had little money of his own. Gloria had given him a large fiambrera, a lunch pail of three tins filled with rice and beans and stewed root vegetables like apio and yautía. He drank fresh water from the many streams along the way. At night, he tethered his horse behind a tree, hoping he had chosen a spot that would keep him safe from the bandits who prowled the country roads. He used his saddle as a pillow and protected himself from the mountain chill with a blanket his mother had given him when she saw that she couldn't dissuade him from leaving. When he had made the trip for Dalia's wedding only a few months before, Raúl Vega had ridden part of the way with him through the most treacherous parts of the road, warning him of the dangers and advising him where to turn off the road at night. This time he was making the journey without his father's help; he reminded himself that he was a man, no longer a scared boy. Vicente huddled under the blanket and stared up at the sky without appreciating the moon or the brilliance of the stars, without hearing the night sounds like the hooting owls or the incessant clamoring of los coquís.

A few days later, Vicente was on the doorstep of her parents' yellow house, hat in one hand, her sister's letter in the other. The girl who answered the door was a proper señorita, from the chaste collar of her white cotton dress to the hem of the long skirt that brushed her shoes.

"It's you," Valentina said.

She stood just inside the door. People walked by them on the street, and one greeted the girl.

"I wanted to see if you were real," he said. "That night—"

"I didn't think that I would see you again." When she gave him a sidelong glance, he knew that he'd never be bored.

"Are your parents home? Your sister Elena?" He fumbled with his hat.

"My sister! What about her?"

He gave her Elena's letter.

"That Elena, que entrometida, always in my business." Valentina handed the letter back.

"I would never do anything to hurt you or your family," he said.

They stood smiling at each other, right there outside her door.

"Can we sit out here en el balcón and talk?" Maybe he could hold her hand.

"Come back when my parents are home," she said. "The neighbors are spies."

He looked for the spies in the painted houses; he turned back at the click of the door. Sometimes in his nightmares, his horse would speak to him. Today he read the horse's thoughts in its big brown eyes not dissimilar to the girl's: *Remember what your mother said? You work for your father, what do you have to offer a strawberry girl?*

After Dalia's wedding, with the exception of Juan Moscoso, who sent an offer via his mother to her mother, no one else offered Valentina a marriage proposal. So after months of boredom in her parents' house, if el viejito Juan Moscoso had promised to take her to Paris immediately after the wedding, she might have joined her life with what was left of the old man's. But Juan Moscoso's mother was too old, too ill, too lonely, too something. Juan Moscoso had said what kind of son would he be if he abandoned his mother, old as she was? Besides, Valentina was young and strong and would be the perfect companion for la doña Moscoso. No, Valentina told her mother. No, she would not be companion to the old lady or wife to the son. Nunca.

Mamá reminded her daughter that it had taken many afternoons of visiting Juan Moscoso's mother to secure his proposal for Valentina; a man didn't reach the age of fifty, sixty years as a solterón without a certain nimbleness required to avoid the married state. When Valentina refused Juan Moscoso, it had put Mamá in a terrible lío with his mother. If Valentina expected men to come to their door begging to marry her, bueno, look around! The men were off to university in Europe or marrying rich girls or too poor to take a wife, according to her mother (or too old or too ugly, according to Valentina), and there was nothing she could do except say a few rosaries while she waited for her youngest daughter to accept what was written in the stars.

"I can't read the stars," Valentina said.

"Don't be such a tontita, I didn't raise you to be stupid," Mamá said. "You'll be a wife and mother, that's what is written in the stars. What else is there for a girl in Puerto Rico?"

"I don't want to marry a viejito."

"Juan Moscoso is here and now," Mamá said. "Snap him up quick before you find yourself an old maid tolerated in the home of some relative."

Valentina watched Vicente from the window. He looked like he was from el campo with his country clothes, not the sophisticated man from the wedding. But he was young. And the way he'd looked at her . . . She thought that he must be very strong, unlike Juan Moscoso. She'd thought about him now and then since Dalia's wedding while she went about her chores and waited for something to happen. Maybe it was the way he looked up at the house, confused and uncertain like a boy, that caused her to feel a tiny pang of—love. No, not love, and not quite affection, but something close to understanding—he wanted her to love him. How long could she wait for someone like Rudolfo to take her to Europe? It was then, at that moment, at her window, that she decided she would consent to be his wife, if he asked her. Surely, as Dalia's cousin, he would want to visit Paris. It was very likely that they could stay with Dalia in Paris for many months, maybe forever.

When Vicente presented himself that evening, the family gathered en la sala. Valentina sat next to her mother on the cane love seat. Mamá held her fan, ready to flick Valentina's wrist if she opened her mouth. After a few minutes of small talk about the difference in weather between Ponce and Utuado, they sat without speaking. The family stared at the prospective bridegroom while Valentina peered at him beneath her eyelashes. Vicente examined every piece of furniture in the room, the comfortable cane table and chairs, the pictures on the wall of the Virgin Mary and of a male saint holding a skull, and the framed needlework of a Spanish coat of arms. He stifled a laugh. His father made fun of Puerto Ricans with a coat of arms, saying how could they all be descendants of Spanish royalty?

Vicente cleared his throat and declared his intentions. His gaze caught Valentina's and she couldn't help smiling.

Mamá tapped her fan on Valentina's wrist.

Papá asked Vicente a few questions about his family then invited him to return the next evening.

At midday when the pharmacy closed for la siesta, Papá went to Dalia's father, who was a wealthy Spanish merchant, to learn that it was true that Vicente's father Raúl Vega owned coffee land. Everyone knew that Puerto Rican coffee was prized all around the world and commanded high prices. To Papá's surprise, Dalia's father didn't recommend the marriage; Vicente was beholden to his father for some years, and even though Puerto Rican coffee was prized today, that could change tomorrow. Better to wait for a more desirable offer.

"I'm still going to marry him," Valentina said.

"That's what you think, señorita," Mamá said.

"Mamá, I've only had two offers. This one and the old man's."

"And you refused the superior one," Mamá said.

"Mamá, do you want your daughter to become a solterona como Tía Evangelina?"

"I—" Mamá pursed her lips.

"Valentina, don't be so impulsive," Elena said.

"You're still young," Papá said. "There's no hurry."

"Ponce is Ponce. With your farmer, you'll be stuck out in the country with nothing to do. Except the cooking and cleaning," Elena said.

"You never even learned to cook," Mamá said.

"They must have servants," Valentina said. "He's related to Dalia's family after all."

"We won't see you more than once a year," Mamá said.

"The farmer's life is a hard one, always at the mercy of the weather and the markets," Papá said. "Think it over carefully."

Valentina appealed to their sad faces. "He came all the way from the country for me. Isn't that romantic?"

Elena took her sister by the shoulders and shook her a little. "Don't let a few kisses persuade you. This isn't a French novela."

"¡Besos! For shame!" Mamá said.

"¡Basta!" Papá raised his hand. "Valentina, do you realize this young man's family might not approve because he is so young? It could put you in a very bad situation."

"I'm sure his family approves," Valentina said. "Otherwise he wouldn't be here."

"He's so young," Mamá said. "He still works for his father."

"Papá works for his brother-in-law," Elena said.

"That's different," Mamá said.

"I like that he's young," Valentina said. "I can help him."

"You!" Mamá said.

"You!" Elena said.

"I'll be a good wife," Valentina said.

"I don't know—" Papá shook his head.

Valentina took her father's hand. "Vicente will work hard for me. I know he will."

"How do you know that? You know nothing about him," Mamá said.

"You don't have to worry about me," Valentina said. "I promise that we will have a good life."

"I hope so, Valentina." Papá looked into his younger daughter's eyes and saw something in them he'd never seen before, was it determination? "Bueno, if you're sure this is what you want, I will give you my blessing."

Valentina embraced him. "Thank you, Papá!"

"¡Teodoro!" Mamá grasped her husband's arm.

"From now on, she'll be her husband's responsibility," Papá said.

"Que Dios te bendiga." She made the sign of the cross on her daughter's forehead.

Elena looked straight into her sister's eyes. "I wish you all the luck in the world, Valentina. You'll need it."

It all happened so quickly—a whirlwind wedding because the young bridegroom had to attend to his coffee plantation, and his mother was on her deathbed—or so Valentina's mother would say to anyone who asked. All that was necessary was to pay for the priest's services and for the wedding license at the ayuntamiento. Elena helped with the wedding dinner, very small, only their close relatives—again, the mother on her deathbed—and she promised to send on Valentina's things to the bridegroom's home up the mountain in Utuado. And then there was the wedding night. No fancy house for la luna de miel, as Valentina's friend Dalia had enjoyed. Instead, los novios retired to the bride's childhood bedroom. Vicente stood in the doorway peering inside at the bed covered with the white bedspread, at the frilly touches in the girlish room. He was twenty-one years old and he'd never been with a woman before. His father had often laughed at his lack of romantic encounters; perhaps it was because his father had so many that Vicente had never been interested in fleeting dalliances.

"Aren't you coming in?" His bride, wearing the gown she'd worn for Dalia's wedding, stood by the bed.

He stepped into the room and closed the door.

"¿Vicente?"

He straightened his collar with a trembling hand.

"Don't be scared." Valentina took his hand.

"I'm not scared."

"I am," she said. "Un poquito."

"So am I," he said. "A little."

She laughed. Vicente laughed because she was laughing, this strawberry girl who was now his wife.

He helped her undress, unbuttoning the buttons and untying ribbons, taking care that his farmer's hands did not snag on the delicate gossamer of her gown. He took out the pins from her hair. She helped him with his shirt and pants.

"Bésame." She inclined her face.

He kissed her.

They fumbled that first time they made love; he squeezed too hard here, her elbow poked his eye. Afterward, they lay on their stomachs without touching, cocooned in the bed sheathed in mosquito netting.

"It wasn't anything like in books." Valentina brushed her hair from her face.

"You read about this in books?" He twirled a lock of her hair around his finger.

"You didn't?"

"I dreamed about it."

"Me, too."

"You did?" Vicente propped himself up on his elbow, taking a closer look at his bride.

"Don't be so surprised!" She laughed at him.

"¿Y qué? It was better in the books?" La vergüenza if she said yes.

"¿La verdad?" She propped herself up on her elbow, taking a closer look at her new husband.

He took a few seconds to answer. Did he really want to know? He was discovering how much he cared about her, and it scared him a little.

"The truth. Even if it stings," he said.

"Yes, better for the woman," she said.

He looked in her dark eyes; he wanted to spend his life looking into them. "Show me, I want to learn."

Valentina took his hand. "Touch me like this."

He did.

Later, she asked, "When did you decide you would come for me?"

"I don't know."

"You don't know? That's not very romantic."

How could he explain what he didn't understand? That he hadn't known he needed her until he got Elena's letter?

"We're husband and wife now; that doesn't matter." He leaned against the headboard.

She lifted the mosquito netting and got up from the bed. She poured water into a glass from the pitcher on the dresser. After she drank it, she refilled the glass and brought it to him.

"Why did you wait so long to come for me?"

"I had little to offer you except for my strong arms." He drank the water.

"I like your strong arms." She touched them.

"You smelled like strawberries." He set the glass on the bed table.

She grinned. "Mamá dusted my breasts with strawberry-scented powder."

He bent to kiss them.

They listened to the roosters crowing morning.

"So this is the room you grew up in?" Vicente's whisper tickled her ear.

"Elena and I shared it until she married," Valentina said. "What will our home be like?"

"Querida, we'll have to live at my parents' for now, sleep in the room I once shared with my brother Luisito until he married." He hoped that she wouldn't be too disappointed, because the similarity ended with the mosquito netting over the bed.

"How long do you think that will be?" She sat up, and the bed covering fell to her waist.

"Bueno, that all depends." He didn't want to tell her about the complications, not on their first morning together.

"On what?"

"Querida, let's not get up yet? We should rest a little before we start home to Utuado." He drew her back into his arms.

CHAPTER SEVEN

LUNA DE MIEL

The newlyweds set out in the delightful early December weather. Elena tried to calm Mamá's fears that she would never see her youngest daughter again, despite Valentina's assurances that she would make the trip down to Ponce three or four times each year. Mamá handed Valentina a parasol, and Elena gave her sister riding gloves, because how would it look to her in-laws if Valentina arrived with the sunburnt hands of a laundress? Mamá's parting warning was that Valentina wouldn't want to arrive at her in-laws a brown girl and have them think that Vicente had married a parda.

On the outskirts of Ponce, they rode past a settlement of bohíos of yagua leaves. Poles separated two huts shaded by palm trees. A white woman and her barefoot children of various black and white hues watched them as they rode past their hut. Some of the children held out their hands, and Valentina gave one of the little girls a piece of bread from their basket. They passed a quartet of black women on their way to market; the women were mounted on small island horses, their straw baskets empty, kerchiefs tied over their hair.

Vicente commented to his bride that there were many more black people in Ponce than on the mountain where he lived. There had probably been more slaves in Ponce, she pointed out. Then he told her about his brother Raulito, who had a black mother. Valentina said that she always wanted a brother.

It would take the newlyweds six days to traverse the distance up from Ponce to Utuado, one day more than it had taken Vicente to make the trip down. Because Valentina wasn't used to the hard traveling, they would stop to rest often. To reach Utuado, Vicente explained, they would travel la carretera, the excellent road from Ponce to Adjuntas, and from there they would follow the mountain trails called vecinales that joined one town to the other. These roads were rough, Vicente warned, but at least the rainy season had ended in November. Then, it was almost impossible to travel because there were many places where there weren't bridges, and when the rivers became swollen, bueno, people had been known to drown.

Did Valentina know that, for years, Puerto Rican prisoners had worked on the construction of la carretera, but because it was taking too long, slaves and prisoners had been brought in from Cuba and Spain? Did she know that Cuba had Chinese prisoners? That many prisoners had died because it was brutal work? When the carretera was completed, the king of Spain had commuted the sentences of the survivors. The Spaniards promised to take back los chinos who wanted to return to China, but the story is that the Spaniards threw all the Chinese overboard. Vicente shrugged. Is it true? ¿Quién sabe? My father says so. No Chinaman ever wrote to say he made it home. Did she know that every man from sixteen to sixty years old who lived near the carretera had been required by law to work one day a week on the road? Had her father worked on the road near Ponce? Valentina laughed. Papá breaking rock with a pick and ax? The idea!

After just an hour, Valentina's waist and back ached from riding sidesaddle. From then on, she rode astride, her skirts bunched up, her legs in white stockings for all to see—the birds, the trees, the sky, people they passed on the road—despite her bridegroom's protests that he felt the vergüenza that she lacked.

They stopped for coffee and pan de agua at little roadside shacks; they bought limonada and alcapurrias, fried fritters made from yuca. Vicente was grateful for the small purse of coins that Valentina's father had given them for food and shelter during the journey; he'd tried to refuse it out of pride, but his father-in-law had insisted that it was a wedding present. The other wedding gifts would come later, when they could find someone to make the journey.

•

They rode nineteen miles in five hours on the excellent limestone road, finding surprises at each twist: a gorge six hundred feet below; the hollow roar of hidden cataracts that shouted to them but were too shy to appear; another twist, and a waterfall for the gods gushed from a great height onto the rocks. Tree ferns cascaded in nature's haphazard, playful beauty. At every turn, there were rivers or streams that shimmered over glossy stones. Valentina cavorted with her new husband with the joie de vivre of any French mademoiselle under a waterfall whose showers transformed the mountain rock into the turquoise of the Caribbean Sea. They stopped at the casilla de camineros built of limestone and inhabited by el peón caminero responsible for the upkeep of a section of the carretera between Ponce and Adjuntas. Valentina found it curious that the house had two corbertizos: one shed was for cooking with two large fogones, and the second was a letrina with a toilet. El caminero's wife insisted that Valentina rest in front of one of the large windows while she prepared café con leche. Valentina played the role of the married dama as she imagined Elena or Mamá would—she was polite and friendly but not too friendly, as was appropriate when others were only peones. She and Vicente rode through thick forests into a world inhabited only by trees. Valentina was grateful for her long sleeves as branches brusheΔ2d her arms. Mosquitoes flew into her face and bit her through her clothes. A bee followed them some distance because Valentina didn't ignore it as Vicente had instructed.

"The road gets rougher from here," Vicente said. "Don't be scared."

It seemed to Valentina as if the journey had no end.

Adjuntas could only be reached through the mountains by this camino real. They rode up and down and up the steep mountain road for miles and miles. Only Vicente's surety quelled Valentina's fear that they were lost. On one particular stretch that Valentina would never be able to recall without a shudder, Vicente kept the horse on the well-traveled path despite a smooth length of road. When Valentina pointed to it, Vicente said that travelers never used it because it was too close to the edge. At various times, Vicente called out to his bride to duck under a branch or hold on tight over the next uphill path whose vertical plane terrified her, and she was sure that they would fall backwards to their deaths. When they didn't, she exclaimed to her new husband that she'd never experienced anything more thrilling. Once they reached the high, sharp crest of the mountain range, seventeen hundred feet above sea level, they looked down at the valley of Adjuntas. Vicente pointed in the direction of the ocean.

"I imagine that only one other place on earth could possibly be more beautiful," Valentina said.

"What could possibly be more beautiful than Puerto Rico?" Vicente removed a canteen of water from the saddlebag.

"Paris, of course." Valentina drank from the canteen.

"In France? That Paris?"

"Tontito, is there any other?"

"My cousin Dalia is in Paris," Vicente said, as if Valentina didn't know.

"When we visit, she will insist that we stay with her." Valentina wiped water from her lips with the back of her hand.

"We'll never see Paris." Vicente drank from the canteen.

"Never see Paris?" Valentina stared at him as if he had threatened to throw her off the cliff. What did she know about him, this stranger?

They turned at the flutter of wings: an eagle swooping overhead. Vicente laughed because now that he had a wife, he doubted that he would ever again dream of eagles.

Valentina wondered if the eagle could fly as far as Paris.

A family of beggars slept under a tree en la Plaza Pública de Adjuntas. For Valentina, the ordinariness of Adjuntas's Catholic church and its brick plaza was a disappointing reward after their perilous journey. When she said so, Vicente pointed out the homes of some of the people persecuted in 1887, a few years previous, during El Componte, the year of terror that the newspapers called "El Año Terrible."

"I'll have to write Papá and tell him," Valentina said.

"Your father? Why?"

"Papá read to us the stories in the newspapers about how la Guardia Civil tortured people who didn't like the Spanish government," Valentina said. "Did you know that a favorite torture was los palillos? They would take these small sticks and pegs, about three, six or seven inches long, tie the smaller ends close together, and insert them with string between the fingers of the victim, pressing them together to crush the bones!"

"I don't want to criticize my new father-in-law, but that doesn't sound like the kind of thing that should be read to girls," Vicente said.

"Papá said that the Guardia Civil still favor palillos," Valentina said. "Did anything happen to your family?"

"No, but some neighbors weren't so lucky."

"Papá knew a man in Ponce whom la Guardia Civil took to jail in Juana Díaz, and then they put him on a boat to San Juan, where he was jailed in El Morro," Valentina said.

"What happened to him?"

"Probably nothing good."

"Nobody was safe, not even the women," Vicente said. "La Guardia Civil came for you at midnight on a rumor."

When the newlyweds reached the town of Utuado, as a special favor to her husband, Valentina rode sidesaddle. She was glad to see all the people on the streets and the yellow stucco church and the large houses of gente pudiente that surrounded the flagstone plaza. Perhaps they could return on that very next Sunday, attend Mass, and afterward promenade around la plaza, stopping to speak to friends and buying a little dulce or limonada the way they had in Ponce. The foot trail to Utuado led through a narrow mountain valley, and there they crossed a stream and stopped to fill the canteen.

The air was perfumed with the fragrance of ferns and flowers, many of which Valentina had never before seen. She felt like she was in the Garden of Eden.

"Look! Another waterfall!"

"It's dangerous to be on the road when it gets dark," Vicente said.

"You don't want to play Adam and Eve?" Valentina took off her traveling dress and ran to the waterfall.

Much later than Vicente had planned, they went over a footbridge—an engineering feat that made Valentina clutch her husband's waist with her eyes closed. Now and then on the mountain, they overtook barefoot boys with stacks of leña for the cooking fire balanced on their heads, and young barefoot girls bent sideways from the large tins tucked under their arms filled with fresh spring water. Vicente bought Valentina a banana from a jíbaro with a tree branch over his shoulders, balancing rhizomes of bananas. The bag of coins from Valentina's father was almost empty.

Bohíos perched like birds on the side of the mountain; a strong storm would send them flying over the valley.

"These bohíos are different from the ones in Ponce." Valentina pointed to las chozas típicas clustered on the mountain. "They're like triangles with sloping roofs. That one has a giant palm leaf for a door."

"A little further down we'll see more huts and la tienda de raya, where the workers buy food and clothing."

"A store? Would we shop there?"

"It's not your kind of store, Valentina," her husband said. "It's owned by a big coffee hacendado who pays his workers with metal tokens called piches that they can only use at the store."

"You're angry." Valentina touched his arm.

"Because it's robbery. Everything at the store is overpriced and often spoiled. The laborer is forced to take food on credit. It keeps him in debt to the hacendado forever," Vicente said. "The stores in town sell at better prices, but the workers can't use their piches there."

"That's terrible! Why is it allowed?" Valentina imagined her mother's anger if she couldn't shop where she wanted.

"That's the way it's always been for los pobres," Vicente said. "Peones are lucky if they eat once a day."

"There were many poor people in Ponce," Valentina said. "Muchos hambrientos."

"There are many poor people everywhere in Puerto Rico," Vicente said. "My mother said it's always been like that."

They rode on.

The house with the shingled roof rose from the ground amid a great profusion of trees and flowers. Wood shutters were closed against the afternoon sun. A woman who wasn't Vicente's mother welcomed them at the door. Valentina could see that the woman had never been pretty.

"Gloria has known me since I was born, isn't that so?" Vicente smiled at the servant still in his embrace. "I want you to teach my wife to cook all my favorite foods."

"I've never cooked in my life." Valentina looked about for Vicente's mother. She hoped that after a few pleasantries, she could take a bath and a long nap.

Vicente and Gloria stared at her, mouths agape.

"You can't cook?" her husband and the servant asked in unison.

"My mother cooked, or the servant," Valentina said.

"You won't have a cook when we live in our own house," Vicente said. "Gloria can teach you."

"We'll start today," Gloria said.

"Not today," Valentina said.

"It was a long journey." Vicente smiled at Gloria. "And she's not used to riding a horse."

"You don't cook, you don't ride horses." Gloria inspected Valentina the way she looked over the chickens before choosing one for pollo fricasé. "I hope you have strong hips to bear Vicente's children."

Valentina looked down at her dusty shoes.

"I hope she's stronger than she looks," Gloria said. "It's hard work to be a farmer's wife."

"Don't scare her, Gloria! She might run away!" Vicente pinched Gloria's cheek.

"She'll have to run because she doesn't ride horses," Gloria said.

When Vicente laughed, Valentina looked out the open door at the road. Would her parents be too ashamed to take her back?

"Where is Mamá? Le quiero presentar a mi mujer." Vicente put his arm around his wife.

"La doña is in her room. She is expecting you."

Vicente took Valentina's hand.

"Only you," Gloria said.

"Not me?" Valentina held tight.

"Wait for me en la sala." Vicente kissed her hand. "I'll explain all about you."

Vicente disappeared with Gloria. Valentina couldn't help but feel that her husband's family was mal educada; she doubted very much she would have been abandoned in the house of Juan Moscoso. What kind of woman didn't welcome her son's new wife? It must be true what the townspeople said about mountain folk's lack of good manners.

Valentina wandered about the room and picked up a cigar box. She rearranged a trio of porcelain figurines of Spanish dancers. She sat in a cane-backed rocking chair. She longed to fling open the shutters, let in sun and air, but it would only make the room warmer. The furniture was of good quality, although the wood needed polishing and some of the cushions in the wicker chairs could stand to be mended. Her mother wouldn't have permitted such disregard for her possessions; she'd taught her daughters to sew and care for their things.

In her parents' house, la sala was where they had often gathered on evenings when they didn't sit en el balcón to watch passersby or exchange a word or two with the neighbors. Sometimes they tossed coins to the black women with baskets of sweets like dulce de coco, who called out "Dulce" as they passed the houses, or to the vendedor ambulante who sold agua de coco from a homemade wheelbarrow piled high with coconuts. They admired the peddler's skill with the machete when he cracked the coconut with one swift chop. Mamá loved agua de coco so much that she often splurged on the fresh coconut water. On the evenings when the sisters strolled to la plaza to meet friends, Mamá had accompanied them. On festival days or during the public concerts, they had gawked at the very rich holding court in their elaborate carriages parked along la plaza.

When they stayed home, Papá read choice bits of news aloud to them from la *Gaceta de Puerto-Rico*, the Spanish government's thrice-weekly newspaper, such as a census report about the racial breakdown of the island's population. They learned that the majority of former slaves had moved to coastal towns such as their own Ponce. Papá told them that in 1873, one year after Valentina was born, the Spanish crown had abolished slavery. Papá described how Spanish law had forced the emancipated slaves to work three years longer for patronos. Papá also relayed the amount of silver that Spain had compensated the slave owners, but nothing for the formerly enslaved—surely the nuns taught the girls facts, and not just to read French and say prayers? Prudencia, what do these girls learn? Mamá reassured Papá that their daughters received all the education that a woman needed in Puerto Rico. Some evenings Valentina or Elena read aloud from a book while la sirvienta served café and delicate almond cookies or cinnamon cucas. On special occasions Papá brought home from the pharmacy a box of the famous chocolates from the town of Mayagüez. The family had enjoyed many evenings with Valentina and Elena reading novels aloud. Valentina recalled in particular Benito Pérez Galdós's *Marianela*. The girls teased their father every time the character named Teodoro turned up in the story, giving him pointed looks and calling him *Doctor Teodoro*. Papá had enjoyed his daughters' teasing and even Mamá had joined in, saying that if only he were a famous ophthalmologist like the Teodoro in the story, then she would be the famous Señora Doctora, his mujer. The whole family was sorry when they finished reading the book. Mamá lamented that Pablo could be so false as to reject the good Marianela, but the sisters agreed with Papá that no one should be expected to look across a table at an ugly face.

As she waited for her husband, Valentina picked up an antimacassar from the back of a chair, her fingertips tracing the mundillo stitching along the border. She was surprised to see that her mother-in-law had the skill of an artist. The nuns had taught them embroidery. How she wished her sister would walk into la sala and offer her unsolicited but always practical advice. Valentina would confess to Elena that perhaps she'd made a mistake. Vicente was not interested in taking her to Paris, and he preferred his mother's company. She heard Vicente laughing again. For the first time she wondered if she had any power over her husband. A man who abandoned his bride of only days to run to his mother might not be so easily swayed. She opened her hand and let the antimacassar drop to the floor. Ashamed at her pettiness, she picked up the delicate lace and draped it over the back of the chair.

The newlyweds were the first ones at the dinner table. Valentina was determined to show that Vicente had chosen well. Is my hair pretty, Vicente? He reached to touch her coiffure. Stop it! I arranged it specially for your mother. See how I tucked in the orchid? There are so many around the house, and this one reminded me of the sun. No, not of the orchids when we went out in the garden alone! Please, Vicente! Don't tease me like that in front of your mother! I forbid you! Promise! Thank you. It smells so lovely, don't you think? Smell it, yes, you can smell it, but don't touch my hair! Tell me, Vicente. Yes, again. Tell me what you talked about when you abandoned me. Yes, abandoned. Let's not quibble over a word. We both know that you abandoned me. If you didn't abandon me and she didn't already hate me, then why didn't she come out to greet me, to welcome me to the family? What does it matter that it was la siesta? Is she an old lady? No? Well then! And who is Inés again? Her companion? Is she an old lady also in need of a nap? Why do you laugh like that? Will your father be at dinner? Why not? What do you mean I'm talking a lot? Why do you ask if I'm nervous? Claro, I'm nervous!

Valentina heard the damas before she saw them. Her fingers went to the orchid in her hair. Two women entered arm in arm: a short, plump one dressed in black wearing a mantilla around her shoulders; the thin, tall one wore a dress that after many washings had faded to a soft blue, the color of her eyes.

"Mamá, te quiero presentar a mi mujer, Valentina Sánchez," Vicente said. "Valentina, this is my mother, Doña Angelina Maldonado Vega."

"Bendición, Mamá." Valentina bowed her head for her mother-in-law's blessing.

"Llámame doña Angelina." Her mother-in-law's kiss of welcome splashed like cold water against Valentina's cheek.

"¡Mamá! Why so formal?" Vicente put his arm around Valentina's waist. "This is your new daughter."

Her mother-in-law's black widow's peak drew Valentina's attention to the judgment in her eyes. She reminded Valentina of a black-and-white drawing of Medusa that Dalia had brought back from one of her trips. Angelina didn't have a nest of snakes in her gray-streaked hair, but Valentina had the urge to turn away lest she be turned to stone.

Inés was not quite forty years old; and even with her faded beauty, Valentina thought that Inés would have inspired fanciful passages in a French novela.

Inés embraced her, complimenting her loveliness and congratulating Vicente on his good fortune. Valentina decided to secretly pretend that she was Vicente's mother. During dinner, Valentina couldn't keep her gaze from the women. They must be related in some way because otherwise why would a woman like Inés be a companion to a stern woman like her mother-in-law? As she listened to the familial conversation that excluded her, Valentina wished she were back at her parents' table, where she'd never had a rock lodged in her stomach. When she felt a sudden urge to wail like a child, she knew that she was just being silly like any bride. She shouldn't expect too much too quickly, her mother would say. Her husband didn't know her very well, and her mother-in-law not at all. She must remember that she was a wife now and not a silly girl soon to be eighteen. The time would come when she would feel like family to them and they would feel like family to her. She would try her best to please them.

Valentina picked at the codfish stew. Papá had declared bacalao manna for slaves and jíbaros. It came to her that she was now a jíbara, one of those country people that ponceños laughed at. Maybe one day when she returned to Ponce, people would laugh at her for the plainness of her dress and mock the way she walked, saying that she limped like someone who only put on shoes for special occasions.

"If only we could have killed and roasted a pig," Inés said. "There is nothing Vicente loves more than lechón."

"I'll kill a pig tomorrow," Vicente said.

"Have you killed a pig with your bare hands?" Valentina stared at the hands that touched her with such tenderness.

Vicente made a slicing motion on his neck.

"You'll need your father's permission to kill a pig," his mother said.

"We can have a little party for the newlyweds," Inés said. "A fiesta. What do you say, Angelina?"

"¡Una fiesta!" Valentina clapped her hands.

"A hog is expensive." Angelina poured herself a glass of guava juice from the carafe on the table.

"You should talk to Raúl," Inés said. "We could invite the neighbors. Luisito could bring his wife."

"Where is my father?" Vicente gestured to Inés to pass him the bread and butter.

"He went to Ponce." Inés passed Vicente the basket of pan de agua and the tin of Danish butter.

"Ponce!" Valentina chewed a forkful of bacalao. "Vicente, your father could have come to our wedding!"

"What is Papá's business in Ponce?" Vicente buttered his bread.

"If you'll forgive me, Valentina"—Angelina turned to her son—"your father meant to stop you from marrying."

Valentina choked. Vicente patted her back and Inés went to the kitchen for water.

"Vicente, I don't often admit that Raúl Vega has razón," Angelina said, "but you shouldn't have married without your father's permission."

"Angelina, not in front of Vicente's bride." Inés handed Valentina a glass of water.

"Mamá, soy hombre," Vicente said. "I don't need my father's permission."

"You do as long as you eat at your father's table and sleep in his house."

"I wouldn't worry, Vicente. Your wife is sure to dazzle your father," Inés said.

"Maybe he'll hate me," Valentina said.

"On the contrary," Inés said.

"He's going to love you, Valentina." Vicente's smile was that of the young man who'd come to her door.

"That is certain." Inés refilled Valentina's glass of guava juice. "I told Angelina that you must have met at Dalia's wedding."

Vicente winked at his wife. "I couldn't resist the strawberries."

"What's that about strawberries?" Inés smiled.

"Only that I love strawberries," Vicente said.

Angelina clicked her tongue.

When the bedroom door closed behind them, they had their first argument.

How could you, Vicente? You married me knowing that your family wouldn't approve? Your father traveled to Ponce to stop it! Imagine the scandal if he had arrived on our wedding day! My reputation and that of my family would have been ruined! ¡La vergüenza! Don't touch me! Don't you dare touch me! And now that I'm here on some mountain in the middle of nowhere, no one wants me—I'm not finished, don't "amor" me! Your mother, your father!

The next morning, Valentina sat with las damas in the shade of el balcón. She had promised her husband that she would try to make friends with his mother. Vicente had gone to a neighboring farm to work as a laborer. She didn't understand why he couldn't just work on the family farm. Angelina rocked in her chair while Inés sat with a mueble de mundillo on her lap, a wood box the size of a small drawer with wood panels six inches tall and an inch wide that anchored a cyclical pincushion on which she had pinned a pattern drawn on papel de estraza. Dressmaker pins outlined the images on the pattern. In each hand, Inés held a pair of bolillos, smooth wooden sticks, each a little shorter and thicker than a pencil. With sleight of hand, she wound fine thread around each bolillo from right to left and then twisted and crossed and exchanged pairs of bolillos from hand to hand, tapping and clacking them against each other.

"It's beautiful, Inés. What are you making?" Valentina leaned forward in the wicker chair to examine it.

"A cloth for the table," Inés said.

"Are these lemons and oranges?" Valentina traced the fruit with her fingernail.

"Yes, and the next series of designs will be berries like fresas and frambuesas. It's a pattern of my own invention." She paused to show Valentina. "As a child I used to draw patterns on leaves and break off the thorns from a bush to use as needles."

"Were you also born in Utuado, Inés?" From the corner of her eye, Valentina could see her mother-in-law was listening.

"I come from the town of Moca. In Puerto Rico, mundillo lace began there, that's why Moca is called the cradle of mundillo." Inés smiled at her.

Valentina picked up a bolillo, admiring the glossy wood. "Didn't the Spanish bring mundillo to Puerto Rico?"

"Yes, but my mother thought that it was invented in Flanders during the Middle Ages." Inés waved a bolillo like a wand, looping the thread around several pins before adding pins to keep the thread in place.

"I read a story once about a girl who came from Flanders." It wasn't true but she wanted Inés to like her.

"She must have worn a mundillo collar to protect the neck of her dress." Inés moved the pins to the next section of the pattern.

"I recall she wore a lace collar," Valentina said. "And lace cuffs, also."

"Angelina, did you hear that?"

Valentina's mother-in-law stopped rocking in her chair. "I heard."

"Here, Valentina, let me show you how to wind the thread." Inés handed her a bolillo. "Like this."

Angelina resumed rocking. Valentina imitated the flick of her wrist.

"Very good! Did you see that, Angelina?"

"I saw."

How could Inés like such a grumpy woman?

"The Italians were the first in Europe to make mundillo lace and to sell it to Spain. All the Spanish ladies love lace."

"Do you come from a Spanish family?"

"My mother never talked about her family, and I never knew my father."

"You never knew your father!"

Angelina stopped rocking. "Inés, you don't need to tell people about the past."

"I stopped being ashamed years ago." Inés took the bolillo from Valentina.

"It's your business."

"That's right, Angelina," Inés said. "When my mother died, I was sent to live with an aunt who wasn't very nice to me. I've had to make my way as best as I could."

Angelina resumed rocking. Valentina watched Inés work the mundillo lace, listening to the clacking bolillos and the creaking rocking chair. She flicked her fan even though it was at least ten degrees cooler than in Ponce. The fragrance of citrus wafted from the orange and lemon and grapefruit trees, giving her un antojo for that morning's fresh-squeezed grapefruit juice. How lovely the birdsong, it seemed like there were many more birds than in Ponce, each with its own particular melody. Flowers of every variety and color dangled from vines and trees and bushes that would surely inspire envy in the gardeners of the island's great houses.

A small brownish lizard scurried up the wood railing. Valentina watched the lagartijo until it was out of sight. She was glad that she hadn't screamed in front of her mother-in-law. The breeze through the trees whispered to Valentina: *El lagartijo didn't bite you. Inés said that you were pretty. Angelina doesn't hate you. Only that you married her son. Vicente's father is sure to like you, Inés said so.*

Vicente's mother removed a cigar from a box.

"May I try one?" Valentina held out her hand. "I read a book where a French girl smoked cigars."

"Do you have my son's permission?" Doña Angelina clipped the top of a cigar with a tiny knife before dropping it in the cigar box.

"Permission for what?"

"To smoke."

"Do I need it?"

"You always need it." Her mother-in-law closed the box.

"Angelina, why be so strict?" Inés pinned the lace she had just woven.

"It doesn't make sense to begin a habit that you won't be able to keep up," Doña Angelina said. "You'll be lucky to be fed and clothed."

"Are times so very hard?" Vicente had hinted that they didn't have money, but the farm, the cook . . .

"It's often difficult for a young couple," Inés said.

"Times are always hard when you're farm people. That's why a man doesn't marry until his twenty-fifth birthday." Angelina tapped the cigar against the banister. "A son works for his father until then."

"Your son came for *me*." Valentina was proud that she sounded brave.

"The beautiful Valentina is here with us now," Inés said. "Let's be happy for Vicente."

Angelina studied the cigar between her stained fingers, then brought it to her lips.

"Valentina, look at that rooster." Inés pointed to the batey. "We named it Raúl."

A rooster as beautiful as any peacock pranced up and down the batey, kicking up dirt with its gnarled feet.

"Why did you name him after Vicente's father?"

"The rooster is always after the hens," Inés said.

"This one, that one, he has them all." Angelina tapped the cigar against the banister.

"What do you mean?"

Neither dama answered Valentina. She looked from one woman to the other and tried to decipher what was left unsaid.

A ruckus in el batey drew their attention. Raúl the rooster danced around one of the hens, dipping his wing down like a caballero asking a señorita to dance. He flapped his wings and flew up in the air. As he came down, he mounted a hen. Her squawks made Valentina laugh. Even Inés and Doña Angelina smiled.

"Raúl the rooster reminds me of this pirate in a French novela," Valentina said. "He fascinated all the ladies on his travels."

"How can a rooster be like a pirate? That doesn't make sense." Doña Angelina blew out smoke.

"You speak French?" Inés said.

"Not much, but I can read it," Valentina said. "The nuns taught us."

"The nuns permitted you to read French novelas? I never heard of such a thing!" Angelina tapped her cigar against the railing.

"We girls hid the books from them," Valentina said. "They're very exciting stories with lots of dashing pirates and handsome scoundrels and duels and love triangles. Everything you could want."

"Nothing like real life," Angelina said.

"In one of my favorites, a French mademoiselle took many lovers, all of them rich and handsome and brave. Some of them were killed in duels. Everyone wanted to win the hand of the beautiful maiden," Valentina said. "It was so thrilling."

"I don't think the subject of multiple lovers is appropriate for the wife of my son." Valentina's mother-in-law stubbed out her cigar on the wood.

Inés looked up from her handiwork. "What harm can French novelas do to a young girl? Especially in the countryside, where there aren't any pirates?"

"There are plenty of scoundrels in the countryside, as you well know," Angelina said.

Gloria came out to tell Valentina that she was about to make the arroz con pollo that Doña Angelina had ordered for dinner. Valentina excused herself to go to the kitchen. A little while longer with her mother-in-law and she would have betrayed all of Mamá's good training. The sooner they lived in their own house, the better.

.

Valentina dipped the washcloth into the basin of warm water she had
heated on the stove. Elena had predicted that Vicente's family cooked
on one of those crude tabletop fogones put together with twigs and a tin
can. She would write her sister that the stove was a brick charcoal pit,
and that she was learning to cook like a good country wife. When Valentina wrote down Gloria's recipe for sofrito, the servant, who couldn't
read or write, didn't hide her pleasure. She had to guess at Gloria's más
o menos instructions. Gloria said, "Add a spoonful of salt, más o menos,
measure más o menos three cups of rice to feed six people, to the beans
add one or two or three handfuls of minced culantro and cilantro and
cebolla, you'll know how much when you do it, don't forget la calabaza
chopped into small pieces. Use the blade of the knife to smash ajo. Not
like that—see how I hold the knife? Now watch how I use the palm of
my hand. Did you know that garlic takes the sting out of bee stings? Sí,
that is my little joke, but it's true! Achiote oil will give the food color.
If it's too pale, add more. To make achiote oil, soak the annatto seeds
in olive oil until it takes on a burnt red color—a day or two should do
it, más o menos—or if you're in a hurry, then heat the oil—use the
seeds again until they lose color. We have an annatto tree in the yard.
You know it? It has red pods, kind of spiky. Don't worry, I'll show you."

She would write Elena about the strange couple Doña Angelina and
Inés made, how her mother-in-law hated her and smoked cigars that she
didn't like to share. And the bedroom didn't have a looking glass, would
she mind sending her the one in her old bedroom along with her trunk?
Once Vicente spoke to his father, they would make plans for their own
home. Perhaps Vicente could persuade Gloria to come along with them
to do the cooking and housework, and she would get a peona to do the
washing. Also could Elena send on her things as soon as possible? A
woman needed her things, even en el campo.

She wrung the washcloth over the basin. If Vicente had come back
from la finca, they could have gone to the river to bathe. She had already
promised him that she would never bathe in the river alone because the

current could be strong and it was dangerous for a woman alone. This little wash would have to do. The door opened behind her.

"Slowpoke, come wash my back." Valentina looked over her shoulder.

"It would be my pleasure," he said.

¡Ay bendito! The washcloth slipped from Valentina's fingers. The scream caught in her throat. She covered herself with her hands as she looked for the drying cloth.

"You're not Vicente!"

"Raúl Vega, a la orden." He didn't bother to disguise his delight.

"I'm Valentina." She bit back hysterics. "Vicente's wife."

"Welcome to the family, Valentina," he said.

"Will you please go?" The cloth. If only she had the cloth.

"You shouldn't be ashamed of a man's admiration," he said.

Though his eyes were so like Vicente's, she recognized that this man was nothing like her husband. He tipped his hat and closed the door behind him.

Valentina grabbed the drying cloth and hurried to push the chair against the door; the rooms in the house didn't have locks. The rooms in her parents' house didn't have locks, either, but if a door was closed, one was supposed to knock. She rubbed the goose bumps on her arms. Raúl Vega, her husband's father, her new father-in-law, had seen her naked! She sat down on the chair. Should she tell Vicente?

Her father-in-law congratulated Vicente on his bride and gave her a chaste kiss at dinner como nada, as if nothing had ever happened.

Gloria served the chicken and rice that Valentina had helped her make.

"¿Arroz con pollo, Gloria? It's not Sunday," Raúl Vega said.

"La doña ordered it specially." Gloria looked at Angelina.

"It must be to celebrate the newlyweds." Inés ate a forkful.

"Thank you, Mamá," Vicente said. "Valentina, wasn't that thoughtful of my mother?"

"Muy amable," Valentina said to the arroz con pollo.

The meal was eaten in silence. Valentina kept her eyes on her plate,

afraid to look up and see everyone staring at her. Afterward, Doña Angelina called Vicente to her side as soon as they entered the sala. Valentina sat next to Inés as she worked her mundillo lace, straining to hear
Vicente and his mother over the tapping of the wood handles. Why was
her mother-in-law whispering? Perhaps she knew that her husband had
seen Valentina? Maybe Gloria had seen her father-in-law enter her room.
When Valentina heard Vicente return from the finca, she'd hurried to
remove the chair and put on her dress. She had greeted him como nada,
but what if she had said, Vicente, this is nothing to get upset about. It
could have happened to any woman—to Inés, even to Gloria. And perhaps Vicente might have laughed it off and told her these things happen in a family house. But what if Vicente said, What do you mean my
father came into the room? Why were you taking a sponge bath? Why
were you naked? Why did you leave the door open? No? You're sure that
you didn't leave the door wide open? She could have tried to explain,
He must have been looking for you, yes, I'm sure he was looking for you.
But what if Vicente said, My father has never looked for me! I go to
him! ¡Coño carajo! ¡Que falta de respeto! I will kill him! So, what good
would it have done to tell Vicente? Or Doña Angelina? Or even Inés? It
would have caused a big revolú within the family. No one would have
thanked her. It was certain that Doña Angelina wouldn't like her any
better. Once something like that is revealed, something must be done
about it. And what would that be? Vicente would fight with his father?
His father would banish them from his house? Throw away Vicente's
chance at his own coffee farm?

So she didn't tell him.

That evening, Vicente and his father smoked outside on el balcón. Bats
flew over their heads and around them, whizzing by in the blink of an
eye; the sweet smells of the night flowers like la dama de noche lingered
in the air. The moon was crescent-shaped, and Vicente thought that he
would ask Valentina to come out and see it with him.

"Explain yourself," Raúl Vega said over the incessant chant of the
coquís.

"Papá, there's not really much to say. I met Valentina and I couldn't stop thinking about her so I had to marry her."

Raúl Vega took a drag on his cigarette, flicked ashes over the banister. "You had to marry her? ¿Ella está encinta?"

"Of course not!" How dare his father!

"¿Entonces . . . ?"

Vicente looked at his father. "Papá, if you could give me a bit of land, just a few cuerdas, I could build Valentina a house and start my own coffee farm."

"Hombre, I'm not a rich hacendado like my father was. Once, half this mountain belonged to Don Luis Manuel. He paid five dollars a cuerda. Maybe less." Raúl Vega stubbed out his cigarette against the balcón's railing.

"I don't need a lot, just a few cuerdas, five or six—"

"And what will you do for money to build this little house of sueños? How will you buy the coffee bushes? Or even the coffee seeds?"

"But you helped my brother." Vicente squashed the cigarette butt with his shoe.

"When Luisito married, las cosas no estaban tan malas como hoy," his father said.

"When do you think things will get better?" He studied his father in the moonlight.

"¿Quién sabe?" His father shrugged.

Vicente hurried past the sala and didn't stop when his mother called out to him. Valentina followed him to their room.

"What is it, Vicente?"

"Give me water," he said.

Her hand shook as she poured water from the pitcher on the bureau. "Before you start thinking crazy, remember that there is an explanation for everything."

"What are you talking about?" Vicente took the glass and drank a few swallows.

"What are you talking about?" Valentina drank the rest of the water.

"We'll stay here," Vicente said. "Maybe in a year or two we can build our house."

"A year or two? Your father won't help us?"

"I don't know if he can," Vicente said.

"Live in this house with your parents." Valentina sank down on the bed.

She stared at the empty glass in her hand.

"I'm no better than a peón." Vicente sat next to her. "You'll probably regret marrying me."

When Vicente couldn't sleep, he got up from their bed as quietly as he could, so as not to disturb Valentina. As upset as he was, he couldn't help smiling at the loud chant of the coquís; that first night Valentina had asked him to check under the bed, sure that there was a coquí family in residence. When he'd reminded her that there had been coquís in Ponce, she'd said not like this, not an invasion of coquís.

He let himself out of the house and stepped into the night fog. He couldn't see the stars or even the moon but if he followed a certain trail up the mountain, he would come upon a familiar bohío.

CHAPTER EIGHT

BROTHER

Years ago, Angelina had known that her sons would hear talk around the mountain, so she told them herself: their father had another son from a young girl descended from la familia Cortés, the people who had once owned half the mountain. Vicente, still a boy, went up the mountain to find them.

A black girl only a few years older than Vicente stood in the opening where the door made of plant fiber had been removed. His mother would say that she was very pretty for a black girl. Vicente thought her beautiful, but he saw that she was missing all her front teeth; he didn't know that due to poor nutrition, many jíbaros lost their teeth before they reached adulthood.

A small child pulled at his sleeve.

"I'm Raulito," the boy said.

Little Raúl.

Vicente looked at his father's namesake. He was black like Eusemia, not a mixture of black and white—pardo—as he had expected. But the boy had his father's hazel eyes—his, Vicente's, eyes. The boy laughed at Vicente, merry bubbles escaping from his open mouth. This child, this happy child, was his father's child with this girl.

Vicente took off his hat. His father was such a bastard.

"A la orden," he said, polite as any caballero. "Mi nombre es Vicente Vega."

"I know who you are," the girl said. "You look just like him."

Vicente looked down at his hat.

"Soy Eusemia," she said.

A hammock dangled from the ceiling. The door was against the wall.

In the back room he saw a crude bed, the mattress stuffed with corn husks instead of feathers. There was a wood box that held clothes or whatever else they possessed. A few articles of clothing hung on hooks— a dress with a torn hem, a little boy's shirt.

Vicente took a seat next to Raulito on the wood bench. The boy was eating beans and boiled green banana with a wooden spoon.

"I live here." Raulito's mouth was full of guineo. "Where do you live?"

"Down the mountain." Vicente waved his hand.

Eusemia poured water from a gallon with *Aceite de Italia* embossed on the label into a cup made from a coconut shell.

The little boy pointed his spoon at his mother. "That's my mamita. Do you have a mamita?"

"Yes."

"A papá?"

"Yes." Vicente wished that he could deny his father.

"Your papá lives with you?"

"Yes."

"My papá comes and goes."

"Hush." The boy's mother set a plate of beans and green banana in front of Vicente.

The little boy tapped his spoon on the table. "A spoon for Vicente! A spoon for Vicente!"

Eusemia took the spoon from her son and handed it to Vicente.

Vicente was ashamed to take it. He would get her another spoon— two—from his mother's kitchen when Gloria wasn't looking.

"Gracias," Vicente said.

"¡Gracias! ¡Gracias! ¡Gracias!" Raulito sang.

"Aren't you going to eat, Eusemia?" Vicente ate some beans.

"I'm not hungry," she said.

Only later would Vicente realize that Eusemia had given him her meal.

Neither his father nor his mother would have approved, but Vicente was drawn again and again to that little shack up the mountain where the soil was too rocky to plant coffee. He was careful that his visits did not coincide with his father's.

Whenever Vicente visited, Raulito would rush his legs and knock him down. The brothers would laugh as they rolled together in the dirt. Sometimes he would bring small gifts. A favorite was a toy boat with a cloth sail that had once belonged to his older brother. Raulito set the boat on the water in the rain barrel.

"Raulito should learn to read and write. A maestro ambulante taught us to read and write when we were his age." Vicente recalled the traveling teacher in his threadbare clothing, whom his father had hired for a few cents plus room and board.

"Hijo, I can't read or write," Eusemia said. "No one in my family ever learned."

It annoyed him that she called him "son." Shame came next. It had never occurred to him that Eusemia might not know how to read or write. On his next visit he brought paper and pen and began to teach both mother and son the alphabet.

Vicente realized that he'd been standing in the batey for some time. Tomorrow he would take Valentina to meet Raulito and Eusemia. He would work very hard to please his father so that soon he and Valentina would have a little house where they would live together happily ever after.

CHAPTER NINE

BROTHER, SISTER

Vicente sat with the damas at the table while Gloria served them their morning café con leche. When he informed them that he was waiting for Valentina to finish dressing so he could take her up the mountain to meet Eusemia and Raulito, he didn't expect their response.

"¡Dios libre!" his mother said.

"Raulito's mother? That's not a good idea," Inés said.

"Not good." Gloria brought the pan in which she had mixed together black coffee, milk, and sugar.

"I promised Valentina I would take her."

"Óyeme, it's not that you can't take your wife to meet Eusemia." Angelina passed Gloria the porcelain cups.

"No?" Vicente reached for a piece of bread.

She served her son his coffee.

"I know that shack, it must be falling apart." Inés passed him a jar of Gloria's homemade lechosa preserves.

"And you're going to shame Raulito's mother by bringing your young bride there?" Angelina reached for Vicente's bread and spread the jam on it for him.

Vicente munched on the bread, talking with his mouth full. "I don't see what all the fuss is about."

"That's because you're a man and you don't understand women."

"Eusemia might be embarrassed and you wouldn't want that," Inés said.

"I don't know about Eusemia pero yo me abochornaba." Gloria brought a pitcher of fresh-squeezed jugo do toronja. "I thank God that I don't live in a bohío."

Vicente looked at the trio of women and they stared back at him, willing him to acknowledge that they knew better.

"Bueno, I'll think of some other way for Valentina to meet Raulito."

"I'm glad to learn that sometimes you follow your mother's advice." Angelina spread jam on another piece of bread for him.

Valentina couldn't understand why Vicente had changed his mind about taking her up the mountain to meet Raulito and his mother. What did las damas have to do with it? Why was it their business? She had been so looking forward to the outing. But then he promised her a picnic by the river. He'd be back in a while, don't go away, he'd said, as if there were anywhere else she could go.

As Raulito waited for his brother under a mamey tree, he reached up and plucked a white flower from among the dark green leaves. Already it had been a good day because Vicente had come up the mountain to get him and given him a ride on his horse. He'd left him under the mamey tree, promising to return with a wonderful surprise. Maybe Vicente was bringing pasteles. Last year during las Navidades, his brother had brought them pasteles—la masa made from a mixture of yuca, calabaza, and guineos and filled with a savory mixture of pork and olives and raisins— and his mother had cried when she'd eaten it. He rushed over, scared: she'd never cried before. Eusemia told him that the pasteles had tasted like something dropped from heaven, and that it had made her wish that her mother Ysabel were still alive.

Vicente rode up on his horse with a lady sitting behind him, her arms around his waist.

The lady waved.

He waved back.

"This is your surprise, Raulito." Vicente dismounted and helped the lady down.

"The horse?"

Vicente and the lady laughed.

"Mi mujer," his brother said.

Raulito looked down at his feet.

"Hay que lindo," the lady said.

"This is Valentina, mi mujer, your new sister."

His brother's smiling wife embraced him. Raulito didn't know what to do with his hands. No woman had ever embraced him, not even his mother.

"I always wanted a brother," she said.

"Mi hermana." Raulito never knew he wanted a sister until now.

Valentina's laugh reminded Raulito of water cascading over the rocks in a certain part of the river.

"Bring the goodies," his new sister told Vicente.

Raulito stared at the pretty dark-haired girl who ordered his big brother around. He followed Vicente and carried the canteen of grapefruit juice, and his brother carried the saddlebag filled with bread and nuts and apples and little candied fruit wrapped in brown paper that his sister told him she'd brought all the way from Ponce just for him. He'd helped her spread a cloth on the ground that she sat on, her legs in white stockings; he and Vicente sat on the grass. Raulito tucked his dirty, bare feet beneath him.

Utuado
January 13, 1890

Querida Elena,

Sister, how I miss you! If only we could talk in my bedroom as we used to do when we were girls. Elena, I have something to tell you that I cannot tell Vicente and I cannot possibly write in a letter. If only you were here or I there! If only you could give me your wise counsel! Elena! Elena! If only—!

How did you pass las Navidades? I wish we'd stayed in Ponce for the holidays. I missed las parrandas and dancing en la Plaza Las Delicias so much! Vicente took me to a neighbor's house and we danced till dawn, but only the one night.

Kisses to our parents and to you and your family,

Besos y abrazos,

Valentina

P.S. Don't give Mamá even a hint of what I've written. There is no need for her to worry.

P.P.S. I met Vicente's half brother. He's a darling negrito of almost ten. Mi suegro es un mujeriego.

Ponce
February 7, 1890

Dear Valentina,

How can I tell Mamá anything? I've no idea what you're talking about! I'm imagining so many wild things! It's frustrating to have to wait weeks for your letters. Why couldn't you have stayed in Ponce? Maybe Juan Moscoso wouldn't have been so bad after all! (Although your Vicente must be very good with his hands, being a farmer and all!)

You'll be pleased to know that we have found someone embarking on a journey to Utuado who has promised to deliver your things.

Our parents send their love.

Muchos besos,

Elena

P.S. I can't say that I'm shocked about Vicente having a half brother, considering what men are, but that he is a negrito! I won't tell our parents.

Utuado
June 4, 1890

Dear Dalia,

Thank you so much for the wedding present—such a lovely pair of silver candlesticks! I keep them on my dressing table to admire them every night. And they came all the way from Spain! Pity me and describe your typical day! I promise not to envy you. Or, at least, not very much, because I am quite happy on the mountain with your cousin! Why did you never tell me about him? I forgive you because if he'd never come for your wedding or if you'd never invited me, then we'd never have met! How funny life is!

This morning, Vicente brought my coffee to me in bed despite his mother's disapproval. (I fear that tu tía doesn't like me. But Vicente reassures me that she will, in time!) I'm always busy here. Gloria (¿tú las conoces?) is training me in the art of housewifery. By the time we move into our own love nest, I'm sure to be an excellent ama de casa. Inés (you know Inés?) is teaching me mundillo. Claro, her lace is quite fine and worthy of one of your Parisian gowns, but she says that I'm improving.

Write me soon! It takes so long to get your letters. Of course it's because mail must come by ship halfway across the world and up from San Juan to Utuado's general store. (That part of the journey probably takes as long as the voyage due to the terrible roads!)

Regards from tu primo, and we send ours to your husband and to España!

Besos,

Valentina

P.S. When will you go to Paris?

Utuado
June 4, 1890

Querida Elena,

Vicente just brought me your letter. It was a lucky thing that his father sent him on an errand to town, otherwise it might have been several months before I received it. Unfortunately, that is where the mail is picked up and delivered. Everything is such a production here; so much effort is required for the littlest thing! How are you and the family? I thank you for your letters. It helps me to feel that I haven't been forgotten by my family. Thank you for finding someone to bring my things, I can't wait to get them. It's been almost six months since we married! Sometimes it feels like a minute; sometimes, five years. Oh, don't mind me. Tengo un poco de depresión. Gloria warns me to watch out because a city woman like me is prone to un ataque de nervios. Gloria is the servant I told you about. Sometimes I think that I'm the other one. Vicente's mother, Doña Angelina (yes, I still call her doña), says that I'm learning to be a proper ama de casa, but some days I think that I'm in training to be a servant. Do I really need to learn how to make starch from scratch? Can't I just buy it at the pharmacy like we did in Ponce? It seems that we can't, because there is no pharmacy nearby, and people en el campo make everything themselves! Unfortunately, Vicente's family isn't wealthy like Dalia's. (I don't understand how that could be because they're the same family!)

Elena, I'm sorry! I didn't start this letter intending to worry you. It's only that I was thinking of Dalia in Spain living mi sueño when Doña Angelina called me to help pick the bones out of the codfish we're having for dinner. ¡Sí, bacalao! Don't tell Papá. I wouldn't want him to know how much of a jíbara his daughter has become. And it's not that I'm really unhappy (or don't like bacalao, because I do!), it's just that while Utuado is very beautiful, it's so far away from Ponce, from you, and our parents. Sometimes I feel so alone.

There is la doña again calling me to the kitchen. She probably wants me to help Gloria wash the pots. The other day, Vicente's mother made me clean the—la doña is at the door! I must go!

Muchos, muchos besos,

Valentina

P.S. As to that other thing, I still can't tell you in a letter! But I'm hoping that it will come to nothing.

P.P.S. I think I might be encinta! No one knows yet, not even Vicente. I know he'll be glad, but it's too soon!

CHAPTER TEN

RAULITO

When Raulito scavenged for food, he looked for edible roots for his mother to boil for soup. He threw stones at birds, even though he didn't like to kill them. He picked fruit from trees that grew along the trails or about the mountain like mamey and quenepas and his favorite, jobo, which tasted deliciously of both pineapple and mango. He stole bananas and plantains from his father's trees, careful not to get caught. Vicente told Raulito that his mother would give him rice and beans and eggs—they kept hens. But he never went because his mother Eusemia had forbidden him. A few times, he snuck onto his father's land and dug out vegetables. Eusemia had warned him against taking anything from other farmers, but there were times when he disobeyed her and used the machete Vicente had given him to chop a few ears of corn from a field. Raulito was already experienced with a machete. As a special treat for his mother, he walked miles for cocos. One by one, he picked up the brown coconuts from the ground, shaking each and holding it to his ear, listening for sloshing liquid—no sloshing and it was fully ripe and the coconut meat would be ready to munch on or grind or boil in water to make coconut milk, a little liquid in the coconut and they could eat the meat with a spoon. It was a feat to climb a coconut palm for the green nuts filled with his mother's favorite coconut water. He wrapped his arms against the rough bark, the soles of his bare feet gripping the trunk. He never worried that a coconut might bash his head in as he climbed, or that he might lose his grip and fall thirty-sixty feet. He thought only of the coconuts, of chopping the fronds and tossing the fruits on the ground until he had enough to fill a whole sack for his mother. She'd take them out one by one until there was a pile of coconuts in their bright green or brown shells at her feet. And then she'd give him one of her rare smiles, and he would smile back.

CHAPTER ELEVEN

WAITING

It began the way such things always begin—with a glance that was more than it should be, with a phrase tinged with promises whispered in the ear. Naturally, Valentina was not experienced in such affairs, but she was young and pretty and all young and pretty girls enjoyed or tolerated such behavior from the males in their circle. When her father-in-law's gaze lingered a moment too long, when he complimented the delicacy of her complexion, the fineness of her hands, the luster of her hair, she'd come down with a nervous stomach and Gloria would make her té de jengibre. The servant would hold the knob of ginger between her fingers and say, Valentina, feel this ginger, see how it's firm, that's how you can tell that it's good, now watch how I use the tip of the knife to pare its skin, how will you learn to be a good wife if you don't pay attention, muchacha, you won't have me to make you ginger tea.

Now Valentina worried all the time that Vicente's father might approach her in a way that would make it impossible to live in the same house with him. And then what would she and Vicente do, especially now that she suspected she was pregnant? Valentina would be in the kitchen with Gloria—Valentina, this is the proper way to iron your husband's shirt, heat the iron on the hot coals, the shirt should be a little damp, if not, sprinkle it with water, next, sprinkle it with a few drops of starch, which should be at hand, I taught you to make starch the other day. You forgot? Did you write it down? See this plant? Looks like a lily? This is a yautía plant. The tubers are in the earth. I will show you how to dig it out. This stone molino is what you use to grind corn into flour to make sorullos, this is how you soak beans, this is how you boil the guayaba for pasta de guayaba, because Vicente has a sweet tooth, this is how you tell the difference between culantro and cilantro, they are cousin herbs or maybe brother and sister—and Gloria would snap her fingers in Valentina's face. ¿Muchacha, dónde estabas? Your mind should be in this pot of beans.

One day, the woman's stare unnerved Valentina.

"Oye muchacha, te doy un consejo." Gloria carried a coconut and a cleaver over to the table. "Never be alone with Don Raúl."

"But he's Vicente's father, mi suegro."

With the tip of the cleaver, Gloria poked a hole in a soft part at one end of the coconut.

"Bring over that glass."

Valentina set a glass on the table.

Gloria flipped the coconut upside down, filling the glass with coconut water.

"He tried his pocas vergüenzas with me long ago when I first came, but Doña Angelina threatened to cut off his thing when he was asleep and that was that."

Valentina gasped.

"Pay attention." Gloria balanced the coconut on her palm and gave it a couple of whacks with the cleaver.

"I couldn't do that! I'm afraid of large knives."

Gloria set the cleaver on the table and broke the coconut in two with her hands.

"You'll learn."

"What should I do about Don Raúl?"

Gloria picked up the cleaver. "If he tries anything, he'll have to deal with me."

"¡Gloria! ¡Eres loca!" Valentina laughed, and Gloria did, too.

CHAPTER TWELVE

DON RAÚL, MUJERIEGO

It had never happened to him before. Never. He'd never believed in it when others spoke of it or wrote about it in poems or décimas. For Raúl Vega it was a thing invented by silly poets or men who liked their liquor. Until Valentina, he'd never understood the passion of men who killed each other for falda—not when there were so many women. Still, he doubted that what he felt was love; it was more of a hunger. From the moment he saw Valentina naked, the washcloth in her hand, Raúl Vega determined that he would have her just like he would any other woman. That she was his son's wife only made it a little bit more exciting and dangerous. But Raúl Vega didn't waste time in introspection. He spent his days in coffee, his nights in the arms of women who weren't his wife. For years, he'd taken the women and girls, mostly willingly, but not always, for his own pleasure; and if the woman or girl was also pleased, so much the better. He married out of family obligation, and because Angelina had done the same, he did not need to consider her feelings as long as he kept a roof over her and did not bring another woman into the house—as some men had been known to do. Raúl Vega fathered two sons and went about his business. His wife did not quarrel with him about this. When she brought Inés into their bedroom and moved him out, he didn't even object.

CHAPTER THIRTEEN

SOME DAYS

Vicente usually worked for his father, and if he labored nearby, he returned for the midday meal. These were Valentina's favorite days. She would hear his voice calling her name as he rode his horse up to the batey, and she would drop whatever she was doing—learning a mundillo stitch from Inés, rinsing a blouse, chopping garlic.

"Los amores." Gloria would shake her head in mock disapproval.

Vicente would carry his wife into their bedroom, kicking the door shut behind him. Gloria and las damas heard the creaking of the bedsprings, their murmurs and laughter; the women paused to recall a time in their lives when they had succumbed to midday lovemaking, overpowered by a force stronger than reason.

One particular morning when she was alone at the table, a spoonful of sugar poised over her coffee cup, Raúl Vega sat next to her. She put down the spoon.

"I'm thinking of giving Vicente a few cuerdas of land so that he can build your casita," he said.

"Don Raúl, how wonderful! Vicente will be so grateful." Valentina looked into the hazel eyes so like her husband's.

"What about you? Are you grateful?" His fingers grazed her wrist.

"Of course, Don Raúl." She looked down at the cup; it was real porcelain. Angelina had told her that the china set had been a wedding present.

Gloria came into room. "Valentina, I need you in the kitchen."

Valentina picked up the cup and saucer and went to the kitchen with Gloria. They heard the door slam.

·

Raúl Vega began to send Vicente to the outer reaches of his farm so that he couldn't return until he finished work. It happened on one occasion that Valentina had un antojo so strong for grapefruit that she had to satisfy her craving. Las damas had retired to their room to rest when Valentina went to the citrus grove carrying the fruit picker, a long pole with a net at the end. Valentina raised the picker up in the tree's crown toward the golden globes. She moved the net back and forth until her arms and shoulders ached, but still she couldn't grasp the grapefruit.

Raúl Vega came up behind her and wrapped his arms around her waist.

Valentina dropped the picker on the ground.

"I've dreamt of this." Raúl Vega stuck his face in the soft spot between her neck and collarbone.

She pushed at his arms, trying to break his embrace.

"Valentina! Valentina!" Someone was calling her.

"¡Que diablo!" Raúl Vega released her and she sprang toward the voice.

Her legs tangled in her long skirt and she braced herself for the fall.

"Valentina! Are you hurt?" She looked up to see Raulito kneeling on the ground beside her. He helped her up and she brushed the dirt from her dress.

"I was bringing you a plant from my mother," Raulito said. "I dropped it somewhere."

"I had a taste for grapefruit."

"I'll pick some for you."

He maneuvered the pole among the branches; a bird with a green back and a black-and-white head flew out of the foliage. Raulito picked a dozen grapefruits and took off his shirt to carry them back to Valentina. She told him to take half to his mother and thank her for the plant.

They lay on their bed, his hand caressing the imperceptible swell of her stomach.

"It seems impossible," he said.

Valentina laughed because he was so silly, because he loved her, because in his arms she felt that the world was wonderful.

"Should we tell them now?" Vicente kissed her belly.

"Not yet. It's too soon." Valentina ruffled his hair.

They heard las damas' voices as they passed their room.

"I have to work," Vicente said.

"Me, too, if I know your mamá." Valentina watched her husband get dressed.

"Do you think we could have our own house before the baby is born?"

"Amor, won't you need help with the baby?"

"We can take Gloria with us."

"She's not a person to take, this is her home," Vicente said.

"I didn't mean it like that."

"I know you didn't."

Gloria knocked on the door. "Vicente, you'd better hurry if you want to eat something, Don Raúl is waiting for you."

"Do you really have to go?" Valentina reached her arms around his neck.

"Papá is waiting." Vicente kissed her.

The day came when Inés also began to watch over her. Whenever Raúl Vega returned to the house, either Gloria or Inés chaperoned Valentina. When he ordered Gloria to the kitchen to make him coffee or cook him some eggs, Valentina went also. Inés was not so easily commanded, and would continue working on the mundillo stitching that was always at hand.

The women were shelling beans; Angelina had gone to her room to rest. Valentina wanted to tell Vicente that his father's behavior made her uncomfortable.

"What good would that do? Vicente would have to fight his father." Inés dropped shelled beans into the big bowl on the table.

"Don Raúl would kill his own son," Gloria said.

"¡Dios libre! Don't talk such boberías, Gloria," Inés said. "But Valentina, Raúl might throw you and Vicente out, and then what would you do?"

"We could go back to Ponce, live with my family." Valentina dropped the shells in a second bowl.

"Vicente in a city? He'll never leave the countryside, and I can't see him living in someone else's house." Inés paused in her work.

"I'm living in his parents' house," Valentina said.

"It's different for the man," Inés said.

"I don't see why. My father could help him get a job someplace."

Gloria picked out a few small beans among the shells. "Valentina, you dropped beans in the shells. Be more careful."

"Vicente lives for coffee," Inés said.

"Maybe he'll have to live for me instead," Valentina said.

"You'll have to take him away at gunpoint," Gloria said.

Utuado
August 16, 1890

Querida Elena,

You're about to become a tía! Our baby will arrive in November. Vicente says that our baby will be a coffee farmer because he is waiting to be born after la cosecha. How I long to have my baby in Ponce with you and Mamá. Vicente reminds me that I am in a house with women who can take care of me and help me with the baby. I'm trying not to complain because I know it bothers him that we're still living with his parents. (But not as much as it bothers me!)

And how are you, dear sister? Our beautiful parents? Your husband and children?

Siempre,
Valentina

P.S. I had a letter from Dalia. She saw Rudolfo at some ball in Sevilla with a beautiful señorita on his arm. I knew he wouldn't be faithful!

P.P.S. Where is my trunk? Don't make me come get it!

THE TASTE OF SUGAR · 113

Utuado
August 16, 1890

Dear Dalia,

I have news for you! Your cousin Vicente and I are about to have a baby! We're so happy, and as you can imagine, so are your aunt and uncle. We are getting ready to move into our own little house any day now, although the damas are begging us to stay until after the baby is born. They love waiting on me hand and foot. They can't do enough for me!

What a happy coincidence to meet Rudolfo at a house party in Sevilla. Rudolfo was always a picaflor. Like you, I'm not surprised that he had the most beautiful girl on his arm. Please give him my regards, and don't forget to tell him how ecstatic I am with my farmer.

I'm including the recipe for Gloria's arroz con gandules as requested. She asks that you let her know how it turns out. She doesn't think that Spanish cooks can be as good as cocineras criollas.

Abrazos,
Valentina

CHAPTER FOURTEEN

THERE ONCE WAS A MOTHER

Lesson number one from Doña Angelina: Why are you still in bed, Valentina? It's after eight o'clock. A quien madruga, Dios lo ayuda. It's not good for a pregnant woman to stay in bed like one of those Victorian maidens in your books. Get up and into the fresh country air. Si te molesta caminar, or if you're too lazy, then you can always stand in front of the house and breathe. Gloria has fixed you something to eat. After that, I'm going to take it upon myself to teach you how to survive in the country. I promise you that if you do as I say, you will be prepared to live in your own house. One day, you'll be grateful. Go to your parents in Ponce until after the baby is born? ¡Que ridículo! Travel on our country roads that are barely roads? You want this baby, es verdad? Entonces, olvidarás esa locura. Don't even mention it to my son, because his father won't be able to spare him. Why do you need your mother when you have three women already? Get dressed!

In the country, you won't be able to buy medicines for aches and pains like in your father's pharmacy. What? Your father was a clerk? Not a clerk? But not the owner? I see. Regardless, you'll have to learn about plants. What's that about a notebook? Bueno, if you think you won't remember something so simple as a plant. This is the verbena cimarrona plant, sí, muy bella with the purple flowers, but the green hojas are what we'll use; mash them in el pilón to make a topical paste or brew a few leaves for a tisane, it's good for digestion and skin infections, Gloria has a special recipe that can cure head lice; this vine is verbena legítima, used in teas or baths to fight fevers or colds. And this plant over here is the one you use to clean your teeth, la raíz de limoncillo, yes, it tastes like ginger, I hope Vicente told you to chew it and then spit it out; you swallowed some of it? Lo que no mata, engorda, but try not to; this plant is malva de caballo and is used for poultices or teas for coughs. You're drawing it? That seems a little frivolous, bueno, hurry up about it, now let me show you . . .

The first time Angelina held her newborn grandson, she inspected the baby in the lamplight. "He's beautiful, exactly the way Vicente looked."

"Surely there is something of Valentina in the child." Inés smiled at the baby in Angelina's arms.

Angelina glanced at her daughter-in-law propped up against the pillows, pale and listless after eighteen hours of labor.

She shook her head. "No lo veo."

"¡Angelina! That's not nice!" Inés touched the baby's cheek.

Gloria wiped Valentina's face with a cool cloth.

In the dim lamplight, Valentina could see how her mother-in-law must have looked with her own sons.

"When you're finished with Valentina, tell Raúl to send el peón for the wet nurse." Angelina rocked the baby.

"No, Angelina." Valentina sat up in bed.

Inés and Gloria exchanged a look. It was the first time Valentina had called her mother-in-law by her name.

"No? What do you mean, no?"

"I'll nurse my baby," Valentina said.

"Things aren't so bad that we can't pay a peona a few plátanos to nurse Vicente's baby."

"I want Vicente."

"I'll get him," Gloria said.

The baby began to cry.

"He's hungry." Valentina held out her arms for her son.

"Gloria, bring some sugared water. That will quiet him until we get the wet nurse," Angelina said.

"Just put him to your breast, he knows what to do." Inés took the baby from Angelina and brought him to his mother.

Angelina turned to stare at Inés, who answered her unspoken question. "Before I became a widow, I had a baby girl."

"You never told me," Angelina said.

Inés shrugged. "My daughter died. Nothing to tell."

Valentina had gone into labor while Vicente and his father were working on the farm. Vicente had returned home alone. Unwelcomed by las damas during the birth, he'd been banished from the bedroom. For hours, he'd paced back and forth, first la sala, then el batey, then back to la sala, tortured by his wife's screams.

Vicente hurried into the room and knelt by the bed.

"¿Querida, estás bien?" He caressed her face, then his baby's head.

"We have a son, Vicente." Her dark eyes filled with tears.

"Querida."

"Let's leave them alone," Inés said, taking Angelina's arm and leading her out; she closed the door behind them.

"Why are you crying? It's over now." He took out his handkerchief and wiped her eyes.

"If only Elena and my parents could see our baby."

"I know, querida."

"I was with Elena when she had her twins."

"I'll go to town tomorrow and send them a telegram."

"Will you? But the expense—"

"A son isn't born every day."

"No, not every day." Valentina smiled down at the baby.

"Your screams were horrible, Valentina." He brought the chair over to the bed. "Did it hurt so very much?"

"You have the next one." She looked down at the baby nursing at her breast. Her hair fell along her face like a curtain.

"The next one?" Vicente caressed his son's cheek with a finger. "He looks like you."

"That's not what your mother says."

"You expected something else from my mother?"

They smiled at each other.

"I don't mind if he looks like you." Valentina switched the baby to the other breast.

Inés and Gloria came into the room.

"Pa'fuera, Vicente. La mamacita needs her rest." Gloria carried some cloths and a basin of warm water.

"But Gloria, this is where I sleep—"

"Not tonight," Inés said.

"I pushed together some chairs en la sala," Gloria said. "It's that or blankets on the floor."

"But Valentina might need me—"

"Not tonight," Gloria said.

Vicente turned to Valentina, who had fallen asleep, the baby nursing at her breast.

Utuado
November 21, 1890

Dear Titi Elena,

Gracias for the congratulatory telegram! Vicente and I were excited to send and receive one, so cosmopolitan. You asked for details. Javiercito was born a week ago por la noche at 10:59 exactly after eighteen hours of labor! Elena! ¡El dolor! ¡Ay bendito, Papito Dios! Still, it was worth it all to have this sweet child who is this moment nursing at my breast. Did I tell you that my mother-in-law thinks he weighed as much as Vicente did? Seven pounds. La doña said the baby is exactly like Vicente, and she is right that he does have his father's eyes.

I can't wait for you to meet your nephew. Do you think that you could visit? Maybe even bring our parents? The children are welcome, too. We'll make room for you here. I would go to you but las damas say that I must not exert myself too much for the first forty days or bad things will happen to me. (I think that's an old wives' tale, but they are determined.)

Elena, again, I implore you to send me my things! Why can't you find someone to bring my trunk? I've been married almost a year! Bring it yourself if you have to! Please do!!

Querida hermana, give my love to our parents and please try to visit me and meet your new nephew! I miss you so much!

Love you,

Valentina (or Mamacita, as Gloria calls me)

Ponce

December 10, 1890

Querida Valentina,

How are you and your little family? I'm sorry that we haven't been able to meet our precious Javiercito, but Ernesto couldn't get away from his post. Obviously, I couldn't undertake the treacherous journey without him. Oh, how I wish that we could sit on your bed and talk like old times. Did you dress the baby in the little gown I added to your trunk? I'm sorry about your things taking so long to get to you. You've no idea what a trial it has been to find a reliable person. Why do you have to live so far away on some mountain? With a husband tan guapo como Vicente, I knew it wouldn't be long before you got pregnant! Mamá was horrified to learn from your letter that you do not employ a wet nurse. Perhaps that is the custom of the country? Don't you find it a little barbaric? We ponceñas are more delicada! Sorry, but you are no longer a ponceña, Valentina! I almost forgot to give you the most important news! Soon, I won't be a ponceña, either! We are moving to San Juan! The capital! I'm so excited to live in the city that everyone calls the most Spanish in all the Americas! Do you recall that Ernesto's family is from San Juan? His father died, and Ernesto is to take over the business for his mother and sisters. A stationery store. Our parents are to come with us.

I must go now, so much to do! I will send gifts for you and my nephew. Some things are from my own children, but they're such good quality that I didn't want to give them to a beggar who wouldn't appreciate them.

¡Feliz Navidad y Prospero Año Nuevo from all of us to your family!

Your loving sister,

Elena, the soon-to-be ex-ponceña

Utuado
April 17, 1891

Querida Dalia,

I hope that this letter finds you and your family well in Paris. Paris! How exciting! I know you're as happy as I am on our lovely mountain with your cousin and our new baby. Dalia, you said in your last letter that you sent a present for the baby. I haven't thanked you for it, not because I'm ungrateful, but because I've yet to receive it! I'm heartbroken over it! Maybe it will turn up, if God grants a miracle. What was it? I can at least imagine it coming to us all the way from Paris, France.

Javiercito is always at my breast, demanding to be fed. It is exhausting! Sometimes I think that maybe I should have accepted your Tía Angelina's offer of a wet nurse, but then he closes his little hand over my finger and gazes at me with the eyes of his father. I'm glad then.

Your house in Paris sounds un sueño. I used to dream of such a house as a silly schoolgirl. But I have happy news, also. We are moving into our own house. Vicente's older brother Luisito came to help him build it. Luisito doesn't look at all like my Vicente, who is tall and lanky while he is short and stocky, but he has those same hazel eyes that all the males of the family seem to inherit, including Javiercito and even Raulito. (I wrote you about him.)

Next time you get a letter from me, I will be una ama de casa and mother of soon-to-be two! (Sí, estoy encinta.) You can address your letters as before—Valentina Sánchez Vega—and send it to the general store. I'll get it eventually.

Un abrazo fuerte para tí y otro para París,
Valentina

Utuado
June 4, 1891

Querida Elena,

I'm sending this letter to the address of the stationery store, as you instructed. Yes, I'm feeling much better, over my morning sickness. How are you and the family? Was the journey to San Juan a good one? Vicente said that traveling the road from Ponce to San Juan is like walking from la sala to la cocina! (How I long to make that walk!) Tell me about your new house. How is San Juan? Elena, you don't know how I envy you! You get to live in the most cosmopolitan city on the entire island while I'm stuck here on this mountain! It doesn't seem fair that you have all the luck! I'm sorry, hermana, I don't mean that, not really. I'm glad for you. It's just that the little house that Vicente is building for us is not quite what I thought it would be. He warned me that I wouldn't have any luxuries, but I didn't believe him. The house is made of wood with a corrugated-iron roof. (The roof panels come from England.) We'll have four rooms, una sala, two bedrooms, the smaller one for the children, and the kitchen—Vicente said it's much nicer than many people have. Most important, it'll be our own little place. I remind myself of that, especially when I think of you and Dalia in your fancy houses.

How do our parents like San Juan? Write me everything.

All my love,

Valentina

San Juan
June 4, 1891

Dear Valentina,

How are you and the family? We are well here in San Juan! This city is so different from Ponce that sometimes I feel as if I moved to another country and only the vista of the same sea, so familiar from Ponce, keeps me moored to our island. The main streets of San Juan are all cobblestone (and hurt my feet), and narrow except for those by the governor's palace, el Palacio de Santa Catalina, which are quite as wide as any in Ponce. The house of Ernesto's family—I should say "our house," is in a quite good location, within walking distance to the harbor. We get a nice breeze off the ocean. (Luckily, we aren't close to the rows of shanties where the poor people live. Ernesto says that often three or more families live in one room! Imagine! I asked him to take me to see for myself but he refused, saying it was no place for a dama decente.) When Ernesto's grandfather built this house that is now ours, he planned the shop downstairs and the family's quarters upstairs. The kitchen and dining room are on the main floor, connected to the shop by a door that is never to be opened during shop hours. Ernesto was very unpleasant toward one of the clerks who made that mistake! We have two servants, one is a cook and the other a general housemaid like Mamá had when we lived at home, and, of course, we send out all the laundry and linens to a lavandera, of which there are plenty in San Juan. We also have a woman who comes in once a week to do the heavy cleaning, and another who comes to iron. Domestic help is so cheap! Isn't that lucky? When I saw the lavandera the other day with her little children in tow, I thought of you. Do you recall how one day you wanted to buy shoes for the laundress's children? And you couldn't understand why our parents didn't lend you the money? You were always the sweet one.

Must go now. I'm off to do the marketing with a list from the cook. Mamá is eager to go with me. You know how she loves to haggle with the vendors.

Much love,

Elena

P.S. I'm sending you some stationery and ink from the shop. And stamps! Write!

(letter continued)

Dearest Valentina,

The servant forgot to post this letter. I don't know if she is just stupid or if it's because she doesn't read or write, the address on the envelope looks like scribbles and she can't tell a letter from a scrap of paper to throw away! Mamá says that servants were so much more diligent in their duties in her day—something about being afraid that they would be sent out into the streets to beg. I must tell you about our trip to the market en la Plaza del Mercado. It was very exciting. Let's just say that it's not a place where a decent dama should go alone. I kept my arm linked through Mamá's, and my basket firmly clutched in my other hand. Everything you can imagine was for sale. One man had set up a fogón and was cooking whole pigeons on it. It smelled divine and I was very tempted, but Mamá said that a person could get yellow fever from street food. Los jíbaros came in from the countryside to sell plantains and bananas and piles and piles of pajuiles and naranjas and anón cimarrón and eggplant and asparagus and every other kind of fruit and vegetable. We bought asparagus and stone fruit like pajuiles and citrus like cidras and naranjas. (I wanted to buy anón cimarrón but you know it is quite a large fruit and we couldn't carry it.) The fisherman wrapped our freshly caught fish in our cheesecloth. Our basket grew quite heavy. Mamá said that next time, we should bring the cook or the maid so that I won't have to carry our purchases.

We stopped to watch a seamstress sew on a tiny machine set atop its wooden box. Mamá asked if she could sew for us if we provided her with the fabric and thread. (An enthusiastic yes! She is coming tomorrow. We need new napkins and a tablecloth.) I pitied the poor woman, not much older than me, working under the hot sun, her barefoot children gathered around her, all rags and big eyes. I gave the oldest child a few coins. I'm saving the things my children outgrow (good-quality things) for your children, otherwise I'd be tempted to give them to these needy creatures. On our way home we passed ancient mendigas in front of the Farmacía Guillermety. Mamá said that it was sad that old women had to beg; she hadn't noticed that so much in Ponce.

Ernesto and I went to see the regatas in the harbor. Everyone who was anyone in San Juan was there. The dresses, Valentina! You would have swooned. (My dress was adequate, but if the day ever comes that the shop does very well, I will order a dress from Paris! As I know you would!) I have to say that the procession of ships decorated with flags and colorful streamers as they glided down the water did much to relieve my homesickness for Ponce. Do you miss it as much as I do?

Your sister,

Elena

CHAPTER FIFTEEN

EXILE

Querida, we built the house on stilts to protect it from flooding during the rainy season; it's the way of the country, you'll get used to it. Look, two barrels for rain so that you don't have to always go to the stream; I rigged up a ducha to catch rainwater so my strawberry girl can have her showers, I built this tiny shed so you'll have privacy from passersby—you don't care if the birds see you, do you? Out there, only a little ways, is the outhouse, I put in a floor, that way it wouldn't get all muddy and disgusting, but we'll have to keep an escupidera to use at night, don't look at me like that, mujer, it's too dark at night to walk all the way to the letrina, what do you mean, who will empty the chamber pot? You're a country girl now, bueno, I will, but we have a son who will soon be peeing like un macho, and you'll be glad of it. Yes, I will teach him not to miss. Valentina, we put in a window in each of the rooms except the children's, houses like ours don't have so many windows! Luisito doesn't have as many windows in his house, but I wanted to make it extra nice for you. Did you notice the furniture? I built it. Mostly. Yes, me. I built the bureau in our bedroom and the smaller one in the children's room, you didn't know I could do that, did you? Papá taught us to work with wood when we were boys; I built the cupboard for the dishes. I know there isn't any furniture in la sala yet, but that will come, you'll see, don't forget, Mamá promised that you could have her rocking chair; do you like the kitchen table? Yes, it is beautiful. No, I didn't make it, no, it wasn't Luisito, either, it was Papá, yes, my father; he insisted that he wanted to give you something special; the old man came around, didn't he?

"I can't believe Raúl made this." Valentina passed her hand over the table of fine reddish wood that resembled mahogany. She switched three-month-old Evita to her other hip. "Is this caoba? It smells like cedar."

"Cedro español as good as caoba," Vicente said. "Papá wanted you to have the best."

Raúl's table was devoid of flourishes yet it was something to be passed down through the generations. Why had he gone to such trouble and expense? It was a matter she would have to ponder later, perhaps even discuss with Gloria and Inés.

Valentina sat down in one of the cane-backed chairs that Angelina had given them. Two-year-old Javiercito, sitting on his father's shoulders, demanded to be set down. He ran to his mother and she took him on her knee.

The lean-to shed housed el fogón on a narrow table that Vicente had built for it.

Vicente opened two wooden shutters the size and width of the window. "You can let out the smoke from el fogón. Here is the palangana. You can wash dishes while you look out the window. When you're done, you just tilt the basin with the dirty water out the window. Luisito and I put in the window specially."

He looked at her, waiting.

Valentina, the baby on her lap, Javiercito clutching her shirt, stared out the window—an opening without glass or a screen. Cook on a fogón, throw the dirty dishwater out the window like a peona—she couldn't believe she had come to this.

"Querida, don't you like it?" Her husband's smile had faded.

She roused herself. He'd tried to please her, to help make her chores easier.

"Claro, que sí."

"I know it's not like Mamá's house—"

"It's not that, I'm just a little overwhelmed."

"Mamá said she would send Gloria to help you to get settled." Vicente gave her a look she knew well. "Let's put the children down for a nap and then we can go to bed, too."

"But what if Gloria comes and we're—"

"You don't want to?" Vicente's smile was hard to resist.

Valentina opened her blouse to nurse her children. "I'll hurry."

There was much that she liked about the house. It was on a particularly beautiful spot surrounded by flowers like orchids and dalias and margaritas. A variety of fruit trees perfumed the air with citrus like toronja or china. There were mango trees and a tree that grew her favorite lechosa—they grew so big she had to carry one with both hands. She fashioned a sling along her chest to carry Evita around the new property, and she enlisted Javiercito to help pick aguacates or delicate fresas that grew the size of his thumb. They popped red berries into their mouths right off the bushes, the sweet juice dripping down their chins. Valentina would sit under the shade of a tree, shrug off her blouse, and nurse a child at each breast. Sometimes she untied her ribbon and let her hair cover them like a curtain, but mostly, she didn't bother.

The hours between her husband's departure and return were long and lonely. She yearned for company, for another woman's kind voice, for a helping hand. Valentina had long ago realized that her mother and sister had been right. Here she was on a mountain where nothing exciting ever happened, where no one interesting ever came to visit or passed by except for barefoot jíbaros. She missed Inés and Gloria, who had become like mother and aunt to her. In her loneliest moments, she even missed Doña Angelina.

It was a hard life, la campesina life—too many chores like filling the water containers, the preparation of food, the making of the fire, the cooking, the cleaning, the nursing of the baby and toddler, who wasn't ready to wean himself. There were days when she didn't have Vicente's midday meal ready; it seemed as if she just set the pot on el fogón and there he was. She cried the first time that happened. He'd taken her in his arms, reassuring her that he wasn't that hungry. There were days when he tried to make it easier for her and didn't come home for lunch but went to his mother's house instead. Valentina felt the sting of his absence, but she was also relieved. She had to draw on everything she had in her to prepare a simple meal, and some days that was all she could do.

And so months passed for the young family in the little wood house with Valentina doing her best as a jíbara wife, putting to use what Gloria and Angelina had taught her and even recalling some of the lessons of economía from her mother. Not a single scrap of paper went to waste. For example, the brown papel de estraza that the country store used to wrap food and bacalao was washed, dried, folded, and put away to be used for writing lists, for covering a hole that had appeared in the out-house roof, etc. They grew their own tubers like yautía and batata and also tomatoes and cucumbers. Corn and other vegetables came from Vicente's parents. They raised chickens. They bought rice and bacalao at the country store with the money Vicente made from selling aparejos or mangos or bananas. When she cooked a chicken on the occasional Sunday—Vicente had to kill the bird, pluck the feathers, and chop it for her—she simmered the remains of the carcass with a diced potato, an onion, and a few cloves of garlic smashed with the back of the knife to make a broth that she fed to the children. One Sunday, while the children were napping, Valentina and Vicente sat at the kitchen table drinking café puro. Vicente was rhapsodizing about coffee. Although his trees were still young, he knew that they would one day bequeath berries as red as little Evita's lips, and that when roasted, they would be the color of Valentina's eyes. Remember he'd told her that Puerto Rican coffee was the only one good enough for the Vatican? One day the pope would drink their coffee! ¡El Papa!

"In a Parisian café, a woman will drink our coffee with a handsome Frenchman," Valentina said.

"I'll be able to pay the merchants because of lovely ladies like you drinking coffee with Frenchmen." Vicente reached for her hand.

"When, Vicente?" She curled her fingers around his.

"It'll be at least four years before we have our first harvest."

"That long?"

"Querida, this isn't news to you."

"The children will be old enough to be left with your mother for a few months while we go to Paris and drink our own coffee in a Parisian café!"

He laughed.

She let go of his hand. "I'd like to have enough money to eat chicken more than once a week and bread once in a while."

"We're doing all right."

Valentina refilled his empty cup with coffee from the enamel coffeepot. "I would like to buy myself a new dress even if I've nowhere to wear it."

"You know we don't have money." Vicente picked up his coffee cup.

"Maybe if we grow other crops to sell? Maybe pineapple? And other fruits and vegetables," Valentina said. "I can help you once the children are a little older."

"Fruit and vegetables would rot on the journey to market." Vicente looked at his wife over the rim of the cup. "You remember how long it took to get here from Ponce?"

"It was a lifetime ago." She drank her coffee. "We should grow rice and corn and things like that for our family and to sell." Valentina set her cup down. "You could get Raulito to help you."

"Raulito and Eusemia have to eat, too."

"Give Raulito part of the crop." Valentina pushed away her empty cup.

Vicente shook his head. "It wouldn't work."

"What about if we exported mangos? We have so many mangos from our trees. When I lived in Ponce, I'd never tasted a mango as luscious and juicy as we have here."

Vicente finished his coffee. "Remember that the journey down the mountain to market is a costly and dangerous one. Even if the mangos didn't spoil along the way, we would never make up the transportation costs."

"But you export coffee."

He reached for her hand but she went to the window. "I can mortgage the land to plant because the merchants want to buy coffee, it doesn't rot like fruit, and the export system is already in place."

He wished that Valentina could be satisfied taking care of the home and children. His mother would never have dreamt of interfering with his father's business and he wouldn't have stood for it. Vicente didn't think that a man should be so harsh as to forbid his wife to offer her opinion—unless it was absolutely necessary.

"I'll be an old lady by the time I see Paris." Valentina stared out the window.

"Paris isn't for the wife of a coffee farmer with a bit of land and lots of debts." Vicente left with one last look at his wife. Why did all the women in his family stare out the window?

San Juan
May 30, 1892

Dear Valentina,

How are you? My handsome brother-in-law? ¿Los niños? Everyone is fine here in San Juan. We had a little excitement just the other day. We went to the Plaza de Armas to see the unveiling of the statute of Cristóbal Colón. Hundreds of people dressed in white took part in the special procession to honor the great Christopher Columbus. The orchestra played—

[Valentina skipped to the end of the five-page letter.]

And that's just a few of many wonderful things to see and do in San Juan. Our parents send their love.

Kisses and a great big hug,

Elena

P.S. I will send a package soon with lovely things (only slightly used) for the children. If only we were the same size, I'd send you some of my old dresses! (Ernesto says that I've gotten a little stout! He is the one who is stout! But maybe I will send you a dress or two—I'm sure you can remake it to fit you!)

CHAPTER SIXTEEN

THE VISIT

Valentina was glad that it was only a twenty-minute walk from Vicente's parents' home. Sometimes Gloria took pity on her and came to help with the children or the cleaning, or Inés visited and worked on her mundillo while Valentina went about her many chores. La doña never came, but Valentina would have welcomed her.

One day, Raúl Vega came to visit just as Valentina was putting the children down for a nap.

"You're getting to be un gran macho." Raúl picked up Javiercito and swung him up in the air.

"Don Raúl, I didn't expect you." Valentina carried Evita on her hip.

"Don Raúl," Javiercito said.

"Mariposa," Evita said.

"You must say 'abuelo,'" Valentina said to her son.

She frowned at her father-in-law. "Vicente isn't here, he didn't come home for lunch."

"He couldn't. He's working on the furthest part of the finca."

Raúl Vega flipped the little boy upside down, then right side up.

"Abuelo." Javiercito giggled.

"Mariposa." Evita held out her hands.

Laughing, Raúl set the boy down and held his arms out to Evita. She giggled as he tossed her in the air.

Valentina stared at her father-in-law, openmouthed.

"Mariposa, mariposa," the little girl said.

"Where is the mariposa?" Raúl Vega pretended to look for it.

"She's crazy about butterflies," Javiercito said.

"Is that so, preciosa?" Raúl held the giggling girl up in the air.

Valentina couldn't help smiling. Could this man be the same Don Raúl?

Raúl held Evita in one arm and picked up Javiercito with the other. It reminded her of Vicente's way with his children. "Don Raúl, you're getting them too excited. It's time for their naps."

"Niños, your mother said it's time for sleep." Raúl bounced the children in his arms. "Shall I fly you to your beds?"

"Fly! Fly!"

"¡Mariposa! ¡Mariposa!"

He followed Valentina to the children's room and set Javiercito down in his cot. Valentina took Evita and tucked her inside her little hammock that the country people called a coy.

"Mariposa, mariposa." Evita reached up her tiny hands.

"Is that all you say?" Raúl peered inside the coy.

"She can say 'Mamita,'" Javiercito said.

"Calladito, no more talking." She looped colorful ribbons around the ankles of each of her children—yellow for Evita, green for Javiercito—and knotted the ribbons to the iron railing of Javier's cot. It was a country custom that Valentina had once found quite barbaric, but with children so close in age, and no servants, she had discovered its usefulness.

Valentina motioned to Raúl Vega to follow her out of the room. Javiercito always fell asleep as soon as he closed his eyes, but two-year-old Evita fought sleep like any child who had just learned to walk. Evita was her laughing girl, eager to touch and explore everything around her. Valentina liked to watch her daughter in her lemon dress chase butterflies, flitting between the trees.

Valentina closed the door to the children's room. "Why did you come when you knew Vicente wasn't home?"

"Can't I visit my grandchildren?"

"You never did before."

"There's always a first time."

He was standing so close to her, she walked around him to the kitchen.

The table stood between them.

"I like the way you look at the table." Raúl passed his hand over the tabletop. "Two beautiful things."

"It *is* beautiful, I thank you for it." Valentina put on her apron.

"May I sit?"

"You may."

Raúl sat in the chair. "Won't you offer your father-in-law a cafecito?"

"Yes, of course."

Valentina's hand shook as she filled the enamel coffeepot with water. She added ground coffee from Raúl's own trees to the strainer basket. She went to the lean-to, carrying the coffeepot to el fogón; she flicked a match and lit the kindling before setting the coffeepot on top of the stones.

"You're really a jíbara now." Raúl leaned back in the chair.

Valentina busied herself with the preparation of sofrito. Vicente had made her a wood cutting board; she minced cilantro and recao and added them to the pilón. Aji pepper.

"You probably never even knew what a fogón was until Vicente brought you to el campo."

Two cloves. Valentina smashed the knife's blade against the garlic.

"If it bothers you so much, you could buy me a stove like the one Gloria has."

"That could be arranged," he said.

She didn't look up. She minced the onion using the wrist-and-hand movement Gloria had taught her.

Raúl took a handkerchief out of his pocket and held it to his nose. The fragrance of fresh herbs and coffee filled the silence between them.

"There isn't any milk." She added the onions to the pilón.

"Not even for the children?"

She didn't answer but went to get the coffeepot and then she prepared his coffee, adding two teaspoons of precious sugar. She served the coffee. She thought, as she always did, that Vicente would look like his father in another twenty years, with a little silver at the temples.

"I don't think Vicente would like you visiting me when he's not home." Valentina pounded the pestle in the pilón. "And what if someone saw you and started talking bochinche?"

"I like the way that sounds," Raúl said, sipping his coffee.

"What? People spreading gossip?" She paused, the pestle in her hand.

"Me visiting you."

She looked into his eyes, so much like her husband's. "Don Raúl, you've been very kind to us, but please drink your coffee and then go. You don't want to regret anything."

"I don't think I would regret it."

"Don't."

The pestle still in her hand, she went to the window and stared at her favorite flamboyán tree. It had recently blossomed with flowers so deep a red that the tree appeared to have burst into flames. There wasn't a cloud in the sky. Orchids grew in wild and glorious profusion where she dumped the dirty dishwater. The birds sang and the rooster crowed en el batey as it stalked the hens. When she heard the chair scrape on the wood floor again, she turned around, the pestle raised.

"Are you going to beat me to death?" Raúl Vega stood by his chair.

She felt herself blush. He hadn't moved any closer. He respected her position as his son's wife. Finally.

"Come, we're family." Raúl Vega held out his hand.

She was ashamed that her hand trembled; he gripped it for too long. She breathed in the scent of his tobacco, the smell of his horse; she felt his heat, the physical power of a laboring man.

If only she trusted him.

"I'll just finish the coffee." He sat back down in the chair, his legs sprawled as if he were in his own house.

They heard Javier call out, and she turned toward her son's voice, sighing with relief.

Valentina left the kitchen and went to the children's room.

"Is Don Raúl here?" Javier was standing up in bed.

"You mean your abuelo."

"Is Abuelo here?"

"Yes, but not for long." Valentina untied the ribbon from Javier's ankle. "Is your sister awake, too?"

"Evita's gone," the little boy said.

"Gone?" She peered into the empty coy, then flipped it upside down, as if the girl had done a magic trick. Valentina picked up her son and ran to the kitchen.

"Evita is gone!"

"What do you mean, 'gone'?" Raúl Vega took the boy from her.

"Gone! She's not in her bed!"

"Tranquila, Valentina." Raúl put a steadying hand on her arm. "Have you checked the other rooms?"

She dashed to the other rooms, calling out the child's name. She looked under her bed and inside the large trunk that Elena had sent with her things and where she now kept the family's clothes. She checked the small balcón in the front of the house. No little girl.

Raúl and Javier had followed her outside. "No te pongas histérica, Valentina. We will find her. Maybe some neighbor took her as a joke."

"A joke! Kidnapping a child is a joke?"

"It's not kidnapping, only a practical joke. It's an old country custom for neighbors to take a little child like Evita—"

Valentina grabbed her father-in-law's shirt. "Find my baby!"

Raúl Vega told them to stay in the house while he searched for the child, but Valentina ran out with her son in her arms. They—even Javiercito, who thought it a game—called out "Evita" again and again.

Much later, Raúl Vega returned to the house carrying the little girl, the yellow ribbon dangling from her wrist. He'd found Evita facedown in the stream.

CHAPTER SEVENTEEN

MARIPOSA

The silence was what broke her—not hearing Evita calling out mariposa for the chair, mariposa for the table, mariposa for her brother, everything mariposa; it was the loss of the little girl just learning to say "Mamita, Mamita"; it was not hearing all the words Evita would never learn. The first days, Valentina kept to her bed. Gloria came to care for her while Angelina and Inés took Javiercito home with them. That first night, Vicente cried with her, promising that they would have other baby girls. Then came the days of shadow. Morning when the rooster crowed and the birds performed their concerts, she knew it was a new day, but what had happened to the day before? What had happened to the night?

CHAPTER EIGHTEEN

EL TIEMPO MALO

Utuado
October 14, 1893

Dear Elena,

I write with terrible news that our sweet baby girl Evita was drowned. A tu hermana le dio un ataque de nervios pero casi está bien. Las damas have helped us during Valentina's nervous breakdown. Mamá takes care of Javiercito, and Gloria takes care of Valentina. You don't need to worry. Please give your parents the sad news.

Con cariño,
Vicente

San Juan
November 1, 1893

Dear Vicente,

How we cried to learn about our little niece! We are so sorry for you and my sister. We're terribly worried about Valentina. Does she need anything? Do you? Please let me know, con confianza. I will write my sister in a separate letter.

Con cariño,
your sister,
Elena

San Juan
November 15, 1893

Darling Sister,

I don't know how to begin this letter. Querida, I'm so sorry about your sweet Evita. I would do anything in the world to ease your pain. Ernesto and our parents send their love. The day we received Vicente's letter, Mamá and I went to the Catedral de San Juan Bautista to give the priest money so that he could say misa for your baby girl. El padre told us that because Evita died so young and was without sin, she is now an angel in heaven. It gave Mamá comfort to know that Evita is a sweet angelita, as I hope it does you. Mamá also insisted that we make a novena for Evita, and we invited people we knew to our home for nine nights to pray the rosary. Yesterday was the ninth night and we said three rosarios, como es la costumbre. I know that this can be but little comfort to you.

Darling Valentina, what can I send you, what can I say to help ease your pain? I can only imagine how you feel, being a mother of two myself. Querida hermana, if only I could hold you in my arms. Know that I— we—have you in our prayers, that you are never far from our thoughts, and are always in our hearts.

I send you and your Vicente the love of your sister and your family.

Siempre,

Elena

Although she didn't want to, sometimes Valentina dreamt that she took an evening stroll down les Champs-Élysées or the Luxembourg Gardens on a lovely spring day, arm in arm with her old friend Dalia. Sometimes she sat in a café, a tiny cup of coffee or a glass of red wine on the table, and her companion, a mysterious well-dressed gentleman, whispered something in her ear that she could never hear but that caused her to frown or her eyes to fill with tears.

San Juan
January 30, 1894

Querido Vicente,

I hope all is well with you and Valentina and my nephew. I'm writing to ask that you tell me truthfully the condition of my sister. Mamá is considering traveling to Utuado to take care of her, but she is not as strong as she once was. I've heard the roads are rough and the journey perilous. I would make the trip myself except that I have two young children and the responsibility of the household, our parents, and my husband. Still, I will drop everything and come to Utuado if you think it necessary for the well-being of my sister.

It seems almost sacrilegious to wish you Feliz Año Nuevo, but I do wish it, with all my heart. I hope that this coming year is filled with the blessings that you and darling Valentina so deserve, and that time will ease your pain and that of my sister.

Con mucho cariño,

your sister,

Elena

Utuado
March 4, 1894

Dear Elena,

Valentina has recovered from the shock of our dear baby girl's death, but sometimes she stares out the window for a very long time. If I ask what she is looking at, she only shrugs or doesn't respond at all.

My mother says that once we have a new baby, your sister will be so busy that she won't have time to dwell on sad thoughts. I hope she's right.

Con cariño,

your brother,

Vicente

•

Valentina saw Evita as she slipped her hand from the lasso of ribbons. She saw her jump off the bed and land on her bare feet. Evita poked a finger into the ear of her sleeping brother. Her tiny fingers lifted one eyelid, then the other. When he turned on his side, she ran out of the room and out of the house. She ran into el batey, chasing the rooster and hens. Valentina saw the little girl dart behind the trees and bushes. Valentina followed the yellow dress down to the stream. She couldn't go beyond that; she couldn't see Evita facedown in the water, her dress floating about her.

Utuado
October 14, 1894

My dearest Elena,

Sometimes when I wake I hear the children in their room. Javiercito is singing to his sister and she is giggling, talking the nonsense talk of a two-year-old. I turn on my side, smiling, listening to them, but then I recall that Evita is gone, and I don't hear them anymore.

Don't tell Vicente what I wrote you. As a mother yourself, you must understand how I feel. I am well, I promise. Very well. Your letters and packages have helped me so much this past long year. I have felt your love and presence, and it's almost as if we were together again. How I long to see you and our parents. I know that one day, we will see each other and it will be as it used to be.

I have news. We are expecting a baby in March. I hope that it will be another boy. I'm not sure if I can bear to have another daughter.

Siempre,
Valentina

P.S. Kisses for everyone, especially our parents.

Utuado
March 14, 1895

My dearest Elena,

I write to tell you of the birth of your niece, whom we have named María de Lourdes. When Inés placed her in my arms, I tried so hard not to cry. Doña Angelina scolded me because tears sour mother's milk and sicken the baby. I know that you and Mamá find my nursing repugnant (don't deny it!) and believe that only a certain class of woman would do such a thing. We don't have money to pay for a wet nurse, even for a peona who asks only for plátanos and rice. Vicente's parents would pay for it, but they have been so good to us already. (If you send money like you did last time, I won't use it to pay for a wet nurse, but for necessities. Be warned.) When I hold my baby to my breast, I am so overwhelmed with love that I pity every mother who gives her child to a wet nurse. Yes, even you. (Don't be angry, darling Elena.)

Oh, how I miss you. I had to be apart from you all these years to know how much I love you. Don't worry so much about me. (Vicente said you wrote him again.) Vicente is always very tender with me.

All my love to our dear parents, whom I love so much and never appreciated when I was at home. Please beg their forgiveness for me. I send my love to Ernesto and the children and especially to you, my dear sister.

Siempre,
Valentina

San Juan
January 7, 1896

Dear Valentina,

By the time you receive this letter, it will be a month old and las Navidades will be just a pleasant memory, but you should know how much we always miss you during the holidays! Remember how we loved to go to concerts en la Plaza Las Delicias? We met our girlfriends at the ceiba tree and circled la plaza to bat our eyelashes at the boys. What fun times we had! The holidays always make me melancholy. It's when I most wish that our children were growing up together. Why did you have to go and marry a farmer from the backwoods? Excuse me—mountain.

Mamá and I dream that one day we will all be together for Christmas. We send you our love and best wishes para un Feliz Año Nuevo. Look for a package with a few French novelas (don't ask me how hard it was to find them!) and gifts for the children. Kisses for my handsome brother-in-law.

All my love,
Elena

P.S. Write soon and tell me how you are!

Utuado
November 11, 1896

Dear Elena,

I hope you and our parents and the family are well.

You asked in your last letter what you might send me. Clothes for the children are always much appreciated, but if you could also send me a primer of mathematics and one for Spanish grammar so that I might teach Javiercito. Vicente was taught by a maestro ambulante, but no teacher has come this way seeking work. I'm sure that I can manage, especially if I have the proper books. You never saw me as a teacher, did you? You would be surprised at what your little sister has had to do since you last saw her. This new Valentina has vowed to devote herself to her family and to put away all childish dreams.

Siempre,
Valentina

Utuado
June 11, 1897

Dear Elena,

Vicente can't stop worrying about coffee—every day, it's the coffee prices this, the coffee harvest that—will it rain?—why won't it rain?—why is it raining so much? Vicente does his best pero a cada santo una vela, always the creditors. To think that I once thought a farmer's life one of leisure! What a foolish child I was! Pero no te preocupes. Next year, our harvest will be better, and the year after that will be even better. We'll survive as long as Cuba, España, and other European countries continue to drink Puerto Rican coffee. In the meantime, I've learned la economía (Mamá would be proud!), and with your gifts of clothing, etc. (hint, hint), we are able to sobrevivir.

Kisses to our parents, your family, and especially to you,
All my love,
Valentina

San Juan
October 7, 1897

Dear Valentina,

I hope you and the family are well? There is much excitement in the capital with the expectation that Spain will give Puerto Rico autonomy. We went to hear Don Luis Muñoz Rivera speak on how Puerto Ricans are capable of governing themselves. The newspapers are full of the coming war with the United States. Have you heard that en el campo, too? (We think that is why there are more beggars than ever in San Juan. You can't walk out the door without a dozen people holding out their hands!) I've begun to take an interest in politics, particularly when it concerns women. Our parents and Ernesto aren't too pleased! There are some damas here who are suffragettes. Have you heard of suffragettes? (They believe that we women should have the right to vote, etc.)

Valentina, I'm going crazy with boredom! Ernesto has plenty of help in the store because you don't have to pay clerks very much. I can't be like our mother and live for the marketing and economizando. Must go now. I have been invited to a meeting of damas to discuss the woman's place in the Puerto Rican home.

As always much love,
Elena

P.S. I am sending you a parcel of canned goods and a bottle of Spanish olive oil. Mamá can't believe how the prices of groceries have skyrocketed!

CHAPTER NINETEEN

DROUGHT

In 1898, Raulito failed to find work as a sharecropper. He didn't know that his great-grandfather Juan Cortés had once been a sharecropper, too. At seventeen years old, Raulito had nothing to offer a landowner except the labor of a malnourished peón, and there were thousands of malnourished peones like him. Raulito wandered the countryside, oblivious to the fact that some of the land had once belonged to his family.

All his life, no one would tell him about his ancestors—that his great-grandfather Juan Cortés had gone from landowner to agregado to jornalero forced to work for a plantation. Or that his grandfather Alegro Villanueva had been a freed slave with a gift for picking coffee; or that his grandfather had been shot in the back by the Guardia Civil on his way to the penitentiary for stealing a few apples for his hungry children. Raulito's mother didn't want to bring up the past. His brother Vicente could have told him that on their father's side, their grandfather Luis Manuel Vega had bought the land cheap from the family of Juan Cortés, but eventually sold most of it to pay off debts. And because he read the newspapers and talked politics with his father and other men whenever he went to town, Vicente could have told Raulito how it was an especially bad time to be poor in Puerto Rico. Spain was preparing for war with the United States, and while it wanted to keep Cuba, the Philippines, and even Puerto Rico, their tiny island was not as important—it was an afterthought. Vicente could have told his brother about the newspaper editorials denouncing the terrible economic conditions on the island. Or that no group—political or professional—was able to solve the hunger crisis. If the island's mayors or leading intellectuals had ideas, they didn't know how to get money to implement them. He could have told Raulito that the Spanish crown had granted governing concessions to the Puerto Rican and Cuban criollo intellectuals who had agitated for years for autonomist rule, and so now Puerto Rico was on its own to manage its problems.

All this and more Vicente could have told his brother Raulito. But even Vicente didn't quite understand that in the early months of 1898 when the new autonomist government began under the leadership of the Honorable Luis Muñoz Rivera, Puerto Rico had no gold in its coffers. Spain still required its island subjects to use tax money to pay for necessities like horses, saddles, and uniforms for the Spanish soldiers who would defend Puerto Rico from the United States, "el Colosal Norte." So there wasn't money to hire laborers like Raulito to repair the neglected bridges and roads or to provide medical care to the sick or food for the starving. There was no money for Puerto Rico or Puerto Ricans.

The drought began with the dawning of 1898. Merchants refused credit to farmers, and workdays were cut or workers fired "por economías." They were told, "No hay trabajo."

Everywhere Raulito sought employment—the sugarcane plantations, the alcaldía, etc., he heard the dreaded phrase, "No hay trabajo." At first, he thought it might have been because he was black, but then he heard it everywhere, and blancos heard it, too. It was the cry of the countryside, "No hay trabajo," and in every single town on the island nation of Puerto Rico.

As Raulito walked through the countryside, he met many people who from a distance he mistook for specters. In town, there were hundreds of these skeletal people, holding out their bony hands for a piece of bread.

In February 1898, only a month after the new autonomist government of Luis Muñoz Rivera took office, fewer Spanish supply ships arrived in Puerto Rico, and when they did, they carried only a fourth of what was needed. Until the government worked out deals with other countries, there were limited supplies of everything. Unscrupulous merchants seized the opportunity and doubled the prices of their goods, cheating the poor—it was common knowledge that no store gave sixteen ounces for a pound. Milk and wine were doctored, causing harm to those who drank them. Merchants refused credit to the poor because they feared they wouldn't be able to pay their debts. Everyone agreed it was a war against the Puerto Rican people, and surely the new government would take action against the Spanish merchants and the homegrown crooks. Small fines and even shaming the culprits by publishing their names in the newspapers did little to deter the practice, especially when some of the guilty were members of the town councils. Los hacendados reverted to the plantation feudalism of the past four centuries and paid their workers una miseria in paper or copper tickets redeemable at their stores for rotten meat and spoiled bacalao. Many of the desperate killed themselves or turned to alcohol or gambling; children were abandoned on the street and in the countryside.

Los hambrientos emigrated to large towns like Ponce in search of food and work, hoping for help from politicians whom they had voted into office. Ponceños complained about "the invasion of the paupers" come to imperil the economy. The authorities discussed putting the beggars in jail. Everywhere on the island, people fainted on streets and pavements, there were stories of starving men collapsing on the doorsteps of the rich only to have the dogs set on them. Tiznados, bands of armed men with faces blackened with charcoal, terrorized the Spanish hacendados taking revenge on the landowners that had abused them. Throughout Puerto Rico, assaults and robberies became common. Cattle and oxen were stolen and mutilated, with the starving sometimes eating the meat raw.

In the newspaper La Bruja, Vicente read that "hunger knocks on our doors and the only voice that answers is one of necessity," while in El País, he read, "The only thing in abundance on the island is salt."

That February, Raulito joined the barefoot and hungry en la plaza, just like any mendigo. He was one of thousands who gathered in the town plazas and shouted prayers for rain at the cloudless sky. When a kind lady or gentleman tossed a handful of pennies on the ground to the child beggars, Raulito lamented that he couldn't be among them scrambling on his hands and knees. The priest passed out bread some Fridays, and made the sign of the cross on the dirty foreheads of those who stopped to say gracias. But more often, la Guardia Civil chased the poor—Raulito and the children included—from the plaza, sending them back to their humble homes (those who had them), where there was nothing to eat. Raulito usually hid behind a building or a tree until the police left, and then he, like many others, returned to la plaza hoping that someone would show mercy.

CHAPTER TWENTY

RAIN

Once-lush green leaves dangled from branches, yellowed like dry corn husks. There was little wind to ease the heavy heat that made a night's sleep impossible. Vicente's feet kicked up dust and it lodged in his throat and left a tickle. He knew this drought was different; he was afraid for his coffee trees and the shade trees like the plantain, whose fruit was necessary for the jíbaros' daily meal. No shade trees, no coffee.

Vicente reassured Valentina that her root vegetables like batata and malanga were safe because they grew in the ground. He'd taught her how to plant them when they first moved to the little house. It had pained him to see his Valentina on her knees, hands in the dirt like any peona. He tried to cover his dismay by teasing her and calling her a jíbara. She'd looked at him in surprise, her hair tucked into a straw hat she'd tied under her chin with a faded yellow ribbon. Yes, she said, it's true. I'm a jíbara.

That February, the rainwater cisterns had run dry. He went every day to the stream to get water for the household. Birds flew above the burnt crowns of the trees, squawking *Rain, Rain*.

Vicente rode to the family house; the horse trod with slow, labored steps on the cracked dirt road. He would have to sell the animal, something he should have done already. His anxiety kept him from sleeping, and he'd taken to roaming the mountain at night. Valentina worried that he would fall off a cliff and break his neck. She'd insisted that he ask his father for advice, surely Raúl must have survived droughts before.

The family farm was better situated, closer to the river. When Vicente passed it, he was shocked by the low water level.

Some things didn't change with the drought—Angelina and Inés fussed over Vicente, as they always did. Gloria made Vicente a fresh cafecito. He felt guilty drinking coffee. At home they'd drunk the last of their own, but since Gloria had already brewed it, he might as well enjoy it. Sitting on el balcón with las damas, Vicente told them about Valentina and the children. They talked about the terrible drought, about the necessity for un tremendo aguacero that would bring salvation to the island.

They watched a beggar approach the house, each step a feat of will.

"Another hambriento," Inés said. "Pobrecito, I know what it is to be hungry."

"I hope that you were never that hungry." Angelina smoked a small homemade cigar.

Inés was decorating the collar of a dress with mundillo. She looked up from her lace.

Angelina sent the mendigo round to the kitchen.

"La piña está agria," Inés said. "Especially for los hambrientos."

"Gloria has taken to hoarding what we have," Angelina said. "That beggar will get something, but not enough to satisfy his hunger."

"I'm thinking of selling my horse," Vicente said, "but I don't think I'll get more than a few dollars for it, the way things are. He's worth much more."

"You need your horse! Everything will be more difficult if you sell it," Angelina said.

Vicente got up to leave. "I can't wait any longer for Papá."

"Talk to your father before you do anything."

"More hambrientos coming." Inés pointed to the horizon. "Que tragedia."

"We'll give them something," Angelina said.

Vicente kissed his mother's cheek. "You're a kind lady."

Once a week, Vicente went to town to get the newspapers and to learn what people were saying about the impotence of the autonomist government, the taxes imposed by the Spanish, and the upcoming war with the Americans.

Vicente had just reached the plaza when he saw Raulito.

Several makeshift stoves, with kettles as big as cauldrons, had been set up en la plaza in an attempt to feed some of the hungry a daily meal of stew. It shamed Vicente that his brother was among those beggars—los lameollas, the potlickers.

Vicente ducked, hoping Raulito didn't see him. He was ashamed that he'd given so little thought to his little brother these last few months. He would ask Valentina for something and take it to his brother.

The first raindrops began to fall at the end of April; people began to hope again and farmers began to plant crops. Newspapers like El País reported that hunger was still a greater enemy to the Puerto Rican people than war. Government flyers began to appear exhorting farmers to plant food crops so that in the future no one would be hungry, but the government couldn't and the merchants wouldn't lend the farmers money for seeds or laborers. Los frutos menores that Vicente and his father planted had suffered from lack of rain; it would be months before any could be harvested. En los campos, May through September was a time of little employment, until the coffee harvest began in October.

When news arrived in late April of the war in Cuba, the Honorable Luis Muñoz Marín begged the mayors of the municipalities to do what they could for los hambrientos. It wasn't much. As food became more scarce, robberies and assaults by bands of tiznados became more frequent. Made up of laborers and the sons of small farmers, the tiznados avenged years of ill treatment by Spanish hacendados and merchants, surprising them in the middle of the night. They stole rice and sugar and coffee; sometimes they burned down their houses or stores, assaulted or murdered the men, and raped the women. As war with the Americans became more likely, tiznados began also to rob criollos, Puerto Ricans, like Vicente.

THE TASTE OF SUGAR · 151

Utuado
May 3, 1898

Dear Elena,

This early morning we woke to Raulito at our door to tell us—I'm sure you've heard—that the Spanish fleet had bombed New York! Everyone was talking about it en la plaza, about how that great American city is in ruins and hundreds, if not thousands, of people have died! The war has begun! (I hope this victory means that the war is over.) We hurried and got dressed to go to town because it wasn't every day that nuestra Madre España conquered New York! I wore my best dress—the blue one you sent with the ruffles—and Lourdes had on her pink. I was able to find a shirt of Vicente's for Raulito, and we went down to town complete with a picnic basket with our lunch. (Lourdes and I rode the horse.) La plaza, really the entire town, was filled with people cheering the soldiers. There were rumors of a great naval triumph in Manila. Hats were passed around for donations for the war, rich or poor dropped in their coins. I was against even a centavo going into that basket, but everyone was looking and Vicente dropped in a few coins, despite my protest. (Later I know he regretted it because we couldn't buy the children the piraguas they wanted.) Tomorrow, when Vicente returns to town to sell some fruit, he'll mail this letter and buy the newspapers sure to be filled with details of the victories. What have you heard?

Recibe un abrazo de tu hermana,
Valentina

P.S. Kisses to our parents, Ernesto and the children, and to *you*!

San Juan
May *11*, *1898*

Dear Valentina,

How are you and the family? The entire city of San Juan was en fiesta yesterday. A fleet of Spanish ships docked at port resplendent with the flags of la Madre Patria. Houses throughout the city, including ours, were adorned with Spanish flags and ribbons. Over a thousand young men have volunteered for the Spanish army. Papá says it's because they're hungry and the army will feed them, but I think it's because they're patriotic! The damas have signed up for the Red Cross, even me! Doctors and nurses and the high-class San Juan ladies set up makeshift hospitals and ambulances. Hundreds of workers marched into the city, their machetes raised in the air. Everyone shouted, ¡Viva España! ¡Viva la Madre Patria! ¡Viva Puerto Rico! ¡Abajo con los yanquis! ¡Viva la guerra! San Juan is ready. The whole island of Puerto Rico is ready. The newspapers say so. Let the Americans come if they dare!

Love,
Elena

PART TWO

THE AMERICANS

San Juan
May 25, 1898

Dear Valentina,

We have returned to our house after several weeks away from San Juan. In the early hours of May 12, we were still asleep when a blast of noise rocked us in our beds. The American warships bombed the harbor! We ran from our room and screamed for the servant to get Mamá and Papá while Ernesto and I gathered the children. We fled the house in our bedclothes and not much else. Ernesto stopped to lock up the door even as I yelled at him to leave it. (Afterward, I was grateful.) Ernesto and the servant carried the children while Papá and I helped our mother. We ran and choked on smoke. Cannon fire from El Morro returned the Americans' attack. It was pandemonium, Valentina, a terrible nightmare, and were it not for the feel of cold cobblestones on my bare feet or the night breeze through my nightgown, I might have thought myself asleep. People ran out of their houses in their nightclothes, as we had; one of our neighbors was naked, his hair wet as if he'd been in the bath; everyone was screaming and pushing to make their way to the road to Río Piedras. A man covered in blood lay on the road. Someone shouted that he was dead, and people stepped on him to get past. The Church of San José had a gaping hole in its roof. Vendors on their way to market from the countryside dropped their wares and scampered for dear life, except for the bread vendors who raced with baskets of fresh bread balanced on their heads. The milkman had abandoned his cow and calves; they bleated and blocked the road. The vendedor de aves had dropped his wooden crates of birds, and they flew against the bars, unable to escape. We took refuge in a friend's house some distance from the harbor. Later that day, we returned to pack a few things before driving in our carriage to the house of Ernesto's sister. (Ernesto decided to go back to San Juan to attend to our business.) One of our neighbors left San Juan in his sailboat; we could see the parade of white sails as we drove by the harbor. The American warships had vanished, but one of the grand houses in San Juan had its entire top story blown off. (We found out later that the Spanish had done it, thinking it was an American warship.) Ernesto heard from our customers that the next day many merchants and regular citizens sent the soldiers in El Morro cases of champagne, cognac, wine, sausages, dulces, etc.

Some of the familias pudientes have left for their grand haciendas in the countryside or taken the steamships to Europe, or have chosen to recuperate in the hot springs of los Baños de Coamo for the duration of the war.

Mamá has not stopped shaking, and I fear that she has suffered un ataque de nervios from which she might not recover. The doctor says to wait and pray. Valentina, remember when we thought Mamá seven feet tall and as sturdy as the trunk of the coconut palm? Now I have to talk to her in whispers because any loud sound will startle her and bring on tears. Our father, on the other hand, whistles all the time. He is the only one who can calm Mamá. Dear sister, how I wish you were with me to help with this burden that God—or shall I say the Americans—has placed on me, but I know that you have your own troubles.

All my love,
Elena

P.S. One of our neighbors found a projectile on the street. It weighed over a hundred pounds!

CHAPTER TWENTY-ONE

PROCLAMATION, JULY 28, 1898

To the inhabitants of Puerto Rico:

In the prosecution of the war against the kingdom of Spain by the people of the United States, in the cause of liberty, justice, humanity, its military forces have come to occupy the island of Puerto Rico. They come bearing the banner of freedom, inspired by a noble purpose, to seek the enemies of our country and yours, and to destroy or capture all who are in armed resistance. They bring you the fostering arm of a nation of a free people, whose greatest power is in justice and humanity to all those living within its fold. Hence the first effect of this occupation will be the immediate release from your former relations, and, it is hoped, a cheerful acceptance of the government of the United States. The chief object of the American military forces will be to overthrow the armed authority of Spain, and to give the people of this beautiful island the largest measure of liberty consistent with this occupation. We have not come to make war upon the people of a country that for centuries has been oppressed, but, on the contrary, to bring you protection, not only to yourselves, but to your property; to promote your prosperity; and to bestow upon you the immunities and blessings of the liberal institutions of our government. It is not our purpose to interfere with any existing laws and customs that are wholesome and beneficial so long as they conform to the rules of military order and justice. This is not a war of devastation, but one to give to all within the control of its military and naval forces the advantages and blessings of enlightened civilization.

Nelson A. Miles

Major General, Commanding US Army

San Juan
July 30, 1898

Dear Valentina,

We are very upset that the Americans devalued our peso to fifty cents to the US dollar! General Miles stepped one boot on la playa de Ponce, and by the time he set down his second boot, he'd raised our cost of living! There is a rumor that our silver pesos are ending up in the US Treasury, where they are adding five cents' worth of silver to remake them into American silver dollars! We were also shocked to read in the newspapers that we are now the island of Porto Rico! Ernesto is furious because Porto is not even a Spanish word. I hope you are well.

Siempre,

Elena

CHAPTER TWENTY-TWO

THE DEVIL

When Vicente's father taught him about coffee, he said, "El café es brujo." As a young boy, he understood that coffee was the devil the first time he picked the berries and his hands became swollen from mosquito bites, his neck red from the pricks of the plumillas. But it was more than that: coffee was at the mercy of nature and commerce. It had been a brutal year but finally, in July, the weather became more moderate and Vicente thought that his first harvest would be a profitable one.

That morning in early August, Vicente had gone with Raulito and Javier to the finca. They had brought fruit picker poles and empty sacks with them. After checking the condition of his coffee berries and pronouncing himself satisfied, Vicente reached the pole into the guava tree, plucking a guava.

He brought it to his nose. "Perfecto."

Raulito picked one. "Perfecto."

"Javiercito, smell this guava." Vicente put the fruit under his son's nose. "Smell it?"

Javier nodded.

"Hold out your hand."

Vicente placed the guava in Javier's hand.

"Feel it. Gently. That's how you know a guava is ready to eat."

Javier bit into the red flesh, smiling.

"Not sour? Or too sweet?"

The boy shook his head.

"That's what you want in a guava," Vicente said. "That's what we want with coffee, isn't that right, Raulito? A little sweetness."

"That's right." Raulito bit into a guava.

"But coffee isn't sweet," Javier said.

"There is a very subtle sweetness, just a hint of the taste of sugar that only those who live for coffee can taste," Vicente told him. "That only people who need coffee as they do water can know."

Javier tossed the pit on the ground.

Vicente pulled down a coffee branch. "See these green berries, Javiercito? They're not ready yet, but by October they will be."

"Can we take lots of guavas to Mami? So she can make us pasta de guayaba?"

"Who doesn't love pasta de guayaba?" Raulito reached his pole into the guava tree.

They heard horses and the sound of marching men. Javier ran to the slope.

"Soldiers!"

Vicente and Raulito set down their poles and walked to the slope, where they watched the cavalry climb the hill.

"Americans," Vicente said.

"Hundreds of them," Raulito said.

"¡Americanos! ¡Americanos!" Javier waved. "¡Bienvenidos! ¡Bienvenidos!"

A jíbaro dressed in white led the US Cavalry—American officers on big, healthy horses and hundreds of foot soldiers—and a hundred of their barefoot countrymen mounted on the island horses that looked like runts. The soldiers wearing cloth hats carried rifles and bayonets along with tents and other supplies strapped to their backs and gray blankets slung over their shoulders, reminding Vicente of burros; he pitied them their sunburnt faces. Some looked only a year older than Raulito. They awaited orders, sweating in wool uniforms and thick canvas leggings. The commander was a tall American, spare of build and dark haired, but with eyes so light they appeared almost colorless—just as Vicente imagined the eyes of all Americans to be. Vicente exchanged looks with Raulito. What would the Americans want from them?

The jíbaro on horseback, one of the few of his countrymen who wore shoes, announced in a hoarse voice that seemed yanked from his vocal cords that he was Emiliano Morales, the Americans' guide and interpreter. He introduced the captain of the cavalry; the soldiers were from Illinois, America, and the men in white were Puerto Rican patriots.

Vicente gave the customary polite salutation, introducing himself, his son, and his brother.

"Your brother?" Emiliano Morales looked down at Raulito from the height of his horse.

"That's what I said." Vicente crossed his arms.

The guide dismounted. "Caballero, I promised these americanos some Spanish soldiers to string by their thumbs, and I haven't found even one dirty Spaniard."

Vicente waved his hand. "This is my farm. There aren't any Spaniards here."

"We're searching for filthy Spanish soldiers hiding out as jíbaros." Emiliano Morales turned to Javiercito. "You see any filthy Spaniards hiding like cowards?"

"Don Miguel is a filthy Spaniard," Javier said.

Vicente put his hand on Javier's shoulder. "Don Miguel's family has lived on this mountain for three generations—as long as my family."

Emiliano Morales explained that he came from nearby Adjuntas, where not so many years before, citizens suspected of wanting independence from Spain had been arrested and tortured. "Where I come from, we hate the Spanish."

"We're all Puerto Ricans here," Vicente said.

Emiliano spoke to the American officer, then turned back to Vicente.

"The Americans couldn't have crushed the Spanish without our help. We told them when and where to attack. Puerto Ricans were waiting on the beach at Guánica to guide them."

Vicente had read in the newspapers about the Americans landing in Guánica, and that ever since the invasion, there had been a rush at the ayuntamientos throughout the island as Puerto Ricans registered their children as Americans. Most likely, there were now hundreds of children named Jorge Washington. So many Abraham Lincolns and Tomás Jeffersons born that first week alone. Vicente looked at Emiliano Morales, a skinny man whose face and neck were burnt dark caramel by the sun, one of many Puerto Ricans who believed that the Americans had come to save them.

"The men must be thirsty," Vicente said. "My boy can take them to the stream."

"Here, boy." Emiliano Morales held out the reins of his horse to Javier, and Vicente nodded permission. Morales relayed to the American officer Vicente's offer and Raulito and Javier led the cavalry and the others to water.

"The Americans don't want to be our masters, like the Spanish." The guide took off his hat and wiped his brow with a kerchief.

"Glad to hear that," Vicente said.

"You sound like a Spanish-lover," Emiliano Morales said, taking an American cigarette from a pouch around his waist. "Don't you know that America is 'the land of the free'?"

"I know coffee," Vicente said.

Two days after they met the US Cavalry, Vicente and Javier started down the mountain just as the fog began to lift on Cerro Morales. They walked alongside the horse, laden with sacks of guavas to sell in the market. When they reached the edge of town, they heard the cannons. Boom! Boom! Boom!

Javier reached for his father's hand. "Is it an earthquake?"

"Did you feel the earth move beneath your feet? No? Then it's not an earthquake," Vicente said.

Utuado's main street was crowded with delirious people who were cheering the way they had a few months before, when they thought Spain had bombed New York and won the war.

"It's the Americans!"

"How pale they are! How young!"

People leaned out windows and shouted greetings to the cavalry, waving handkerchiefs and American flags. Pretty señoritas draped themselves over wrought-iron balconies and tossed garlands of roses and orchids on the parade of American soldiers. Women ran up to them with cups of fresh, sweet water and juicy mangos, while the men passed out little cigars made from homegrown tobacco.

The American flag now flew from the flagpole of the ayuntamiento, where the town's citizens registered the birth of their children and paid their taxes. The Spanish flag had been tossed on the ground somewhere behind the mayor, who shook the hand of an American officer. The mayor proclaimed that after four hundred years as a Spanish colony, 1898 would go down in history as the year Puerto Rico became a free country.

"Surely the great poets will immortalize the Americans, the liberators of our beautiful island, who have broken the chain that has shackled us as a colony," the mayor said. "¡Viva Puerto Rico americano! ¡Viva los Estados Unidos!"

The crowd cheered. Flowers and papelitos, tiny paper disks, rained down on the soldiers. The military band played "The Star-Spangled Banner."

An old man next to Vicente shouted over the crash of the cymbals.

"Puerto Rico americano," the old man said.

CHAPTER TWENTY-THREE

FOR THE PRIVILEGE

It had been only weeks since the American invasion and Vicente didn't know how to tell Valentina about the new tax that he'd learned about en la plaza. He went to his parents' house, where his mother told him that Raúl Vega had already left for la finca. Vicente rode to the coffee farm. Raúl Vega had tied his horse to a tree branch, and Vicente dismounted and did the same. He found him at the top of a small hill, looking down at the grove of trees.

Vicente called out as he approached, "Papá, have you heard that el Presidente McKinley—"

"I heard." Raúl Vega didn't turn around.

"The Americans are trying to destroy us," Vicente said.

His father took out a cigarette from his pocket and struck a match. "As soon as General Miles devalued el peso, I knew it wouldn't turn out well for puertorriqueños."

"What will happen to us? To our coffee?"

Raúl Vega opened his arms as if he could encompass all the land he saw in front of him.

"This was nothing but wild grass and woods when your grandfather Luis Manuel came in 1825. He probably stood on this very same hill."

Father and son looked down at the shade trees, the guama and guava trees, the banana and plantain, the protective canopy above the coffee trees. They stood without speaking for a few moments as they admired the beauty of the vista. They heard the neighs of the horses and felt the sun on the back of their necks. It was the kind of day they'd hoped for all that long year—when the drought had come and gone, the war had ended, and they could dream of a good harvest.

"My father was a hard man. Fuerte, like men had to be in the old days. He was tough with everyone, his slave Benedicto, the people who worked for him—los agregados, los jornaleros—with me. Fuerte."

His father had never spoken like that. "Papá—"

"This new tax will ruin us," Raúl Vega said.

"The Americans say that it's to pay for the military government." Vicente adjusted his hat. "The United States is making Puerto Rico pay to be occupied!"

Raúl Vega brought the cigarette to his lips. "Puerto Rican coffee can rot in its own bean as far as the Americans are concerned."

They stood there for a while, father and son, not talking, staring out at the green mountains in the distance.

San Juan
August 18, 1898

Dear Valentina,

We have just come from la Plaza Alfonso XII. As we waited en la plaza under the hot sun—everyone was there, rich and poor alike—no one spoke. A company of American soldiers lined up in front of el Palacio de la Real Intendencia, while on the rooftop terrace, others waited holding an enormous American flag. On the second terrace, on one side in full uniform, were the American generals—Miles, Grant, Sheridan, etc.—and, on the other side, the former president of Puerto Rico, the Honorable Don Luis Muñoz Rivera, and the rest of our government officials. The old bell clock struck twelve times and still no one spoke. Then we heard cannon fire from El Morro and from the American warships. The soldiers raised the Stars and Stripes onto a flagpole on the rooftop terrace of la Intendencia. We watched it flapping in the wind. We stood there in silence while the military band played "The Star-Spangled Banner." I swear that at that very moment the sun eclipsed, bathing the city in an orange light.

Ernesto says a new era has begun for Puerto Rico. Dios quiera, that it will be a good one.

I hope that you and the family are well, as we are, considering Mamá's condition. I will write again very soon.

Siempre,
Elena

Utuado
August 28, 1898

Dear Elena,

The Americans are turning us into paupers. We had a good harvest this year, a miracle, Vicente says, considering the long months of drought. But what good is it when Vicente and Raúl have to practically give away their coffee to the creditors because the merchants can't sell it to Cuba or Spain or France! And except for some place called the Hamptons, Americans don't like Puerto Rican coffee! Nobody buys Puerto Rican coffee! And that means that the merchants won't buy from farmers! What is to become of us?

My love to our parents and Ernesto and the children and especially to you,

Siempre,

Valentina

San Juan
October 22, 1898

Dear Valentina,

San Juan is filled with Protestant missionaries. They came with the army and you can't walk down the street without one waving a Bible in your face. More than a few ladies have had their heads turned by the soldiers. I know of at least two society damas planning marriage with Americans. It's true that some of the soldiers are handsome with their blond hair and eyes the blue of el Caribe. I'll be sure to keep watch over my daughter because she reminds me of you—headstrong, always day-dreaming. The day she mentions the word "pirate" is the day she enters the convent. Luckily, there is one here in San Juan!

Everyone gathered at the harbor to watch the Spanish soldiers board the lighters that would transport them to the Spanish ships. The Span-ish military bands played. They're such wonderful musicians and we'll miss them. The crowd waved and wished the soldiers a pleasant journey. Many of the soldiers had Puerto Rican wives and children, and it was heartbreaking to see these families torn apart, but the Americans insist on the departure of all Spanish military. Valentina, even these brave soldier-husbands/fathers were crying. Most of them will probably never see their family members again unless the soldiers are allowed to return to Puerto Rico or can afford to have their families make the voyage to Spain. What will happen to the wives and children left behind? It's a tragedy.

On October 17, we woke early to go to La Fortaleza. Our stationery shop was closed by official decree, as were all the shops in San Juan. Yanqui soldiers with bayonets guarded every street corner. Dressed in our best clothes, we went to el Palacio de Santa Catalina, where the Americans had built a grand speakers' platform like an offering to the gods, complete with roofs and awnings in red, white, and blue stripes. Valentina, I wish you had been here to enjoy the spectacle with us!

The whole town was draped in the American flag, some as large as the buildings. All the Spanish flags had been collected from the townspeople beforehand (upon risk of a fine if they weren't turned in) and stored away who-knows-where. Newspaper boys sold la *Gaceta de Puerto-Rico* with the American eagle on the front page instead of the Spanish coat of arms.

There was a story in the newspaper about some yanqui soldiers who caused a ruckus at the restaurant La Mallorquina. The yanqui general apologized to the people of San Juan and all the people of Puerto Rico for the shameful behavior of the yanquis from Wisconsin. We think it had something to do with the indecent way some of the American soldiers have accosted women on the street.

We cheered as the American flag was raised over the governor's palace. The military band played the American national anthem. (It sounded almost musical.) Who would have guessed that we Puerto Ricans would be such yanquifilos?

All my love,
Elena

P.S. In another parcel, I will send you *Idioma inglés en siete lecciones*, sold on every street corner in San Juan. Ernesto is studying it because he says he wants to learn English and read the news in the yanquis' own words.

CHAPTER TWENTY-FOUR

A MAN'S HOME

Vicente woke to the neighs of horses and the muffled voices of men. He wrapped his arms around his wife under the bedspread and touched his lips to her ear.

"Wake up, los tiznados están en el batey."

She opened her mouth to speak, but he squeezed her hand. "Go to the children," he said. "Under no circumstances are you to come outside."

Valentina ran naked to the children's room. Vicente reached under the bed for the gun his father had given him just a few weeks before. Raúl Vega had stopped by one morning to warn Vicente that a neighbor had been attacked by a band of tiznados. He'd hoped he would never have to use it.

Vicente went to the front of the house without bothering to pull on his pants; he opened the wood shutter just wide enough to slide out the nose of the gun. It was the kind of night when spirits and men up to no good wander blind in the fog. The men on horseback huddled en el batey; he heard them but could not see them. Vicente decided not to speak, but to wait the men out—to try to discern how many there were. He had only the bullets in his gun. His hand shook. He'd never shot at a man before, but he knew he would kill to protect his family. They'd heard that the men who had robbed Isidro Santiago down the mountain of his coffee harvest had also raped his wife. He'd kill all of them before they could touch Valentina.

"Come out before we torch your house," a voice shouted.

Where had he heard that voice before?

"I'm giving you a chance to save yourself," the voice said.

Vicente remained at the window, his gun peeking through the shutter. Something calmed inside him. He fired his gun toward the voice; he heard a groan. He ran to another window and fired again in the direction of the voice; at a third window, he fired a third time.

Somebody shouted, "There's a bunch of them!"

Los tiznados rode away, but Vicente held his gun at the ready until he could no longer hear the horses. He sank to the floor, the gun hot in his hand, and waited for his heart to return to its regular beat. He found Valentina and their sleeping children curled together in Lourdes's bed.

"Thank God you're all right, Vicente!" Valentina looked up at him through the mosquito netting.

Vicente pushed aside the netting; he took her hand and drew her to Javier's cot.

"You're trembling." He pulled the bedcover over them and wrapped his arms around her. He breathed in her scent that he knew so well and settled his thighs beneath hers.

"I would have killed any man who dared touch these." Vicente cupped her breasts.

"You don't mean that."

"Of course I do, querida." Vicente kissed her shoulder.

"Don't start anything."

"No?"

"The children might wake up."

"The shots didn't wake them, I wouldn't worry."

Later, when Valentina fell asleep, Vicente realized they were breathing in unison. When they had made love, the children asleep in the next cot, she'd pressed her mouth hard against his so that he could swallow her moans. He loved that about his wife, his Valentina, how loud she was, how free she was in their lovemaking. Once when Javiercito was a toddler, he'd come into their room, crying because her screams had woken him. Papi, why are you hurting Mami? Valentina had carried the boy back to his bed. Vicente could hear her say, Sweetheart, your father wasn't hurting me. Those were happy cries from Mami. Now go to sleep, I want you to stay in your bed until morning. She returned to him, her hair half covering her face so that he couldn't see her expression in the moonlight that slid in through the wood shutters. He loved her like that, when she made love to him like that, wild like that. She needed him then, wanted him then. He was sure that she didn't wish for other things, not then, things that he wasn't able to give her, would never be able to give her. Only when they made love did he feel that.

As he closed his eyes, he remembered where he'd heard that voice in the batey.

The morning after los tiznados tried to raid his home, Vicente hurried his horse down the mountain. He asked everyone he passed along the way if they knew Emiliano Morales. Somebody said, Oh, Emiliano Morales, I heard he's in the hospital, had an accident while he was cleaning his gun, things like that happen when you clean your gun in the middle of the night. He was loco like that, the kind of man who would clean his gun in the middle of the night while decent people slept, but why did he, Vicente Vega, a peaceful family man, want to see Emiliano Morales? Not such a good idea, not after the things people were saying about Emiliano Morales.

American soldiers were everywhere—en la plaza, at the ayuntamiento where Vicente appealed for time to pay his taxes. He had begun to hate the Americans the way his father hated them, as others did, including some of the newspapers. He didn't have faith that the well-being of the island was a priority for the Americans. Didn't General Miles realize that when he set the price for the Puerto Rico peso, he only made life harder for Puerto Ricans? That many more people went hungry? Hadn't they welcomed the Americans with flowers and mango slices served from the fingertips of pretty señoritas? Then why did they need the military to run their island?

An American flag now flew in front of the police station. Hat in hand, Vicente was taken to the captain. He was invited to sit while he told them about los tiznados and how he'd shot a man in the dark.

"So, you're the one who shot Emiliano Morales." The captain was drinking coffee, and he signaled to a policeman to bring Vicente a cup.

Vicente folded his hands in his lap to hide their shaking.

"We found Morales half-dead in la plaza. How do you know him?"

"He came up the mountain with the US Cavalry while I was in my finca." Vicente accepted the cup the policeman brought him.

"That makes sense," the captain said. "The Americans have been protecting their guides. Letting them rob the Spanish hacienda owners and not doing anything about it."

"Why would they do that?" Vicente took a sip of café and was soothed; it was delicious, definitely Puerto Rican coffee.

"The Americans hate the Spanish." The captain removed a folder from the desk drawer. "And they won't help them unless it affects American interests."

"I never killed a man before." He spilled a drop of coffee on his shirt.

"He's not dead yet." The captain opened the folder.

"That's good," Vicente said.

"And even if he dies, who can say it was your bullet?" The captain looked down at the report. "You know who the others were?"

"It was dark," Vicente said, "but Morales has that voice that rasps against your skin, so rough that you check for blood."

"These bands have even ambushed la Guardia Civil," the captain said, "but because they blacken their faces, it's not so easy to capture them. Sometimes they rob their own relatives and they don't recognize them."

Yelling could be heard from the other rooms in the station. Vicente's hands started to tremble again.

"It's probably lucky that you shot him, Vega," the captain said.

"How so?"

"Some of these bandits have been known to disrespect the women in the family," the policeman said. "The shame has led to a suicide or two."

"No me digas," Vicente said. "Of the husband or the wife?"

"Mostly it's the husband who kills himself, sometimes it's the father if it was his daughter who was assaulted. The shame a man suffers when his women have been violated." The policeman shook his head. "Can't say I'd blame him."

"I'd kill the man first." Vicente picked up the coffee cup again, and this time his hand didn't shake.

San Juan
December 14, 1898

Dear Valentina,

¡Feliz Navidad y Prospero Año Nuevo to you and yours! How are you, my dear sister? Please kiss my handsome brother-in-law and your children and tell them that their Titi Elena sends love from the whole family and especially from los abuelos.

Since Mamá's nervous breakdown, I must employ an additional servant. Fortunately, servants ask for very little—room and board and perhaps a few coins—the country is full of unemployed people. How dull are the duties of an ama de casa. I don't know how you've tolerated it all these years. Or do you spend your days staring out the window at the flamboyán?

Only last week, the Americans gave out flags to all the schoolchildren. Such a to-do en la plaza! Business is beginning to be very profitable for us, despite the devaluation of the peso. It seems I've inherited Mamá's accounting skills. Ernesto has learned a few words in English and much of our trade is American. Many of the soldiers can read, and do they write letters! Ernesto and I have talked about one day traveling to Paris to buy *papier à lettres*. Don't be jealous, it's only a dream.

All my love,
Elena

P.S. I send the usual Christmas package with a few extra things for you. Thank the American soldier who loves to write his mama!

CHAPTER TWENTY-FIVE

HAPPY 1899!

S he sipped the cognac, loving the way it glided down her throat, its delicate warmth still on her lips. She and Vicente sat at the table and finished off Dalia's French brandy. In the fading light, she felt a rush of feeling for her husband; it wasn't the usual lust, no, not that, or even love, but something akin to gratitude for their years together, that they had each other when they had lost Evita. Then Vicente told her the merchants wouldn't lend them any more money. "That's bad news for us," Vicente said.

Valentina braced herself.

"We can't take out a loan against the farm." He rubbed his eyes.

"Why would we want to do that?"

"You know that we don't have any money, Valentina." He stared inside his glass, at the golden liquor. "This year would have been a pretty good year for us. We would have been able to settle our debts and survive until next year."

"But we can't sell our coffee," she said.

"We can't sell our coffee, nobody can. And the only way we can get money without selling land is to mortgage it."

Valentina got up and brought the kerosene lamp to the table. A moth fluttered around it. Vicente caught and smashed it between his palms.

"The merchants and the Americans are buying up land cheap when the debtors can't pay off the loans," he said.

She poured the last of the cognac into their glasses. When Vicente had told her that they had to have a serious talk after the children were asleep, she'd gotten out the bottle from where she kept it on a high shelf hidden behind the small tin of Spanish olive oil and the big tin of

American lard that had long been used up and where she now stored a small bag of flour.

"We could go to your parents."

"Valentina, no. We can't." He picked up his glass.

"They'll help us. I know they will."

"Papá is in the same situation. And he has three women to support."

"What about Luisito? He's your brother. Or Elena? I can write her."

"Querida, no. Luisito is in bad shape, too. And Elena has helped us enough through the years."

"Then—" Her voice shook.

"We need a miracle." Vicente raised his glass.

She raised hers. "To a miracle."

They finished the last of the cognac.

CHAPTER TWENTY-SIX

A MYSTERY IN UTUADO

Vicente had just left his mother after an errand for Valentina—to ask Gloria for annatto seeds from the achiote tree that grew in front of the family home—when several men approached on horseback. He was surprised to see that they were from la Guardia Civil.

"Buenos días," one of the policemen said. "Are you Raúl Vega?"

"Vicente Vega, his son, a la orden."

"Is your father home?"

"No."

"Do you know where he is?"

"No."

"When will he return?"

Vicente shrugged.

At that moment Raúl Vega rode up on his horse, seemingly unsurprised to see policemen. The policeman who had first spoken to Vicente asked if Raúl Vega knew a man named Claudio Mora Ruiz.

"Somewhat," Raúl Vega told them.

"We'd like you to come with us to town to answer a few questions," the policeman said.

"I was on my way home."

"We insist, Don Raúl." The policeman put his hand on his gun. "We don't want any trouble."

"I'm not one to make trouble," Raúl Vega said.

"You, too." The policeman pointed to Vicente.

At the police station, they learned that a certain Claudio Mora Ruiz, the nephew of one of "los grandes" de Utuado, had been shot twice, once in the heart, and his body dumped on Caonillas Road. Vicente wanted to ask about the second shot but didn't dare. Raúl Vega didn't seem nervous, he was whistling.

The captain's pen was poised over a notebook. "Señor Vega, witnesses say that you once had an argument with the deceased. Do you deny that?"

"We had words once." Raúl Vega crossed his legs.

Vicente stared at his father, openmouthed.

"Why was that?" The captain leaned forward on his desk.

"I don't recall exactly, but I think there was some question about a few acres of land." Raúl Vega took some cigarettes out of his pocket. He passed them around. One of the policemen offered him a light.

"What was the argument about?" The police captain brought a cigarette to his lips.

"It was some time ago."

"Try to remember."

"Mora Ruiz claimed some of my land belonged to him."

"Did it?"

Raúl Vega shook his head. "I filed a complaint in court."

"And?" The police captain stared at him through the cigarette smoke.

"The court ruled against me," Raúl said. "There were no hard feelings."

"Where were you on January 20th?" The police captain leaned forward in his chair.

Raúl Vega considered his cigarette. "My son Vicente and I were together on the farm."

The captain turned to Vicente. "Is that true?"

Vicente looked from his father to the captain. "Yes, it's true."

"How do you happen to recall that date specifically?"

"Afterward, Papá came to my house. My wife cooked dinner." Vicente remembered that it had been a rare visit from his father. Valentina had made tembleque with coconut milk and cinnamon.

"She's a good cook," Raúl said.

"Señor Vicente, how well do you know Mora Ruiz?"

"I've never met him," Vicente said.

"Why do you think he was killed?" Raúl Vega knocked the cigarette ashes into an empty cup on the captain's desk.

"All I know is that there are bands of men meting out their own brand of justice in the middle of the night. Maybe we'll let the American military handle this one." The police captain stood up. "Buenos días, caballeros, I don't think we need trouble you again."

Father and son rode through the plaza like two strangers with the same destination. Yes, they had been together on January 20th, but still, it was all so strange. Vicente patted his pocket for the packet of annatto seeds. What had happened to it?

CHAPTER TWENTY-SEVEN

VALENTINA READS THE CONSTITUTION

One day Vicente returned from town with Raulito, whom he had found standing around en la plaza with other men hoping for work or food. He'd insisted that his brother come home with him. Vicente also brought a week-old *La Democracia* dated July 4, 1899, in which the US Constitution had been printed in Spanish.

They drank coffee while Valentina read bits of an editorial aloud.

"Listen to this: 'Read the Constitution because a people constituted on a basis so free and democratic cannot bring forth tyrants. That is the reason why we trust in the justice that will be given to us: the offspring of those who signed that Declaration of Independence can do nothing less than give liberty to our people.'"

"Haven't the Americans been in Puerto Rico a year already?" Raulito dunked a piece of hard bread into his coffee.

Valentina looked up from the newspaper. "Yes, they have, Raulito."

"Keep reading," Vicente said.

Valentina turned a few pages. "It's long."

Vicente stirred his coffee with a spoon, though there was no sugar in it; they'd run out months ago.

"This is called the Preamble. 'We the people . . .'"

While Valentina read, the children wandered outside, Raulito dozed off, and Vicente refilled her water glass twice.

"Beautiful words," Valentina said when she finished.

"Beautiful lies," Vicente said.

"I wonder if this newspaperman read the Constitution before he wrote his editorial," Valentina said.

"He's probably one of the American lambe ojos, there are plenty of them around." Vicente took the newspaper from her to see who had written it. "Yup, just what I thought. Lambe ojo."

San Juan
July 10, 1899[*]

Dear Valentina,

How are you and the family? Mala suerte, we're not quite as well as we once were. Many of the American soldiers are being sent back home to the States, and that means less money for all the businesses. We've had to let one of our clerks go and I'm spending more time in the store. Papá has been very helpful; he's the one who goes to the post office every morning to get the mail. Mamá is the same. Every little sound from the street frightens her.

Ernesto is up to date on the tariffs and we are worried about your family. What are your plans? Can Vicente's father help until the Americans ease their regulations? I hate to think of you suffering. You can always sell the farm and come stay with us until Vicente finds some kind of work. Try to convince him. It would be lovely to be together again.

Love to everyone and especially you,
Elena

P.S. We can still manage to send you a few things and I am preparing a large package of food tins and cans that Papá will take to the post office.

[*] Letter returned to sender

CHAPTER TWENTY-EIGHT

THE HURRICANE

It was difficult to sleep in the terrible heat of the first days of August 1899. There was something unusual about the air that escaped Valentina's notice but filled Vicente with a sense of foreboding. Up on the mountain, he smelled flowers native to the coast. Then the night came when Vicente observed reddish clouds in the east instead of the west.

"The stars have lost their brilliance," he told his wife, pointing to the sky. "Look at that curious white band on the moon. I've never seen anything like it."

Vicente took Valentina and the children to his parents' house before setting out again to get his brother. He brought in the bundles. His father was carrying a gallon of water under each arm.

"You prepared your house for the hurricane, Vicente?"

"Not yet."

"What are you waiting for?" He went to the kitchen.

Angelina called from the kitchen, "Vicente, don't stand there all day talking to Valentina."

"I'd better go," Vicente said.

"I don't like to stay in your father's house without you," Valentina said.

"Why not, when my father likes you best?" Vicente teased her. "It's safer here."

"Really, Vicente, I think you're exaggerating the danger."

"I've never seen that peculiar moon."

"The moon, the stars."

"And you." He smiled at her as if he weren't worried.

Vicente stopped back at their little house to nail pieces of wood to the windows and doors. He considered locking the pig inside, but better for the pig to brave the wrath of the hurricane than his wife's fury. He drove the pig into the shed. He wished that he had slaughtered it earlier in the summer, and invited their neighbors to feast on lechón; they could have celebrated surviving a year of the Americans. He took one last look at the house he had built for Valentina, with its roof sloped in four corners in the traditional cuatro-aguas style. He rode past the chicken coop sheltered by mango and citrus trees. The wind blew cool on the back of his neck. He shivered in the sun, disconcerted that he could smell the coffee flower so far away from the coffee trees.

Vicente rode his horse up the rocky slope that curved around the mountain. Even those mountain-born like Vicente had to be cautious of the steep trail. He rode alongside a village of bohíos built of straw or corn husks until he reached the hut Raulito shared with his mother. Vicente found Eusemia sitting under the shade of a mango tree, fanning herself with a large leaf.

"It's you," she said.

"It's me," he said.

"I expected you," Eusemia said. "This heat is a terrible thing."

Vicente took off his hat and wiped his brow with his kerchief. "I came to take you to my father's house, Eusemia. You and Raulito."

"You've always been kind." Eusemia stood to pluck mangos from the tree.

"You'll be safer there." Vicente looked at the hut made of plant fiber.

She followed his glance, then held out the fruit. "It has survived other storms. Here, take these to your mother."

Vicente put them in his saddlebags. "You won't come?"

"I can't be with those white people," Eusemia said, "but I give you thanks."

Vicente knew she meant that she couldn't be in the same house with his father. "Raulito won't come without you."

"Make him go," Eusemia said.

Vicente found Raulito inside the bohío, adding yagua rushes to its thatched roof. There was a pile of straw on the floor.

"I came to take you and Eusemia to Papá's house," Vicente said.

"I'm staying here," Raulito said.

Vicente stared for a moment at his little brother, knowing he wouldn't be able to persuade him.

Raulito pointed to the roof. "It leaks when there is an aguacero."

"This one is sure to be un tremendo aguacero at the very least."

"Did you see the moon? It's going to be a bad one." Raulito packed some straw into the wall. Vicente helped him. Before he left, the brothers hugged each other.

When Vicente rode past the rows of bohíos, he saw men carrying palm leaves or plant fiber to prepare their homes for the storm. Women cooked on fogones while their children, the little ones naked, played in the dirt. The children ran alongside his horse, laughing as they raced it. Vicente returned their smiles, wishing he could do more than just wave goodbye. He wasn't a man who prayed, but he mumbled a heartfelt plea for the safety of the people in their straw huts.

Vicente wished that his family didn't have to shelter in his father's house. But at least Valentina brought out the best in Raúl Vega, everyone said so. It made Vicente a little uneasy. He had once heard his mother comment to Inés how only when Valentina was in the house could she recall the charming rascal who had come to call on her once upon a time. Wasn't that so, Inés? Remember how charming he could be? Inés said, Yes, Angelina, of course she remembered, once upon a time Raúl Vega had charmed her into becoming his mistress. Vicente had a vague recollection of the day Inés had come into their lives, because that day was the only time Vicente had ever heard his mother raise her voice to his father. Mostly Angelina spoke to her husband in veiled sarcasm. Vicente wasn't sure what had taken place between his parents, only that from that day forward, the widow Inés had slept on a pallet in his mother's bedroom and he and his brother had carried their father's things to the other end of the house. Vicente was in his teens when he realized that Inés was no longer called "la viuda Inés," but just plain Inés, that she was his mother's special friend, and that the pallet was gone from the floor. Inés and his mother shared a bed, but what was wrong with that, Vicente had once said to his wife, sisters often slept in the same bed, wasn't that so?

"Elena and I didn't," she said.

Valentina had given him a look that he chose not to interpret. All that was important to him was that his mother didn't stare for hours out into the horizon, as she had before Inés.

The rain had already begun when Vicente arrived at his parents' house. In his old bedroom, Vicente changed out of his wet shirt and pants and into the clothes Valentina had brought for him. His shoes were soaked but he didn't have another pair.

"The barefoot jíbaro has arrived," Raúl Vega said as his son entered the kitchen.

Vicente greeted his father and kissed the women, receiving blessings in return.

Valentina was helping Gloria peel root vegetables. Vicente planted a kiss on her cheek; she smiled at him.

Raúl Vega was reading the pro-government San Juan News that islanders had nicknamed "el Esnú," mocking the English name. Vicente's father either proclaimed every article preposterous and an outright lie or called his countrymen who collaborated with the US government lambe ojos for kowtowing to the Americans. More than once, Vicente had witnessed his father tear the paper to shreds.

"Eusemia wouldn't come," Vicente told him, "and Raulito wouldn't come without her."

"It's going to be a bad one." His father put down his newspaper. "Did you notice the moon?"

"Maybe if you had gone it would have been different." Vicente waited for his father to defend his negligence or to express remorse.

"Only if I'd forced them a la mala," Raúl Vega said.

"I hope that you locked up your house very well." Gloria handed Vicente a cup of coffee.

"I even locked up the pig." Vicente smiled.

"Not in our house?" Valentina looked up from a half-peeled batata.

"No, querida." He sipped his coffee. "Luisito isn't coming?"

"Your brother probably decided to stay with his wife's family." Angelina lit one of her tiny cigars. "They live closer to them than to us."

Vicente sat down at the table, picking up the newspaper pages his father had discarded. Lourdes climbed into his lap. Javier sat next to Raúl Vega.

They ate Gloria's homemade blood sausage with boiled malanga and yucca and batata and Eusemia's mangos. Lourdes helped Gloria wash the dishes.

And they waited.

Raúl Vega went to a cupboard and took out a bottle of rum. Gloria got up for glasses and he poured rum for everyone, even a splash for Javier; Valentina put her hand over the glass meant for Lourdes.

And they waited.

When they needed to relieve themselves, they stepped into the other room, where Gloria had set an escupidera, and then they hurried back.

Gloria lit candles; Inés brought over the kerosene lamp. Valentina looked at Inés's long fingers, bereft of her mundillo, restless on the tabletop, tapping out a song that no one could hear.

Lourdes fell asleep on her father's lap while Javier slept with his arms cushioning his head on the table.

In the hour between night and day, the leaves on the trees ceased to whisper, animals became mute, and nature held its breath.

Then there was wind and rain that came in torrents; lightning buried electrical bolts into the ground. They sat at the table listening to the sounds of crashing objects outside; one thunderous clamor and violent vibrations shook the ground beneath the house. Vicente thought the earth might crack open.

They wouldn't have been able to hear each other if they had spoken.

Huddled together, the adults sat wide-eyed, the children hid under the table. The rain pounded the house, and lightning flashed through the cracks in the boarded-up windows, illuminating the fear on their faces.

In the early hours of the morning, Angelina and Inés rose from the table. What they said was lost in the rain. Vicente put his arms around his mother, his words imploring her to stay unheard. Valentina grasped Inés by the hand and Inés kissed it; she made a tiny sign of the cross on the younger woman's forehead. Then Angelina and Inés took one of the candles and left.

The rain pounded the door of the house, demanding entrance. Vicente realized that he'd never heard such wind. He thought of his brother Raulito and Eusemia, just two of the peones who lived in the countryside in their huts made of straw and coconut palm; how could they survive such a storm? Would they? Yes, yes, they would, he told himself. And his coffee trees, could they survive? Soon the coffee would be ready for picking. Vicente rubbed his forehead to banish the vision of his coffee trees tossed on the ground like matchsticks, the berries scattered to the ends of the earth.

Finally, there was a lull in the wind.

Vicente went to check on his mother and Inés but the women weren't in their bedroom or in the house.

"Mamá and Inés aren't here!"

Vicente ran to the entrance of the house, his father behind him. When they couldn't open the door because the wind pushed against it on the other side, Vicente ran to the wall for the pick to pry open the shuttered window.

Raúl Vega tossed one end of a heavy rope to Vicente.

"Tie it around your waist and knot it well," he said.

Vicente followed his father out the window and bumped into him when he stopped short.

Gone were the citrus trees—lemon, orange, and grapefruit—that had provided fruit and perfumed the air. Mango trees, gone. Vines of roses and orchids that his mother had planted, the trellises she'd wrapped them round, gone. Bushes of herbs—cilantro, recao, marjoram—everything, gone. Gloria had often sent Valentina annatto seeds from the achiote tree that grew alongside the house. Gone. The chicken coop, gone. The shed with the sacks of coffee from last year's harvest that no one wanted to buy—gone. The horses, gone.

The day had the darkness of night.

The rain slashed their faces. The rope gripped tight in his hands, Vicente followed his father like a blind man. They stumbled over the trunk of a twenty-foot palm tree that had been snapped in half. It seemed like hours before they reached the river, now swollen to twice its usual depth. A wild procession of dogs and cats and cows and horses and uprooted trees and beds and chairs flowed downward as if a giant hand had hurled them onto a river of mud. Men and women and children bobbled up and down and then disappeared, the river swallowing their screams. Bohíos, intact and with their occupants still inside, careened in the water. The wind picked up again, and the men knew it was the second front of the hurricane. They risked being carried away. Father and son turned back toward the house, pushing against the wind. A cow flew over them, upside down on its back, hooves and udders flapping like wings. A boy, his arm sliced off at the elbow by a flying blade of zinc, appeared, then disappeared, like an apparition. Vicente shouted over the din; he felt his breath in his diaphragm, but he couldn't hear a sound.

Raulito clutched his mother Eusemia's hands as they sat huddled together on the cot. It reminded him of how as a small boy, his mother had carried him to her bed when he had woken up crying about spirits; he was forever dreaming about spirits. (It didn't help that Eusemia often saw her dead relatives—her mother and father and grandparents wandering the mountainside or next to her when she picked coffee.) His mother had explained that the spirits had once been human beings, but because of terrible tragedies they had suffered when they were alive, they couldn't make their way into the spirit part of the world. There is only one world, Eusemia had said, everyone lives in it—the living and the dead. Raulito had cried because he didn't want to live with his dead relatives. The spirits meant him no harm, his mother had reassured him, but they were among them always, whether he wanted them to be or not.

Now he pledged to protect his mother, this woman whose hands were rough like bark. Rain came through the thatched roof. His eardrums felt as if they would burst. Hours later, when the wind abated, his ears popped, and he clutched his head in pain. Mother and son stood outside their bohío, staring in silent horror. The few trees that remained had been snapped like kindling. The huge mango tree from which Eusemia had picked mangos for Vicente's mother the day before, gone. Many of the bohíos had vanished. Some of their neighbors drifted in dazed circles or ran about in a crazed state; toward what, or away from what, it was impossible to tell. Later Raulito would realize that the people were naked.

The wind picked up again and they returned to their home of straw and plaited palm. Raulito reached for his mother's hands again. He was sure that the terror on her face was reflected in his own. He fought against the scream that rose in his throat, even though no one would hear it. The rain came down in furious waves and carried off the hut's thatched roof. Water gushed down over them like a waterfall. He felt himself lifted up.

When Raulito was a small boy, his father Raúl Vega picked him up and tossed him high up in the air and he flew up up up; Raulito flew up into the sky.

The mosquitoes and the rains came the day after the hurricane, but still the men prepared to go out to look for the missing women. They didn't know that it would rain for twenty-eight days. Together, they set out; Raúl Vega and Vicente found the road to town impassable. They stepped over or around corpses of dogs, cats, oxen, horses, and sometimes, people. They turned over the bodies of young men and women who might have been Raulito and las damas. Each time, Vicente breathed a sigh of relief that it wasn't one of his loved ones. As they followed the river a ways to look for the women, bodies floated past them. On a bank they found two little girls, facedown in the mud. Vicente couldn't help crying out for a moment remembering Evita, even as he turned them over on the chance that they might still be alive. They returned home before dark, their shirts fashioned into slings filled with what fruit and vegetables they had picked up along the way.

The next day the men went out again; the women had brushed the dry mud off their clothes that morning while they ate their breakfast of coffee and cornbread spread with Gloria's pasta de naranja, a sweet orange marmalade that was Vicente's favorite. The women and children were instructed to stay inside because it was too dangerous. Valentina promised to preserve what she could of the fruit and vegetables they had found.

Father and son took the opposite direction from the day before. The trails they'd known well had disappeared; they walked one behind the other up the mountain using broken branches as walking sticks. Sometimes they stopped to get their bearings, other times they stopped because they were dumbfounded by the devastation. Where once there had been a hill with groves of coffee trees or with dozens of straw bohíos, some with families they had known well, now there was just sunken earth.

Another day they were able to make it all the way to Raúl's coffee farm. The hurricane had picked up the coffee trees and shaken them like maracas, scattering the still-green coffee berries all over the mountainside before tossing a few trees back down. Vicente snuck a look at his father, but he'd pulled his hat low on his face to protect it from the rain. Most of the shade trees had disappeared—the banana, the plantain, the guama, and the guava. The few that were left bowed their giant leaves in surrender.

They helped pull corpses out of the river. Each time they turned over a woman who could have been his mother or Inés, Vicente cried, his tears disguised by rain. Each time it wasn't either of las damas, he felt ashamed of his relief.

On the tenth day of rain, they were able to reach Vicente's farm. He told himself that whatever they found, he still had his health, his wife, his children, Gloria, and even his father. And perhaps he would find

Raulito and las damas. People were what mattered. People. Not coffee. Not land.

All the trees had been carried off, and the ground was saturated with water. Vicente stood in the batey, his shoes sunk in the mud. He stared at the house that he had built and where he had lived with Valentina and their children. Where they had kept vigil through the night for their little girl, where Evita had lain in a tiny white coffin set on the fine table his father had built. A huge palm tree had fallen on the house; the hurricane had taken the roof. It was as if someone had punched him in the gut.

His father stood beside him; they didn't speak.

The shed he had used to store coffee still stood. It seemed impossible that it had survived while the house had not. Perhaps the pig had survived. Inside, Vicente found a naked man on the ground.

"¡Raulito!" Vicente shook his shoulder.

Raulito sprang up and threw his arms around his brother.

"The hurricane took her," Raulito mumbled into his brother's shoulder.

"You're coming with me." Vicente patted his brother's back.

"But your house—"

"To our father's house."

"He won't want me." Raulito tried to cover his nakedness with his hands.

Vicente took off his shirt and gave it to him.

"He's here, don't worry." Vicente put his arm around his brother.

It had begun to rain again. They walked around the palm tree inside Vicente's house. Raúl was looking at the broken pieces of the table he'd made for Valentina.

"Maybe we shouldn't tell Valentina about the table just yet."

"Papá, I found Raulito in the shed."

"¡Raulito?" Raúl Vega turned around.

"Don Raúl." Raulito didn't raise his eyes from the floor.

Raúl Vega looked at his sons, one naked from the waist up, the other from the waist down. For once, he didn't make a sarcastic comment.

"And Eusemia?" he said.

"Desapareció." Raulito tried not to cry.

Raúl Vega nodded as if he had expected it.

Vicente found Raulito a pair of pants and a shirt; the clothes were wet, but then so were they. They carried what they could salvage and walked home in the rain.

CHAPTER TWENTY-NINE

THE PUEBLO ASKS FOR
WORK AND BREAD

They were to learn that almost two thousand people had died in their district; that the hurricane had been named San Ciriaco because it had landed on the saint's day; that every single bohío in Utuado's countryside had vanished, the inhabitants presumed dead; that the rivers had swept up more than five hundred houses, with a hundred persons drowned in a single house, forty people in another; that the entire town had flooded, the current dragging twenty houses and their occupants down to the river; that the hurricane destroyed most of the houses, including the infirmary, the telegraph station, the Catholic church, the schools, and the cemetery; that almost the entire coffee crop and most of the food crops had vanished, even the tubers in the ground had been blown away. Later they would learn that in one town on the island, people saved themselves by passing from balcony to balcony and climbing into borrowed boats; they would learn of the deaths and devastation in other parts of Puerto Rico including the city of Ponce, where over five hundred people had drowned, most of them los pobres who lived in shanties; ships arriving in the port of Ponce reported dead bodies floating in the sea. The island-wide damages totaled over twenty million dollars. Three thousand three hundred and sixty-nine people dead, and thousands more homeless.

Utuado had sent a contingent to San Juan to meet with Governor Davis en La Fortaleza to plead for immediate help, informing him of the desperation of its citizens, of the many hundreds homeless and starving. General Davis pledged to provide money to construct a bridge at the entrance to Utuado after the rainy season ended, but unfortunately,

Puerto Rico would have to wait for emergency funds until they figured out how to distribute them in an organized manner.

At the post office and the ayuntamiento, Vicente added Angelina and Inés and also Eusemia to the list of the missing. He reasoned that as long as they didn't find his mother's body, there was the possibility that she was still alive. One night he dreamt of his mother and Inés hand in hand at the edge of the raging river during the night of the hurricane. In his dream, he shouted at them to turn back, but they didn't hear him.

More than half of the island's food supply was destroyed. One-fourth of Puerto Rico's population, half a million people, were destitute or homeless. The newspapers were filled with horror stories. Vicente read in *El Pan del Pobre* that a man had slumped over dead from hunger on Calle San Francisco, and that campesinos from the town of Morovis had taken to roasting cadillo seeds instead of coffee beans to make a breakfast of dandelion coffee. Armies of los hambrientos spent their days in aimless walks around the pueblos. Skeletons in tattered clothing slipped barefoot down country roads swollen with mud. Only up close was it possible to see that the walking bones had once been José Valderrama or Joaquín Sandoval Hernández or Cristina Mercado Ortiz or fulano Santiago or fulana Castillo or any of thousands of puertorriqueños. Rather than watch their children starve, people drowned themselves in the streams and rivers. Girls and women sold themselves for a piece of bread. More than once, Vicente came upon a man dangling from a tree branch.

When Vicente met other Puerto Ricans after the usual greeting of Buenas, how are you, and the answer, Luchando, at least I'm alive, the questions they asked each other were always the same: Why don't the Americans help us? Why are so many American soldiers doing nothing but eating good food and sleeping in real beds? Why didn't the American military feed the people—the thousands of starving men, women, and children?

They read the newspaper editorials that asked: Where was the help that the people of Puerto Rico had expected from the great Republic to the North, the country of Washington and Hamilton and Lincoln?

A letter sent by the representatives of Utuado to the newspaper *La*

Correspondencia said: "The pueblo asks for work and bread. Tomorrow thousands of campesinos from twenty-five barrios will arrive in Utuado, calling for trabajo y pan. How can we provide that when in all of Utuado there aren't provisions enough for eight days?"

Vicente and Valentina read that the United States didn't have a special budget for calamities, but that the two million dollars that had been collected from taxes on Puerto Rican products imported to the US since the military occupation would be returned to the island to help the Puerto Rican people. The newspaper *El Diario de Puerto Rico* wrote that because the US government shouldn't have charged the tariffs in the first place, the money returned was justice, not charity.

Then, on August 22, 1899, another tropical storm hit the island, causing extensive damage in the capital of San Juan.

They didn't know that only a week after the hurricane, President McKinley ordered the military in Puerto Rico to pass out rations. The military government didn't know how to help—they'd never before had such a human catastrophe on their hands. They came up with a plan for charity and offered a sweet deal to the planters. All they had to do was make sure that the hurricane victims worked for their food and clothing, which the charity board would provide from funds donated by the American people. The planters would get free labor to repair their properties and plant and harvest their crops. With the help of the military government, in September 1899, less than two months after the hurricane, the plantation owners had reestablished Puerto Rico's centuries-old feudal society.

Raúl Vega told Vicente that the best thing that ever happened to the owners of the big coffee haciendas and sugarcane plantations was Hurricane San Ciriaco.

CHAPTER THIRTY

LOS FLAMBOYANES

Valentina prayed it would never come to this—that she would
be back in Raúl Vega's house.

It was dreadful that Angelina had vanished in the hurricane. And Inés—Valentina had to put away the bolillos and the cushion
for mundillo to keep from crying for Inés. One day, Lourdes had taken
an antimacassar from la sala and pinned it to her hair, and Valentina
burst into tears, scaring the poor child.

At first, she refused to believe Vicente when he said that their own
house was uninhabitable, that it needed repairs that wouldn't be possible for a while, not until las cosas se mejoren, and who knew when that
would be.

"Mujer, you're better off here." Gloria slapped at a mosquito on
her arm.

"But our house is empty." Valentina swatted a mosquito on her thigh.
"Our things are there."

"¡Malditos mosquitos!" Gloria looked at the new red mark on her arm,
only one of many.

Valentina rolled up her sleeve. "Look! They feed on me in my sleep
even with the mosquito netting."

"We'll look for peppermint or some other plant for the mosquito
bites," Gloria said.

"You better wait until the weather gets better," Vicente said.

"But Vicente, what about our things?"

"You should go get your things," Gloria said.

"I'll get them for you, Valentina," Raulito said.

She smiled at him. "We'll go together."

They started off early in the morning on foot. Raúl's horse had been found in a nearby pasture, but not Vicente's. She didn't recognize the route home. The once-lush vista was a barren yellow and brown. The red flamboyanes that had turned the road into a blaze of fire had disappeared.

Vicente took her hand. "Querida, you must prepare yourself."

She cried out when she saw the palm tree sticking out of their house.

"I didn't want to tell you—" Vicente put his arm around her.

Valentina shook her head. "A palm tree. There weren't any palm trees near the house."

Valentina picked her way around the palm tree and entered where once there had been a wall. She looked down at the table in disbelief; this was where she served her family their meals, where she and Vicente lingered over their coffee, where she had written her letters to Elena and Dalia. She had sat at this very table nursing her children.

Vicente came up behind her. "Querida, it was only a table. One day, I'll build you another."

Valentina couldn't speak without bawling, so she didn't. She walked around the tree to their bedroom to view the damage and decide what could be salvaged.

They took the linens off the beds and tied the sheets together like sacks. Javiercito filled them with the kitchen things like pots and pans, while Lourdes was instructed to take the pillows and mosquito netting. The men took apart the beds. Valentina went to her trunk and examined the contents. Everything was soaking wet—her wedding dress, her letters, and the stationery Elena had sent her. She took everything out and laid them on the floor to dry. What they couldn't carry, they would return for tomorrow with Raúl's horse.

CHAPTER THIRTY-ONE

HAPPY 1900!

Vicente had picked up the newspapers in town after trying to appeal his taxes to the American at the government office. Was it his fault that the hurricane had taken all his coffee trees? How could he pay his taxes if he didn't have coffee to sell? The American had told him through his translator to return with his land deed. Vicente wasn't sure what would happen next, but he did know he still wouldn't be able to pay his taxes.

It had become a habit for the adults to gather at the table at the end of the day and read the newspaper aloud by the light of the kerosene lamp. This time, Vicente read while Valentina lengthened the hem of Javier's pants. Raúl smoked, Raulito whittled a tiny horse from a scrap of wood for Lourdes, and Gloria rested in a chair with her eyes closed.

Vicente read that President McKinley had signed a new law especially created for Puerto Rico, called the Foraker Act, that would allow for civil government.

"What's the catch?" Raúl Vega took a drag on his cigarette. "No way the Americans are going to let the Puerto Ricans run our own island."

"It could happen," Valentina said.

Raúl smiled at her through the cigarette smoke.

Vicente read: "'The governor and officials will be Americans and appointed by the president.'"

"What did I say, Valentina?" Raúl tapped the ashes into a glass.

The Congress of the United States had decided that the US Constitution gave them the right to levy taxes on Puerto Rico—taxes on food and land and what-have-you—taxes that would pay for the appointed administrators and schools and infrastructure.

Valentina had looked up from her sewing.

Vicente read: "'The Foraker Act is named after its sponsor, Joseph Foraker, a Republican senator from Ohio. Senator Foraker reported that the committee decided against the proposal from US General Davis for free trade with Puerto Rico. "We are here to legislate for the whole United States, not only the island of Porto Rico," Senator Foraker said.'"

Vicente smacked his hand against the newspaper.

"What's that?" Raulito looked over Vicente's shoulder and pointed to a black-and-white drawing in the newspaper.

They all got up to look at a cartoon reprinted from an American newspaper of Uncle Sam patting the head of a black child in diapers and a straw hat. "Puerto Rico" was written on the diaper. The child smiled up at Uncle Sam and waved an American flag. The caption read: "Don't worry, boy, we'll teach you!"

"¡Malditos cabrones americanos!" Raúl Vega said.

CHAPTER THIRTY-TWO

VALENTINA TO RAÚL VEGA

I will never be your querida. ¿Entiendes? Never. There is no "we'll see." I hope that you will not force me to tell my husband, *your son*. Of course I don't want to! Why would I want to cause him pain? I love him. Yes, I love him! It's not up to you to say whether or not I love my husband. I don't care if you don't believe me! Listen to me, Raúl Vega, we've been able to behave like civilized people these last ten years, let's continue to do so. That is the only way that I can live in your house. If you can't promise to leave me alone, to respect my position as your son's wife, then I have to do something about it. Like what? I could— convince Vicente that I can't live here and make him take us to my sister's in San Juan as soon as the roads are passable. You doubt that he'll go? That won't make him a beggar! For the last time, stay away from me, because a woman can only take so much!

CHAPTER THIRTY-THREE

THERE ARE ALWAYS ROOT VEGETABLES

The men were out en la finca when a woman came to beg for bread. Valentina invited her to rest en el balcón. Gloria was in the kitchen when Valentina entered to fix the woman a plate. Gloria said, "Don't you dare to give her our food."

"Gloria, she's starving."

"We'll be starving soon, too. You know we lost our crops and we don't have money to buy food, not at the prices the robber merchants charge."

"We still have root vegetables." Valentina touched Gloria's arm.

"You remind me of your mother-in-law," Gloria said, "que descanse en paz."

"Doña Angelina was always generous."

"Bueno, just a piece of malanga and yaútia." Gloria gave in. "You can't keep giving to every beggar who comes to the door."

Valentina kissed her cheek as she left the kitchen.

"I mean it!" Gloria called after her. "Next thing you know, all the beggars in the countryside will be here!"

Valentina handed the woman the plate of food.

"I haven't eaten for three or four days." The woman looked into the house. "Your mother? Is she very angry?"

"No te preocupes," Valentina said.

As the woman ate, she told Valentina how she had just returned from the town of Arecibo.

"Señora, have you ever been to Arecibo?" The woman gulped down a bite of vianda.

"No, I haven't been anywhere since I came here from Ponce," Valentina said.

204 • MARISEL VERA

"If you came from Ponce, then you know the carretera you have to travel," she said.

"It was in another life," Valentina said. "I barely remember."

"I walked that carretera," the woman said. "I walked all of that and more."

"You walked that? Ay bendito, pobre mujer." Valentina looked at the woman's dirty feet that peeked out from under her skirt. Her toes looked like they had once been broken.

"I used to live in a bohío not too far from here." She pointed up the hill. "We heard that there was food in Arecibo from the Americans." The woman wiped her eyes.

"Tranquila." Valentina touched the woman's arm. "No te preocupes, you don't have to tell me."

"I want to." The woman composed herself. "Arecibo is so very far. Some of the roads had disappeared with the hurricane. We were afraid that we would drop dead from hunger and exhaustion, or that we would fall off the cliffs."

Valentina waited while the woman finished the last of the viandas. She wished she could offer more, but Gloria was still in the kitchen, most likely standing guard over the stove.

"Somehow we managed to get there. Sixty-five of us. Women with children and old people," the woman said.

Valentina looked out at the horizon where once there had been a grove of glorious citrus trees that perfumed the air with lemon. Only a few stumps remained.

"The mayor said he couldn't help us, that Arecibo had nothing to give—not for us pobrecitos from Utuado, not for anybody," the woman said.

"What a tragedy," Valentina said.

"We cried, especially the old people," she said. "The children cried from hunger, but the old people—"

They stared out at the tree stumps.

"What did the mayor do?"

"He went to the Americans, to the army, but they told him they had nothing to give," the woman said. "And then the mayor sent us back to Utuado in an oxcart."

"An oxcart?"

"Sixty-five of us—women, children, old people—in an oxcart." The woman stared down at her empty plate.

When Valentina went to the kitchen, she placed her share of viandas on the plate to give to the poor woman because, ay, Gloria, there were some things that un ser humano shouldn't have to endure.

San Juan
June 1, 1900

Dear Valentina,

The newspapers are filled with stories about the poor jíbaros who are starving in the countryside, including in your Utuado! Valentina! Can this be true? I don't mean to imply in any way that Vicente isn't providing for you or his family, I only ask because you must come to us—all of you—Vicente and the children—if this is true. Write soon so as to reassure me!

Siempre,
Elena

P.S. The new American governor, a Mr. Allen, arrived with plenty of hoopla—the governor's mansion was wrapped in flags—from our house we could hear the cannons and the military band, but we decided to stay home. I think it was raining.

Utuado
July 14, 1900[*]

Dearest Elena,

I realized that it's been more than ten years since I last saw you and our parents. Ten years! I could cry but I don't have the tears. Not anymore. It's as if you and our parents live on another planet or in another country on the other side of the world. You might as well live in my beloved Paris. Elena, how it pains me to realize that we might never see each other again, that I will never be a true tía to your children, or you to mine. I fear never hearing your voice again, and that I will never be able to ask our mother for her blessing or to listen to Papá read tidbits from the newspapers. Ay bendito, to hear Papá read government statistics like he used to! How bored we were! I yearn for those dull moments of our childhood, which now seems so idyllic. (No te preocupes, it's only momentary silliness on my part.)

Darling Elena, I must say that your letters and parcels have helped me keep some dark thoughts at bay, especially during the bad times like when we lost Evita. I can hear your worry. Sweet Elena, Vicente and I have each other and our children. Somehow sobreviviremos. Know that you are always in my heart. Dear, dear hermana, my love to you and yours and our parents.

Siempre,
Valentina

[*] letter lost by United States Postal Service

San Juan
August 16, 1900

Dear Valentina,

I've had a long talk with Ernesto and Papá and we've decided that you and Vicente and the children must come to us. You must persuade Vicente. Why don't you make preparations to come to us after the hurricane season? Think of it! You could be with us by Christmas! I'm enclosing some stamped envelopes. Write soon!

Love,

Elena

CHAPTER THIRTY-FOUR

EL SUEÑO

Early one morning in the hour between night and day, Vicente eased out of bed, careful not to wake Valentina. He put on his pants and shirt, then tiptoed out of the bedroom, carrying his shoes and closing the door gently. He passed Raulito asleep on a cot en la sala; his brother stirred but didn't wake. Vicente left the house, pausing to put on his shoes. The mountain was still encased in fog. He buttoned his shirt against the chill. A múcaro garbled, other birds cawed and cooed good morning. Something touched his hair. The boy Vicente would have screamed, thinking it was a spirit, but the man Vicente thought a murciélago had flown too close. The clamor of the coquís comforted him. He walked the mountain he knew so well, listening to his footsteps, feeling the cool mist on his skin, breathing in the freshness that is the predawn air; he wiped something from his eye and walked on.

PROHIBIDA LA ENTRADA. PROPIEDAD PRIVADA. Vicente stared at the sign in front of what once had been his farm. In a flash of anger, he grabbed it with his hands, trying to pull it out of the ground. It had been well anchored, but he tugged and tugged until he succeeded in yanking it out. Then Vicente tossed it in the dirt. He walked on.

He sat on a tree stump. He heard a bird whistle, the tune mournful. Vicente looked at the land bereft of trees and saw it as it once had been: green and fertile with canopies of shade trees sheltering his coffee trees, plantain, guamá, and guava trees, the guavas trailing their white flowers. He didn't know if there was a more beautiful sight than coffee trees in bloom, the berries brilliant as rubies in the dark green foliage, so

pretty that perhaps the tediousness and difficulty of coffee picking was
forgiven. Vicente watched the sun rise over the graveyard that had once
been his farm, trying to etch the colors into his memory for the days to
come when he would need to recall it. He promised himself that one day
he would return and buy back the land and live on it with Valentina and
their children and with Raulito and Raulito's children.

Before the sun became too strong, Vicente asked Valentina to join him
for a walk.

"A walk? What's wrong?" Valentina was shucking ears of corn and
slicing off kernels with a knife.

"A walk? What's wrong?" Gloria looked up from the stone molino
where she had been grinding corn into flour. The women were going to
make la masa for sorullos.

"Can't a man go on a walk with his wife? Don't get excited,"
Vicente said.

"We're jíbaros," Valentina said. "Townspeople walk for pleasure, while
country folk walk because they don't have horses."

"You're crazy if you think you're leaving this kitchen without telling
us what's wrong," Gloria said.

"Gloria, this is between a husband and a wife—" Vicente took the
knife from Valentina's hand.

Valentina wiped her hands on her apron. "Now I know something is
wrong."

"There are no secrets in this house," Gloria said.

Valentina took off her apron. "Don't worry, I'll tell you later."

They went outside.

"Wait, Vicente!" Valentina ran back into the house, returning a
moment later with a parasol.

"Remember this? Mamá gave it to me when we were leaving Ponce.
It survived the hurricane in my trunk." She opened up the parasol, then
took his arm. "A lady must have her parasol."

They walked past his father's shed, which the men had rebuilt. The
countryside was beginning to recover from the hurricane and leaves

were sprouting on the branches and flowers on the bushes or the base of trees. Vicente pointed out flores that looked like coral.

"Vicente, this isn't a Sunday stroll through the plaza. What do you have to tell me?" She stopped walking. "You're scaring me!"

"I wish I didn't have to tell you." He took her hand.

"After Evita and losing Angelina and Inés, nothing can be so terrible," she said.

He was afraid of the disappointment he was sure to see in her eyes.

"We lost our farm," he said.

"What are you talking about?" Valentina stared up at him.

Vicente took a folded newspaper page already a week old out of his pocket; she looked down at the section he'd circled.

She read aloud. " '*Utuado: Coffee farm, government auction. Fifteen cuerdas, family farm—*' "

Valentina looked up from the newspaper. "I don't understand—"

"We can't pay the new American property and land tax," Vicente said.

Valentina stared at the circled ad; a dozen words in the newspaper that would change their lives forever. "Couldn't we have sold some of the land to pay it?"

"Not enough to pay off our debts and begin all over again," he said. "Not at five dollars a cuerda. Before the hurricane, we would have gotten forty-five dollars."

Utuado: Coffee farm, government auction. Fifteen cuerdas, family farm—

She'd thought they had experienced the worst that could befall them, but now this—the parasol slipped from her grasp.

He placed a steadying hand on her arm. "The American governor confiscated our farm."

"The American governor confiscated our farm. The governor?" Valentina paused after each word. "Our farm?"

"Not just ours." Vicente took the newspaper from her; he ran his finger down the list of ads. "Forty farms for auction. Forty!"

212 · MARISEL VERA

"Forty farms." Valentina sat on the grass, head in her hands.

Vicente sat next to her. "That's forty farms last week. Who knows what Governor Allen will do this week?"

"Can he do that?"

"It seems he can." Vicente opened the parasol, holding it over her head. They looked out at la naturaleza blooming again.

CHAPTER THIRTY-FIVE

BROTHERS

One November morning, the brothers walked down the mountain so that Vicente could vote in the local mayoral election. They hoped that there would be news about construction work.

"Raulito, I've been meaning to talk to you about calling our father 'Papá,'" Vicente said.

Even after more than a year of living in his father's house, when it was necessary for Raulito to speak to Raúl Vega, he called him "Don Raúl." If he happened upon him alone in a room reading or looking through papers, Raulito greeted him as Don Raúl, bowing his head. Sometimes his father returned his nod.

"¡Papá!" Raulito stopped walking. "I couldn't!"

Vicente stopped, too. "Don't look so scared. At least call him 'Raúl,' the way Valentina does."

"I could never do that!"

"Why not?"

They started walking again.

"Even my mother called him Don Raúl," Raulito said.

Vicente shook his head. "I don't like the way he treats you, I'm going to talk to him."

Raulito tugged at his brother's shirtsleeve. "Don't! Estoy bien."

"Did I ever tell you that when we were boys, Luisito and I called Papá 'el General'?" Vicente chuckled.

"I saw you a few times with Luisito. I used to wish I was your brother so that I could live with you." Raulito's smile was shy; he was missing several teeth.

Vicente's smile was wide, his teeth white and strong. "You are my brother. We'll always be brothers."

"But then I thought that I would have to leave Mamá and live in your father's house."

"Our father's house."

"Don Raúl's house."

"You're hopeless, hermanito." Vicente patted his brother on the back, laughing.

They heard the shouting as they reached Utuado. En la plaza, a crowd of men shouted accusations at a group of a dozen others, calling them traitors for selling out to their masters, loan sharks who cared only about filling their pockets, choosing American dollars over their country and countrymen.

They went up to a barefoot jíbaro. Raulito nodded a greeting. "¿Qué pasa?"

The man pointed. "The plantation owners and merchants don't want those men here."

"Who are they? Americans?" Raulito looked over at the men.

"Can't be," his brother said. "The plantation owners and the merchants love the Americans."

"No son americanos, son puertorriqueños," the jíbaro said. "They're looking for men to cut cane in Hawaii."

Raulito asked el jíbaro, "Where is Hawaii?"

He shrugged; Vicente shrugged also.

A fistfight broke out; some people placed bets. The police came; the brothers walked away with el jíbaro, not wanting to get mixed up in el revolú.

Raulito waited with his brother in a long line of men, many of them barefoot, for Vicente to vote. Afterward, Vicente bought a newspaper. They stopped at a stream on the way back up the mountain for a drink of water.

Vicente tossed the newspaper at Raulito. "Read what *La Correspondencia* has to say."

Raulito read: "'The Puerto Ricans who come into our mountains and pueblos to snatch up our hungry countrymen to work on the Hawaiian sugar plantations are a new pla—pla—'"

He pointed to the word; Vicente looked over his shoulder.

"'Plague,'" he said.

"'—plague on Puerto Rico.'" Raulito paused. "What's 'plague'?"

His brother took out his handkerchief and dipped it in the water. "It means another disease for puertorriqueños, like la tuberculosis."

"You think that?" Raulito trailed his fingers in the stream, then touched the back of his neck, relishing the coolness.

"I don't know." Vicente wiped his face. "There's no work in Puerto Rico. What is a man to do?"

Raulito held out the newspaper. "But what it says here? And those men in the plaza—"

Vicente waved away the newspaper. "Those plantation owners pay the Puerto Rican fifteen to twenty centavos a day, and the merchants rob him at their stores or with their interest rates. They're a plague, too."

"Keep reading?" A few sprinkles had dropped on the paper; Raulito blew on it to dry it.

"Read on." Vicente stretched out on the ground, covering his face with his hat. "You read very well, Raulito. I'm proud of you."

Raulito felt the prick of tears; his brother was proud of him. He wiped his eyes with the back of his hand and read on.

In the afternoon when the coquís began their chant, they started back home. Raulito liked the sound of the coquís. When he was a little boy, he tried hard to catch one of the tiny tree frogs. He never could.

"If you went to Hawaii, I would go with you." Raulito glanced at his brother from under the brim of his hat.

"I wouldn't go to Hawaii without you." Vicente put his arm around his shoulders for a quick hug.

Raulito thought about the men in the plaza, not the plantation agents, but the other men, the barefoot ones in rags. There wasn't any work for those men and they were forced to beg for food. He'd still be one of those men if not for his brother.

When they reached the batey, Vicente stopped and Raulito stopped, too.

"I wouldn't say anything to anyone about Hawaii," Vicente said. "There's a lot to consider."

"Valentina?"

"Yes, Valentina," his brother said. "Everything."

"Not a word," Raulito said.

CHAPTER THIRTY-SIX

¡AL HAWAII! ¡AL HAWAII!

I n town there was the battle of the handbills. *Work in Hawaii! Honest Labor in Hawaii! Free Transportation for the Whole Family from One US Territory to Another US Territory! Free Housing and Medical Care in Hawaii! Schools for Your Children! ¡Compañeros, Don't Abandon Your Madre Patria! Better Country Than Food! US Plans to Rid Puerto Rico of Its Citizens! Puerto Rico for the Americans!*

Vicente tucked an advertisement into the band of his hat. He walked around with the leaflet for days and took it out to read often, although he had memorized every word. It seemed like the answer to all their problems. Decent pay for a day's labor. A bonus paid every year. He would be able to save the bonus money since he wouldn't have to pay for housing or medical care. They'd be back in Puerto Rico in two or three years. Four. By then there would be work to be had on the island. Maybe he could buy back his land from the American company that owned it. If he saved all he could, it might be possible. (Yes, it was a dream, but sometimes dreams come true, yes?) When they returned to Puerto Rico, he would plant coffee trees and take on other work, as he'd done before. One day again, he would harvest his coffee crop. The reality was that here, in Puerto Rico, when he swung his machete, he, Vicente Vega, former coffee farmer, former landowner, was a peón. Would it make any difference if he were a peón in Puerto Rico or in Hawaii? It would, according to the advertisement for workers for the Hawaiian sugarcane plantations.

.

Vicente showed her the handbill with EMIGRACIÓN PARA HAWAII in large block letters in the privacy of their bedroom when they were getting ready for bed.

Valentina smoothed out the creases in the paper.

"I think it's the best opportunity for us right now," Vicente said.

She finished reading it. "Why not go to San Juan? Elena and her husband would help us."

"We don't want to go to your sister like mendigos, Valentina." They sat on the bed. "And what will I do in San Juan? I'm a farmer. I don't work in a store like Elena's husband."

"But Vicente, we'll have to leave Evita, and to think that I'll never see my sister or my parents again—"

"Querida, Evita is gone."

Valentina nodded. She stared down at the paper; her hair was loose, hiding her face. Vicente took her in his arms.

"Querida, there is nothing here for us in Puerto Rico, no future for our children. You know that, don't you?" He felt her nod against his bare shoulder, her tears wet and cold on his skin.

Raúl Vega waved *La Democracia* newspaper under Vicente's nose.

"Look! Your name is in the paper! My name is in the paper! ¡Vega! Right here on the list of men going to Hawaii."

"In the paper! Why would they put my name in the paper?"

"So that other poor suckers like you will join up." His father tossed him the newspaper.

Vicente read: *Vicente Vega de Utuado.*

Raúl Vega pounded the table with his fist. "That's what they want—Governor Allen and all the Americans—they want Puerto Ricans to leave Puerto Rico so that they can have the island for themselves. It's all there in the newspaper. All the reasons why the Americans want us to leave, all the reasons that we shouldn't."

Vicente read:

The native subagents working for Hawaiian sugar are willing to sell their countrymen for a dollar a head. Do not forget your heritage! Fellow Puerto Ricans, take care that you not fall into the traps of the American flesh merchants, take care that you not end up slaves in a strange land. Take a lesson from the way Americans treat us on our own island! Better to starve in your own country than in a strange one!

Vicente pushed the newspaper away. "Better not to starve at all."

"We can continue to live together in this house," Raúl Vega said. "Of course Raulito can go to Hawaii, if he wants. But you have Valentina—"

Vicente looked at his father. "You don't care if Raulito goes? He's your son, too."

"He's been living under my roof since el huracán, hasn't he? He can't complain." Raúl picked up the newspaper.

Vicente shook his head. "You haven't been cruel, that's true."

"Exactly." Raúl Vega turned the pages of the newspaper. "Think this locura over carefully, Vicente. Don't believe anything the Americans promise you."

When one of the town's committeemen lectured Vicente about how he was wrong to leave the island, to turn his back on la Madre Patria, Vicente said, What country are you talking about? The Puerto Rico once ruled by Spain, or the Puerto Rico with its new American masters?

CHAPTER THIRTY-SEVEN

GLORIA

W hy are you crying, muchacha? What has Vicente done? Tell me, let your Gloria comfort you. There, there, Dios mio, it must be something terrible for you to go on like this, it isn't like you to be such a llorona. Was it Don Raúl? I'm going to make him some special tea and he'll suffer such a terrible itch that the only way he will be able to ease it is by taking a blade and slicing—what's that? Not Don Raúl? Bueno, then it can't be anything so bad, because the worst has already happened to this family, no crees? It's like that time the American preacher came to the house, remember, Valentina? Spoke English and nobody knew what disparate he was talking, but then he took out some paper and started drawing all these terrible things, pointing to us, we thought he was talking about el huracán, but then when he drew locusts and frogs and X's on doors, somebody, was it you or Vicente, no, it was Don Raúl who figured out it was the story about plagues in Egypt that I never knew about, and we all stared at the preacher drinking our coffee, and finally he left, the papers still on the table and I fed them to the stove, what do you mean, I'm not making any sense, you're the one crying and laughing at the same time, muchacha, dime, what is it?

Hawaii? What is this, Hawaii? ¿Qué? So far away? Eres como mi hija, Valentina. The daughter I never had. I'll go with you.

CHAPTER THIRTY-EIGHT

OFFERINGS

The beans and root vegetables that Raúl Vega and his sons planted after the hurricane now provided most of their daily meal. Gloria had gone to the vegetable plot to pull up some tubers like ñame and malanga for their dinner. Carrying a small sack, Raúl Vega came into the kitchen while Valentina and Lourdes were shelling beans.

"Lourdes, go help Gloria," Raúl Vega said.

Lourdes did as she was told.

"What's in the sack?" Valentina looked up from the beans.

Raúl Vega placed it on the table. "Open it."

Valentina reached for the bag. "Rice! How did you get it?"

"I'll do anything for you, Valentina," he said.

"Please, Raúl, you've been behaving very well lately," she said.

He had been waiting for the right time to persuade her, but she would be leaving soon. "Don't go to Hawaii. Stay in Puerto Rico, with me."

"You must be out of your mind to suggest such a thing," she said.

"I feel a little crazy," Raúl Vega said.

The way she looked at him, her dark brown eyes wide in surprise, reminded him of the girl he'd seen naked all those years ago.

"We can continue to live in this house together, you and me, Javiercito and Lourdes. And even Gloria."

"Raúl, I appreciate that you let us stay here and how much you've helped us." Valentina stood, putting the table between them.

"Things are harder now than they were before, but I'm sure you're better off with me here than you'll be with Vicente in Hawaii," he said. "I can give you more than my son can."

"Vicente is my husband, I love him, not you," Valentina said. "You must accept that."

"When you leave, it will be like losing the sun," he said.

She smiled a little. "That's sweet."

Raúl sat down slumped at the table. Gloria and Lourdes came into the kitchen, arms full of vegetables.

"Valentina, look at all these—"

Raúl got up; they watched him leave.

"What did he want? Is he up to his old pocas vergüenzas?"

"¿Qué pocas vergüenzas?" Lourdes dropped the vegetables on the table.

"Go wash your hands," her mother said.

The women marveled over the sack of rice and Valentina told Gloria everything.

"Poor Raúl," Gloria said. "Las damas are in heaven having a good chuckle."

CHAPTER THIRTY-NINE

GRATITUDE

One day in late November, Vicente brought home a newspaper and asked Valentina to read it aloud because her voice was so lovely it even made bad news sound good. She announced that Governor Allen had decreed a holiday in Puerto Rico called "Thanksgiving." Governor Allen reminded Puerto Ricans to give thanks that all was right in their world: in the last twelve months, under the influence of good government, the crops had improved, the farmland had recovered, industrial and financial interests had become more profitable. Aside from the hurricanes, the island hadn't been visited by pestilence or other calamities, and the general health of the public was excellent.

Valentina looked up from the newspaper and found everyone staring at her.

Utuado
December 1, 1900

Dear Elena,

Prepare yourself for terrible news—we are leaving Puerto Rico for the Hawaiian sugarcane fields. No queremos, pero Vicente no tiene otra opción. Ay bendito, Elena, to think that I've fallen so low. I can't help feeling ashamed. I wish—oh, I don't know what I wish! Yes, I do know— I wish for a miracle.

Raulito and Gloria have chosen to come with us. We leave from the port of Ponce on December 26th. I was last in Ponce so many years ago, I'm sure I wouldn't know it. I would like to take a last look at our hometown, walk by our old house, and show our children where their mother came from, but we are to be picked up by oxcart and taken directly to the harbor. Elena, how I wish that I might embrace you and our parents one last time, that I might kiss your children that they might know their Titi Valentina, and for you to kiss ours so they might know their Titi Elena.

Siempre,

Valentina

PART THREE

HAWAII

CHAPTER FORTY

¡ADIÓS, PUERTO RICO!

T he oxcart driver slept on the floor of la sala because traveling at night was dangerous. Before dawn, the oxcart was loaded with the family's possessions. The children carried their bundles laughing and chattering, they were so excited about their new adventure. At the last moment, Gloria refused to climb into the cart.

The old woman threw herself on Valentina. "Ay Valentina, no puedo, hija, I can't."

The children jumped down from the cart; they wrapped their little arms around the old woman, everybody crying.

Valentina patted Gloria's back, making soothing sounds even as she wanted to beg her to keep her promise. How could she leave her behind, Gloria who had been like a second mother to her, who had taught her how to be a good country wife, who had cared for her like a daughter when Evita died, holding her hand in silence on days so unbearable that if Gloria hadn't anchored her to the earth, she might have drowned herself in the river.

"I will write to you, Gloria, and tell you how we are so you won't worry." Valentina hugged her tighter, feeling the woman's frail bones through the thin fabric of her dress, Gloria who had been plump and round once upon a time.

Gloria raised her tear-streaked face. "Hija, you know I can't read."

"Raúl will read my letters to you. Won't you, Raúl?" Valentina called out to Raúl.

Raúl came over to the women, a package in his hand.

"Don't worry, Gloria, I'll read all of Valentina's letters." He handed Valentina the package. "I had Gloria pack up things that Inés made."

Valentina pressed the package to her breast. "Raúl, thank you!"

Raúl took her hand; she let him hold it for a moment.

"Que te vaya bien, querida." He brought her hand to his lips and kissed it. With a little bow, he went into the house.

Vicente came and put his arm around Gloria's shoulders. "I'll miss you."

Gloria cried some more.

"I wrote to Luisito. He'll come to see you and el viejo." Vicente kissed the old woman.

"Ay Vicente . . . Vicente . . ." Gloria pressed her face into his chest.

The children gave the old woman a final hug and ran back to the oxcart.

Raúl Vega came back carrying a machete.

"Raulito, come here," he said.

Raulito had been helping load the oxcart; he obeyed, standing next to his brother.

"This is for you." Raúl held out his machete.

Everyone looked at the machete that no one but Raúl Vega had ever used.

Raulito took it. "Gracias, Don Raúl."

Raúl nodded.

The oxcart driver called out that it was time to leave. In a flurry of kisses and goodbyes, Raúl Vega embraced his grandchildren and then Vicente and, of course, Valentina. At the last moment, he shook Raulito's hand.

Vicente sat next to the oxcart driver while Raulito sat with the children on top of their bundles. Valentina perched on her trunk, which Vicente said was too large to take on the ship; she turned back to look at the house that had been her home on and off for the ten years of her married life. She waved and waved to Gloria and Raúl, blowing kiss after kiss, sending pieces of her heart back to her old life. When the oxcart took a curve on the road and the house and its occupants were no longer visible, Vicente reached for her hand, giving it a quick squeeze.

The mist lifted on the horizon, revealing an orb of orange fire, its tentative rays spreading across the sky as blue as any sea. The road was still in terrible condition even more than a year after the hurricane, and Valentina felt every bump. She recalled that other journey, when she was a young bride holding onto her new husband, riding with him on his horse, when everything had been green and golden. When Evita died, she'd thought there could be nothing in the world that could hurt her so much. She still knew that to be true even now, but still . . .

The children wanted to see the big town of Ponce and the house where Valentina had been raised. And hadn't she told them about a big red-and-black firehouse, and that Ponce had the prettiest plaza on the entire island? That Ponce is Ponce! When she didn't answer the children's questions, Vicente turned around to look at her and told the children to let their mother rest. When the oxcart climbed the steep slopes, the children screamed in terror and delight. Vicente pointed up the mountainsides and told them how before Hurricane San Ciriaco, people had built everywhere, some had even perched their bohíos at the very edges of the cliffs, the way some birds build their nests.

When they reached the town of Utuado, peddlers were just coming to market; the children waved to mounted police on their way to rout the homeless families sleeping en la plaza. They drove by the yellow stucco Parroquia San Miguel Arcángel. The children recalled the day they'd had a picnic. What day was that, Papi? Vicente didn't say that was the day utuadaños went mad over the rumor that Spain had bombed New York and was winning the war with the Americans. Instead he said, Wasn't that a fun picnic? We'll stop for lunch and have another, would you like that, niños? Of course the children said yes.

The oxcart driver didn't want to stop to see the view of Adjuntas from the mountain road, but Vicente spoke to him in a voice the children had never heard before, a voice that reminded everyone of Raúl Vega. They climbed down from the oxcart; Vicente lifted Valentina by the waist. Clouds wafted like waves in the sky above the mountain range; golden dry splotches scattered along the green valley below.

Vicente pointed over the valley. "There were groves of giant shade trees and every other kind of tree. Remember, Valentina? Flamboyanes and palmas and—"

"I'm cold," Javier said.

"I'm cold, too," Lourdes said.

"Wrap yourselves in the bedding." Valentina linked her arm through her husband's.

Raulito took the children back. Valentina and Vicente stood there for another minute looking out into the valley; in the distance they imagined the sea.

When they passed the trail to Lares, the oxcart driver said he was born there. He shook his head when Vicente asked him if his family had fought in el Grito de Lares.

"Why is it called 'el grito,' Papi? Why were the people from Lares shouting?" Lourdes tugged at her father's sleeve.

"It's not a pretty tale for little girls," her father said.

"Tell her." Valentina opened up her paper fan.

"Valentina—"

She fanned her face. "She'll soon learn that life isn't pretty even for little girls."

Vicente glanced at his wife; there were lines furrowed between her eyes. He twisted in his seat to look at his daughter. "Most of the time grito means a shout, just like you said, Lulu. But in this case, grito means a declaration of independence."

Javier said, "What's that?"

"Don't interrupt, Javiercito." Valentina flicked her fan on his arm.

"Independence means to be free." Vicente cleared his throat, a little nervous, but that was silly, he was talking to his own family.

"Just like the Americans now, when the Spanish were in Puerto Rico they had lots of laws that weren't good for the Puerto Rican. Like a tax for everything, a tax to have a fiesta, a tax to sing a song, or if you bought a bed, you'd have to pay a tax on that bed, and not just when you bought it, but every single year that you owned that bed. The Spanish government was also very cruel and put a lot of people in jail. Puerto Ricans were unhappy and some people wanted to do something about it. They decided to fight against Spain so that they could be free. These brave people had what is called a revolution."

Vicente glanced at Valentina; she was smiling.

"Puerto Rico had slavery, then, and black slaves joined the revolution," he said.

"Black slaves like Tío Raulito?" Lourdes looked at her uncle.

"I'm not a slave," Raulito said.

"Your uncle isn't a slave," Vicente said.

"For shame." Valentina flicked her fan on her daughter's arm.

Lourdes began to whimper.

"Stop that." Her mother tapped her again with the fan.

Lourdes stopped.

Vicente continued. "One September in 1868, there were over a thousand men up there on a coffee plantation in Lares ready to fight the Spanish, but there was a little problem."

Javier leaned forward. "What problem, Papi?"

This time, Valentina didn't reprimand him. Everyone was listening, even the oxcart driver.

"They didn't have hardly any guns, and the Spaniards had a whole army with lots of guns," Vicente said.

No one spoke.

Vicente began to enjoy himself.

"The Puerto Ricans captured the town of Lares and proclaimed a new government, and then they went to San Sebastián, where the Spanish army was waiting for them, but they didn't know that."

"The Puerto Ricans didn't become free?" Javier said.

"No, Javiercito," his father said. "We Puerto Ricans aren't free."

"You know Puerto Rico is American now," Lourdes said to her older brother.

Vicente looked over the children's heads. Valentina mouthed, Muy bien, Vicente.

·

They ate the food that Gloria and Valentina had packed and filled their tin cups with water from the streams along the way. When night came, the driver stopped under some trees in the town of Adjuntas and crawled under the cart to sleep. The family slept under the stars, and the children insisted that their Tío Raulito sleep near them while their parents laid out their bedding nearby. When Vicente whispered in Valentina's ear, she turned her back, saying she was tired.

They passed the casilla de camineros where, over ten years ago, they had stopped on the way up to Utuado. Valentina recalled how once she'd thought herself too fine a lady, how haughty she'd been when la ama de casa had invited her to rest and offered her coffee. If only la señora could see her now.

Early on December 26, 1900, when they reached the city of Ponce, the driver wanted to take them straight to the harbor, where they were to meet the ship later that day.

"Señor, por favor, just a quick ride through town so that our children can see where their mother came from," Valentina said.

The driver shook his head. "I was paid to take you to the harbor, and that's where I'm going."

As the cart rode toward the harbor, Valentina stood up. "Señor, I won't get on that boat! Not a single member of my family will get on that boat!"

"Señora, sit down!" The driver turned to look at her.

"You can explain it to the people who paid you why we aren't on that boat—"

"Valentina, sit down, you'll hurt yourself." Vicente reached for her.

"Señora, I told you to—"

"Hombre, are you going to take us through town or are we going to jump off this wagon?" Valentina tossed a bundle over the side of the wagon.

"¡Señora! Yes, yes, I'll take you!" The driver stopped the cart.

Valentina thanked the driver and sent Javiercito to pick up the bundle.

She couldn't help feeling disappointed as they drove through town. Everywhere the damage from Hurricane San Ciriaco was still visible, even en la Plaza Las Delicias.

"See over there, niños? See, Raulito? That's the Catedral Nuestra Señora de la Guadalupe and that red-and-black building is the fire station, el Parque de Bombas. It was built for an exhibition in 1882, our parents took Elena and me see it. An exhibition is like a big fiesta with music and dancing and lots of food and new things to see. It was right here en la plaza. We wore our best dresses and Papá bought us dulces. I always asked for chocolates from Mayagüez. I ate too much and got a terrible stomachache! El Teatro La Perla is that building. Isn't it beautiful? ¡Ponce es Ponce! Our parents went to concerts there and also a play, once they took us to—look! La Gran Ceiba de Ponce! Raulito, have you ever seen a ceiba tree that huge? It's hundreds of years old! Driver, por favor, if you turn here, here, yes, gracias, a little ways more, there, that's Dalia's mansion, and where I met you, Vicente, do you remember, and if you drive just down this street a ways, you'll find la Iglesia de la Santísima Trinidad, where we got married, and in another few blocks, you'll see my house, my parents' house, there . . . there it is, ay bendito, what happened to it?"

Her parents' yellow house and those on either side were abandoned, partially destroyed by the hurricane. What had happened to their neighbors? To the people who had bought her parents' house? The oxen plodded along down the streets and through the crowds of people, some well dressed, many others ragged and seeking shade under trees. San Ciriaco had struck a great blow to the beautiful city of Ponce, and it had yet to regain its luster. Valentina kept her gloveless hands hidden in the folds of her dress. She thought she recognized somebody. She turned away.

When the oxcart driver dropped them off at the Ponce harbor, there were hundreds of Puerto Ricans waiting for the ship: four hundred people—men, women, and children—many of them barefoot and in rags; some of the children wore only hats. Friends and relatives had come to see people off. There was laughing and singing and guitar playing and güiro scraping and maracas shaking. Somebody played an accordion. Vicente and Raulito carried Valentina's trunk. Valentina unwrapped the package Raúl had given her. She found the mantilla Inés had made for Angelina but that she rarely wore, declaring it too fine for el campo. She fingered the beautiful lace on the edges of the shawl and thought of Inés.

Somebody passed Vicente a jug of ron caña; he took a swig.

Valentina put on the shawl and held out her hand for the jug; he hesitated.

"It'll burn your throat, Valentina," he said.

"I don't care," she said.

He gave it to her.

She wiped the opening with her sleeve, then took a long swallow of fire. She had a coughing fit, her eyes flooded with tears. La gente laughed at the pretty dama.

"What did I tell you?" Vicente patted her back.

She took another swallow, this time only a little one just to prove something to her husband, though she didn't know what. She hardly coughed.

"¡Brava!" The ron caña man took back the jug.

"It's like a party." Vicente put his arm around her.

Well-dressed people had also come to see the Puerto Ricans going to Hawaii, and Valentina hoped that she wouldn't see anyone who knew her. She knew it shouldn't matter to her, but it did. A group of men who someone said were plantation owners came to try to persuade them to stay, assuring them that sugar refineries would be built very soon by the Americans and then there would be plenty of work, if they wanted to work.

．

They boarded the ship, carrying everything they owned; for most that wasn't much, and some had nothing. One man balanced a chair on his shoulders; others clutched their guitars and instruments. The accordion player didn't board. Several women shouted from the shore the names of their husbands, saying that they were trying to evade their familial obligations by going to Hawaii. Those men were found on board and sent back to shore. A couple of the Puerto Ricans carried roosters tucked under their arms. When the Hawaiian plantation agents tried to take them away, the men refused to get on the ship without the birds. The roosters boarded, too.

Vicente and Raulito carried Valentina's trunk between them, and the children went on ahead holding the bundles, and Valentina the bedding.

One of the agents pointed to Raulito. "You there! Where do you think you're going?"

"Hawaii," Raulito said.

The agent blocked their way; the brothers set the trunk down.

"They don't want black men in Hawaii," the agent said. "No negros."

The brothers exchanged a glance.

"My brother doesn't go, I don't go." Vicente signaled to Raulito to pick up the trunk.

The agent stepped aside.

The plantation agents searched the ship before it left the harbor and removed all the black men they could find, but not Raulito. Only three hundred and eighty-four Puerto Ricans, including children, set sail on the steamship.

Some of the Puerto Ricans were in good spirits and full of pity for those poor unfortunates not going on the great adventure.

"Adiós, Puerto Rico, sentimos por los que se quedan . . ." They waved from the deck of the *Arkadia* steamship and called out to those left behind, "Goodbye, Puerto Rico, we're sorry for those who stay."

CHAPTER FORTY-ONE

HARDSHIP

The wail pierced the din of steerage. That hideous sound! If only someone would make it stop!

Vicente Vega cradled Javier in his arms. When he woke, he would need nourishment. Fruits and vegetables. Rice and beans. Raw eggs. There had to be hens aboard the ship. The American passengers must surely eat eggs. He would beg the steward for an egg or two for the boy. If only he had something to trade . . . no importa. Somehow he would get that egg!

It was stifling hot in the ship's hull. Sweat dripped down Vicente's neck into his already damp shirt. Vicente kissed his son's forehead. The poor boy had ceased to tremble, but his skin was cold. Maybe he should call out to Valentina to bring a mantilla to cover him. Javier, age ten and gangly; who from the moment he could walk, had trailed behind him every day. Whom Vicente had raised with the love a father should have for his son. Javiercito, who, as a toddler, would reach up for Vicente to lift him onto his horse; Javiercito, whose tiny fingers grasped at the horse's mane as Vicente urged the animal into a gallop; Javiercito, whose laughter would anoint Vicente like an afternoon shower.

When Javier became well, he would be like the other boys again. He would do the mischievous things the other boys did, which he had once done. He would escape from steerage to go above deck and breathe in the fresh ocean air. He would run away from the stewards to explore the ship and spy on the Americans. That very day, the other boys had returned from their adventure to describe the endless platters of food served to the above-deck passengers: chicken and fish and meat. Was it beef? It might have been beef. The boys had never seen beef, so they weren't positive, but yes, it might well have been beef. They had seen tureens of soup so big that they had to be carried by two men. Bread in baskets waist high. Cakes! Brown cakes, white cakes, even pink cakes! Also, every kind of fruit, like mangos and oranges that they used to have aplenty in Puerto Rico before the hurricane. Vegetables like they used to have, too! The Puerto Ricans in steerage, who ate tasteless soup or stew ladled out of what looked like slop buckets, whose supper was rice or potatoes with bread and something brown that they guessed might be meat (it was surely not beef), yelled at the boys to *shut up!* The boys' parents rewarded their lies with cocotazos, the customary hard raps on their heads.

Javiercito weighed so little; Vicente had carried heavier sacks of coffee. Vicente vowed that when they reached the new country—this Hawaii—if he had to cut cane every day of the week, every week of the year, every hour of the day, he would provide a good life for his family. They would have food and housing and medical care.

Where was the steward? He would ask the steward for a live chicken and offer his machete as payment if necessary, but somehow, somewhere, he would procure a live chicken, even if he had to steal it. He would wring the chicken's neck with his bare hands and pluck its feathers. Valentina would cook it, careful not to waste a speck of its nutritious blood. Vicente would spoon the life-giving broth into the boy's mouth drop by drop. A few servings of his mother's chicken and rice soup and Javiercito would be like the other boys. And if that wasn't possible, if he couldn't get a chicken, then they would make do with one of the roosters that had pecked their way around steerage until their owners realized that they might soon become soup, the food was so bad. Now they tied their legs together to keep the roosters from wandering, never letting them out of their sight. Yet every morning despite the darkness of the ship's belly, the roosters woke them at dawn.

A hand on his shoulder. Words, English and harsh to his ear. Hands pried loose his fingers. That dreadful howling again! Why did his brother Raulito weep? He would have a talk with him. Raulito was twenty, old enough to know that men shouldn't weep. Vicente took a deep breath.

Again, that terrible sound! That hideous cry that was more animal than human! Would somebody make it stop! He bit hard on his tongue. The taste of blood in his mouth. Sailors tugged at his arms and tried to break his embrace. No! He wouldn't let go! Never! His son was not dead, no! His compatriots occupied the gloom of the ship's hold. Illuminated only by a few kerosene lamps, candles forbidden in steerage, they were but shadows. Someone lit a candle that revealed the father's anguished face and those of his compatriots. A sailor barked a command and the flame went out. Later, when Vicente thought about this day and how his compañeros flickered in and out of light like apparitions, he would think that what he had glimpsed on their faces was not pity but relief, because God had seen fit to spare their own sons.

"Don Vicente." The respectful salutation commanded his attention. It had been so long since he'd been so addressed, and only out of courtesy by his father's peones. He hadn't enough money or land or age to merit the title. The speaker was the plantation agent Albert E. Minvielle, who had astounded them by speaking Spanish as well as English. It was rumored that his mother was a Puerto Rican.

"I'm very sorry for your loss." Minvielle pointed to the sailors: sunburnt, rough-looking men. "They're here for the boy."

His son. His boy.

Minvielle took his handkerchief out of his breast pocket. The stench of hundreds of unwashed emigrants and their normal bodily functions was so vile that the ship's doctor held a handkerchief to his nose whenever he was obliged to descend to steerage and tend to the sick.

It wasn't as if the Puerto Ricans couldn't smell the terrible odor, but what could they do about it? Stick pieces of cloth in their nostrils for the duration of the voyage? They had to breathe, didn't they? What choice did they have when nobody listened to their petitions? When they were met with silence whenever they asked for water to wash or to empty their chamber pots? The very unlucky had cots near makeshift water closets.

Strangers and acquaintances alike moved out of Vicente's way as if Javier had died of some contagious disease. Bare feet shuffled on the wood planks as they parted for their fellow compañero and his dead son.

Hushed murmurs ceased. Valentina and their daughter huddled together on their cot. Lourdes, now Vicente and his wife's only living child, cried at her mother's side. Valentina gathered the boy to her breast as she had when he was her newborn baby. She whispered a mother's nonsensical murmurings as Vicente watched helpless in his grief and guilt. Minvielle reminded him that the sailors were waiting. Vicente bent to take their son.

"¡No! ¡Vicente, no!" Valentina slapped at her husband's hands.

"Querida—" Vicente knelt down and wrapped his arms around his wife and their daughter. The plantation agent tapped his shoulder. *Time to go.*

Vicente followed the sailors up some steps. A gust of wind from the ocean chilled him and he braced his legs against the ship's oscillations. He thought he might fall, but he righted himself, the boy heavy in his arms as only a sleeping child can be.

The small room was bare except for a table and a few chairs. A kerosene lamp, a cloth, a bowl of water, a swathe of heavy canvas, and a sewing box were on the table. Minvielle relayed instructions from the sailors and they left him alone to prepare the body. Vicente washed and dried his son's face, his hands, his feet, noting, without realizing it, the crooked toe on Javier's right foot, the same as his father's. His fingers trembled as he moved the needle with coarse thread in and out; he sewed his son's nostrils closed. He remembered their departure from the port of Ponce, when Javier played monster, chasing his little sister up and down the pier. Vicente had thought the boy too old to be so childish, especially in front of strangers, and had been about to reprimand him when Valentina placed her hand on his arm.

Minvielle returned with the sailors, who carried a plank and a piece of heavy chain. They wound the chain around Javier's ankles and placed him in the sack. Vicente asked that they give him time to sew the sailcloth closed, but when Minvielle conferred with the sailors, he was told it would take too long. The sailors balanced the sack with the boy's body on the plank. Vicente heard the sharp clack of their shoes on the wood deck; he wondered what had happened to Javiercito's shoes, perhaps Valentina had them. He saw his brother Raulito with his arm around Valentina, his wife's face hidden behind a black lace mantilla. A crowd of spectators, both steerage and cabin passengers, had gathered on deck for the burial at sea. The murmuring swell of excitement rushed against Vicente's temples.

Behind the captain and a minister in clerical collar, the sun sank into the ocean like an aureole. The Puerto Ricans bowed their heads at amen. The sailors balanced one end of the plank on the railing. The sack with his son slid down into the black water and disappeared into the mouth of the sea monster.

Minvielle told him that it was a terrible thing what had happened, but soon they would be in Hawaii. It was a good place, this Hawaii, a country of aloha. Vicente would have work in the sugarcane fields. Good hard work. Steady work. What every man needed. Minvielle advised Vicente to bid adiós to the past and aloha to the future, that's what the Hawaiians say. A strange word, aloha, it meant both hello and goodbye. He could never figure out why that was. But Vicente didn't have to worry about that. Talking Hawaiian, he meant. Even if he ever did meet any Hawaiians, he would be too busy on the sugarcane plantation to talk to them. Hard work would do him good. Hard, steady work in the Hawaiian sugarcane fields. Hawaii would do more good for him and his compatriots than the whole island of Puerto Rico had done since before the great Hurricane San Ciriaco, since the Americans, and even all the way back to the old days of los españoles. That's what they all needed, the Puerto Ricans. Hard, steady work in the Hawaiian sugarcane fields.

Vicente held onto the rail, unaware that he was alone on deck and had been for hours. His fellow Puerto Ricans in their steel cages dreamt of the island breeze that once swung their hammocks, and the chant of the coquís that used to lull them to sleep. Vicente didn't hear the hum of the ship's mechanical workings or the sailors as they went about their duties.

Well-dressed cabin passengers paused in their evening stroll for a closer look at the man whose child was now at the bottom of the ocean. The men had supposed that he'd be more of a brute; the women hadn't expected a tragic hero. He didn't look like a savage native. Of course they'd had very little contact with the natives, especially the negros. There were the servants, of course, but one didn't notice servants. Porto Ricans played in the native orchestras, but one didn't actually look at the musicians. The cabin passengers all agreed that the island of Porto Rico was very beautiful, and the parties in the Spanish-style homes of the island elites quite acceptable as far as provincial island entertainment went. So exotic to see palm trees while dancing, wouldn't you say? Quite fascinating how travel broadens one, they all agreed as they returned to their spacious staterooms and comfortable beds with the bedclothes turned down by the stewards.

The sailor assigned to make sure Vicente didn't jump into the ocean brought him a flask of whiskey, compliments of the captain. Raulito snuck on deck, and they stood vigil through the night. The stars illuminated the waves that moved the ship further away from all they had known and all they had lost.

CHAPTER FORTY-TWO

RON CAÑA HELPS

No sky for days—five days. No sky for a people born into sun. Streaks of light, too dim to give courage or hope, came in through portholes that they couldn't open to dispel the stench. In the cavernous hold of the ship, the men were separated from the women and children, they slept on pallets of straw in iron cages set in double banks, row after row, tier upon tier. The women hung their mantillas or whatever they had for privacy.

They shivered in their thin cotton clothing when the steamship *Arkadia* docked at Port Eads Harbor in the chill of a New Orleans winter. They complained that they had never felt so cold, not even after Hurricane San Ciriaco, when some of them had been naked and without shelter, no señor, not even then. They were allowed on deck when they reached port and watched in amazement as stevedores carried crates filled with bananas off the ship. Bananas were mother's milk! They shouted, "Minvielle, Minvielle, why didn't you give us bananas?" When they saw mangos carried off by the hundreds, they thought it was but a dream. Why weren't they given mangos? The cabin passengers disembarked, men and women brilliant like peacocks in their fur-cloaked plumage. A Puerto Rican child called out to one of these lovely ladies, who waved a fur muff in condescension.

"The doctor is coming." Minvielle pointed to a tugboat sputtering up to the ship, its yellow flag flapping in the wind. "Everybody has to be inspected."

"What are we? Cattle?" the Puerto Ricans complained.

"What about them?" Vicente gestured to the cabin passengers.

"They're not emigrants," Minvielle said.

"Or Puerto Ricans," Vicente said.

The men refused to leave their womenfolk, despite being directed to a separate line. The doctor had no choice but to conduct a cursory examination on deck. He took from his pocket an instrument that looked like a hairpin to check underneath their eyelids.

Minvielle told them that the ship would dock at the Algiers pier for a day or two before they could continue their journey. Not to worry. There was plenty of food and water. It could be worse; on the first trip, they'd had to wait for someone in the United States Customs Office to decide whether or not the Puerto Ricans were American citizens because US law wouldn't permit foreign immigrants to work in the territory of Hawaii. US Customs had declared them Americans. ¡Oye, americano! In Puerto Rico, they weren't citizens—neither American nor Puerto Rican, and certainly not Spanish, not since the war. Look how they were already ahead! Minvielle, maybe we'll get paid more now that we're Americans?

"Probably best not to get too excited." Minvielle turned to leave.

Vicente called out to Minvielle, "¿Somos americanos? Do we Puerto Ricans have the same rights as people in the United States?"

Minvielle shrugged. "I'm just doing my job. I work for the Hawaiian planters just like you."

They passed the time in steerage playing music, dancing, and telling stories.

"Óyeme bien," said a man from Adjuntas who reached for a jug of ron caña making the rounds. "I swore that I would never again leave my beloved country after the Cuba Company and the iron mines. I had an old mother to support and three unmarried sisters. We starved in Puerto Rico like everyone else, and when a man has four women to feed, he will do anything, even go down into hell."

Murmurings. Agreements. Calls for the jug of ron caña.

"It was like a voyage to hell. On la *California*, an American ship. Half of us barefoot and in rags. All of us skin and bones, some men were sick or dying from the hunger. They gave us something putrid to eat, que ni el diablo la comía, and dirty water for coffee. Vomitando y durmiendo tirados en el piso. Sleeping like animals on the deck. A thousand men. More. When a man died, they stuffed him in a sack of sand and threw him in the sea. By the second day, almost all of us were sick. Por fin, half dead, we arrived at a little town called Daiquirí where americanos—grandes, gordos y colorados—picked out two hundred and fifty men. The ship sailed to another town, where more fat Americans picked out another couple hundred men. At Nipe, the third stop, some yanquis came on the boat and took seventy-five men. Ese tiempo, I was one of them. That left over four hundred puertorriqueños, negros, todos. They could all be in the sea, for all I know."

"Ay bendito, Santa María," somebody said.

"Nobody cares about los negros," somebody else said.

Raulito looked around steerage; he was one of the few black men. What if it were worse in Hawaii for a black man than it had been in Puerto Rico? He looked at Vicente, sitting with Valentina, and he knew that as long as he had his brother he would be all right.

"How did you get back to Puerto Rico?" Raulito recalled the stories the family had read in the newspapers about the Cuban mines.

The miner put his hand out for the jug. "Alive, gracias a Dios."

Laughter.

"Escucha mi cuento. Soy Gómez de Peñuelas," one of the Puerto Ricans said. "The day before San Ciriaco, I was to take the boat to Santo Domingo to work the cane, but there was this woman—"

"Ay los amores," somebody said.

"Women got that sweet stuff that healthy men can't resist." Gómez touched his hat. "Perdón, damas, Mamá didn't raise me to be so crude."

"That's what my father always told my mother when she complained about his pocas vergüenzas," somebody said.

"A woman is always ready with her sugar when a man is weakest," Gómez said.

Laughter.

Vicente put his arm around his wife. He couldn't bear the pain in her eyes, pain that he felt, too, but that they couldn't express to each other without two or three hundred people witnessing it.

Gómez was still telling his story.

"This woman used to be my wife, but certain things occurred, as they often do when a woman is cursed con mal genio. If a man wants to take another woman or even two, well, who can blame him? Still, except for certain episodes, she was a good wife. I only had the shirt and pants—the ones I have on—and she washed my clothes on Saturday so I didn't have to shame myself when I went to town on Sunday. Muy buena mujer, but she wanted a saint, not a man. Soy hombre. The day came when I said ¡Basta! I was sick of her quejas. I heard there was work in Santo Domingo. She said that a curandera had told her to stop me from getting on the boat. I don't believe in brujería, that witchcraft stuff, but because she was a woman, one thing led to another, and by the time I got to Mayagüez, the ship had already left the harbor. The sky had a strange tint to it and the wind was a demonio. It was the hurricane coming. San Ciriaco. I survived el huracán without a scratch in the home of a kind family. And the ship—all those puertorriqueños and their families going to Santo Domingo—the hurricane picked it up and threw it down, but la gente survived, sí señor, I helped to bring them out of the water."

Gómez crooked his finger for the jug.

"Everybody lived except for two little girls."

The jug of ron caña was passed around; another jug appeared.

"We are born to die," a woman said. "Dying is part of life. Just like being born, just like having children. And being buried out in the ocean is much better than being buried in dirt."

Valentina felt as if the woman were talking only to her.

"You know how we bury the poor. Los muertos are carried to the cemetery in a rented coffin and dumped in the graves." The woman took a swig of ron caña. "My father was the keeper of the cemetery, and part of his job as a palero was to dig up the bones to make room for the new dead."

Valentina was tempted to tell the woman to *shut up*.

"We grew vegetables in a tiny plot near the boneyard," the woman said. "Mamá said that's why our vegetables weren't very big, because they came from the graves of the poor, there weren't enough vitamins in the earth."

"Coño carajo," somebody said.

Valentina accepted the jug from the gravedigger's daughter and took a long swig that ended in a fit of coughing. Vicente patted her back.

After the second day, the Puerto Ricans were herded off the steamship and into small boats that took them to the pier. They searched the gray sky for snow. Someone said it was 40 degrees. Surely that was cold enough for snow! Stevedores from other ships loaded onto the pier crates of vegetables and fruits like asparagus and oranges. Valentina recalled a story her father had read to them from a newspaper long ago, about six Italian sailors who had been lynched in New Orleans, the murderers were never found. The Puerto Ricans, mostly country folk, marveled at the fancy carriages and the horse-drawn milk wagons transporting huge containers of milk. It had been years since they had drunk milk, not even the children could recall the taste of it.

The massive iron and steel machine was as terrifying and foreign to the Puerto Ricans as Columbus and his ships must have been to Puerto Rico's Tainos. They stared up at the black monstrosity. Thirteen tourist cars had been added specially to the Southern Pacific Railroad freight train for the trip across the country. It started to rain. Wind blew through the women's thin mantillas, and the rain ran off the men's straw hats. Children covered themselves with bundles. Mud splashed the women's long skirts as they hurried down the sidewalks to the arched causeway that led to the railroad depot.

"Frío, frío," they called out as they ran on the wet pavement.

Near the depot, a group of indios, Native American men and women, passed out blankets to the Puerto Ricans, who thanked them in Spanish.

The train whistle blew loud and insistent. Men hired by the Hawaiian sugar planters urged them on in English. Sailors carried the ill on stretchers. "Quickly! Quickly! Everyone on board the train! No, this isn't

Hawaii, yes, those are real Indians, no, I don't know why they're here." Minvielle waved them toward the train. "Yes, you have to get on the train. No, it's impossible to walk!"

Valentina looked out the window at the rain. Vicente sat next to her and Lourdes in front with her uncle. The train passed by farms and houses and towns too quickly. She would have liked to examine them, anything to keep her thoughts away from Javiercito. She had pleaded silently with God. She had made promesas she would have kept if Javiercito had recovered: she would attend Mass, baptize the children; she would never again envy other women for their clothes, and she wouldn't complain about whatever was in store for them in Hawaii. But God hadn't taken her up on her promesas. Valentina couldn't rid herself of one question: What had she done to deserve the loss of two children? She tried not to cry because she didn't want to upset Vicente. He'd taken it so hard. Javiercito, their precious boy, tan dulce. She reached for Vicente's hand.

Her lower back ached from the hard wooden seat of the third-class car, and she doubted she was the only one who longed for steerage's iron cots and thin pallets. The Puerto Ricans marveled at the vastness of the country, the towns they passed, the bales of hay coiled in rolls as if for giants, the horses seen at a distance running wild, the buffalo, the herds of cattle, the cowboys, the flatness of the land, the rise of the hills, and they talked about the family they'd left behind in Puerto Rico, the money they would make in Hawaii, and what they would eat once they could buy food.

Valentina held onto ropes that had been tied to each side of the car platforms to prevent the Puerto Ricans from falling or jumping off. They had to pass through many carriages to eat their meals and wait in long lines for water closets, where they were not even able to wash. They suspected that the Americans must not be very clean.

•

They ate cabbages and Irish potatoes with onions and parsley, salted meat and codfish, rice and runny whitish grits that Vicente compared to rice pudding made by a very poor cook. Those like Vicente and Valentina, who, once upon a time, had been among the more fortunate, longed for pollo fricasé and arroz con gandules y sancocho de guineo and café colao made from homegrown coffee beans.

Vicente worried that Valentina would have un ataque de nervios like the one she'd suffered when Evita died. His beautiful Valentina who'd had so much misfortune during their marriage, and now the loss of a second child. Yes, it had happened to him, too, but he would take on her pain if he could. Vicente brought her hand to his lips and he kissed it.

Valentina lied to her daughter. Everything will be fine, Lulu. It won't be much longer. They promised us a little house, and you'll go to school, too.

It'll be just like before the Americans, before the hurricane, a woman told Valentina. Like when the Spanish were in Puerto Rico, except better. In Hawaii there'll be food and no Spaniards. And we won't have to live in bohíos.

It was the sixth of January, Three Kings' Day. Vicente listened as his countrymen recalled the fiestas to celebrate the arrival of Los Tres Reyes Magos, who brought gifts of gold, frankincense, and myrrh for el Niñito Jesús. Lechón and arroz con gandules. Postres, like funche con leche and turrón, the almond and honey nougat made specially for Christmas. Nuts like avellanas, which were Valentina's favorite. Rum. Maví. Jíbaro musicians played all night long; they'd danced all night long. Lourdes was squished between her parents on the hard bench. She said that last year, she and Javiercito had tucked boxes filled with grass under their beds, and in the morning they'd searched the grass for candy. Vicente told her that when he was young, Raúl Vega would give ron to the jíbaro musicians while Gloria fed them asopao de pollo. Someone said how sometimes el hacendado would throw coins into a barrel of water for the poor children to catch with their teeth. Several homesick souls cried. Somebody strummed a cuatro guitar. People started dancing in the narrow aisles. Raulito danced with Lourdes. Vicente felt a tickle in his throat. Last Christmas they'd danced until the early morning at a neighbor's house and then they'd gone home, Raulito and the children to sleep. He and Valentina had made love and discussed plans for their future. Now, Valentina stared out the window, where there was nothing to see because it was night. He put his arm around her; she rested her head on his shoulder.

The train stopped the next day to pick up supplies in a small town without any sign of life. The Puerto Ricans joked that they would have run away, too, just as the townspeople must have. Then somebody said that Indians had killed the townspeople. Vicente said the people hadn't run away, the Americans had killed the Indians just like the Spaniards had slaughtered the Tainos.

"Papi, look!" Lourdes tapped on the window.

Guards pointed their rifles at a young puertorriqueño named Juanito Ramírez. The Puerto Ricans yelled and pounded on the window glass. The guards forced Juanito Ramírez onto the train and into his seat.

"Calm yourselves, ladies and gentlemen." Minvielle had come from another car to investigate the commotion. He sent the guards away and everyone talked at once.

"That poor boy reminds me of Raulito. Do something, Vicente," Valentina whispered to Vicente.

Vicente stood up. "Why the armed men, Minvielle? Juanito isn't a criminal."

"The Hawaiian Sugar Planters' Association hired the guards for your protection," Minvielle said. "Just like they hired all of you, just like they hired me."

"What were they protecting Juanito from?" Raulito leaned forward in his seat.

"You don't understand," Minvielle said. "There was trouble on the first journey to Hawaii."

"What trouble? Tell us what happened." Vicente crossed his arms.

Minvielle cleared his throat. "The planters don't want trouble."

"I don't want trouble." Juanito Ramírez stood up. "I only want to go back to Puerto Rico."

"I'm sorry, but that's not possible." Minvielle took a handkerchief out of his pocket.

"I want to go back to my mother," Juanito Ramírez said.

"It cost a lot of money to get you to Hawaii." Minvielle wiped his brow with the handkerchief. "On the last trip, three families refused to get on the train in New Orleans. They sent them back to Puerto Rico but dropped them off on the opposite side of the island from where they came from."

"Pobrecitos definitely won't get back home, not with how bad the roads still are after the hurricane," somebody said.

"But they're back in Puerto Rico." Vicente sat back down next to Valentina.

"The planters won't do that again," Minvielle said. "Cost too much."

Minvielle patted Juanito Ramírez's shoulder. "Take my advice. Go to Hawaii, save your money, and then go home to your mother."

The Puerto Ricans had plenty to say when Minvielle left the compartment.

"From Cuba, you could swim to Puerto Rico," Gómez said.

"And be eaten by sharks," somebody said.

"The Americans are like the Spanish," Vicente said. "We shouldn't forget that it's all about money for them."

The Puerto Ricans sat on the hard wood benches and stared out the windows; they listened to the wheels of the train that churned, *you'll never go back you'll never go back*. WELCOME TO SAN ANTONIO flashed before Vicente's eyes, but he was back on the mountain, one hand shading his face as he looked up at his coffee trees.

•

Juanito Ramírez jumped off the train as it was traveling thirty miles an hour through El Paso, Texas. The train halted in its tracks with a blast of the horn and a screech of the brakes that jostled the Puerto Ricans on their benches. The guards chased him. Vicente imagined Juanito Ramírez dodging the pedestrians as they hurried on their errands in the afternoon drizzle. He heard the birds in the sky as they cawed, *Run, Juanito, run.* He saw Juanito run to the door of the grandest house he ever saw, grander than any on the island that now belonged to the rich American sugar planters, lovelier than the Spanish-style houses owned by the coffee-growing hacendados of Utuado. He imagined Juanito free.

The Puerto Ricans were disappointed when Juanito Ramírez was dragged back onto a different part of the train. He didn't stand a chance against men with guns in a strange country where he didn't even know the language. Pobre muchacho didn't even have shoes.

The Puerto Ricans demanded that Minvielle explain why Juanito Ramírez, a boy who hadn't committed a crime, had been so shamefully mistreated.

Minvielle held out his hands for order. "Damas y caballeros, it's only for his own protection."

"What's going to happen to the boy?" Valentina stood so Minvielle could see her.

"It's not up to me," Minvielle said.

"Please send him back to his mother," Valentina said.

"I don't have any authority, señora," Minvielle said. "I'm just doing my job as best I can."

Poor Juanito Ramírez, the Puerto Ricans said, he was only a boy who wanted his mother. It didn't seem like Minvielle was on the side of los puertorriqueños.

"Minvielle has to earn his daily bread just like us." Vicente felt sorry for the plantation agent, who was a decent man.

"If only el pobre muchacho could be sent back to his mother," Valentina said.

CHAPTER FORTY-THREE

YELLOW

The wheels of the train chanted Javiercito was dead . . . Evita was dead . . . Javiercito was dead . . . Evita was dead . . . Javiercito was dead . . . dead . . . dead . . . over and over, mile after mile, town after town. Valentina sought out a flash of yellow. A daffodil in a field of weeds or a yellow tablecloth hanging on a clothesline. Javiercito, she couldn't think about. Not yet.

CHAPTER FORTY-FOUR

THERE ONCE WAS A SEÑORITA

In San Francisco, the ship that would take them to Hawaii had yet to arrive, which meant another night on the train after four long days cross-country. By now the Puerto Ricans had learned that the Hawaiian Sugar Planters' Association would do anything to save money. The pain in their backs! The ache in their thighs! The next morning, they were herded off the train without breakfast. They shivered in the January chill and the Puerto Ricans, wrapped in the blankets the Native Americans had given them, sent los indios bendiciones. A dozen naked children huddled together on the platform, including a little girl with a kerchief. Valentina parted with one of Javier's shirts, and it hung on her like a dress. The women wore mantillas intended for tropical nights. They walked past small wood houses that squatted close to the road. Painted ladies leaned out of windows and called out invitations. There was a girl selling roses. The cable cars clacked along the wharf. They dodged horses that pulled freight wagons and delivery carts, and tried to avoid the horse droppings that dirtied the streets and the hems of ladies' dresses.

The bay's murky water wasn't the brilliant blue of the Caribbean Sea. It smells! Lourdes told her mother. It stank like fish. Valentina recognized only the Spanish, French, and American flags waving from dozens of ships.

Lourdes pointed to everything. Mami, look at the ships, look at the people, and look at the vendors selling so many strange things!

Javiercito would have been so excited about the ships.

The harbor was packed with San Franciscans whose favorite pastime was to greet the arrival of ships. Lourdes tugged at her mother's skirts and pointed to a large group of men near the pier.

"They are chinos from China," Valentina said. "China is in the Orient, remember we read about the Orient in the book Titi Elena sent?"

Fashionable people rode by in horse-drawn carriages or strolled down the pier. Well-dressed San Francisco gentlemen accompanied ladies in huge beribboned hats. Fathers bought their children nuts that peddlers roasted in steel drums and scooped into paper cones. A peddler sold vanilla ice cream from a cart. Lourdes was about to ask her mother to buy her a cone, ice cream already a dream in her mouth, helado that she had never tasted, but one look at her mother's face and she swallowed her request.

There were tall ships and a fleet of small fishing boats with green triangular sails. The names of saints were painted on the hulls—Saint Thomas, Saint Joseph, Saint Geraldo, and a few female saints like Saint Magdalena and Saint Veronica.

A fisherman sang:

Di Provenza il mar, il suol
chi dal cor ti cancello?
Al nation fulgente sol
qual destino ti furò?

Valentina placed her hand on her chest, so overcome that for a moment she couldn't speak. The music recognized her heartbreak, the loss of her children Evita and Javiercito, and of her parents and beloved sister and her home and everything that had ever meant something to her.

"Mami, are you thinking of Javiercito?" Lourdes took her mother's hand.

Valentina nodded.

"The sailors are singing in Spanish," Lourdes said.

"Italian," Valentina said. "That kind of singing is called ópera."

"Ópera," Lourdes said.

"When I was your age, la ópera came to Ponce and my parents took your Titi Elena and me." She remembered it as if it were something that had happened to someone else. She told Lourdes how she had worn a white dress with many flounces; Elena's dress had two extra flounces because she was taller. Their mother's gown was a delicate thing of the purest blue; a Spanish comb glittered in her dark hair.

Ma se alfin ti trovo ancor,
se in me speme non fallì,
Se la voce dell'onor
in te appien non ammutì,
Dio m'esaudì!

She told her how Egisto Petrilli's opera company had come to Ponce. For months, her mother had spoken of nothing else. It had annoyed Papá so much that he'd had to resort to long evenings at the pharmacy.

Their attention was drawn to a woman in a fanciful hat with ostrich feathers. She said something to her companion and pointed a gloved hand toward Valentina for emphasis. She wore delicate leather shoes that peeked out from under the hem of a gown in Valentina's favorite color. Valentina was sure that the woman was criticizing her worn dress and her unkempt hair.

She had a strong urge to call out, If you please, madame, once upon a time, I, too, had a lovely dress in that same shade of rose. I had loving parents and a beloved sister and my own home where my children could sleep in their beds. If I were to tell you how I came to be in rags, you would not believe me. Or, she might say, Madame, you must understand that when you have eaten and slept in your clothes day after day, night after night, first in the bowels of a ship and then on a train, for so many days you couldn't wash like a human being, if you had experienced all this, then of course you would be filthy, your clothes would smell and you would stink!

Oh, why did she care? It was so stupid.

She looked down at her daughter, her third and now only child. Her anger left her; how silly she was to care what a stranger thought, a woman with whom she would never exchange a single word. Lourdes looked up at her with her sad brown eyes. Valentina didn't know why the stars had determined that their lives would unfold like a tragedy, but she would try to be strong for her daughter.

Valentina wiped away a streak of dirt from her daughter's cheek. "Ay Lulu, I wish you could have been a silly girl like me."

CHAPTER FORTY-FIVE

INSTRUCTIONS FOR THE CARE AND FEEDING OF THE PUERTO RICANS

T he water of San Francisco Bay was choppy, but the Puerto Ricans, along with forty black men from the southern United States and two hundred Chinese, crowded the deck of the *City of Peking* for a last glimpse of San Francisco nestled in the blue hills. The foghorn blew with the finality of church bells during a funeral procession. The sun chased away the last of the haze and speckled the algae-strewn water with flecks of gold. Minvielle pointed out the Golden Gate Bridge, which was so different from all the bridges the Puerto Ricans had known on their tiny island. A newfangled object swayed in the sky above them. A huge straw basket dangled from a hot-air balloon that swung to and fro from the ropes of the red, white, and blue balloon. People shouted down at them from inside the basket. The Puerto Ricans gasped at the whoosh of fire, sure that the balloon and all would come crashing down on the ship.

The children jumped up and down in delight.

"One day I will fly in a basket over the ocean," Lourdes said. "I'll wave to Javiercito."

"I'll come with you," Valentina said.

Vicente leaned over the railing. "So will I."

"Me, too," Raulito said.

The voyage to Honolulu was so rough that Valentina would look back on the accommodations on the steamer *Arkadia* as luxurious. They were crammed hip-to-hip in the hold of the *City of Peking* for eight days. Somehow the black men from the southern states ended up in the passenger cabins after talking to the captain. Los puertorriqueños kept a close eye on their women and children. It was never quiet, day or night, but how could it be? Six days of huge oscillating waves that tossed them about, causing most of the steerage passengers to become seasick. The stewards were slow to empty the sick pails. People threw up because of the foulness of the water closets. In one of her lucid moments, Valentina begged God to have mercy and kill her already. Vicente, one of the few not to get seasick, pleaded with her not to tempt Him.

Three Puerto Ricans had their wishes granted (some said) and died, their bodies thrown overboard without even a prayer from the captain.

Allowed on deck, the Puerto Ricans cheered the sight of an island spotted in the distance. Oahu, Minvielle said. The gray mountain peaks were unlike the lush green mountains of Puerto Rico. Numb with exhaustion, they sat on their bundles and stared out onto the glistening water. A giant fish jumped up from the sea and sprinkled those nearest the rail with salt water. Startled into laughter, the Puerto Ricans quickly fell back into languor. As they sailed closer to land, the sea turned into a kaleidoscope of colors and Oahu rose like Atlantis from the coral reefs.

Men loaded and unloaded supplies from ships that flew American flags. Coal was stacked in giant piles and ash rose from the smoky chimneys of the factories. Standing on the pier under the hot sun, Vicente swatted away flies and mosquitoes as he waited with his family and all the other Puerto Ricans, their possessions piled by their feet. He didn't realize that the crowd on the Pacific Mall Wharf had come for a glimpse of the barefoot natives from Porto Rico, the new American possession. Vicente didn't know that the Hawaiian newspapers had written about them for months and had announced the date of their arrival.

Lourdes said she was hungry and thirsty. The Puerto Ricans had been provided with food twice daily since their departure; it hadn't been the tastiest, but it had sat heavy in their bellies and helped them to believe that they had made the right decision. As he looked for Minvielle to remind him that they hadn't eaten since the day before, Vicente was pushed into a row of men—Puerto Rican, black, and Chinese. A hand-ful of white men walked down the row, inspecting and selecting laborers.

Minvielle and other plantation agents called out from a manifest the names of los puertorriqueños. Sánchez. Serrano. López. Cruz. Soto. Ruiz. Velázquez. Miranda. Castro. Villanueva. Vega. They hung numbered metal disks—four-digit bangos beginning with the number 9 for Puerto Ricans—around their necks like leis and then rushed them toward the interisland ferry.

"Another boat? But this is Hawaii." Vicente eyed the boat with suspicion.

"Some of you will remain here with me on this island called Oahu," Minvielle said. "The *Ke Au Hou* will take the rest of you to the Big Island of Hawaii."

They had not been on the *Ke Au Hou* for more than a few minutes when they heard shouting. Someone said there was a revolú! One of the Puerto Ricans had a knife, the sheriff was coming, and everyone would soon be in jail! Raulito! Where was Raulito? Valentina, have you seen Raulito? Vicente searched for his brother in the frenzied crowd. He pushed his way to the front of the boat. Why hadn't he kept an eye on his brother? But Raulito was twenty years old, a man. He could take care of himself, couldn't he? Vicente stepped on pieces of bread. "What the hell, Baltazar?"

A Puerto Rican who was not Raulito held a knife to a sailor's throat.

Vicente had come to know Baltazar Fortuno in the first days of the voyage, when Javiercito's feverish shakes began. Baltazar Fortuno had gotten the steward to bring hot soup to stop the boy's escalofríos.

"Compai, do you see how they treat us? That bread—that's our break-fast, lunch, and dinner." Baltazar Fortuno pointed to the bread with his free hand. "All day they don't feed us, and then they throw bread at us like we're cattle!"

"¡Malditos yanquis cabrones!" Vicente kicked a piece of bread. "We're not cattle!"

"We're men!" Baltazar's hand on the knife was steady.

"But why the knife, compai?" Vicente hoped that Baltazar was a reasonable man.

"This boat stays here until we're treated like men." Baltazar Fortuno nodded to the captain, standing with some of his men. "I had him send for the sheriff."

Vicente thought that, yes, sometimes it was necessary to hold a knife to a man's throat, even an American's, or maybe especially an American's. Baltazar was right that these americanos should know right here right now that they weren't cattle, and coño carajo they wouldn't put up with their disrespect!

Minvielle arrived in a tugboat with the sheriff and his men, who had drawn their guns.

"Señores, this is madness," Minvielle said.

"Don't take another step." Baltazar Fortuno's knife flashed silver.

"This is Sheriff Brown." Minvielle pointed to the sheriff.

"What seems to be the problem?" Sheriff Brown put his hand on his revolver.

"¿Qué es el problema?" Minvielle took out his handkerchief and wiped his brow.

"You see that bread? On the ground? That's our breakfast, lunch, and dinner." Baltazar Fortuno moved the knife down an inch. "We are men, not cattle."

"Nothing good can come of this," Minvielle said.

"Es un falta de respeto, Minvielle," Baltazar Fortuno said.

"What kind of place have we come to, Minvielle? Where human beings are treated like cattle?" Vicente saw the ship's captain and the sheriff talking, possibly hatching a plan to subdue Baltazar Fortuno, who had stood up for what was right. He couldn't let him act alone.

"We're men, not cattle!" Vicente yanked off his bango and tossed it overboard.

Los puertorriqueños followed Vicente's example and yanked off their tags and threw them into the ocean. They shouted, "We're men, not cattle! We're men, not cattle!"

"¡Señores! Your bangos! Don't take off your bangos!" Minvielle put out his hands to stop them.

Vicente felt a little sorry for Minvielle, who had been as decent as could be expected of somebody working for the planters.

Sheriff Brown pointed to the bread strewn on the deck. "Why dump the bread in the hatch in the first place?"

"They're not lords and ladies," the captain said. "Besides, didn't they eat on the *City of Peking?*"

"Captain, I authorized a barrel of salmon, another of pork, and some rice," Minvielle said. "Why didn't you serve them that?"

"Captain, if you had provided them with decent food in the first place, that knife wouldn't be pointed at your man's jugular," Sheriff Brown said.

"The Puerto Ricans have been brought to work on the sugar plantations," Minvielle said. "It's important to the Hawaiian Sugar Planters' Association that we treat them well."

"They're just a bunch of immigrants—" the captain said.

"The planters hired you to convey their laborers," Minvielle said to the captain. "You'll have a lot of explaining to do if they're not in good condition."

The captain sent to shore for food.

"This isn't going to look good if it gets in the papers," Minvielle said.

"No sirree, it won't look good in the papers," Sheriff Brown said. "Best pretend it didn't happen."

Before Minvielle left the ship, he told the Puerto Ricans that they shouldn't have tossed the bangos overboard; it was sure to cause a big headache for the plantations. Soon afterward, Vicente realized that Raulito wasn't on the boat.

CHAPTER FORTY-SIX

RICE

The Puerto Ricans slept in montones, piles of people, squeezed together on the deck of the *Ke Au Hou*. They wrapped themselves against the night breeze in the blankets from los indios. The sun beat down on them during the day, and there wasn't enough water for everyone. During the four-day voyage, there was only bread to eat: they hadn't eaten a full meal since the one after the uprising. Like many of the passengers, Valentina suffered from seasickness. Sometimes she lay with her head on her husband's lap and he waved her Spanish fan over her face.

Three times the vessel had to round the southern point of the Big Island. The captain of the *Ke Au Hou* unloaded the Puerto Ricans fifty at a time onto small boats to take them ashore at various stops along the coast. They called out to each other, "¡Adiós! ¡Adiós! ¡Nos veremos! ¡Hasta pronto!"

Valentina didn't expect the mountain that came out of hiding along the Hamakua Coast, or the turquoise blue water that was almost as beautiful as the Caribbean Sea. Somebody helped Vicente carry the trunk ashore. Valentina was so tired; she would need a month of Sundays to recover from the journey.

Plantation men carrying rifles were waiting with horse-drawn wagons on the wharf. They didn't speak Spanish and the Puerto Ricans didn't speak English. One of the men pantomimed swinging a machete. Los puertorriqueños protested that surely they weren't expected to cut cane the very day they arrived. They were exhausted, every single one of them. Thirsty. They hadn't eaten a full meal for four days! Mañana, they could work mañana. They needed to make a home, eat a plate of food. Rest. The men corralled the Puerto Ricans into wagons, gesturing with their rifles.

Vicente called to Valentina to be brave. She wanted to cry out that for once she didn't want to be brave! Lourdes sat on the trunk gripping the bedding, eyes wide open, past crying. As the men were driven away, waving to their families, Valentina remembered that Raulito had the bundle with the mosquito netting. Pobre Raulito, she hoped that he would be all right, that he'd turn up soon, once the plantation realized that he was meant to be with his brother.

One of the plantation men gestured to the women and children to get into wagons. At first, the women objected to going away with strange men, but the man insisted. They climbed into the wagons, complaining about the terrible way they'd been treated since they'd left San Francisco. Valentina pleaded for the wagon driver to help her with her trunk, putting her hands together in prayer, and although he didn't understand Spanish, he called over to somebody to help load it. Wagons took the women and children down a dirt road through fields of cane twenty feet high. All they could see were waves of green cane and red hills. They fanned themselves and rolled up their sleeves to try to cool off a little. One of the women sobbed.

Valentina wished she would stop crying. She was tempted to say, Señora, save your tears. You might need them later.

Lourdes moved closer and Valentina put her arm around her. She kissed the top of the little girl's head. Pobrecita, she'd been through so much.

The wagons stopped at the plantation store—a small wood building crammed with shelves of tinned meat and sardines. Lard and shortening. Rice in fifty-pound bags. Sacks of flour and sugar. Barrels of beans and salt.

Lourdes tugged at her mother's sleeve.

"What is it, Lourdes?" Valentina stared at the sacks of rice.

Valentina wanted rice. She could make arroz blanco to eat with habichuelas guisadas. Arroz con pollo, if she could get chicken. Arroz con dulce, if she could get raisins and sugar. Arroz con coco, if she could get ginger and cloves and azucar morena, and surely, on an island, there must be plenty of coconuts—Lourdes tugged again on her sleeve.

"I'm trying to think—" Valentina looked down at her daughter.

Lourdes pointed.

"It's not polite to point." Valentina gently lowered her finger.

A man behind the counter crooked his finger at them.

"Or to wag your finger at someone," Valentina told her daughter before walking up to the counter as if she were still an ama de casa with a proper home.

"Your husband's name and bango number?" His pen was poised over a ledger.

She stared at him.

"Bango! Bango!" He pointed to his neck, to her neck.

Valentina touched her neck. Ah, he wanted to know Vicente's number. Well, the bango was somewhere in the ocean. The man kept shouting. She stared at him in the same haughty manner the fashionable ladies in San Francisco had looked at her.

"Will you write down your husband's name here?" The man at the counter pushed the ledger toward her. Now he spoke to her in a normal tone and she deigned to look down at the ledger. He handed her a pen and she wrote Vicente's name on the ledger. He sighed, so relieved that Valentina smiled. Las puertorriqueñas who couldn't write asked her to hacer el favor and put down their husbands' names, then each woman marked an X.

Buy now, pay later. They were to choose whatever they needed for their new homes. Anything. Everything. Canned goods, candles, pots. Food was sold in bulk, like the twenty-pound sack of flour. Everything was sold at a minimum of ten cents' worth, whether it was salt or onions or garlic or candles or tobacco. The store didn't sell batatas and yautías. It didn't stock gandules or cornmeal. Valentina gasped aloud when she saw bacalao at twenty cents a pound! Ten cents a pound for rice! In Puerto Rico, after the Americans invaded and devalued the peso to half its worth, rice was still four cents a pound. Now, here in Hawaii, they wanted ten cents! Ten cents! Vicente was to earn fifteen dollars a month the first year. Valentina tried to decline the purchase of cloth sacks, but the clerk insisted that she take two and he put it on Vicente's account. Later they learned that these sacks were sleeping pallets to fill with straw.

"I'm going to get everything I want," one woman said.

Valentina tapped her arm. "Con permiso, but did you notice that everything costs so much more than in Puerto Rico? You'll be in debt to the plantation store forever."

"That's my husband's business," the woman said.

"What does it matter what we buy today?" another woman said. "We might all be dead tomorrow."

"Claro, tiene razón." Valentina was determined to never again give unsolicited advice.

One woman who had been on the wagon with them bought rice that was sold only in fifty-pound sacks. Valentina made a mental note of which women bought what. Valentina bought beans, powdered milk, dried codfish, and oil. Beef jerky. Hard bread. Matches. A galvanized pail. Salt and coffee. She decided against sugar, because it came in twenty-pound sacks. Some women bought cookery items like pots and pans, but Valentina had packed hers in the trunk. They bought salt pork, rice, plantains, and flour. Eggs. A clerk was kept busy wrapping bacalao in brown paper. It was as if the women had gone mad. They laughed and called out, "Dios mío," and "Carajo, que sueño," as they bought up staples that they hadn't been able to buy for years; to some it seemed but a dream. Some of the children sucked on sticks of peppermint candy. At first, Valentina ignored her daughter's pained look. Then she remembered Javiercito. Just this once, she told Lourdes, who flung her arms around her mother's waist.

They followed the clerk who was carrying the bag of rice for one of las puertorriqueñas. She and Lourdes carried their bundles and purchases from the plantation store. It took all her effort to lift one foot after the other. But she couldn't pass out in a faint, not when she had to care for Lourdes, not when Vicente was cutting cane on an empty stomach.

She helped Lourdes climb into the wagon.

"I bought everything I could so I can cook a proper meal for my husband for the first time in years." A woman propped her feet on the sack of rice.

"Did you buy sugar, too?" Valentina wanted sugar.

"Of course I bought sugar!" the woman said. "What is coffee without sugar?"

Valentina decided right then to become the woman's best friend.

She held out her hand. "I'm Valentina Sánchez and this is my daughter Lourdes. My husband is Vicente Vega."

The woman shook it. "My name is Dolores Cruz and I'm married to Eugenio. This is my Tomás."

"Encantada." Valentina avoided looking at the son. He was close in age to Javier.

"You're the woman who lost her boy," Dolores said. "I don't know how you can be so calm. Some people said it was unnatural how calm you were. I would still be screaming if I lost my Tomás."

Shut your big mouth, mujer, Valentina wanted to tell her, but then she remembered the rice. And sugar.

Valentina pointed to the sack. "Fifty pounds! I don't think there was that much rice left in all of Puerto Rico."

"I know you're right!" Dolores said. "I see that you didn't buy any."

"What with everything—" Valentina didn't have to pretend to be sad.

"Pobrecita." Dolores touched her arm.

"My poor daughter will just have to make do without rice." Valentina pinched Lourdes's arm. She cried out.

"Poor things," Dolores said.

The wagons stopped at a row of trees. The wagon driver pointed down a dirt road. He shoved Valentina's trunk onto the grass. The women struggled with all their parcels. They stared at a great house in the distance. Pretty houses dotted the red hills, and Valentina was foolish enough to hope that the little houses might be for them.

The women planned how they would fix up the little houses they'd been promised. They would plant vegetables, because it would be wonderful to have fresh vegetables again. Maybe there would be a mango or lemon tree as there had been in Puerto Rico before the hurricane. Weren't those pretty houses?

"There's no plaza, no church," one woman said.

If only not having a plaza or church were the worst of it. Valentina dared to hope that the houses they'd been promised had stoves, that she could find kindling, that there would be a freshwater stream, and that she could set about cooking a decent meal before she dropped off to sleep in a real bed.

If only.

Valentina looked up the hill at the grand house, and then down at the pretty little houses below it.

The women turned toward the pretty little houses, but one of the wagon drivers shouted at them, pointing down the hill.

Valentina looked in the direction he pointed, and her gaze followed a cement ditch alongside the dirt road. It couldn't be!

"It stinks." Lourdes pressed her nose into the bedding that she was carrying.

Valentina whispered for her to hush, better to let the others figure it out themselves. She left the trunk where the driver had dropped it. She wouldn't be able to carry it; Vicente would have to bring it whenever he came. She left her parcels also so she could offer to help Dolores carry her fifty-pound sack. The women walked on with their heavy bundles, speculating about the source of the faint odor.

Lourdes had run up ahead with the other children and called out to her mother, "I think they had a hurricane, too!"

Surely Lourdes was right; a hurricane must have swept through. It had picked up the crude shacks and thrown them on the ground in splintered and broken pieces. Misshapen steps led up to shanties cobbled together to form a communal roof and floor separated only by walls of wattle.

Some of the women cried. For this, they'd journeyed thousands of miles over sea and land and sea, yet again? Valentina and Dolores dropped the sack of rice on the ground. Valentina made her way to the first shanty. She stood outside the door, afraid of what was on the other side. Lourdes held onto her mother's sleeve. Valentina took a deep breath and was immediately sorry. She buried her nose in her shirtsleeve.

They entered their new home. One large room with a wood floor. No bed. Not even a shelf. A plain wood table with benches. Valentina was never happier to see a table in her whole life. Lourdes dropped her bundle on top of it.

"I hope it's better at the end of the row." Dolores stood in the doorway.

"Let's take your rice to your new house," Valentina said.

They passed round brick ovens with the insides burnt black from smoke, which they would later learn had been built by the Portuguese who had once been sugarcane workers like them. They looked inside a wood barrel.

"Rainwater," Valentina said. "I hope there is a river or stream nearby."

The smell became stronger as they walked. Dolores would soon realize her terrible mistake, but it wasn't Valentina's place to advise her. Look what happened the last time she stuck her nose into someone's business.

Las puertorriqueñas were exhausted but there wasn't time for rest. They had to unpack a few things and set about preparing dinner. Dolores talked about how hungry she was and how she couldn't wait to cook up a banquet for her husband and son. Valentina had seen that stick of a husband of hers, hadn't she? But then, they were all sticks, weren't they?

"Mami, it smells so horrible," Lourdes said.

She shook her head at her daughter.

"A little longer, Valentina," Dolores said.

Something must be wrong with Dolores's sense of smell. She claimed the last shanty and her new home. It was empty except for the usual insects. The woman next door watched them through the cracks in the wattle.

"Damas, I wish I'd drowned in the ocean," the woman said.

"Don't say that! This is the dama who lost her son at sea." Dolores glanced at Valentina.

"Ay bendito, you're that mujer," the woman said. "Lo siento, but I still wish I had drowned in the ocean."

"You're attracting el mal de ojo." Valentina wished it for the woman.

Dolores squashed a bug with her heel. They dropped the sack of rice on the table.

"How am I to cook? In Puerto Rico, even the poorest peona had a fogón." Dolores wiped her hands on her skirt.

"Once upon a time, I had a stove." Valentina recalled it like a dream, but it came out of her mouth like a lie.

"Bueno, at least I have rice." Dolores patted the fifty-pound sack.

"Dolores, if you could share some of your rice with me, I would really appreciate it." Valentina blinked tears from her eyes.

"Rice? You should have bought some at the store."

"I know, I know, but I didn't."

"No, you didn't."

"I can give you something in return, or I can sew something for you."

"You can sew? That's wonderful," Dolores said. "Of course I can give you rice."

"And a little sugar?"

"Sugar? I hope you brought a needle with you," Dolores said. "And thread."

Valentina spread her mantilla on the table and helped Dolores lift the sack; the rice spilled like seed pearls on the black lace. Valentina thought she'd never seen anything so pretty.

CHAPTER FORTY-SEVEN

WE ARE MEN, NOT CATTLE

On the first day, the Puerto Ricans learned that sugar was called poho. They also learned to hate the men on horseback who shouted at them in Portuguese, which they didn't understand; they learned to despise the boss, who was called the luna, and fear the plantation police with their guns and truncheons. The wagons rode over dirt roads no better than the trails in Puerto Rico. Only in Hawaii five minutes and already they were separated from their families, cabrones! Hombre, a man should be allowed to collapse! Instead they were loaded onto wagons like cattle! ¡Malditos cabrones! Vicente glanced back at the road that led to Valentina and Lulu. He hoped that Valentina would find a pretty little house with a bit of dirt where she could plant vegetables and herbs, and that Raulito would turn up soon.

Some of the Puerto Ricans like Vicente had their own machetes, but for those without, the cost of the machetes would be added to their accounts at the plantation store. At the luna's bark, the cane workers bent to the cane. Vicente reached for a stalk and chopped it twice, then tossed it on the ground. He was so thirsty and the heat inside the cane so intense that he was sure he was in hell. When it began to rain, he cut a dozen more stalks before stopping. Surely they wouldn't be expected to work when they could barely see the cane.

"Hana! Hana!" the luna shouted, and galloped off to round up the Puerto Ricans who had ceased to work. He and his henchmen rode up and down shouting "Hana! Hana!" By now los puertorriqueños knew it meant, "Work! Work!"

·

It was evening when the guards led los puertorriqueños off the cane fields. They didn't have the energy to complain, even among themselves. They passed men still at work, and somebody said they were Japanese.

Vicente saw Valentina's trunk in the dirt. He asked one of his compatriots to help him carry it.

Valentina told Lourdes to watch for her father from the open door. She'd planned to wave her hand around the hovel and say to Vicente, *For this, you made us leave Puerto Rico? I left my sister and parents and Evita for this? I lost Javiercito for this?* But one look at her husband, wet and exhausted, his hands blistered and swollen, one look at him, and instead she handed him a drying cloth.

For dinner, she served him a piece of bread and beef jerky.

When they finally lay together on the feather mattress, Vicente thought that he'd never been so tired. Lourdes was asleep on the floor, her face smushed on a bundle. He told Valentina how somebody had stood next to Raulito on the pier in Oahu and now that man was here but Raulito wasn't. He must have been sent to another plantation, perhaps in Oahu. Damn the Americans! These malditos cabrones americanos doing things so slapdash, not giving a damn about the Puerto Ricans, but when had they ever? And did she know there was a woman who was left with a child and no husband to support her, her husband someplace else, just like Raulito?

"Poor things! How can they survive?"

"She'll think of something."

"You mean selling her body to the sugarcane workers? She won't earn enough fucking peones for a bowl of rice."

Vicente turned to look at his wife in the candlelight. "Valentina! You've never talked like that before! It's not like you."

She closed her eyes. "Let's not quarrel, Vicente."

The neighbors on the other side of the wall made loud love; they could hear everything through the wattle wall.

"They might as well be lying next to us," Vicente said.

"They had a good idea," Valentina said.

They laughed, and it surprised them.

Valentina jumped into Vicente's arms at a terrible sound, a blaring noise so insistent and insidious that it shook them. Valentina looked over to Lourdes, who stirred but didn't wake. They dressed and hurried outside, sure that the world was ending, sure that the heavy fragrance of flowers in the evening breeze would be the last thing they would remember as they traveled to the other side. Death came at them on a horse riding down the row of shanties, but as the rider drew nearer, they saw that it was a plantation policeman shouting at them and waving a truncheon until they went back inside. Finally the terrible noise ceased, and soon the Puerto Ricans would know it was the evening siren commanding them to sleep.

The next morning, the siren woke them from a sound sleep.

"Jiralue dem poro rico jana jana! Jiralue dem poro rico jana jana!" Someone pounded on the door. Vicente reached for his machete. The door of the hut flung open.

"Jiralue dem poro rico jana jana!" A plantation policeman cracked a whip against the floor.

Vicente sprang up, machete in hand.

"Vicente, don't!" Valentina tugged at his arm.

"Jiralue dem poro rico jana jana!" the policeman said, before backing out of the shack.

Valentina closed the door. "You lunatic! What did you plan to do? Kill a policeman on your second day?"

"You're naked!" Vicente set down the machete to pull on his pants.

"Of course I'm naked," Valentina said. "You undressed me last night, don't you remember?"

"That policeman saw you naked!" Vicente looked at his wife as if it were her fault.

"I can't be the first naked woman he's seen," Valentina said.

"That policeman was lucky I didn't slice him up!" Vicente waved his machete.

"Don't be ridiculous," Valentina said. "What would happen to us if you went to jail?"

"What is it?" Lourdes, her dark hair in a braid down the back of her nightdress, sat up on the sleeping sack.

"Your father has to go to work." Valentina slipped on her dress. "Go back to sleep." Vicente went outside. Goddamn policeman. Piece-of-shit shack it might be, but while he lived in it, it was his piece of shit. Later Vicente and the other Puerto Ricans would learn that "Jiralue dem poro rico jana jana!" meant, "Get up, you Puerto Rican, work work!"

When the Japanese walked past their hovel, they stared straight ahead. Only the children snuck glances at the Puerto Ricans. All the men carried machetes, but the women and children carried what Valentina would learn was a hoe for weeding. Valentina claimed one of the brick Portuguese ovens. She would make a crude fogón for cooking until Vicente could make her something better. Lourdes helped her fold the bedding and she put it inside the trunk. Valentina placed on top of it the packets of gandules and annatto seeds she'd brought to plant. She and Lourdes went out in the light rain for kindling and rushes to make a broom. When the sun came out, Valentina spread them out in front of the hut to dry.

"Let's look for the mother and daughter your papi told me about last night," Valentina said.

But Sonia and her little girl found them.

"Doña, por favor, ten misericordia, have pity on us. We need a place to stay." Sonia set down her bundle. She was a skinny woman with a big smile and green eyes. "This is my Mirta. She looks as old as your daughter."

Valentina sent Lourdes with Mirta to get more kindling while Sonia told Valentina her story—she'd lost her husband somewhere on the journey, they'd stayed the night with Dolores, who had turned her and Mirta out that morning, but she was so grateful to Dolores, don't think she wasn't, because if it weren't for Dolores, she and her daughter might have had to sleep in a cane field. She'd gone down the row of huts and asked for shelter at each. Every dama had said lo siento but the huts were so small, barely enough for her own family, and yes, it was true that the huts were small, but Señora Valentina, what would she do if someone didn't have the heart to take them in? The only good thing was that each dama had given her a little something either out of mercy or guilt. Here Sonia offered her bundles.

Valentina took them. "If you stay, we'll share everything."

When Vicente returned from la caña, he found Sonia Fernández and her little girl in the hut.

"Don Vicente, I saw the spirit of my husband," Sonia said.

"That kind of talk scares the children." Vicente took off his shoes. It was important to preserve them; who knew when he could buy another pair of shoes.

"I saw mi Pedro like I see you at this very moment," Sonia said. "He was always rambling on about how the Americans had stolen the island and money right out of the Puerto Ricans' pockets."

"He got that right," Vicente said.

"I don't know why he said that because we never had money," Sonia said.

"Permit me to educate you," Vicente said. "First, the American general said our silver pesos were only worth fifty cents, and then McKinley, el presidente americano, said that our dollars were worth sixty cents! So the Americans came with empty sacks and they filled them up with our pesos and took them back to America. You know what happened to our silver pesos? Those ladrones americanos added five cents' worth of silver to our silver pesos!"

"Vicente, not again," Valentina said.

"And you know what those ladrones americanos got?"

Sonia stared at Vicente, who pointed his fork at her.

"American silver dollars!"

"¡No me digas!" Sonia looked at Valentina.

Valentina dished up rice and bacalao onto a plate.

"Five cents!" Vicente took the plate of food.

"Eat your dinner." Valentina placed a gentle hand on his shoulder.

"The Americans stole my farm." Vicente looked down at his plate.

"I don't understand these things," Sonia said.

"The Americans are thieves. What's there to understand?" Valentina washed the rice pot in the galvanized metal pail.

"And then they taxed our—" He stabbed his fork into a piece of bacalao.

"Please don't start with the tariffs, Vicente."

"The Americans may be devils, but you and your señora are angels, taking us into your home," Sonia said.

"What's this, Valentina?" Vicente's fork clacked against the enamel plate.

"They have to sleep somewhere."

"Not here," Vicente said.

"Have mercy, Don Vicente!"

"It's only until her husband turns up," Valentina said.

"Take a look around." Vicente waved his fork about the hut. "There isn't room."

"They slept in the cane fields," Valentina said. "With the rats."

"We'll die in the cane fields," Sonia said. "The rats will eat Mirta."

Both little Mirta and Lourdes began to cry.

"Niñas, no need to cry," Valentina said.

"Don Vicente, if you don't open your heart, what will become of us?" Sonia knelt in front of Vicente. The little girls knelt down also.

"Everyone get up." Valentina pulled Sonia to her feet.

"Valentina, you know it's impossible," Vicente said.

"That we are even here seems impossible," Valentina said.

Vicente looked at the little girls' tear-stained faces.

"Just for tonight." Valentina put her arm around Sonia. "We can't turn mother and child away."

"Just for tonight," Vicente said. Lourdes hugged him.

•

Sex always helped her forget—where she was, who she had been, who she had become. Whether the neighbors glimpsed them through the cracks in the wattle wall, whether Sonia closed her eyes or kept them open and watched them by the moonlight that silvered inside the hut, the lovers didn't notice, certainly not Valentina. When it came to love-making, it went unspoken that it wasn't proper to comment on it, not even by close friends and relatives; Sonia wouldn't say anything the next morning. It was Valentina and her husband's hovel, and she wasn't even thirty years old, and if she wanted to make love, then coño carajo she would! And if their neighbors heard them, she didn't care. She needed sex to fall asleep so she wouldn't hear the rats hunt through the garbage beneath them; she needed sex to get up in the morning to face another day in this godforsaken place, this Hawaii. She had no proper house, no stove, no bed, no luxury of any kind. She was thousands of miles away from her family—she couldn't even think of Javiercito, not yet—and she would be damned if she gave up sex!

Once when she was particularly loud, Vicente covered her mouth with his hand and it reminded her of another time long ago, when she had bitten the hand on her mouth and drawn the metallic taste of blood, and how its owner had let his hand slip from her mouth in surprise or, perhaps, pain.

Hilo, Hawaii
——Plantation
January 30, 1901

Dear Elena,

Our precious boy Javiercito was buried at sea somewhere in the cold Gulf of Mexico. One day he had a terrible fever—I can't write more about this—only that he's gone—my lovely boy—I try not to think of him—I wanted you to know, tell our parents only if you believe it necessary, but I see no reason to do so. I wish that you could have helped us to avoid this journey—did you not get my last letter?—but here we are on the other side of the world. The day begins with a siren to wake the dead and "Jiralue dem poro rico jana jana! Hana! Hana! Hana!" shouted at us by the plantation policemen. The siren tells us when to wake and when to sleep. It's as if we were indentured servants at the beck and call of a feudal lord. We live in a hut of the meanest sort that is not even good enough for pigs. There isn't a school for Lourdes, as we were promised. No one speaks Spanish here, and as we don't speak English, you can imagine the difficulties. Somehow we lost Vicente's brother Raulito on the voyage—he was sent to another plantation, we don't know where—and Vicente is beyond worried. We don't know what to do or who to ask for help finding him. We've taken in Sonia Fernández, a puertorriqueña, whose husband Pedro has also been misplaced. She has a daughter who is company for Lourdes. If somehow you hear of Sonia's husband, please tell him where to find his family. ¡Ay bendito, Elena! I don't know how or when this letter will reach you, or even if ever. (I have little paper and ink to write more.) I fear I will never see you or our parents again, but you are always in my heart.

Siempre,
Valentina

> *Hilo, Hawaii*
> ——— *Plantation*
> *January 30, 1901*

Dear Raúl,

Our precious Javiercito died at sea. It is almost more than I can bear to think about. Vicente is taking it so hard that we don't even speak of it. We lost Raulito somewhere. Please don't tell Gloria, but say instead that we are well and that our life here is a dream. Raúl, maybe we should have listened to you and stayed in Puerto Rico because it's not what we expected it to be. Your son and nieta te envían recuerdos. My love to mi querida Gloria.

Sinceramente,

Valentina

CHAPTER FORTY-EIGHT

JIRALUE DEM PORO RICO JANA JANA!

The Puerto Ricans lived between the sirens of morning and night. That hideous shrill at eight each evening commanded them to sleep and shattered any illusions they might have had that they were in control of their lives. Where once they had woken to early lovemaking or the birds chirping and the rooster crowing or the soft patter of the morning rain on zinc roofs, now it was the blare of the siren reminding them that their bodies belonged to the plantation.

They were paid on Saturdays, when they worked a half day. Vicente collected his pay along with both Puerto Rican and Japanese workers. Men and women and also young boys and girls who worked the cane lined up outside the plantation manager's office. When it was Vicente's turn, a policeman checked his bango and only then was he allowed to enter the office and approach the desk where Mr. White, the plantation manager, sat with his clerk, an open ledger at his elbow, a pile of cardboard pieces in front of the clerk. The lunas and policemen stood guard behind him and his assistant.

Mr. White and the clerk compared Vicente's bango number against the ledger. They had reassigned bango numbers that first week, four digits on a metal tag beginning with 9. Number 9 meant Puerto Ricans. The clerk wrote in Vicente's notebook and on a piece of cardboard; he handed both to Vicente.

Vicente looked down at the notebook with his name incorrectly spelled and the piece of cardboard in his hand. The clerk had written an amount that was less than he'd expected, and it would be months before he would learn that he was taxed on his pay. Vicente was tempted to take a match to the cardboard. He and Valentina had calculated it one night. This first year he would earn fifteen dollars monthly for working ten hours daily for twenty-four days. They couldn't believe that the total Vicente earned was sixty-two cents for a ten-hour day of cutting sugarcane. Sixty-two cents. In Puerto Rico, they'd thought, well, at least they would have a nice house and a good school for Lourdes and medical care when they needed it, but the housing was a shack and there wasn't a school in sight and who knew about medical care? All this was on his mind, but how could he say this to people who didn't understand him and were sure not to care even if they did?

Instead, Vicente pointed out to Mr. White the incorrect spelling on his notebook.

"My name is Vega, not Vegas," Vicente said.

Neither the plantation manager nor the clerk spoke Spanish.

"I'm a man, not a number." Vicente waved the cardboard under the clerk's nose.

A policeman came up behind Vicente; one of the lunas stepped up to the table, hand on his gun. The clerk waved at Vicente to step aside and make way for Eugenio, husband of Dolores, who was next in line.

"Easy does it," Mr. White said to the policeman. "We need these Porto Ricans."

To Vicente, who didn't speak English, it sounded like Mr. White told the policeman, *You might have to shoot this porrican.*

"I don't know what kind of trampa you're working here. The amount is incorrect, and where is my money?" Vicente rubbed his fingers together in the universal sign for money.

The clerk said something to him and pointed to the plantation store, then to the cardboard in Vicente's hand.

Vicente looked down at the piece of cardboard and then it came to him. "They're paying us in scrip!"

"They're paying us in scrip!" Eugenio looked over Vicente's shoulder.

"¡Me siento como un pendejo bien cabrón!"

"Tranquilo, Vicente." Eugenio put his hand on his compatriot's arm.

•

Vicente considered the armed men. If he struck one of them, the other would surely shoot him, and then what would happen to Valentina and Lourdes and Sonia and Mirta? Anger warred with the injustice of finding himself at the mercy of the plantation, yet again at the mercy of Americans. ¡Coño carajo! His father would say I told you so.

"Mi nombre es Vega." Vicente pointed to his chest. He said his name again to the plantation manager and the clerk, who didn't understand and didn't care, but at least he said it. Trabajo y tristeza, that's what all the Puerto Ricans said life was in Hawaii. Work and tragedy.

That first Saturday afternoon in Hawaii, the Japanese walked through the Puerto Rican camp on their way to their communal baths. Everyone came out of their hovels to see the Japanese in various stages of undress, what they would refer to among themselves as "la desgracia." Some puertorriqueños ran alongside them and shouted their objection to such immodesty.

"¡Que falta de respeto!"

"Put your clothes on!"

"¡No es decente! There are women and children here!"

A few of the Japanese men shouted back. Neither group knew the other's language, but their anger needed no words.

Lourdes pointed to a Japanese man with only a cloth wrapped around his waist.

"How many times have I told you it's not polite to point?" Valentina tapped her daughter's shoulder.

Valentina envied the Japanese women, babies strapped on their backs, wearing light wrappers.

"Walking around half-naked." Sonia shook her head. "That would never happen in Puerto Rico."

"But we're not in Puerto Rico," Valentina said. "I wouldn't mind walking around like that."

Vicente turned to look at her. "Would you, now?"

Valentina smiled at him. "You would mind me walking around half-naked?"

282 • MARISEL VERA

"What are you saying, mujer? That you would walk around like a japonesa if I let you?" Vicente tried to give her a stern look.

"It's probably a Japanese custom, but we could make it a Puerto Rican one." Valentina put her arms around him.

"Maybe I need to be more firm with you, like my mother always said." Vicente chucked her under her chin.

Valentina touched his chest. "I feel hot and sticky. Wouldn't it be nice to bathe like the Japanese? Naked."

"Let's go swimming!" Lourdes and Mirta jumped up and down.

"We'll find a private little spot." Valentina gave him a sidelong look that she knew from experience he found hard to resist.

"Que locura," Vicente said, but it was a weak protest. It was the first time since Javiercito died that Valentina had teased him. He would agree to anything.

"There is a little pond not far from here that I passed one day on the way to the cane," Vicente said. "I don't think anyone knows about it."

They shed their clothes at the pond, everyone except Vicente, who kept his trousers on, embarrassed to be naked in front of the little girls and Sonia, a woman who wasn't his wife. It wasn't proper and it would put him in a terrible lío with Sonia's husband. Vicente kept a little apart from the females as they swam and cavorted in the warm water. No one would ever have cause to blame him. Valentina noticed that Sonia, thin as she was, thin as they all were, had a slight belly. She suspected that her new friend was pregnant, but she would wait until Sonia told her, only then would she tell Vicente. When the children tired, Valentina sent them home.

"Sonia, take the children back, won't you? Vicente and I will be right along," Valentina said.

"Valentina, must I?" Sonia looked over at Vicente the way a woman shouldn't look at another woman's husband.

"Sí, mujer, start cooking and I'll finish up. Then we'll go to the party." Valentina treaded water.

With one last look at Vicente, Sonia left with the children.

Valentina swam over to her husband and tugged at his pants.

"You're shameless." He lifted her out of the water.

"It's the only way I can forget," she said.

Vicente needed it, too.

There was a party set up outside the shacks over by one of the Portuguese ovens. Everyone was talking about the revolú caused by the indecent Japanese and what could be done about it. Somebody said that he would be the first one to punch a Japanese in the face next time he walked around naked in front of his wife and daughter. What kind of place was this Japan? Then somebody said, Let's have some music! Where is that Hawaiian moonshine? What was it called? Okolehao. The women passed out food they'd brought while the jugs of okolehao made the rounds. Some of the women like Valentina took a swig. The musicians strummed guitars, others scraped güiros, and somebody shook el shekere, a calabash gourd covered in strings of beads. The children were sent to play while the adults danced. The okolehao made Valentina care only about music and dancing and her husband's arms around her.

Somebody shouted, Look! Japanese!

A dozen Japanese men in kimonos walked up to the Portuguese oven. The musicians stopped playing, the singers stopped singing.

One of the Japanese men spoke, pointing to the musicians, and by his angry words and expression, the Puerto Ricans knew he was complaining about the music. They murmured among themselves, que nervio, wasn't this the Puerto Rican camp, wasn't it Saturday, the only night they could have a fiesta, wasn't it bad enough to have lunas and blancos and police telling them what to do, now it was the Japanese.

Somebody said, Get the machetes!

"Vicente, do something!" Valentina tugged at her husband's arm.

Vicente walked between the two groups of men. "Mi gente, tranquilos."

Machetes . . . machetes . . . machetes . . .

He held out his hands. "Let's try to settle it without bloodshed."

Everyone watched as the two groups of men glared at each other. Finally, the Japanese men turned around and went home. The Puerto Ricans went back to their party. Play louder, they said to the musicians, and they danced until dawn.

CHAPTER FORTY-NINE

ON A DAY LIKE THIS

"Jiralue dem poro rico jana jana! Jiralue dem poro rico jana jana!"
the luna shouted from the great height of his horse as he rode up
and down the rows of sugarcane. He was a blur in the hard rain.
Vicente reached for a cane stalk and chopped it with the machete; cutting cane was especially dangerous in this weather. Not only was it hard
to see, but the machete could slip from a man's hand and sever something
important to him or his neighbor. The rain abated to a drizzle during the
midday meal. Huddled together between the rows of chopped sugarcane,
the men squatted and brought tins of food close to their mouths. In
Puerto Rico, they could have brought their guitars and played after they
ate, but here they only had their stories. One of the portorros told his.

"On a day like this in Puerto Rico, I went home early to my wife and
she was in bed with another man."

"¡Coño carajo!"

"Hombre, mala suerte."

"¿Un fulano? Or somebody you knew?"

"My younger brother."

"Your brother!"

"Your wife!"

"What did you do?"

"What any man would do. I broke off a switch from a tree. I gave them
both una pela they never forgot! No one blamed me, not my brother, or
my mother, not even my wife."

"Your own brother!"

"A man can't trust anyone with his woman, not his brother, not
his father."

"You didn't suspect?"

"Why do you think I came home early?"

"A man knows if he wants to know," somebody said.

Vicente found his lunch of beans difficult to swallow. He'd always had an uneasy feeling when his father was around Valentina. There had been something curious about the way they stood apart, something that had worried him. But why did he have to think about that now? What did it matter when he was squatting in Hawaiian sugarcane? ¡Coño carajo! If only he could confront his father right now!

The luna rode his horse down the row of sugarcane only a few feet away from where the men ate.

"Look at how they treat us." Vicente wanted to hit someone or something.

"It's like slave times," someone said. "I've got the luna's whip marks to prove it."

"No man except my father ever raised a hand to me in Puerto Rico."

"¡Ay bendito, las pelas papi gave me!" someone said.

"A father is one thing, but I'm not a slave," Vicente said. "We're men, not cattle."

"Hana! Hana!"

The men went back to the cane.

Vicente had stopped to wipe his forehead with his blue kerchief when the luna rode over to him on his horse, flicking his whip over Vicente's back. He cried out at the fire on his skin. Not since he'd become a man had he been treated with such disrespect. Vicente wrestled the whip from the luna's hand, pulling him down. The horse began to trot away, dragging the luna through the rows of cane, his leg caught in the stirrup. Vicente chased after them; he grabbed the reins, yanked them, and pulled the horse to a halt. The plantation policemen rode up on their horses and Vicente put up his hands, guns understood in any language.

CHAPTER FIFTY

SEÑORA, SEÑORITA

Somebody would bring her Vicente's machete.

Valentina peered out the door at the men who passed them on their way to their huts. Despite the slight offensive odor in the air, except when they slept, she always kept the door open for the natural light since the shack didn't have windows. Whenever she chased out a bird, she looked up at the sky, imagining that it was the same sky as in Puerto Rico.

Vicente was the kind of man who always came straight home. Of course, it was always possible that Vicente had a mujer, but he wouldn't be able to keep another woman secret, given the way the Puerto Ricans lived. And if he spent a penny of la miseria he made on another woman, Valentina thought she just might kill him.

Where could he be? It could only mean trouble.

"It's not like Vicente to be late," Valentina said.

"Maybe he met someone and stopped to talk," Sonia said.

When someone called her name, Valentina hurried out of the hut, Sonia and the girls right behind her. She hoped that Vicente hadn't suffered an accident, like the man whose neighbor had chopped off his arm with the swing of his machete.

It was Eugenio, the husband of Dolores.

"Tranquila, Valentina." He patted her arm. "They took Vicente."

"Who took him? Where?" Valentina looked behind Eugenio as if she could see her husband.

"I don't know," Eugenio said. "Jail, maybe."

The little girls began to cry.

"Niñas, a casa," Sonia said to the girls, who ran back inside.

"He beat up the luna." Eugenio held out the machete.

"That's a lie!"

"I can't say yes, I can't say no, but that's what they say," Eugenio said. "I was too far away to see anything."

"Who says he beat up the luna?" She took the machete from Eugenio, wary of the blade.

"The luna."

"He's a liar."

"He did have a bloody nose."

"Vicente?"

"The luna," Eugenio said.

"That's not like Vicente."

Eugenio took out his blue kerchief and wiped his forehead. "The luna whipped Vicente."

" 'The luna whipped Vicente.' " Valentina repeated the words as if she didn't understand them.

"Tranquila, Valentina." Sonia put her arm around her friend.

"Was he terribly hurt?" Her Vicente tan dulce. After everything he'd suffered, whipped.

"The luna? I think Vicente only punched him in the nose."

"Not the luna! Vicente!" What was wrong with Eugenio? She wanted to drop the machete on the ground and take Eugenio by the collar and shake the details out of him.

"It didn't seem so. The policemen marched him off the field," Eugenio said.

Valentina looked out into the road. Somewhere down that road her husband was in jail.

"I'd better go," Eugenio said. "Dolores will be wondering where I am."

"You're a good friend, Eugenio." Valentina tried to sound grateful but she wasn't grateful, she wanted to scream until her husband came home. Instead, she carried the machete inside and hung it on its hook on the wall.

"What will we do, Valentina?" Sonia looked as frightened as the little girls.

"Don't worry. I'll go to the manager tomorrow," she said. "I'm sure we'll have Vicente back home soon."

The women put Vicente's dinner away and then they worked on a dress for Dolores, who'd promised to pay them with rice and flour. Sonia was also a good seamstress. The girls went to sleep. At the blare of the plantation siren, the women put their needles down. Sonia settled on her straw-filled sleeping bag, and Valentina on the bedding they'd carried all the way from home. But Valentina couldn't sleep.

She'd wanted Eugenio to go back to Dolores and the others and say, Esa Valentina, que brava. Didn't collapse into tears because her husband is in jail and who knows when he will get out. You won't see that woman having un ataque de nervios. But Eugenio didn't know that she would get Vicente out of that jail tomorrow! The rats scavenged in the waste under the hut and Valentina plugged her fingers in her ears. Eyes squeezed shut because she wouldn't couldn't mustn't cry, she thought of their little house in Puerto Rico and the very first night when all four of them had slept in the big bed together. Javiercito, still a toddler, had slept facedown in a little ball. She'd woken up to nurse their daughter, and Vicente had woken up, too, looking at her in a way that made her feel a little shy—that someone could love her like that.

Valentina took more care with her appearance than she had for many months; she changed into her good shirtwaist and brushed her hair until it was glossy black. She pinned it up with every hairpin she had to keep it neat, in defiance of the wind.

"Anyone would think you were the patrono's mujer." Sonia inspected Valentina's frilled shirtdress and the shoes she had dusted and polished for her with a tí leaf that grew aplenty around the huts.

"I am going to get Vicente back." Valentina picked up a tiny annatto seed from the precious package she'd brought in her trunk and dipped it in a cup of water, then rubbed it on her lips. She dropped it back in the package.

Sonia passed her a rag. "How? You don't know English."

"I'll manage." Valentina rubbed the red dye off her fingertips. "Échame la bendición, Sonia." Valentina lowered her head for her friend's blessing.

Sonia made the sign of the cross on her forehead and blessed her. She and the little girls kissed Valentina for luck.

Valentina was careful to lift her skirts away from the red dirt. Women came to say that they'd heard about her husband. Was it true that he'd broken the luna's neck? Not that the luna didn't deserve it, but still, you could understand why Vicente was in jail. They didn't want to frighten her, but what if something happened to him—tú sabes, something really, really bad? Like what? Oh, they didn't like to say. Where was she going? No! She wasn't going there! Mujer, have you taken leave of your senses? You'll be eaten alive! One very pregnant woman pushed a twig of a boy toward her. Take Paco with you! He knows English. Take him! He's not doing anything useful around here. Valentina took Paco with her, or, rather, he walked alongside her.

He was about Javiercito's age, but she wouldn't think of Javiercito now. Instead, she thought of two little girls who needed to eat, and Sonia, who most likely was pregnant. The gangly, barefoot boy wore a shirt she guessed might have been white when they'd left Puerto Rico. After all the trouble with her appearance, she'd have to get rid of him.

"Why don't you run off now? Your mother isn't here to see you."

"She's not my mother."

"No?"

"Esa mujer is my stepmother."

"Your stepmother, then," Valentina said. "And it's una falta de respeto to call her 'esa mujer.'"

"Even if she's only a stepmother?"

"Even if she's only a stepmother."

"Even if she's mean?"

"Is she mean to you?" Valentina looked at Paco, who was only a boy like Javiercito had been.

"Not as mean as my father," Paco said.

"That's too bad," Valentina said.

"Will they give us food?"

"Who?"

"Them. El patrono."

"I don't think so," Valentina said. "Why should they?"

"Because we'll be company." Paco picked up a stick and used it as a cane. "In Puerto Rico, when my mother was alive, she gave food to company. When we had food. Hardly ever."

"This isn't Puerto Rico." Valentina lifted her skirts to avoid a muddy stretch. "Besides, we won't be company."

"No food? Mala suerte." Paco threw the branch against a tree.

"You didn't eat this morning?"

"Beans yesterday." His step was full of bounce, not the step of a boy half-starved.

"Poor thing," Valentina said. "How old are you?"

"Ten."

Like Javier.

"How many of you at home?"

"Three boys younger." Paco picked up a rock and skipped it along the dirt road. "Sugarcane gives me the asthma."

"How did you learn English?"

"From the American soldiers," Paco said.

"When we get back, I'll give you something to eat," Valentina said.

The manager's mansion with its spacious verandas and gardens was up on the hill and overlooked the plantation. From the top of the hill, Valentina and Paco looked down at the lovely cottages with well-kept gardens where the luna and the plantation clerks lived. Valentina glanced at a particularly beautiful orchid plant but she didn't stop. They walked up to the front of the house, set on a stone path shaded by a canopy of trees. Someone had placed a white wrought-iron bench under a huge coconut palm. Stupid idea, Valentina thought, but she envied the big house with the large veranda. She was reminded of when she'd first met Vicente at the wedding of her girlhood friend Dalia, which had been held in a home much grander than this one. Her shoes clacked on the pink stones. Valentina looked down at Paco's bare feet, red with dust.

A woman wearing a large apron, her arms and apron dusted with flour, blocked the entrance to the house. Her face had that hard look that often belonged to women who have had to earn their keep from a very young age.

"Buenos días, I've come to speak to the plantation manager." Valentina spoke with the same authority with which she had once spoken to la lavandera.

"Speak English!"

Valentina nudged Paco.

"Purdy sen-you-*ritas*."

The woman stared at Paco, her words stuck in her throat.

"Purdy sen-you-*ritas*."

Valentina stuck her foot in the door as the servant tried to close it.

"Meester White! Meester White!" Valentina shouted through the partially open door.

"Matilda, what is it?" A woman Valentina's age, dressed in pristine white, came to the door.

"They talking the foreign, missus," Matilda said.

The missus stared at Valentina, who was glad that she had taken special care with her appearance. She knew that, despite drudgery and deprivation, she was still a pretty woman. Of course la señora White, who looked at her as if she were some kind of exotic animal, would be hard pressed to believe it, but she, Valentina Sánchez, once upon a time, had also been una ama de casa.

Paco grinned. "Purdy sen-you-*ritas*."

The women stared at Paco in his filthy, threadbare clothes.

"Purdy seño*ritas*, purdy purdy señ—"

The lady of the house turned a shocked face toward Valentina.

"Callate." Valentina touched his shoulder. "Please, I would like to speak to Meester White about my husband." She enunciated the Spanish syllables the way the clerks at the plantation store had spoken English to her, but of course she didn't yell the way they did, as if she were deaf.

"John? What business do you have with my husband?" Mrs. White looked down at Valentina's bare hands. No lady would be without gloves, regardless of the weather. Valentina grew hot with shame, terrible, terrible shame that she had fallen so low as to not wear gloves.

"El señor White. Meester White. Please I must speak to him about my husband Vicente Vega." She hid her hands behind her back; they hadn't been the hands of a lady for years.

"I think we've heard enough," the lady of the house said to the servant. Valentina faced the closed door.

"I don't think those damas spoke English," Paco said.

"Let's try Mr. White's office. We should have gone there first," Valentina said, stopping at the orchid bush she'd passed earlier. She plucked the prettiest and largest of the pink flowers and tucked it in her hair. She took a second one and gave it to Paco, who tucked it behind his ear.

Several clerks sat at desks, leather-bound ledgers opened in front of them. They looked up in surprise when Valentina entered with Paco.

"I *must* speak with Meester White," Valentina said.

"Purdy sen-you-*ritas*," Paco said.

A clerk giggled.

"Hush, Paco." She would have left the boy outside but she hadn't wanted to walk into the manager's office alone.

Valentina wanted to reach over a desk and take the clerk by the collar of his shirt.

"Is Meester White here? Meester White!"

The clerk looked at Valentina as if she were an accounting problem he wasn't quite sure how to figure out.

"I think she's asking for Mr. White," the second clerk said.

"You know Mr. White isn't available to these people," the first clerk said.

"No Mr. White." The second clerk opened the door for them.

"Purdy sen-you-*ritas*," Paco said.

They hurried past the plantation manager's hacienda, past the plantation store, past the doctor's office, empty except when he came once a month, past the tidy wood houses of the lunas, and all the way down the long dirt road to the decrepit row of shanties. She found Sonia with Dolores and the girls.

"I didn't think it would do any good," Dolores said. "You're not the wife of a coffee farmer anymore."

Valentina glanced away from the smug look on her friend's face. Better not to say anything, the woman had a generous nature and she would probably need more rice if Vicente didn't return soon.

"Paco, repeat what you said to the Missus White," Valentina said.

"Purdy sen-you-*ritas*." Paco grinned.

"Sen-you-*ritas*," Valentina said. "What do you think, Dolores? It sounds like señoritas to me."

Dolores smacked Paco on the head. "Stupid boy. Is that all you know?"

Paco raised his hands to protect himself.

"Let him be! Dolores, you should have seen the looks on those women's faces!" Valentina laughed and laughed, and not even the concern on the faces of her friends could stop her.

"Tranquila, Valentina." Sonia hugged her. "Laughing too hard is asking for el mal de ojo."

Valentina bowed her head. "Échame la bendición, Sonia. Maybe it will keep bad luck away."

Sonia touched Valentina's forehead, blessing her.

Again the next day, women came out of their hovels as Valentina was leaving. Where was she going? Why was she looking so lovely? Meester White? Again? They heard it hadn't done any good the last time. They wished her luck even as they turned to one another to say that it wouldn't do any good this time, either, Americans didn't care a coffee bean about the Puerto Ricans. Poor, desperate woman, they were glad not to be in her shoes, even if she was muy guapa and had shoes, which some of them didn't. One or two of them weren't ashamed to admit that they had told their husbands to take the whip if it meant food in their children's mouths.

Valentina hurried, eager to get away from her noisy compañeras and plead her case. She pinched her cheeks and chewed on a petal from yesterday's orchid to color her lips. She knew that, despite her travails, she had rarely looked better. A woman like the plantation manager's wife might look only at the quality of her clothing or sneer at her for being gloveless, but a man, a man who liked women, might be swayed by her face and other features, even if she didn't speak English.

Valentina tried the plantation manager's office but the door was locked, the lights off. She went next door to the plantation store.

Valentina saw the clerk she'd spoken to at the plantation manager's office the day before.

"Meester White, por favor."

The clerk took her arm. "If you'll come with me, I'm sure I can be of service."

His politeness reassured her, although she couldn't understand Americans. Either they were rude, like the plantation manager's wife and servant, or they were polite, like this clerk who showed all his teeth when he smiled.

One of the other clerks called out from across the room, "Maybe you shouldn't, Kurt."

"I plan to be very nice to the pretty sen-you-*rita*." Kurt guided her to the back of the store.

Valentina was surprised when they entered a large storeroom crammed with barrels and shelves of foodstuffs. She stared at the cans stacked in pyramids that reached up to the ceiling, at the rice sacks, and the huge barrels of she-knew-not-what that crowded the room.

Kurt pulled her over to the rice sacks next to a pyramid of sardine cans and pinned her against a sack. He squeezed her breast hard; she cried out in pain. He tugged at her long skirt. Valentina struggled, and then held herself very still. Cool air on her thigh.

"That's it, sweetheart, nice and quiet." He reached between her legs.

When his hands went to his pants, Valentina shoved him with all of her might into the pyramid of cans. She heard the crash but she didn't stop. She ran. She didn't look back; no one ever died from being knocked over the head with a can, but if he died she wouldn't be sorry. Outside the storeroom, she stopped to straighten her dress and to tell herself not to cry. She walked past the astonished clerks with as much haughtiness as if she were Missus White.

She lay on a bed of sardine cans, her skirt pulled up over her face. His fingers dug into her buttocks. She cared only that he not stop. There were fish, large and small, rainbow-colored, that she'd seen in the ocean, a pink-and-yellow one she'd admired in the water near Oahu, and then the dolphin that had entertained them all. Finally, came the shark. Her moan came out as a strangled cry. Sonia murmured in her sleep. Her neighbors on the other side of the wattle wall called out, Tranquila, Valentina, tranquila, try not to cry, try to sleep, everything is always better in the sunshine.

CHAPTER FIFTY-ONE

INSIDE MEN

Vicente was sentenced to two months of hard labor and a fine of one dollar for insubordination to be deducted from his future earnings, but he didn't know it, because he didn't speak English. He thought he was entitled to a fair hearing and to know the charges against him, so he demanded a Spanish interpreter but, of course, he didn't get one. Vicente wanted to report that the luna and his henchmen were quick with the whip, but these men, haoles, americanos blancos, in starched collars and dark coats, considered themselves superior to the foreigners, those Others, those not like them, never like them. Others spoke Japanese or Spanish or any language not English. Others were natives from islands that were all sun and play and populated with lazy men who were like children in need of a firm hand because they were brown or black or poor. Others must be taught how to work and to live and to submit to the higher knowledge of those not foreign, of those not Other. Vicente thought of these men as Inside Men: inside their houses, inside their stores, inside their family circles, inside their missionary heritage, inside their fire-and-brimstone churches, inside their offices where they decided how to make money and how to keep it. Vicente knew that these Inside Men meant to share as little as possible with men like him, the Others who earned their money for them.

These Inside Men puffed on cigars and cigarettes and dismissed him as a troublesome vagrant. Back home, he'd learned what the Americans thought about Puerto Ricans from the newspapers. They believed that the Puerto Ricans had that indolent Spanish race in them, and some African, maybe even a strain of Indian, and that made them less-than.

Only much later would Vicente learn that the Inside Men had

brought the Puerto Ricans to Hawaii because most of them were white enough to satisfy them. The Inside Men had enough problems with the "yellow" Chinamen and especially the Japanese, with their unreasonable demands for better work conditions and higher pay. He didn't know that the Inside Men had wanted men like him to "whiten" the pool of cane workers.

The clang of steel butts against iron and the shouts of the guards roused them. They had stale bread for breakfast and what the prison cooks referred to as "coffee," but Vicente knew that not a single coffee bean had been used in the murky sludge. Then, the prisoners marched in the rain through the muddy prison yard in the still-dark. Vicente's group was assigned to carry heavy loads of crushed stones to areas where they would be raked and leveled to make roads. One day in the dirt of the prison yard, he found an orchid on the ground; he picked it up and tucked it into the waistband of his pants.

In the mess hall, Vicente met a Puerto Rican named Ignacio Nuñez who had left the island on the shipment after him. Vicente asked if the plantation Ignacio Nuñez had been assigned to had a school, and if the workers had real houses, and not la basura his family lived in. And did he get paid en efectivo—cash money—and not scrip?

"Sí, hombre, all of that." Ignacio Nuñez ate his piece of bread; four of his front teeth were missing.

"¿Entonces, qué pasó? I would still be on that plantation if I were you," Vicente said.

"I refused to work in the rain," Ignacio said. "The morning of un tremendo aguacero, the plantation policeman chased me out of my house. After that, I said, 'Olvídate, I'm leaving.'"

Vicente stared at him over his tin cup of sludge.

"It was a thunderstorm," Ignacio said. "There was lightning."

Vicente nodded. "Tiene razón, I knew a farmer who was struck by lightning."

"You understand then," Ignacio said.

Another time, in the jail cell before they were ordered to shut the fuck up and go to sleep, Ignacio shared a different story.

"On the plantation where I worked, all the single men live crowded in barracks. The plantation takes out money from our pay for a cook who prepares our meals—not comida criolla, but terrible food, some kind of hard potatoes and brown meat that was drowning in a sauce that was brown, too—the Americans don't care if we don't like the food. If we don't eat it con ganas on our own, then they call the policeman, who stands over you until you clean your plate."

"That was a bad situation," Vicente said.

"Hombre, I couldn't take it anymore," Ignacio Nuñez said. "It was like being in prison except with dances on Saturday nights."

Vicente nodded. "I lost my brother on the boat. Do you know a Raulito Villanueva?"

"You lost your brother? I left behind five brothers in Puerto Rico," Ignacio Nuñez said, "but I don't know yours."

"That's too bad." Vicente closed his eyes to sleep.

His body hurt so much he couldn't sleep, and Vicente wished he could reach for Valentina. He tried not to think of Javiercito or Evita or the coffee trees. It was better to pretend that they were part of some other man's life, and most days, he was able to do that. He worried about his brother. If only he could find him. He hoped that he had been sent to a plantation where he was treated decently, where it didn't matter that he was both Puerto Rican and a black man. Vicente thought of Lulu, and Mirta, too, but especially of Valentina. How would she survive? How would she and the little girls eat? And Sonia? Terrible thoughts came to him. What would his wife be willing to do to feed the little girls? Sell her body, her sacred body that no other man except him had possessed? No! Valentina was a good woman. Look how Valentina had insisted on taking in Sonia. Without his wife's kindness, Sonia would have had no choice but to prostitute herself to any fulano de tal. Valentina would never do that, not his Valentina. Would she? Sell her body? Valentina was above that, his wife was. She would never make el amor for money.

He was sure of it. She could be so wanton in her lovemaking. But for money? No. She wasn't that kind of woman. What kind was that? One who would do anything rather than see her children starve?

But questions came to him in the middle of the night; questions that had hidden in his mind all these years. Perhaps it was because he didn't have Valentina to help suppress them. Questions such as why had his father been the one to fetch him that terrible day when Evita died? Why had his father been visiting in the middle of the day, when his wife would be alone in the house with the children? Vicente wondered about it now, but all he could think of then was that Evita was dead, his little girl who loved mariposas. He'd cried right there in front of his father.

Vicente stared up at the bars of the cot above him, and it came to him that he'd never asked Valentina why his father had been there that afternoon. When people told Vicente that por lo menos it was his father who had found the little girl, he'd wanted to yell at them without knowing why. Vicente's father had built the tiny coffin that they set upon the table he had built for Valentina. Everyone in the countryside came to hold vigil, even the campesinos and los peones, who stayed outside en el batey, as did Raulito because he didn't want to see their father Raúl Vega or embarrass Vicente's mother.

The night Evita died, Vicente had held his wife in his arms and they'd made love without speaking and without joy, only necessity. Only Valentina knew his pain, only Valentina knew what it was to watch their beautiful baby girl wobbling on her fat little legs chasing butterflies. They could hear the mourners in the other room with their baby girl's coffin; the mourners sang the rosary, their Padre Nuestros y Ave Marías rising and falling above the chant of the coquís.

Vicente recalled other moments that hadn't felt quite "right." It was something in Valentina's manner, the barest skittishness in his wife's behavior when she was in the presence of his father that had given Vicente pause. Suspicions he had cast aside as unworthy of their love and their marriage. In the beginning, when his father had taken an immediate liking to Valentina, Vicente had been glad of it. Who better than his pretty young wife to soften the heart of his stern, tough father?

Vicente recalled once or twice that he'd smiled when Valentina seemed a little awkward around Raúl Vega. She'd blushed at his father's teasing. Vicente had been proud that lovely Valentina belonged to him.

A scream from another cell. He'd seen his mother and Inés exchange glances when his father addressed Valentina.

Vicente banged the cot. He shouted. Some of the men shouted back—*shut up keep quiet go to sleep beat the hell out of you porrican*—English words whose meanings couldn't be mistaken.

How could he possibly suspect Valentina, his wife, of anything—vile? She, who had suffered the loss of two of their three children, of something with his father! Vicente rubbed his temples and tried to clear away such shameful thoughts. If it were true about Valentina and his father, nothing could be worse. Nothing. Except. He stared up at the iron bars of the cot above him. The worst. The very worst. He couldn't couldn't couldn't contemplate it. Because if one, then two; if two, then three; if A, then B; if B, then C. His children. Not his father's. His. Javiercito and Evita and Lourdes. His son. Evita. Six-year-old Lulu, the only child left. Could that be why he'd always been a little harsher with Javiercito than he should have been? Not because he was a boy but because he'd suspected—no!

Lourdes. His. Not. His.

Only after Valentina confessed everything, if there was something to confess, would he decide what to do. No one would blame him, whatever he did. Not even his wife.

CHAPTER FIFTY-TWO

HOE HANA

Hoe hana. Hoe hoe hoe, weed weed weed for four hours in a straight line, no talking. Bent over at the waist, Valentina dug at the red clay earth to prepare it for the planting of sugarcane. Although women and children earned less than half of what men earned, hoe hana was the hardest work Valentina had done in her whole life.

Up with the 5 a.m. blare of the siren to pull on pants that had once belonged to Vicente's father and that she had taken for Raulito. Valentina left the sleeping girls in Sonia's care. The Japanese women wore white scarves that they pulled over the hats. Valentina took to tying a scarf around her straw hat like the Japanese women. Las japonesas sang songs of mourning while they worked, some of them crying. She brushed something from her cheek, surprised that her hand was wet.

Whenever Valentina stood up straight to ease the pain in her back, the luna charged up on his horse and shouted down at her. Hoe hana! Hoe hana! Only when it was necessary to sharpen the blade of the hoe on a stone with hands that trembled from effort and fatigue, only then could she stop hoe hana. Boys younger than Javiercito carried bundles of cane stalks on their backs like miniature mules. The youngest girl was eight years old, only a couple of years older than her own Lourdes. Hoe hana would crook the girl's spine like a tree branch. Some of the Japanese women who worked alongside her had warped spines. She dragged herself home feeling like someone had beaten and kicked her all over.

Valentina was the only puertorriqueña. When the others sat on their hoes while they ate lunch, she did the same. The Japanese brought their food in delicate lacquered boxes. She'd once kept hairpins and ribbons in a lacquered box that was lost in the hurricane. One of the Japanese women returned Valentina's stare. Valentina looked away, hoping she wasn't offended.

The first time Valentina had to put food on credit at the plantation store, she told herself that it wasn't her fault. Because she was a woman, she earned twenty-five cents a day to Vicente's sixty-two cents. (Girls earned twelve cents a day.) She bought bacalao, beans, and powdered milk for las niñas and a piece of liver for Sonia because she was pregnant and needed iron. (Although Sonia still hadn't confessed that she was encinta.) One day when Valentina didn't bring lunch because it was hard to feed four people on hoe hana wages, a Japanese woman offered to share her meal. Although Valentina felt faint from working under the hot sun, she tried to refuse, shaking her head, saying, no, gracias, señora.

The Japanese woman bowed again.

"Valentina." She pointed to her chest.

"Valentina." La japonesa bowed. "Mikioki." La japonesa pointed to her chest and bowed.

"Mikioki." Valentina bowed.

"Ono! Ono!" Mikioki pointed to the rice ball.

She didn't want to eat it but she was so hungry and she didn't want to be impolite. Valentina ate the rice formed into a ball with a surprise in the center of raw fish and a red pickled plum.

"Hmmmm, delicioso." Valentina smiled.

"Hmmmm, ono! Ono!" Mikioki smiled.

The women bowed to each other.

After that, Valentina always brought something to eat. The next payday, she put enough bacalao on credit to make extra for Mikioki. She sent the little girls to pick tí leaves, which she had seen the Japanese women use, and she wrapped the bacalao and rice in tí leaves instead of the banana leaves she would have used in Puerto Rico. Mikioki ate it and said, Ono! Valentina learned that *ono* meant tasty.

When Valentina stumbled home, exhausted after hoe hana, she knew that she looked as ragged as the other field workers. There was nothing left of the old prideful Valentina. Her shoes were dusty with red dirt.

Her friends and neighbors teased her because she wore her father-in-law's pants. She wasted no time thinking of Raúl Vega, but she thought about Vicente, worried about him. When would he return? Would he return? She hoped that los americanos hadn't done something terrible to him. With Vicente gone, it was like she was having a one-person conversation: she asked and answered all the questions, told and listened to all the stories, described problems, proposing what to do or lamenting that nothing could be done. She missed talking to him. Most of all, she missed that he looked at her as if she were still the strawberry girl from Ponce.

CHAPTER FIFTY-THREE

HOME

H is body didn't feel as if it belonged to him, his arms and legs seemed to move of their own volition, his hand rose to shade his face from the sun, something that he'd not been allowed to do on the chain gang. The police had brought him back to the planta-tion. For the first time in months, Vicente walked without a gun pointed at his back, and it gave him the sensation of freedom.

Vicente wished that he'd been allowed to wash. He had stone dust on his skin and under his fingernails. He was ashamed to have people see him filthy like any beggar. He hurried down the dirt road, eager to see the little girls and his wife. He thought of the great big kiss they'd share and how Valentina would linger in his embrace, not caring that he hadn't showered in two months.

"¡Valentina!" He ran the last few yards to their hut, calling out her name.

"¡Papi!" The little girls ran to him.

Vicente lifted them up, one in each arm; their joyous giggles eased some of the pain of what he'd endured. But Valentina, where was Valentina?

"Papi, you stink." Lourdes held her nose.

"You stink." Mirta held her nose, too.

"Oh, I do, do I?" Vicente planted a loud kiss on each little girl's fore-head, making them squeal.

"Where is your mother?" Vicente said to his daughter.

"Hoe hana." Lourdes pointed down the road.

"Hoe hana?" *His Valentina hoe hana?*

"Mami is here." Mirta pointed in the other direction.

He set the girls down and took one last look down the road, but no Valentina. They went to find Sonia, who was stirring a pot of beans in the Portuguese oven.

"Ay bendito, Vicente, it's wonderful to have you home." She hugged him. "You stink! Hombre, you need a bath!"

The little girls watched for Valentina; when they saw her, they ran toward her calling out the news.

"¡Papi is home!" They hugged her waist, taking her lunch pail and hoe, arguing as to who would carry what, telling her that he was real dirty but it was really Papi.

Vicente was back! She took off her hat and scarf and her hands trembled as she tidied up her hair. Vicente was back! If only she'd had some warning, if only she'd had time to bathe. That he should see her like this, her shirt sweat-stained, her hands dirty, and her nails cracked from hoeing weeds, that he should see her in these pants filthy with red dirt. She spit on the back of her hand and wiped her face, leaving a streak of red on her cheek.

Valentina wanted to throw her arms around him and cover his face with kisses, but he looked at her as if he didn't know her, as if she'd never been his strawberry girl. She thought it was because he was ashamed that she was dirty, that she worked in the cane. She didn't kiss him.

He stared at her, a sunburnt Valentina, a pants-wearing woman with her hands on her hips. He longed to take her in his arms, to wipe the dirt from her cheek, to tell her how much he'd missed her.

"What the hell are you wearing?" He pointed to her legs.

"Pants, as you can see." She waved a dirty hand down the length of her leg.

"Where did you get them?" Vicente crossed his arms.

"Not that it matters, but they were your father's."

"My father!"

"Las niñas asked about you every day," Valentina said. "They really missed you."

"What about you? Did you miss me?" Why were they standing in the road? This wasn't what he wanted.

"You don't know how much." She looked into his eyes, surprised that he'd asked.

"You don't show it." His voice was low, a little hurt.

Friends and compatriots surrounded them. Women welcomed Vicente with kisses and murmurs of sympathy for all he must have suffered. Men returned from working a half day, it was Saturday, and stopped to shake his hand. People congratulated Valentina, how wonderful that the police had sent back her husband in one piece. ¡Que gozo they'll have tonight! A little ron caña, a little Hawaiian moonshine, a little song, a little dance. We'll celebrate that you survived jail, that we survived another week in the cane.

Vicente said that a man just home from jail needed to talk to his wife in private. Take your time, Vicente! *Talk* as much as you like. Valentina went to their hut to get some clean clothes for both of them. They left the little girls with Sonia. When they reached the pond, Vicente wanted to ask Valentina if she'd come alone to bathe while he was gone, but he didn't. She took off her shirt and pants. Valentina dropped the dirty clothes on the ground next to the drying cloths and clean clothes. She picked up the bar of soap she'd wrapped in one of the cloths.

"Aren't you coming in?"

He hurried to remove his clothes.

She took his hand, drawing him into the pond.

"Welcome home." She kissed him.

He picked her up and carried her in the water to a depression in the sand where he could stand steady. He held her tight, she wrapped her legs around him. She murmured his name. He called her querida. The soap slipped from her hand.

"Vicente, the soap!"

"Forget it, querida."

"You need it."

"Y tú tambien."

They laughed.

Sometime later, they searched for the bar of soap.

"That soap was a day of hoe hana," Valentina said.

"We'll find it."

"I hope so."

Vicente ducked his head in the stream and came back up victorious, the bar of soap clutched in his hand.

Much later, they walked to the riverbank.

"Was it horrible? Being without a man?" Vicente set the soap on the grass to dry.

"I missed you most at night." Valentina looked at him in that way that he loved.

Vicente laughed. "You have no idea how I missed you."

She handed him a drying cloth.

"You dry me, I'll dry you."

"Everyone is waiting for you. Don't you care?"

"Not really."

Laughing, Valentina moved out of reach.

She wrapped the towel around her waist and shook her hair, twisting it to squeeze out the water.

"Eugenio brought me your machete. It wasn't right what the luna did to you. Then to send you to jail for two months."

"I couldn't stop thinking about you." Vicente didn't want to tell her about prison. Not yet.

"Sugar dreams?" She put on her dress.

"More like worries." He finished drying himself and pulled on his pants.

"I don't make a lot hoe hana," she said.

"I'm sorry you had to do that."

"I had to charge food at the plantation store." Valentina sat down on the grass.

"That's all right." Vicente buttoned his shirt, relishing the laundered cleanliness of the cloth on his skin. "Thank you for the clean clothes."

"You deserve that and more after all you've been through."

He sat next to her. "As do you."

They sat without speaking for a moment, looking out at the pond, turning to smile at each other.

"You know those stories they tell in Puerto Rico about los muertos in the countryside? That's me at the end of the day," Valentina said. "Muerta."

"Querida." He took her hand, giving it a gentle squeeze.

"But las japonesas are very nice." She smiled at him because he was sitting next to her and calling her querida the way he always did. How she'd missed that.

A bird flew down into the pond. They watched it rise out of the water with a fish in its beak.

"Vicente, why don't you go on strike?"

"What?"

"Huelga. You and Eugenio and the others should go on strike."

"They won't care about a bunch of Puerto Ricans."

"They will care. They need you to cut their stupid cane. And what about if you got the Japanese to strike, too? Puerto Ricans and Japanese together. Isn't that a good idea?"

"The Japanese! We don't know any Japanese, and even if we did, we don't speak the same language!"

"I know this woman—Mikioki—she's Japanese. I hoe hana with Mikioki. You can talk to her husband."

"I don't know." Vicente shook his head.

"What is it that you're always saying—you're not a cow?"

He laughed. "We're men, not cattle."

She giggled. "Yes, that's it."

Vicente lifted a long strand of hair; the back of her dress was wet.

"Your hair is still wet."

"It'll dry."

He fiddled with her hair, wrapping a strand around his finger. "I kept thinking about my father."

"Raúl?"

"He liked you." Vicente saw her shoulders stiffen, just a little, but he saw it.

He brought the strand of hair to his nose, it smelled like fresh water.

"I had a lot of time to think," Vicente said. "About us. You. Him."

"You're not making any sense." Valentina flipped her hair in front of her face, her fingers searched for knots.

"I want to see your face." He took her by the shoulders and brushed her hair from her face. He could have been gentler.

"Was there something between you?"

"Why would you ask me that? Jail must have made you crazy."

"Was there?" Vicente looked into her eyes.

She turned her head. "I won't talk to you when you're like this—"

There *had* been something. Vicente's hands became tangled in her hair. "Did he do this—"

"Let go of me!"

He let her go.

Valentina moved away. "You must be crazy!"

"Whenever I think of you and my father, I feel a little crazy."

He looked at his wife, her dark hair falling to her waist, arms crossed over her chest, her brown eyes frightened.

"The day Evita died, he came to see you when he knew I was en la finca."

"You know I don't like to remember that day."

Vicente said, "You were alone with him."

"And the children."

"They were babies."

Valentina sat to put on her shoes. "Why ask me this now, Vicente? After all this time?"

"Why? Why did he come see you?"

"I don't remember, Vicente. It was so long ago—and then—"

The sounds of guitar playing came from the Puerto Rican camp; the party had begun.

"The way my father looked at you," Vicente said. "I should have known he was up to no good."

"We were having such a lovely time, Vicente. Why do you have to go spoil it?"

"Did you let my father fuck you?"

Valentina turned to look at him. "All these years you thought—"

"It was in the back of my mind but I didn't know it." He didn't take his gaze from her face.

She stood up and smoothed down her dress.

Vicente reached for her hand. "You know my father."

"And you know me." Valentina pulled her hand away. "I'm going to the party. You can stay here with your suspicions."

He watched her run until she was only a flash of white.

La gente were sure to gossip about Valentina at the party by herself on the day her husband came home from jail; los puertorriqueños liked a good bochinche. Valentina would be with the women talking, maybe even drinking. She did what she wanted here in Hawaii, though she couldn't dance with another man without Vicente's permission, not when he was around, anyway: although she might be willing, no man would take such a risk. He made his way to the party because it was, after all, a fiesta held partly in his honor. Besides, why shouldn't he go to the party and enjoy himself? *He* hadn't done anything wrong. The breeze wafted the sweet smell of sugarcane, which he could live without smelling. He plucked a red orchid from a bush and touched the red petals with the tip of his fingers; it was delicate and soft the way Valentina had been when he first knew her. But now she was strong; she'd had to be. He had to forget whatever might have happened with his father. And he would. He just needed her to say just once—that there was nothing to tell.

He smelled the freshly cut grass before he saw it. That morning, the older boys in the Puerto Rican camp had cut the grass with machetes to prepare it for dancing.

There she was, his wife, talking and laughing with the other women. She didn't bother to look in his direction. Somebody passed him a jug of okolehao and asked him about jail. What had the malditos americanos done to him? He told them about the chain gang.

"We're men, not cattle," somebody said.

Vicente smiled, remembering Valentina thinking it was "cow." Eugenio passed him a cigarette, the first cigarette Vicente had had since Puerto Rico because he had promised Valentina not to charge anything that wasn't a necessity at the plantation store. He held the cigarette in the palm of his hand and marveled that something of such scant weight could bring such pleasure.

"We're screwed and the Americans know it," somebody said. "There isn't anything we can do about it."

"We can refuse to cut cane." Vicente rolled the cigarette between his fingers. "We can go on strike."

"¿Huelga? ¡Huelga!" passed from man to man.

"We can set down our machetes," Vicente said.

"Huelga," Eugenio said.

"We're men, not cattle," Vicente said. "No man has the right to raise his whip to us."

The men drank.

"Promises were made," Vicente said. "We must demand that they be kept."

"Huelga," Eugenio said again.

"Huelga." The men drank.

"We need to get together with the Japanese," Vicente said.

"The Japanese?"

"We'll organize with the Japanese in the other camp," Vicente said. "We'll strike together, then we'll have more bargaining power with los americanos."

"We don't know anything about the Japanese," Eugenio said.

"We'll learn."

"Do we even know any Japanese?" Eugenio refilled Vicente's glass.

"We will."

"Japanese and Puerto Ricans working together," Eugenio said. "Can it be done?"

"We didn't come from the other side of the world to become slaves in this one," Vicente said. "We have to try."

They drank as they considered it.

"The Hawaiian Sugar Planters' Association won't want the cane to rot in the fields," Vicente said. "We have that in our favor."

"But they have guns," Eugenio said.

They drank as they thought about guns.

"They wouldn't be able to arrest all of us," Vicente said. "Or kill all of us. They need us to cut the cane."

"But nobody talks Japanese," Eugenio said.

"That's a problem," Vicente said.

Somebody began to play the cuatro guitar, Valentina's favorite, then a woman took up a güiro, another shook el shekere. Somebody sang. People began to pair off. When her husband asked her to dance, Valentina walked away, and everyone watched him follow her.

"I don't want to dance with you," Valentina said.

"I don't want to dance with you, either," Vicente said.

They stood next to the Portuguese oven. On its roof was a milk jug of Hawaiian moonshine. She took a slug of the okolehao; Vicente noticed that Valentina didn't cough the way she had the first time.

"You drink okolehao como nada," he said.

She ignored him.

"Did you dance while I was gone? Without my permission?"

"How was I supposed to get it? You were in jail."

"I hope that you didn't wander off with your partner under the stars." Valentina looked at him. "Don't be stupid."

"I'm the one who should be angry," Vicente said.

"You've no right to be angry." She put the jug back on top of the oven.

"But Valentina, my father—"

"Hombre, I've spent the last two months hoe hana and I'm not taking mierda from anyone." Valentina placed her hands on her hips.

"I'm not anyone," Vicente said. "I'm your husband."

"You, either," Valentina said.

They watched their friends laughing and dancing to the normally sedate vals; the music and the beautiful night enticed them to shake their hips a little, as they wouldn't have back home.

"I don't want to fight," Valentina said.

"I don't want to fight, either." Vicente moved closer to her.

"I'm glad you're back," she said.

"You're different," Vicente said.

"Hoe hana will do that to you," Valentina said.

"I don't mean that."

"What did you mean, then?"

"I don't know. Different."

He leaned in to kiss her; she kissed him back and he tasted the sweetness of okolehao on her tongue.

"We won't stay here forever," he said.

"The sooner we leave, the better."

"First we have to pay off the debt to the plantation store."

"We'll both work. That way we can pay it off quicker," Valentina said.

"No, I will work—"

"We could use the extra money," Valentina said. "Sonia will help."

"Even in my nightmares, I never saw my own wife working like a peona." Vicente held her tight.

"I was a peona en Puerto Rico," Valentina said. "Now I'm a peona in Hawaii."

He gasped as if she'd stabbed him, and he let go of her.

"I never wanted it like that, Valentina, I did my best."

"Who says you didn't?"

Valentina reached for the jug and took another drink of okolehao. "You want to know about your father? I'll tell you, but then I don't ever want you to ask me about it again."

So she told him. All these years later, she told him. But she didn't cry because there were worse things to cry about, and she wouldn't cry over those things, not with all their friends watching, not with the little girls running around with their friends, she would save her crying for some other time.

If only she'd told him, he said, if only she'd told him about the first time when his father had approached her. Then he could have—what— what would he have done? Something. He would have done something, he hoped so anyway.

He took the jug from her, then took a drink before setting it back on the Portuguese oven. He noticed for the first time that the moonshine had a hint of pineapple.

"I was afraid, afraid that you'd say that I'd enticed him somehow," Valentina said. "I thought I was protecting you, from what you might do."

"Querida—"

"I was so young, I thought it would cause so much trouble—"

"Querida—"

"And then when Evita died, I thought—that it was my fault—that you would be right to blame me—"

"Blame you? I wouldn't have! It wasn't your fault—"

"I only want to forget," Valentina said.

"We can't forget. Ever. Not Evita or Javiercito. We wouldn't want to forget them." Vicente held her close. "We can't forget Raulito or my mother or your sister Elena or your parents or even Puerto Rico."

"Or Inés and Gloria."

He held out his hand. "Will you dance with me?"

They joined their friends on the grass and danced under the stars until dawn.

The stars twinkled, *Love, love.*

CHAPTER FIFTY-FOUR

SISTER

They stopped to rest on their way back from getting water from the stream.

"You ride Vicente like he's a horse and you have to win the race." Sonia brushed the red dirt from Valentina's sleeve. It was impossible to keep their clothes clean, what with the wind.

"You shouldn't pay attention to what I do with my husband." Valentina retied the kerchief in her hair that had come undone.

"Do you mind my talking about it?" Sonia sat down on the grass.

"Mujer, after everything that I've gone through, there is very little that I mind." Valentina brushed her skirt, wondering why she even bothered.

"When he sucks your tetas, I want to pull down my blouse and give him one of my mine." Sonia pulled her dress down.

Valentina examined her friend's plump breast.

"I wouldn't do that." Valentina sat down next to her.

"No? You once said that we'd share everything." Sonia smiled at her friend.

Valentina laughed. "It's one thing to share food and a floor to sleep on, but my husband has only so much energy after working in the cane all day."

"Maybe one night, if you're too tired?" Sonia tucked her breast back in her dress.

"Look for someplace else to stay," Valentina said, "if you're going to be a nuisance."

Sonia clutched Valentina's arm. "Lo siento, it's just that I'm pregnant."

"Pregnant? ¡Ay bendito! That explains your big tetas." Valentina feigned surprise, as if she hadn't suspected for months.

"I get very horny when I'm pregnant," Sonia said.

"Doesn't every woman?" Valentina remembered how she would throw herself at Vicente the minute he came home from la finca.

"Will you help me, Valentina?" Sonia picked at the blades of grass.

"I already told you—"

"With the baby," Sonia said.

"Do you want to keep it? I can make a concoction of herbs—"

"Have you ever—"

"No, but we'll have to do it soon." Valentina had learned a lot of home remedies from both Gloria and Doña Angelina.

"I want the baby, I hope he's a boy."

"You'll sleep on our bedding until the baby comes."

"With Vicente?" Sonia winked.

"Find yourself one of the single men from the barracks who can keep his mouth shut," Valentina said. "I'd bet there are one or two."

"My Pedro always said that I was tan jugosa when I was pregnant," Sonia said. "I hope your husband can control himself."

"How about when Vicente sucks my tits, you pretend they're yours." Valentina stood and offered her friend a hand up. "Would you like that?"

"Thank you." Sonia took her hand.

Sonia didn't draw men to her with the heady scent of sex and the heavy breasts of a healthy woman. Valentina worried that her sickly, sallow pallor came from la anemia.

One morning, Valentina handed Vicente his lunch. "I'm going to take Sonia to the plantation doctor."

"You speak two words of English," Vicente said. "What good can come of seeing the doctor?"

"He's an idiot if he can't recognize a sick woman," Valentina said.

The doctor came once a month for a few days and worked in a one-room infirmary not far from both the manager's office and the plantation store. Valentina and Sonia waited their turn with Puerto Ricans and some Japanese from the camp next door. They heard a boy's scream and turned to each other in horror. Later they would learn that the boy had been strapped to a chair while the doctor removed an infected toenail without anesthesia.

Inside a man took notes at a desk stacked with jars of different-colored pills. Valentina pantomimed a big belly and cradled an imaginary baby.

"Don't let him touch me." Sonia hid her face in Valentina's shoulder.

"Tontita, you wanted a man to touch you, didn't you?" Valentina was glad for her friend's smile, however weak.

The doctor checked Sonia's pulse, then pointed to his mouth and stuck out his tongue. Sonia gagged from the wooden stick down her throat. The doctor called out to the man at the desk, who scooped up blue pills from a jar and wrapped them in brown paper. Next thing they knew, the women were outside.

They saw Ramón Solis, one of the cane workers, talking to someone waiting in line.

"The luna's presents." Ramón lifted his shirt to show blistered welts on his back. "The doctor gave me pills for the infection and said, 'Hana! Hana!'"

They stared at the blue pills in Ramón's palm.

"¡Mierda! The doctor gave Sonia the same pills!" Valentina examined them.

"¡Coño carajo! ¡Maldito cabrón!" Ramón Solis threw his handful of pills on the ground.

"I'm going to die." Sonia covered her face with her hands.

"I won't let you." Valentina hugged her, careful of Sonia's slight bump. She was seven months pregnant and the baby should have been much bigger.

Vicente and Valentina walked up the hill, as they sometimes did in the evening. It was the only way that the pair could speak without everyone knowing their business—Sonia, the girls, the neighbors, and anyone who passed by the hovels.

"Sonia worries me." Valentina held her husband's hand. "We have to give her better food, vegetables and meat. We'll have to put it on credit."

"Do it."

Valentina rewarded him with a kiss.

"Querida, let's make a baby." He maneuvered her against the trunk of a tree.

"We can't." Valentina placed her hands against his chest.

"We can." Vicente pulled up her dress.

"Let's talk about it another time." Valentina pulled down her dress.

"Why talk?" As he leaned in to kiss her neck, they heard Lourdes calling out for help.

Sonia was in labor, two months early. Valentina took Sonia's hand in hers and told Vicente to get the doctor and to hurry back before the plantation siren. Sonia screamed and the little girls screamed. The neighbors next door called out through the wattle, ¿Qué pasa? What could they do to help the mother? Valentina said, Boil some water, bring me a sharp knife, and clean cloths.

Valentina sent the girls to stay with Dolores. She lit another candle and knelt by her friend.

"Did you have a doctor deliver your baby in Puerto Rico?" She wiped Sonia's face with a cool cloth.

Sonia gave a weak laugh. "Claro, que no. Did you?"

"Las damas delivered my babies." Valentina helped her take off her dress.

"Babies? I thought you only had Lourdes." Sonia was so fragile in her thin cotton sheath of a slip that Valentina had to stop herself from wincing.

"I lost two of my children." Valentina searched her memory for what las damas had done for her.

"Ay bendito, lo siento. I forgot . . . your son . . . the boat." Sonia took her hand and gave it a weak squeeze.

Valentina looked into her friend's eyes, willing her to believe what she hoped would be true. "I don't want you to worry. We will birth this baby together and everything will be fine."

"Échame la bendición," Sonia said.

Valentina made the sign of the cross on her friend's forehead and blessed her.

The baby came in one fast swoosh. He was a tiny thing, all scrunched up and covered in blood, but with Sonia's mouth and nose.

"It's a boy." The baby's bluish tinge filled Valentina with dread.

"Pedro wanted a boy." Sonia closed her eyes in exhaustion. "Does he have all of his fingers and toes?"

"All of them." Valentina touched the perfect toes.

Valentina cradled the baby with one arm while she got the knife the neighbor had brought and passed the blade through the candle's flame. She sliced the umbilical cord with the tip. One, two. Done. Valentina tied the stump of the umbilical cord with a string and wished she had some copaiba oil to dress it the way the midwives did in Puerto Rico. Tomorrow she would ask around if anyone had some. For now, she could clean it with ashes from el fogón. Valentina's hands were gentle as she dried the baby and wrapped him in a piece of cloth.

"He's beautiful, Sonia." She placed him in his mother's arms.

"Precioso." Sonia smiled at her son.

The plantation siren blared. Valentina glanced at the door; Vicente wasn't home yet.

Valentina pushed the trunk behind her friend and helped her sit up. "I want you to sit with your back against this trunk so you can nurse your baby."

The new mother put the baby to her breast.

The baby didn't move; Sonia didn't seem to notice.

Sonia looked up from her baby. "Can I be with Vicente now?"

"As soon as you're strong enough, you can be with him the whole night long." Valentina knelt by her friend; why didn't Sonia see that her baby wasn't nursing?

"Oh, thank you! I won't let him drink my breast milk," Sonia said. "No matter how much he begs."

"How did you know he liked breast milk?" Valentina wiped her friend's face with a wet cloth.

"What man doesn't?" Sonia kissed her baby's head. "I'll call him Manuel, after my father."

The women sat together, their backs against the trunk. Sonia talked about how happy her husband would be, how she felt in her heart that her husband would find her because she believed in miracles, didn't Valentina?

"I always hope for miracles," Valentina said.

Valentina held out her arms for the baby. "Let's make sure that everything that was supposed to come out came out."

She put the baby on the girls' pallet and helped Sonia lie back down. Valentina pressed down on Sonia's stomach. Sonia's screams soared over the hovels; it entered the dreams of the sleeping cane workers in which plantation policemen raised their billy clubs and whips and shouted *Hana! Hana!*

Her baby next to her, Sonia slept on the feather mattress a few feet away. Valentina and Vicente lay on the grass-filled cloth bags.

"I'm so glad you're safe."

"They said the doctor wasn't in." Vicente reached for her.

"I can't hoe hana anymore, I have to take care of Sonia."

"I never wanted you to hoe hana."

"If only the doctor had come." Valentina buried her face in her husband's shoulder.

"They said he wasn't home."

"Was that true?"

Valentina felt Vicente's shrug.

Tomorrow she would have to tell her friend that her baby was dead.

Valentina didn't wait her turn. She walked past the line of the sick, carrying the tiny body wrapped in a cloth like a small bundle of food.

"Get in the back of the line like everyone else," somebody said.

She didn't hear or she didn't care, and she walked unannounced into the doctor's office. Valentina shoved aside some of the jars of pills and laid the bundle on the desk.

"Lady, who said you could come in here?" The doctor's assistant reached for her.

Valentina waved him away and unwrapped the bundle; the men looked down at the baby.

"Stillborn?"

The doctor examined the baby. "That's what I'm putting in my report."

"A boy," the assistant said.

"Better bury it," the doctor said.

Valentina made a sweeping bump over her stomach and pointed in the direction of the hovels.

"Señora. Lady. Mamá. Bebé. ¡Doctor, por favor!" She tugged at the doctor's sleeve and he inspected it for fingerprints.

"Mamá." Valentina pointed toward the plantation workers' hovels.

"I think she wants you to see the mother," the assistant said.

"You make one exception and you'll be making house calls to every hut for a cold in the head," the doctor said.

"You have a point," the assistant said.

"These Porto Ricans are the most demanding of the lot, worse than the Portuguese," the doctor said.

"But not worse than the Japanese," the assistant said.

"Nobody's worse than the Japanese," the doctor said, as the assistant picked up the baby, but not without some care.

A few weeks went by with the little girls helping Valentina take care of Sonia. They pressed cool wet cloths on her forehead, held the cup of water to her lips, picked the aloe vera plant so that Valentina could smooth the gel on her skin, but Sonia spent her days staring out the open door.

"Sonia, please eat something, maybe just a spoonful of rice." Valentina held the spoon to her lips.

Sonia ate a few grains, then turned her head. Valentina knew that she had to do more. If only she could get her hands on a live hen to make a sopón. That was the best remedy for a woman recovering from child-birth, that and hot milk made with chocolate from Spain. Valentina cut open an aloe vera leaf and massaged a little gel on Sonia's bloated stom-ach. Only with Mirta did Valentina see a glimmer of the old Sonia. She had to get her to the doctor, but how? She couldn't carry her; it was too far for Sonia to walk, and besides she didn't have the strength. Vicente couldn't take a day off from the cane without the plantation policeman coming to get him; Valentina didn't want him sent back to jail. Yet the situation was desperate. Valentina couldn't let her friend die; she didn't think she could bear it. And Mirta needed her mother.

When Valentina saw the wheelbarrow in the plantation manager's gar-den, she knew it was the answer. She could easily push Sonia in it. She would steal it somehow. Valentina looked around for the gardener, a middle-aged haole who threw rocks at the children for stealing vegeta-bles. It was one of those sunny days when for a few minutes there was a soft rain. If she hurried, she could be gone before the rain ended and the gardener returned. She pushed the wheelbarrow.

A hand spun her around.

The gardener looked her up and down in the rude way a man looks at a woman that makes her cringe. Valentina wanted to slap him, but instead she smiled and pointed to the wheelbarrow, then to herself. She pantomimed wheeling it away. In turn, he made an indecent sugges-tion with his hand. Valentina backed away, ready to run. Her gaze fell again on the wheelbarrow. She needed that wheelbarrow. No! She still couldn't do what he wanted. Not even for the wheelbarrow. But for Sonia? Could she do it for Sonia? How else could she get Sonia to the doctor? The haole gardener said something else that Valentina didn't understand. She looked again at the wheelbarrow. Sonia would die with-out a doctor's attention. If she did it . . . how revolting . . . Sonia was her friend . . . Sonia was like her sister, she reminded her of Elena . . . that she even considered it . . . shame on her. She couldn't do it. Yet Sonia. The doctor would be gone in a few days, not to return for weeks. Sonia would die by then. If she did it . . . would it be so terrible? No one would ever need to know.

Valentina followed the haole into the shed.

His pants bagged around his ankles . . . dust mites floated in the air . . . guttural, foreign words tumbled on her head as she knelt . . . birds cooed outside the shed . . . the pressure of his hand.

Valentina pushed the wheelbarrow down the dirt road past the Japanese camp and stopped at the path that separated the Japanese camp from the Puerto Rican camp. She pushed the wheelbarrow by a tree, sitting down next to it in the shade. She covered her face with her hands, the tears hot on her palms. What had she done? Why had she done it? She should never have done it. It was terrible. She was terrible. Then she thought of Sonia. She'd done it for Sonia.

"Valentina?"

Valentina looked up through her tears.

Mikioki from hoe hana bowed.

"Okay?" Mikioki pointed to her.

Valentina shook her head. The thought passed through her mind that Mikioki should be working. The Japanese woman sat down next to her. They sat there for a few minutes without speaking and then Mikioki listened, nodding as if she understood what Valentina was telling her in whispered Spanish, the terrible secret that Valentina would never reveal to another soul.

After a time, the women stood, bowed to each other, and went their separate ways.

Dolores gasped.

"¡Que diablo! Tell me everything," she said, but Valentina pretended not to hear.

Valentina wheeled Sonia right past the line of people, apologizing, asking perdón of everyone. The doctor's assistant carried Sonia to the infirmary as if she weighed no more than a sack of rice. Valentina worried that Sonia must be very ill since the doctor hadn't sent her away with blue pills.

The infirmary was little more than a shed with cots, one of which was already occupied by a coughing Japanese woman. Valentina covered her mouth with her kerchief, hoping that the woman wasn't suffering from tuberculosis; that would be sure to finish Sonia off. For a second, Valentina envied Sonia for sleeping in a real bed and was ashamed. Valentina held Sonia's bony hand, which reminded her of chicken feet.

"Vicente fucked me last night," Sonia said, with a glimmer of her old smile. "I didn't dream it, did I, Valentina?"

"You rode him like a horse," Valentina said, making the sign of the cross on her forehead, blessing her.

Valentina cried as she pushed the empty wheelbarrow to her hut. She cried for Sonia and she cried because of the wheelbarrow, what she'd done for it. She had never touched another man except for her husband. And now she had a secret to keep from Vicente, forever, because he could never know. She cried harder because it might have been for nothing.

When Valentina brought Mirta to see her mother, she again ignored the reproaches of the long line of the sick waiting in the rain. The infirmary was empty and she went to the office, where she found only the doctor's assistant. She spoke to him in Spanish and he answered her in English. She wished, not for the first time, that the plantation had someone who could speak Spanish—if not the doctor, then at least his assistant.

Valentina held Mirta's hand. He came around the desk to speak softly to her; she closed her eyes, opening them to his gentle touch on her arm. She nodded and he pointed to a shed up the road.

Mirta ran ahead as she walked past the line of patients again. The sound of a hammer could be heard as they approached the shed; a man in shirtsleeves was building a coffin. Valentina asked him about Sonia, and although he didn't understand her words, he pointed to the shed.

Valentina bit back her scream. Sonia lay in a coffin made of plain wood planks; she was a pale, barefoot wraith playing dress-up in the clothes of a much larger woman. Sonia who was like her sister, Sonia who made her laugh. Sonia. Querida Sonia.

Valentina lifted Mirta over the coffin.

"Is Mami sleeping?" Mirta touched her mother's cheek.

"No, darling," Valentina said. "Your mami is with baby Manuel."

"Is Mami an angel, too? Dolores said baby Manuel is an angel." Mirta braced herself on the coffin's edge.

"An angel like baby Manuel," Valentina said, although she wasn't sure if she believed in angels.

"Mami is an angel." Mirta kissed her mother.

Valentina wondered what had happened to Sonia's shoes. She would have to go back to the infirmary to get them. She could bargain with the shoes or save them for the little girls. But why was she thinking of shoes?

Valentina set Mirta down on the ground and bent over the coffin.

She kissed her friend and whispered, "Querida, I'm sorry I didn't let you make love to Vicente."

The little girl began to cry. "I don't have a mami now."

"You'll always have us." Valentina knelt and took Sonia's daughter in her arms and she cried, too.

CHAPTER FIFTY-FIVE

TIBURÓN

When Raulito realized that Vicente wasn't on the pier in Oahu, he tried to jump in the water to swim after his brother, but several of the Puerto Ricans pulled him back.

"¡Muchacho, estás loco? There are tiburones in the water!"

Raulito tried to break free. "I'd rather be shark meat than lose my brother!"

"Don't be stupid! You won't find your brother inside the stomach of a tiburón," somebody said.

¡Vicente! ¡Hermano! Where are you?

Raulito turned twenty-one on the sugarcane plantation. His mother Eusemia finally started coming to him in dreams, with her hair tucked in a turban of bright colors. In his dreams, she always smiled. In life, her lips weren't accustomed to turning up at the corners of her mouth, and they didn't know that they weren't supposed to quiver.

Brother, where are you?

It was a nightmare, this Hawaii.

From what Raulito had seen of Oahu, it wasn't very beautiful, though it might be up in the mountains, where he heard there was no sugarcane. It couldn't be as beautiful as Puerto Rico because that was impossible. Oahu was the green or yellow of the cane stalks that cut into his palms; it was the scratches on his neck; it was the silk that got caught in his fingernails and made him want to tear them out. It was his body bent to the will of the cane, to the will of the luna. Work, Work, Work. Hana, Hana, Hana. Oahu was lonely, lonely nights. He slept on a bare cot in the single men's barracks, where there wasn't even an escupidera to use as a chamber pot, as he and his mother had always had. He didn't like to do his business outside in the middle of the night when the plantation policemen were patrolling. If they saw you, they threatened you with their guns or nightsticks.

Everyone said that life in the camp was trabajo y tristeza. Some unlucky puertorriqueñas had lost their husbands to death or the planters' negligence and had to earn money however they could. People asked him why he didn't take a wife—there were a dozen pretty girls in need of a husband. Men advised him to visit Nina Pagán, whose husband had drowned in a pond soon after el pobrecito arrived in Oahu.

When Raulito went to introduce himself to Nina, she sent her three children to gather kindling. Stale odors lingered in the one-room shack. He saw that there was no way to make his escape. The shack was crowded with a cot and a table and a bench for sitting. Cooking utensils and several bags of foodstuffs like coffee beans and cornmeal covered the table. An empty oil can was used as a fogón with scraps of kindling.

Nina took off her dress. "Don't just sit there like a tonto. What's wrong? Why are you crying?"

"I'm not crying." Raulito wiped his eyes with his sleeve. Nina sat next to him on the cot.

"Didn't you come to make el amor?"

Raulito looked down at the shoes Vicente had given him after he lost his in the hurricane. Vicente hadn't said so, but he'd known that the shoes once belonged to their father.

"Then why—"

"I can't—"

"You can't? Or you don't want to?"

"I don't want to."

"Why are you here, then?"

"Please let me stay," Raulito said. "I'll pay."

Nina put her dress back on. From then on, Raulito visited Nina every week and he paid her to talk. He listened to stories of how once she had been la ama de casa of her own household. The arrangement suited them both.

"My husband Victorio was a very good man." Nina mashed spices like garlic and onion in a small wood pilón while he smashed coffee beans in a larger one he had made her as a present.

"A very hard worker. Sometimes I think of Victorio and how hard he worked. What good was it? We come here and what happens? He goes to bathe in the reservoir and his foot slips. And he leaves me thousands of miles from home to fend for myself and the children."

After the first few times, Raulito only needed to nod or murmur when she paused, to insert a sympathetic "ay bendito," or an affirmative "claro" or "no me digas." It got to be that he found it soothing to hear her voice in the background of his thoughts, the way he'd listen to the caw of a bird on the mountain. He'd think about how he lost his brother and how he would find him. Once, Raulito looked up at Nina's hands paused in the act of snapping a bean pod. He took a chance and said, "¡No me digas!" Nina snapped the bean.

When Raulito left Nina's house, he strutted around the camp like a rooster so everyone would know where he had been.

Raulito ate, slept, and woke at dawn to cut cane, ate, slept, and woke at dawn to cut cane. A day was forever when one was young and alone in a strange country, with nobody to love and nobody to love you. Others had their families or their women, but not him. He came to enjoy Nina's company, but because he paid to visit, he knew that any friendship they shared would be over if he couldn't pay her.

He ate with the family of a fellow puertorriqueño named Carlito Maldonado, whose wife Soraida cooked for him. Soraida asked why didn't he find himself a woman and make a family? Carlito said he could marry a nice girl and still visit Nina, nothing wrong with that. It was a man's right to have as many women as he wanted, especially if he could hide his querida from his wife. Raulito remembered his father Raúl Vega then. How he'd discarded his mother and never acknowledged him. If he ever had a woman—and he never would—he wouldn't be like his father, no señor; he would be like his brother Vicente.

Raulito liked to go to the parties on Saturday nights. The Puerto

Ricans took turns as hosts; they talked politics, lamented that they'd left Puerto Rico and their fate of trabajo y tristeza. But it was really a dancing and drinking party. Raulito, like most of the Puerto Ricans, loved to dance. The Puerto Ricans danced because they wanted to forget the cane, because it gave their hard lives joy, because they were young, because they were old, because the sun was bright, because the moon shone, because the stars twinkled and the sea was blue, because the music allowed them to pretend that they were still in Puerto Rico. Valentina had taught Raulito all the dances. La guaracha. El seis. La danza. El vals. The dance floor was the largest room of the sugarcane workers' two-room house. El vals, la mazurca, and la polca required lots of spinning and space. The host would announce the numbers of partners and call the direction of the dance. The women waited for the men to ask them to dance after they finished their cigarettes outside. The rules were always the same: Don't dance too close. Don't cut in on another man's dance. Possession rights for all dances were granted to the first man who asked a woman to dance. It didn't matter if the woman didn't like the man. Always ask the husband for the honor of a dance with his wife. To avoid trouble from a rejected suitor, a Puerto Rican girl was trained from a very young age to never, under any circumstances, refuse to dance with a man who asked her. It happened that sometimes a girl or woman would refuse a dance with a man she disliked, or because she preferred to wait for another partner, and then her punishment was to forfeit the rest of the dances. A man had his pride.

The misunderstanding arose because Raulito was always the first to ask one particular girl to dance, the sister of one of the other sugarcane workers, a certain Estrella Vázquez. Raulito thought Estrella deserved her name because her dark brown eyes shone like stars. Estrella was a nice girl, and any man would want her for his mujer, any man except for him. Estrella was a good dancer and she liked to dance. Raulito was a good dancer and he liked to dance. He didn't have to pretend, didn't have to think, and was as close to happy as he had ever been. Soon, Raulito danced only with Estrella and she danced only with him, and now everyone wanted them to get married.

"You and Estrella are so sweet together." Soraida served him rice and beans.

"She's a good dancer." Raulito tried to find his escape in the plate of food.

"That's an indicator that she'll be good in bed. Isn't that so, Soraida?" Carlito cupped his wife's behind.

"¡Hombre, for shame!" Soraida spooned beans onto her husband's plate, but she didn't shake his hand from her behind.

It used to make Raulito squirm to see them touch each other, because he didn't know where to look, but now he didn't even notice.

"Somos amigos," Raulito said to the rice and beans.

"That's not what Estrella thinks," Soraida said.

Girls have to marry young, especially the pretty ones, that's what everyone said. Raulito was relieved when, a few weeks later, Estrella married someone else. He ate lechón and rice and drank ron caña at the wedding party, which would keep Estrella's new husband in debt for months to the plantation store.

Soraida handed him a plate of roasted pork and arroz con gandules. "Your face would break a mother's heart."

Raulito didn't know why he was so sad, perhaps because he'd lost his dancing partner or because he didn't have anyone to love. But that was the moment he decided the time had come to leave the plantation and find his brother Vicente. People would say he left because he was brokenhearted over Estrella. Let them say that. It would be a relief if they said that.

From then on, his decision to leave made him rash, and although it wasn't allowed, he stood up straight in the cane field, looking up at the blue cloudless sky. In Puerto Rico, he would lie on the grass, gaze up at the sun, and dare it to make him blink.

The luna rode over on his horse. "Hey, 9562, hana, hana!"

The luna never called the Puerto Ricans by their given names, always their bango numbers or "porrican." They called the luna "el Cochino Gordo" because he was fat and they were skin and bones, because he was Portuguese, because they envied his horse, because he was cruel.

"¡No más caña!" Raulito waved his machete. He watched the luna ride away, and for the first time in his year in the Hawaiian sugarcane, he wasn't afraid.

"Stupid, you don't tell el Cochino Gordo no more sugarcane!" Carlito ran over to him.

"I'm going to find my brother." Raulito squatted between the rows, thinking no one would find him that way.

"Idiot, you need time to make a plan." Carlito stood over him.

The luna and a plantation policeman galloped on their horses toward them, and Carlito went back to cutting cane.

"Hey, porrican!"

Raulito got up.

"You cane or you cárcere?" The luna raised his whip, ready to strike.

Carlito was right; he needed a plan.

"He a dumb one," the luna said.

"I scare him a little." The policeman pointed his rifle.

"Porrican one of best workers," the luna said. "Hana, hana, porrican!"

The whip struck Raulito's shoulder. He turned his back for the second blow, and then raised his machete to the cane.

Carlito advised him to wait until he heard from Vicente before running off to who knew where. Be smart, muchacho, be smart, but Raulito thought he'd been smart for a year and he was still alone.

The Puerto Ricans were on their way back after a day in the cane, when Carlito's little boy ran up to them.

"Raulito, Raulito! Your brother is in a letter!"

"My brother's in a letter?"

No longer bent over like a viejito, Raulito raced the boy back to his small hut.

"It's from my sister." Soraida waved the letter. "She lives on the Big Island of Hawaii."

Raulito shut his eyes tight. A day in the cane fields worse than the day before, and now no letter from his brother.

"There's something about your sister-in-law in it."

When he opened his eyes, Soraida was the most beautiful woman in the world, even prettier than Valentina. She could read because she had come from a coffee-growing family that had once had a teacher living with them for months.

"Want me to read it for you?" Soraida often read and wrote letters for the Puerto Ricans who couldn't.

"I can read," Raulito said.

"You can?" Carlito asked. "I can't."

"Why didn't you say that your sister-in-law was a madrona?"

"Valentina?"

Soraida handed him the letter, although he was sure that the Valentina he knew would never ever be a midwife.

> *There's a madrona here called Valentina Sánchez, the wife of a certain Vicente Vega from Utuado, who delivered this last one of mine, but Dios mío, I pray no más bebés because it is hard enough to feed the four I have now. Valentina says that she can make me a special concoction of plants and herbs so that this one is my last. She has only the one child so she must have a secret potion.*

"Is that Valentina your sister-in-law?" Soraida reached for the letter.

"It seems so." Raulito's hand trembled. "But I can't see Valentina as a midwife."

"Will you ask her to send me her recipe for no more babies?"

"¿A receta para no más bebés? No entiendo," Raulito said.

"But she will." Soraida took back the letter. "Don't forget, it's important."

They sat on the bench that also served as a bed for one of the younger children.

"They'll never give you permission to work on another plantation." Carlito went to get the bottle of anisette that Soraida had made from aniseed.

"Carlito, it's not even the weekend," Soraida said.

"It's a special occasion, mujer," Carlito set the bottle and two glasses on the table.

"You're not drinking?" Soraida picked up a glass.

Carlito went to get another.

"My sister says that the workers there can leave their plantation when they want," Soraida said.

"But that's not this one." Carlito poured the anisette into three glasses.

"I'm leaving anyway." Raulito took a sip from the glass. He liked the sweet, smoky taste.

"How will you eat?" Soraida served her husband his dinner.

"I'll manage somehow."

"When you get caught—and you will—make up a different name for yourself and tell them that you come from your brother's plantation." Carlito drank the anisette. "Maybe they'll send you there."

"They'll have to believe I'm a shark or something," Raulito said. "This is Oahu. Doesn't Vicente live on the island of Hawaii?"

"What other choice do you have?" Carlito picked up his spoon.

Because Soraida pitied him, she spooned extra rice and beans onto Raulito's plate.

"Ay, mijo, think it over. Your life could get so much worse because that's how life is. Trabajo y tristeza," Soraida said.

"Don't trust anybody you meet, especially Americans," Carlito said.

"Never." Raulito tossed back the anisette. "I hope I don't ever have to speak to one."

"Don't worry about that." Carlito poured more. "They won't waste a civil word on a Puerto Rican."

Soraida wrapped rice and beans in a shiny green tí leaf. She cried, being one of those women who believed the worst would happen.

Raulito tucked the food in his knapsack, along with a tin can to fill with water from streams; the edges had been smoothed out to save his lips. He heard guitar music and the rasp of a fork against a güiro. The Saturday night party had started. Another night of music and dance and comida criolla to help his compatriots forget that they cried out in their dreams for their island and for their mothers and fathers and brothers and sisters and the coquís that had lulled them to sleep. Another night to remember only that they had come from Puerto Rico and that they were Puerto Ricans and would die Puerto Ricans, wherever they might be.

Carlito had a memory for routes and he'd drawn dots and dashes on a scrap of brown paper the plantation store used to wrap parcels.

"This here is the road we sometimes take to cut cane, and you follow the road to here." His finger hovered above a big black dot. "From here, you'll have to walk a long time. Could be a day, I'm not sure. I remember when we arrived, the wagon rode by a stream . . . follow it and you'll get to the harbor. Then you'll have to get on a boat . . ."

At the end of the dots and dashes was Vicente.

CHAPTER FIFTY-SIX

PROMISES

When Lourdes screamed in her sleep, Valentina went to her, brushing the little girl's hair from her face, making soothing sounds.

"Mami, am I going to die like Javiercito and Manuelito?"

Valentina looked down at her daughter's frightened eyes, which she could see in the streaks of moonlight coming in through the cracks in the wattle wall.

"Shhh, Lulu, no." Valentina kissed her daughter's forehead.

"But they died. And Sonia died."

"I know."

"And Tío Raulito."

Valentina shook her head. "No, not Tío Raulito. He is alive and well." She didn't know if it was true, but how she hoped that it was.

"But Abuela Angelina and Tía Inés?"

"Yes."

"Why did they die?"

Valentina took a deep breath.

"I don't know."

Lourdes whispered, "I miss Javiercito."

"I know."

"And Tío Raulito."

"Me, too."

"I'm afraid, Mami."

"Nothing bad will happen to you, Lulu," Valentina said. "I promise."

Lourdes nodded; she closed her eyes to sleep.

THE TASTE OF SUGAR • 337

•

A notice written in Spanish had been posted at the plantation store. This Saturday was a special day, as an interpreter was being brought in to hear the Puerto Ricans' grievances. There was a rumor that the interpreter was a Spaniard. A few of them swore that they would refuse to speak to any Spaniard. The Spaniards had never treated the Puerto Ricans right, they all agreed. Look how, after Hurricane San Ciriaco, the Spanish hacienda owners had kept most of the money for themselves and had made the Puerto Ricans work for what? A piece of bread? A shirt? A pair of pants? Vicente said that the interpreter wouldn't be a Spaniard because the Americans hated the Spanish. Didn't they remember that the American army had encouraged the bands of tiznados, who had smeared charcoal on their faces to hide their identities when they robbed and beat up the Spaniards? The partidas had the run of Utuado and Adjuntas, too, remember?

The Puerto Ricans had a lot to complain about—that there wasn't a school for their children as they were promised; that they lived in shacks instead of decent houses as promised; that they were at the bottom of the hill, breathing in foul garbage and human waste; that foodstuffs were double the prices of those in Puerto Rico. Somebody said that they should appoint a man to speak for them, someone who had once owned a farm and knew how to talk to businessmen, like Ramírez or Vega. How about it, Ramírez? Ramírez said that he didn't have schooling like Vicente Vega, better Vega. How about it, Vicente?

"What do you think, Valentina?" Vicente looked at his wife.

Ramírez and the man next to him exchanged glances. What kind of man needed his wife's permission?

"Ask about the school," Valentina said. "And Raulito, and Sonia's husband."

People called out to Vicente: Ask why the doctor gives out blue pills for everything, and why he sends us back out to the fields when we're sick. Tell how the plantation police drag us out of bed as if we were slaves from olden times. Tell about the shotguns in our backs. Tell about how the luna raises his whip to us as if we were slaves. And what is this about the docking of pay when we take a minute to piss in the fields, or when we cut less sugarcane because of bad weather? Demand that we be paid cash money! As we were promised! Demand the increase we were promised! We've been here a year already! We should have gotten a pay increase! But all we got was a balance due at the plantation store! Remind them that we are to get a bonus in the third year. And would the translator take letters to mothers, fathers, and the newspapers on the island? They weren't sure that the letters they mailed had arrived since they never received responses. Would—could—tell—tell.

The Inside Men, the manager Mr. White and the interpreter, sat outside the plantation manager's office; the guards with their shotguns stood on either side. The Puerto Ricans gathered in front of the table.

"¡Vicente Vega, a la orden!" Vicente was proud that Valentina stood beside him, watching him be the spokesperson. "I have been elected to speak for all of us Puerto Ricans."

The interpreter said he was Mr. Donald Jackson and that he worked for the Hawaiian Sugar Planters' Association. He'd learned his Spanish in the Philippines and Cuba during the Spanish-American War. Please excuse his mistakes, Mr. Jackson said, in that way that made it evident he thought he'd conquered the language.

"The Spanish-American War?"

"You know . . . la guerra . . . why you belong to the United States."

"Ah, you mean the Americans' war against Spain."

"No speak fast," Mr. Jackson said. "Don't understand fast talking."

Vicente exchanged a look with Valentina.

"Señor, we're expected to work in the pouring rain like beasts. The police disrespect us. They kick open our doors and enter where our wives and children are sleeping." Vicente paused after every few words.

Mr. Jackson consulted with the plantation manager.

"The five a.m. to wake," Mr. Jackson said.

"Respectfully, Mr. Jackson, would you like someone to enter your home uninvited?" Vicente crossed his arms.

"Five a.m.," Mr. Jackson said.

"My home may be a hut fit for animals, but no one has the right to come into it when my wife and children are sleeping." Vicente's voice was strong and firm. "Not you or the police or even the plantation manager."

A few of the puertorriqueños looked at Valentina and imagined what she looked like in bed, while their wives took another look at Vicente, so brave.

"I no make the rules," Mr. Jackson said.

"Who makes the rules, then?" Valentina said to Vicente.

"Who makes the rules, then?" Vicente said to Mr. Jackson.

"Five a.m. whistle you wake, that's the rule."

The Puerto Ricans murmured, Que falta de respeto.

Vicente shook his head. "When we are sick, the doctor tells us that we are not sick and sends us back to the cane, where we get sicker."

"Doctor know best," Mr. Jackson said.

"We are men, not cattle," Vicente said.

"Well, now," Mr. Jackson said.

"The luna and his henchmen raise their whips to us," Vicente said. "Tell Mr. White to stop that immediately."

The Puerto Ricans murmured, We are men, not cattle.

"What's your bango number?" Mr. Jackson looked down at a paper.

"Mi nombre es Vega. Vicente Vega, not Vegas like in the account book," Vicente said.

"I asked for your bango number."

"I'm not a bango number," Vicente said. "I'm a man with a name."

"Vicente Vega, what's your bango number?"

Vicente nodded, satisfied. "9643."

"9643," Mr. Jackson said to the plantation manager, who wrote it down.

"We are men, not cattle."

"What's that about cattle?"

"The luna and his men raise the whip to us," Vicente said. "We demand that they stop."

The Puerto Ricans chanted, We are men, not cattle.

Mr. Jackson conferred with Mr. White.

"Mr. White talk to the luna," Mr. Jackson said.

Was there anything else? ¡Claro! Vicente, go down the list!

"Sí, sí." Vicente raised his hand to his compatriots. "We shouldn't have to work in the hard rain. Have you ever worked in the rain, Mr. Jackson?"

"I not sugarcane worker," Mr. Jackson said.

Los puertorriqueños murmured, He's not a sugarcane worker; somebody cracked a joke that he would sell his soul to the devil if he arranged for los blancos grandes, gordos y colorados to work a single day in the cane. Some of the Puerto Ricans laughed.

"You work, you eat," Mr. Jackson said.

"We want to eat, and we also don't want to work in the hard rain."

Mr. Jackson whispered something to Mr. White.

"The lunas decide when you work," Mr. White said.

Vicente shook his head in disappointment; Valentina touched his arm.

The Puerto Ricans murmured, Coño carajo, only animals worked in the rain.

"Mr. Jackson, we want to live like human beings without garbage flowing outside our homes," Vicente said. "Have you seen the hovels we live in? Waste from the house of Mr. White comes all the way down to where we live."

Vicente pointed to the plantation manager's mansion, his finger drawing an imaginary line from the grand house down to the houses of the lunas, then past the houses of the clerks, the plantation police, and down to the shanties.

Mr. Jackson's gaze followed Vicente's finger.

"I don't think anything can be done about that," Mr. Jackson said.

"It's inhumane," Valentina said.

"We'll see what we can do." Mr. Jackson looked at her and she was glad that she'd changed into her good dress.

"The planters brought us here with false promises," Vicente said.

"Lies, lies, mentiras, mentiras . . ." the Puerto Ricans murmured.

"We were promised dollars for our labor." Vicente waved a piece of cardboard. "This is what we get."

Mr. Jackson consulted the plantation manager.

"You buy in plantation store," Mr. Jackson said. "Why you need dollars?"

Valentina told her husband, "Ask him if he's paid in scrip."

"Mr. Jackson, it's a human right to be paid in real money for a day's work. Are you paid in scrip?" Vicente offered the scrip to the interpreter.

Valentina led the Puerto Ricans in the chant, "Dollars! Dollars! Dollars!"

Mr. Jackson conferred with Mr. White, then held up his hand.

The Puerto Ricans' shouts dropped to whispers.

"We will pay in American dollars," he said.

Men slapped Vicente's back.

"Mr. Jackson, why don't we get the full fifteen dollars a month that we were promised? Money is deducted from our pay," Vicente said.

"I think those are your taxes," Mr. Jackson said.

"Taxes! Why are we paying taxes? We don't even vote!"

"All the plantation workers pay taxes."

Taxes, they paid taxes, coño carajo, it was just like being back in Puerto Rico, first the Spaniards and then the Americans . . .

Mr. Jackson raised his hands and called for quiet. "We'll end this meeting right now if you don't act right."

What were they, children?

"If we pay taxes, then we should vote."

Mr. Jackson cleared his throat. "Only men who are Hawaiians or Americans can vote."

Taxes, not votes, the Puerto Ricans repeated to each other.

Vicente shook his head. "What do we pay taxes for?"

Mr. Jackson didn't say that their taxes helped to pay for the cost of the plantation policemen, for jails, for schools for other people's children, for better sanitation in other places, and for salaries of government officials.

"Why can't we vote?"

"You'll have to talk to the US government about that," Mr. Jackson said. "Anything else?"

"Plenty," Vicente said. "We were promised a raise after a year's work, and a bonus after three. In dollars."

"Mr. White, he let you know," Mr. Jackson said. "Maybe raise, maybe no bonus."

The Puerto Ricans talked all at once. Back in Puerto Rico, the agents promised raises and bonuses! Mr. Jackson held up his hands for quiet.

"I have good news. You can write family," Mr. Jackson said. "We'll send on the letters."

Some of the Puerto Ricans said, If only we knew how to write, if only our mothers and fathers knew how to read.

"Ask about schooling and finding Raulito and Sonia's husband." Valentina nudged Vicente's arm. It didn't look like they were going to get raises today, no matter how much talking they did.

"Yes, in a minute," Vicente said. "The men are talking—"

What if Mr. Jackson said, Enough! No more requests granted or denied? Then how would they find Sonia's husband? Or Raulito? How would the children get schooling?

"Patience." Vicente put his hand on his wife's shoulder.

"¿Paciencia? ¡Hombre, I live in a hovel! Don't talk to me about patience!" Valentina shook off Vicente's hand.

The Puerto Ricans moved away from her, the men shook their heads in disapproval. The women, ashamed for Vicente, whispered to each other, ¡Que vergüenza!

"Mr. Jackson, it's very important—"

"Who do you belong?" Mr. Jackson asked.

"He's my husband." She pointed to Vicente.

"You mean, you are his wife." Everyone laughed, even Vicente. The interpreter repeated his little joke to the plantation manager, who laughed along with the lunas and the henchmen.

"Coffee goes down the same way." Valentina raised her voice. Men! They seemed to think the same in any language.

Vicente looked at Valentina. She knew he didn't like it when she raised her voice. *Too bad.*

"Mr. Jackson, we need someone here all the time who speaks Spanish," Valentina said in the manner of a mother to a child. "Even the doctor can't understand us."

"You learn English," Mr. Jackson said.

"We want to learn English! We want to send our children to school to learn English! Where are the schools we were promised for our children?"

Mr. Jackson looked through some papers on the table. "There is a plantation school near Hilo."

"Hilo! Isn't that where we disembarked? Surely you would want your own children to have schooling," Valentina said. "Or is it that you don't care about *our* children?"

The Puerto Ricans said, They don't care about our children . . .

Mr. Jackson's voice was low when he spoke to Mr. White.

"Mr. Jackson, we came halfway around the world to make a better life." Valentina pointed to the hovels. "Look where we live! And you don't even care! And now you tell us that our children have to walk hours to school!"

"You work on the plantation?"

"I have."

"Tú numero?"

"Why do you need my bango number?" Valentina crossed her arms.

"So I know who I'm talking to." Mr. Jackson crossed his arms.

"Then ask me my name," she said.

Vicente looked at his wife in admiration; the Puerto Ricans murmured, Que mujer, que mujer . . .

"¿Tú nombre?" Mr. Jackson tapped his fingers on the table.

"Valentina Sánchez." She gave him a sweet smile.

"Valentina—"

"Señora," Valentina said.

"Señora," Mr. Jackson said.

"Maybe we should move to a plantation where there is a school," Valentina said. "What's to stop us?"

"On Mr. White's plantation, you can leave, no need discharge papers," Mr. Jackson said. "Not yet."

"What plantation has a school and decent housing?"

"Don't know."

As far as Valentina was concerned, this Mr. Jackson knew very little.

Mr. Jackson conferred with Mr. White. "You leave, no bonus. You stay, get raise, get bonus."

Some of the Puerto Ricans slapped each other on the back. They would get their raises and bonuses after all.

Valentina pointed to Mirta. "See this little girl? Her father was sent to another plantation. Her mother is dead."

"Our business is sugarcane," Mr. Jackson said, "not little girls."

"The plantation lost him and the plantation should find him," Valentina said.

"The plantation lost my brother," Vicente said. "Can you find him? Raulito Villanueva."

"Not our business," Mr. Jackson said.

"Not your business! Then whose business is it?" Valentina placed her hands on her hips.

"Señora, these things happen when you import people," Mr. Jackson said. "You can't blame the Hawaiian Sugar Planters' Association."

"Then who can we blame? How can we find them?" Valentina's voice rose again. People might say she was yelling, but why was it yelling when she was speaking with passion?

Mr. Jackson and Mr. White got up and went inside the manager's office. The police waved the Puerto Ricans away. Vicente put his hand on her elbow; she shook it off.

They walked down the dirt road to the hovel.

He tried to take her hand, she pulled away.

"Aren't you glad that from now on, we're going to be paid in cash money?"

"It's so little money! You should have demanded that they find Sonia's husband and Raulito. That they open up a school, right here on the plantation." Valentina knew that she was being unreasonable, but she also knew that they had to leave the plantation. She wouldn't be responsible for her actions if their girls didn't go to school and she had to live in a hovel much longer.

"It seems that I can't do anything to please you," Vicente said.

"You want to please me, Vicente?" Valentina stopped in the middle of the road. "Let's leave this plantation."

"We will," he said.

"Today," she said.

"Today?" He took her hand and this time she didn't brush him off.

"We will get the girls and all our things," Valentina said, "and walk to someplace better where we can live like people and not animals."

Vicente winced. "Raulito might be on his way here, and what about the bonus?"

"You'll only see that bonus in your dreams."

"We still owe at the plantation store from when I was in jail," Vicente said. "That'll be paid off in a month, and then we can save a few dollars."

Dolores called out to them as she wheeled the red wheelbarrow piled with groceries up the road.

"Vicente, you're a poet," Dolores said. "You'll soon be making up décimas."

"A man must take charge," Vicente said.

Dolores gave Valentina a look that said a strong, good-looking man in charge could yield a woman a lot of satisfaction, but Valentina was distracted by the piles of tins and cans and sacks of foodstuff stacked in the wheelbarrow.

"So much food! You already owe the plantation a lot of money!" Valentina wished that she could be more like Dolores and charge everything they needed, but the knowledge that it would keep them tied to the plantation restrained her.

"We have to eat!" Dolores picked up a can of sardines. "Have you tried this? With a little olive oil, it's delicious."

Valentina examined the tin and was disappointed when Dolores took it back.

"Go on ahead, I'll wait for Eugenio," Dolores said. "I'll send my boy over later with the wheelbarrow."

"And maybe a tin of sardines?" Valentina lent the wheelbarrow to the women, who always returned it with a little something extra, like a few carrots or a tin of powdered milk.

Vicente glanced back at Dolores several times. "I've been meaning to ask you, Valentina, what about that thing?"

"What thing?"

"Tú sabes, that red thing." He pointed to it.

"It's a wheelbarrow," she said.

"I can see that it's a wheelbarrow," he said.

"We used to have them back in Puerto Rico, remember?"

"I want to know how you got it."

"I got it to take Sonia to the doctor."

"How?"

"From the gardener," Valentina said. "Didn't I tell you?"

"No, you didn't tell me," Vicente said. "I never heard of a white man giving away something for nothing."

"We were talking about leaving the plantation," Valentina said.

"Tell me about the wheelbarrow," Vicente said.

"Vicente, why are we talking about a wheelbarrow when we have so many more important things to talk about?" Valentina stopped. They had walked to the path that led to the Japanese camp. She pointed down the row of shanties that were a little better than theirs and said, "My friend Mikioki lives here."

"¿Mikioki? Who is that?"

"Mikioki. A japonesa who was very nice to me when I hoe hana," Valentina said. "We should go to talk to her about the strike."

Vicente shook his head. "A woman? We need to talk to her husband."

"Then we'll talk to her husband."

"I guess it's worth a try. We'll go there together."

Valentina smiled, taking his hand and placing it over her heart.

"Feel it? How fast it's beating?"

"For me?" He grinned.

"Yes, for you, Vicente," she said. "But also because we will have to fight for what we want. No one is going to give it to us."

Hawaii
February 14, 1902

My dear Elena,

I don't know if you'll ever receive this letter, but if by some miracle you do—you'll be sure to think that I've risen from the dead. Darling sister, I write to tell you about this fracaso that we find ourselves in.

Elena, can you write the newspapers for us? Tell them some of what I write you? It might help make life better for us here. Write the newspapers that the Hawaiian Dream for Puerto Ricans is more like a Hawaiian Nightmare. In an earlier letter I wrote you about Raulito. He is still lost but Vicente won't give up hope that one day we will find him. There's so much I can tell you, but I must get back to sewing—I make a little extra money this way. I'm trying to bargain with one of the other puertorriqueñas for a sewing machine—like the one Mamá had— somehow she brought one with her on the boat and she doesn't even know how to use it! We were able to pay off our debt at the plantation store, which we took on when Vicente was in prison—another letter, but don't worry, Vicente is still a good man. The planters are liars and brutes and thieves. We are finally getting paid with dollars. We are saving every penny we can—and it is pennies—so that we can go to Oahu, where Vicente thinks he might find Raulito. Eventually from there I hope we can go to California. The journey is not without its challenges—the sea is rough—I considered jumping overboard on the way here, it was that terrible—and we'll have to get to the harbor, which is hours away, but we are determined to get there and to pay our passage to Honolulu. Vicente thinks that he can find work there, and I will start sewing for others or work as a maid. Easy work after hoe hana! You wouldn't recognize me if you saw me, hermana. Certainly our parents wouldn't. (How are they? Is Mamá completely recovered? I hope so. My love to them, and better if they don't know too much.)

Back to the newspapers—the promises Vicente was given—fifteen dollars a month, the first year, sixteen dollars the second—bonuses—housing fit for human beings (not pigs)—good medical care—school for the children—lies, all lies. Vicente gets fifteen dollars a month, and only recently has that been in dollars. (And we pay taxes!) We doubt that we will ever see a bonus. We live in a hut. Because the nearest school is too far, I'm teaching the girls to read—Lourdes and Mirta, mi hija de crianza. Her mother was my friend Sonia, who died. (I wrote you about her.) The doctor didn't even bother to examine her. Mirta's father was sent to another plantation, never to be seen again, and no one cares. The foreman is called a luna and he is very severe with the men. The plantation policemen are quick to arrest Puerto Ricans. Our lives belong to Sugar.

Don't distress yourself, darling Elena. It hasn't all been bad. Maybe el dicho is true: Dios aprieta pero no ahoga—maybe God doesn't abandon you. I'm not sure. I've made some very good friends, and that's the wonderful part. I haven't had friends since I was married. Except for my beautiful Inés. I've run out of paper. I hope you get this letter so that you know how much I miss and love you and our parents. And I miss Puerto Rico and Ponce and my sweet Gloria and even the mountain in Utuado. A little. Ay bendito, Elena, we thought we were coming to something better.

I hope to hear from you, my darling sister.

Siempre,

Valentina

CHAPTER FIFTY-SEVEN

WHEN HE WAS DON VICENTE

After Sonia died, it seemed to Vicente that for Valentina, everything began and ended with her need to leave the plantation. Valentina did the laundry on Sunday afternoon because then Vicente could help her carry the water and tend the fire. Boiling water was the best way to get rid of the dirt that stained everything red. Vicente didn't even mind very much when the other men made fun of him for doing women's work.

"We had such fun with the French mademoiselles, didn't we, Valentina?" Vicente hoped for a smile.

She left the hovel without answering. Perhaps she didn't want to think about French mademoiselles, but he did. On those days when he thought he might fall into despair, he liked to think about when they were first married. Mornings before he went out to the coffee finca, Vicente brought her hot chocolate because a French mademoiselle was served hot chocolate in bed when she had pleased her lover. Mamá had told him to take his head out from between his wife's legs. (Vicente was shocked by his mother's crudeness.) Some men might have thought him pitiful, still in love with his wife after more than ten years. When Valentina brought him a hot tisane of ginger and lemon to chase away the chill of cutting cane in the rain, or massaged his aching muscles with aloe, he wished with all his heart that they were back in Puerto Rico in their very own bed. He recalled the Sundays when Valentina would brew him a tiny cup of café negro with a teaspoon of sugar, and after he drank it, he would go out to see to the chickens and his horse. When he returned, she would spoon sugar into his café con leche, which he would enjoy with a bowl of avena sweetened with honey. Valentina was the French mademoiselle then, and he, Don Vicente the Coffee Farmer.

CHAPTER FIFTY-EIGHT

NO VAGS HERE

Raulito couldn't make out his hand in the dark. On Cerro Morales, where he and his brothers were born, Raulito could find his way even in the fog. He knew that mountain like the lines between his mother's eyes. In this place, Oahu, he stumbled about in the unknown, afraid of white men with guns.

Finally, it was morning, and birds cawed as they flew in the sky. The sounds of insects and critters reminded Raulito of his beloved mountain. He saw green that was not cane as far as the eye could see. Coconut palms. Trees. Ferns. Flowers like orchids, Valentina's favorite. Raulito tucked a pink blossom behind his ear.

That second day, Raulito decided to rest in the tall grasses along the road. He would make himself very small—as small as a skinny man with long limbs could make himself—and he would lie very still. A horse-drawn wagon rambled down the road and he parted the grasses. His gaze followed a yellow bonnet until it became a speck in the distance. Raulito wished that he could wear a yellow hat instead of rags; that he were free to ride in a wagon instead of hiding in the tall grasses.

That night, Raulito walked for hours until he reached a town. It was there that he found the newspaper on the street. He stared down at the drawing of the masked man, barefoot and wearing a straw hat like his, armed with a knife and pistol. He couldn't read English but he could read the words *Porto Rican*. He folded it into a small square and tucked it into his bundle. He would show it to Vicente. He was careful to duck into the bushes or behind a building whenever he saw anyone, even at a distance. Carlito had warned him to avoid people, day or night.

He'd reached the outskirts of town on the morning of the third day. He filled his tin cup from a stream and hid behind some bushes. He used his knapsack as a pillow; when sleep came, Raulito dreamt that he was back in Puerto Rico.

Somebody kicked his leg. Two policemen, so tall they blocked out the sun, were pointing rifles at his head. One searched his bag and found the newspaper article and the map of dots and squiggles Carlito had drawn. He threw the papers on the ground. The policeman stepped on Raulito's hand when he tried to pick them up.

They made him stand with his hands over his head. His legs shook. They asked him questions, and he stared at them, eyes wide.

"This one's deaf and dumb."

"Whaddaya think? Negro? Porto Rican?"

"Same thing."

The stench of men in the cramped jail cell reminded Raulito of steerage on the ship. A galvanized metal pail filled with excrement overflowed in the corner. A bee tapped against the iron bars of the glassless window.

"Is that Vicente's brother?" A man with a crack in his straw hat crushed Raulito in a big embrace. "It's me, Gómez! Gómez from the boat!"

"¡Gómez!" Raulito cried a little on the big man's shoulder.

There was no room on the floor, but Gómez pointed to someone who moved to make space.

"Gómez, have you seen Vicente?"

"I think he went with the group to Hilo, Hawaii. What they call the Big Island."

It was true, then. Vicente was on the Big Island, and here he was on Oahu.

"This isn't a place where a man can be weak." Gómez noticed Raulito's quivering lip.

"I'm not weak." Raulito bit his lip.

Gómez introduced him as Vicente's brother to the Puerto Rican cell mates.

"This is Raulito Villanueva, un negrito pero buena gente," he said.

Several recalled Vicente as the man who had lost his son on the voyage. One man stared at him without blinking, and Raulito pretended that it didn't bother him. He made believe that he was Vicente, strong like his brother. Gómez told him that the Puerto Ricans got along with all the Japanese, even the one who had beaten his wife to death: they didn't hold it against him because that sometimes happened, even in Puerto Rico. Sometimes a woman deserved it and sometimes she didn't, pero, bueno. (Gómez raised his palms in a gesture that meant it was inevitable.) And over there, don't look, don't look, don't look at that white man. He had raped and killed a small boy.

"That one's not human," Gómez said.

Raulito shivered in the white man's gray gaze, which reminded him of the ocean on that bitter day Javier tumbled down to his watery grave.

Gómez asked Raulito if he'd had it bad on the plantation. Raulito shrugged. What was bad, what was good, when there was no one to love or to love him?

The night was broken with the cries and moans of men. In his dream, Raulito was a small boy again and Vicente lifted him up onto his horse. Raulito laughed; the horse's mane tickled his bare legs. His brother let him hold the reins. Don't be afraid, Vicente said to five-year-old Raulito. I'm here.

The judge sat at a table. Next to a deputy was a prisoner whom Gómez had pointed out as Jones, one of the haoles. The judge banged his gavel, and a light-skinned Puerto Rican was shoved forward to the table.

The judge asked the prisoner a question in English and then turned to Jones.

"What is your name?" Jones said in Spanish.

The Puerto Ricans shouted the news to each other. El blanco speaks Spanish!

All this time with us and he speaks Spanish! He's a maldito spy!

The judge pounded the gavel and the deputies shouted at the Puerto Ricans to shut up.

"I learned me some Spanish," Jones said. "During the war."

The judge banged the gavel again.

Jones repeated the question.

"Alberto Rodríguez."

"What do you do?"

"Work," Alberto Rodríguez said.

The Puerto Ricans laughed.

Bang! Bang! The judge sentenced Alberto Rodríguez to a month's hard labor for vagrancy.

A deputy thrust Raulito forward. Jones translated.

"What's your name?"

"Raulito Villanueva."

"What do you do?"

"Work."

More laughter.

"What plantation did you come from?" Jones stared at Raulito.

Raulito looked back at Gómez.

Gómez had warned Raulito that they would return him to the plantation. Even if he never found Vicente, Raulito didn't want to go back there, where everyone would pity him.

"Come on now," Jones said.

The judge shouted at Jones, "Hurry up, man."

"Where your bango and discharge papers?"

"What papers?"

"Giving you permission to leave the plantation," Jones said.

"I lost them," Raulito said.

"Bango?"

"Lost."

The judge sentenced him to one month's hard labor for vagrancy.

"Sorry, boy, you going to jail for vagrancy." Jones said "vagrancy" in English because he didn't know the Spanish word.

"What's vagrancy?"

"It means you lazy," Jones said.

"I'm not lazy," Raulito said. "I was working the cane the day before yesterday—or maybe the day before."

"Hawaii needs workers. You gonna work, whether you get paid or not. Make your mind up to it, boy," Jones said. "One way or another, you gonna work."

Bob the jailer rapped his rifle butt against the bars of the cell. After eating a piece of bread and gagging on coffee the Puerto Ricans swore was mud mixed with water, the prisoners were herded to the construction site of the new railroad. Each clang of the hammer reminded Raulito that he was a slave. The jailers kept their guns pointed at the prisoners; when they shouted at them, Raulito knew that they were saying, *You gonna work, boy, make up your mind to it.*

Raulito lay next to Gómez, foot to head, head to foot, face turned away from the stink of Gómez's feet. His eyes were closed; his thoughts were of a Puerto Rican in the other cell. Raulito looked at him when others weren't looking; the other man looked at him, too. Raulito was happier than he'd ever been his whole life, even happier than when he was with his brother, and Raulito had never thought that possible. He didn't even mind being in prison.

It just so happened that they sat next to each other during the fifteen-minute lunch break. Bueno, it didn't just happen, maybe prison had made Raulito brave.

"Raulito Villanueva from Utuado." He offered his hand.

"I'm Marco González from Peñuelas." His eyes were the brown of tamarind.

The feel of the other man's palm in his, the little extra pressure he gave Raulito's hand, and suddenly what had once been murky was now clear. Marco. Beautiful Marco. Raulito wanted to know everything about Marco. Did he have family? Did he wish he'd stayed in Puerto Rico despite the hunger and desperation?

Tell me, tell me everything, and I will tell you.

They ate bread slathered with meat grease.

"Why are you here?"

"I don't know," Raulito said.

"I don't know either," Marco said. "A bunch of us ran away together and they caught all of us, except José Santos. He might be back in Puerto Rico by now."

"How many more days for you?" Terrible that he wished it, but Raulito hoped that Marco would be in prison as long as he.

"Five," Marco said.

"Only five?" Good for Marco, but bad for him.

Marco's name escaped his lips while he slept, and Gómez shook him awake.

"I didn't know you were that kind," he said in Raulito's ear.

"Gómez—"

"Just don't touch me." Gómez turned his back.

The next day, Marco and Raulito ate lunch with the others so as not to draw attention. Everyone was talking about where they would go after they were freed.

"One day I plan to make my way to Honolulu," Marco said.

"What will you do there? Take the boat to Puerto Rico?" Gómez and the others laughed. Not Raulito.

"I'll stow away on a ship to San Francisco."

"What's there for the likes of you?" Gómez gulped down his coffee.

"Something better than this," Marco said. "I'll earn my living somehow, but not in the cane."

Raulito thought that he would follow Marco to San Francisco if he asked him, but first he needed to find Vicente.

On Marco's last day, they sat apart from the other prisoners. They spoke low, but they didn't whisper. People always paid attention to whispers.

"Gómez is acting strange." Marco nodded in the big man's direction.
"Don't worry about Gómez."

"Does your brother know about you?"

"I didn't know until I met you," Raulito said.

They risked a glance at each other and then looked away, smiling.

"My brother loves me," Raulito said, without looking at Marco.

"You're lucky." Marco looked down at the railroad tracks that they
had been working on before their lunch break.

"When did you know? That you were—tú sabes." Raulito looked at
the railroad tracks, too.

"I can't remember not knowing," Marco said. "I just was."

Raulito nodded.

"I was afraid, too," Marco said. "I had an uncle who liked to sit me
on his lap."

Raulito wished he could take Marco's hand and comfort him. "You
told your parents?"

"I was scared of my father," Marco said. "When I told Mamá, she
slapped me for telling dirty lies."

A flock of birds perched on the rails.

"He was uno de los mayores." Marco picked up a rock and threw it at
the birds; some of them flew away

A guard walked past them. They didn't speak for a minute.

Marco threw another rock.

"Don't do that," Raulito said. "You might hit one."

"I was in love with Salvador." Marco dropped the rock.

No! Raulito wanted to shout.

"The first time I saw him, he was dancing with my sister."

There's never been anyone before you, Marco.

"Salvador loved you?"

"He loved me." Marco lit a cigarette. "But he loved my sister, too."

Raulito's mouth was full of bread. Marco looked at him through the
cigarette smoke. Raulito swallowed.

"Can you love both?" He wouldn't want anyone except Marco.

"Salvador could."

They exchanged another glance. Raulito wanted to look into Marco's tamarind eyes all day, but he knew it wasn't safe.

The guards shouted for the prisoners to get back to work.

Marco stubbed out his cigarette and tossed it on the ground.

Raulito pretended that he had a rock in his shoe; he picked up the cigarette stub, hiding it in the cup of his hand, feeling its warmth, his heart racing because it had touched Marco's lips. He put it in his pocket.

The day Marco left, they shook hands through the iron bars. In that handshake, Raulito said everything he'd ever wanted to say.

"They're sending me back to the plantation," Marco said. "I'll be there for a while."

"You'll be with Salvador?" Raulito looked for the truth in Marco's eyes.

Marco's gaze was steady. "Salvador stayed with my sister in Puerto Rico."

Raulito wanted to smile and cry at the same time.

"I hope you see Vicente again," Marco said. "Isn't your brother named Vicente?"

What about you, Marco? Do you want to see me again?

"Vicente Vega," Raulito said.

"You know where I'll be," Marco said. They exchanged a last glance. In it, Raulito imagined a whole life together.

Marco was gone, and Raulito wished the birds would drop dead from the trees. Raulito was grateful for the clang clang clang on iron so that he didn't have to hear the stupid birds sing. Bang bang bang. Raulito didn't want to think about his brother, who might be lost to him forever, or about living in a world without Marco. Bang bang bang. He couldn't live another minute chained like a dog to a fence, and he looked around the tracks for something to pick the locks of the irons that shackled his ankles. One day he found a sliver of steel on the tracks. He turned his back to the guards as he slid it into the waist of his pants.

Gómez saw him. "Are you fucking crazy? They'll shoot you in the back when they catch you."

"I'll run," Raulito said. "I've always been fast."

"You mean you've always been stupid," Gómez said. "I won't let you do it."

"What's it to you?" He didn't care about Gómez. He cared about Vicente and Marco, and both were gone.

"For your brother," Gómez said. "You want to see him again, don't you?"

Raulito let the sliver of steel drop to the ground.

The men crowded the wagon. Japanese and Puerto Rican. Men just like him. Raulito had served his time and was being taken back to the plantation. If he didn't go back, the white men would brand him a vagrant, and there was nothing worse a man could be in this Hawaii, especially a black man like him.

At the last minute, the judge decided that Gómez hadn't served his full sentence. Raulito was sorry to say goodbye. Gómez had looked out for him the way his brother Vicente would have done, even after he'd learned what kind of man he was.

Raulito didn't want to go back to the plantation. Everyone would point to him as an example of what happened to a man without a woman. Nina would take his money and then put him to work crushing coffee beans in the pilón.

"Oye, can you help me get away?" Raulito addressed the Puerto Ricans.

"Claro," somebody said.

"If they catch you, it's back to the chain gang," somebody else said.

"I haven't done anything wrong," Raulito said.

"You know better than that," somebody said.

"I'm going to roll off the wagon," Raulito said. "Can you make sure the guards don't see me?"

"What about them chinos?" Somebody pointed to the Japanese.

"They got the same problems we have." Raulito looked at the Japanese. They stared back at him; one bowed his head.

"I'll sock them if they try anything," said the first Puerto Rican.

When Raulito saw a group of trees up ahead, he slid off the wagon and rolled onto the dirt road into the brush. He crouched behind some bushes. He ran through the woodland. He gulped free air and wished that he could fly like a bird, over the sugarcane of this terrible Oahu and toward the island of Hawaii, where he would find his brother. He ran until he couldn't lift his legs anymore, then he dropped down onto the soft grass and stared up at the sky. When he was a child, he thought that the birds flew into the sun and worried that they would catch fire until his brother explained how the sun was very far away. The birds here sang the same songs they sang to him in Puerto Rico. Some people thought nature was quiet at night, but it was loud with a thousand sounds. Creatures sang or chanted or buzzed or howled. Trees creaked in the wind. Owls announced the moon.

Raulito dozed off, and when he woke the moon was high in the sky. He ran through the woods, in the direction of Honolulu, where he planned to smuggle himself onto a boat bound for Hilo. Raulito's shoes cracked on a broken branch and the sound pierced the clamor of the night creatures, stunned silent for a moment. He suspected that he was breathing too loud. He ate wild berries and drank from a stream. When he tired again, he climbed a tree, where he hoped he would be safe from animals, two- and four-footed alike, but he fell asleep again and tumbled down onto the grass. Luckily, he didn't split his head open like a coconut! He found more berry bushes. He picked them too quickly in his hunger, squashing them with his fingers. Once again he drank fresh water from streams. He cracked a coconut against a tree trunk, drank the water, and broke the coconut meat into pieces. He thought of his mother.

Raulito ate the last of the coconut meat on the second day, and his stomach grumbled for the hard bread and meat paste of jail, the last real food it could remember. But his stomach didn't rule him. He'd often gone hungry in Puerto Rico, and if he didn't eat until he reached Hilo, then he didn't eat.

•

The dogs came for Raulito when he was doing his business. He yanked his pants up and ran faster than he'd ever run in his life, faster than when he'd jumped off the wagon. He slid on patches of leaves wet from the morning dew. A tree with strong branches called out, *I will hide you in my branches*. If only he could reach it! Faster, run faster! Reach it! Hurry! Marco. Marco. ¡Marco! Shouts! Shouts . . . barks . . . Vicente . . . Hurry! Hurry! So close! Hot breath on his neck . . . smell of wet dog . . . ¡Marco! ¡Vicente! Brother . . . Help! Sharp teeth snapped at his heels . . . pain . . . heavy paws on his back . . . falling, falling . . . a rifle poking his head.

They searched him for discharge papers and his bango, but they only found shards of coconut. Raulito said he was Vicente Vega, and he gave them the name of Vicente's plantation in Hilo. They looked confused. Their questions were in English.

The guard clanged the door shut, leaving Raulito in a crowded cell. Men slept, talked, urinated in a galvanized metal pail. It was more or less like the other jail.

A big man, negro like Raulito, greeted him en español.

"Vicente Vega de Utuado, a la orden," Raulito said.

"Abraham Báez de Guánica, a la orden," he said. "Where did you come from?"

"The Big Island of Hawaii," Raulito said.

"You swim here?" Abraham said. "You a shark?"

"Something like that," Raulito said.

Abraham laughed. "Tiburón. That's what I'm going to call you."

It was then that Raulito thought of going to Marco first; together they could find their way to Vicente.

"Everyone, meet Tiburón," Abraham said. "Let me present our fellow countrymen."

Miguel Romero was a skeleton with a lazy eye. Nobody believed that fifteen-year-old Chico Álvarez wasn't full grown. Luis Compañero swayed as if he were about to fall, and when Raulito looked down at his tiny feet, he understood why.

"What kind of place is this?" Raulito sat on the filthy floor. "Some kind of stone mountain?"

"It's a fortress, stronger than El Morro in San Juan that the Spaniards built," Miguel said. "It's Oahu Prison."

"I've never seen El Morro," Raulito said.

"And you never will," Luis said.

"Welcome to the Reef, Tiburón," Miguel said.

"'Reef' is American for infierno," Luis said.

"I wouldn't wish this place even on los españoles," Abraham said.

"I would wish it on the Spaniards," Miguel said.

"I would wish it on the Americans," Luis said.

"Sí, los americanos," Abraham said.

"I worked on a chain gang before." Raulito leaned back against the wall; it was sticky with something he hoped wasn't blood.

"You're going to look back on that time like you was in heaven," Luis said.

Chico cried out.

"Tranquilo, muchacho." Abraham patted Chico's shoulder.

"There are four different kinds of prisoners in the Reef." Luis held up four fingers from a hand that was missing its thumb. "First kind—only the very lucky are this kind and they are always haoles—is in charge of the storeroom and the hospital and the cooks. These white men eat all the food they want and have real sugar in their coffee."

"Next kind takes care of the stables and horses, they eat second-class food and drink real coffee with real sugar, too," Miguel said.

"Gardeners, shoemakers, tailors, men like that, are the third kind," Abraham said. "Then there are the work gangs—the Makíkí and the Kamoilllli and the Normal School and the Waikiki gangs. These kinds don't eat so well and they don't get sugar with their coffee."

"What kind are the Puerto Ricans?" Raulito held his breath for the answer.

"We're the fucked kind," Luis said.

"No sugar for the Puerto Ricans," Miguel said.

"I can live without sugar," Raulito said, "but I wish I didn't have to."

"You won't get any wishes granted here," Abraham said.

"Judge Wilcox sends us to Captain Henry," Miguel said. "Captain Henry sends us to the Hot Box."

"We call it the Sweat Box," Luis said.

"Sweat Box, Hot Box, infierno," Miguel said.

"The Hot Box? I don't understand," Raulito said.

"You will," Abraham said.

"Is Captain Henry the governor?"

"The grand jailer," Abraham said.

"We call him Satan," Luis said.

"Because he likes to send Puerto Ricans to hell," Miguel said.

"Judge Wilcox hates Puerto Ricans more than murderers," Luis said.

"More than negros and Chinamen?" Raulito thought there was no one more hated than negros and Chinamen.

"More than negros and Chinamen," Abraham said. "Not even God can save you and me."

Raulito knew that nothing could be worse in Hawaii than to be un negro puertorriqueño.

In his office at the Reef, Judge Wilcox liked to say to High Sheriff Henry of Oahu, "Give me a Porto Rican and I'll make that boy sorry he ever been born."

Raulito was sentenced to three months' hard labor.

As Raulito was escorted out, High Sheriff Henry poured the judge a glass of his favorite pineapple juice concocted from the sweetest pineapples, sent to him specially by his pal Dole, the owner of the biggest pineapple plantation in all of Hawaii.

The Puerto Ricans squatted in the prison courtyard. They ate bread and drank foul-smelling liquid that was supposed to be black coffee. The guards prodded the prisoners with their rifles, forcing them down a dirt road. Sunlight streaked through the dark sky; soon it would be dawn. The wind sprayed flecks of rock on their skin and clothes. The perfume of this terrible place, this Oahu, took Raulito back to Puerto Rico, where, in the early morning fog of Cerro Morales, he listened as the tiny coquís croaked their last refrains. He'd never hear coquís again. Raulito wiped his eyes with the back of his hand. It was ridiculous to cry over frogs.

"Move it!" A guard's rifle jabbed Raulito's ribs.

The blast was like dynamite. Though they were still some distance away, they felt the earth shake. It reminded Raulito of the small earthquake after Hurricane San Ciriaco. Raulito tried not to piss on himself. When the wind blew, bits of stone fell through the foliage of the trees. When they reached the quarry, they saw a mountain broken open, revealing a world of stone the color of bones. The noise was like that of a small avalanche. They ducked the flying rocks.

"The Hot Box." Abraham pointed.

Smoke escaped from the monster's gaping mouth. A slab of stone the size of a train caboose dangled from its iron teeth.

The guards fed the Puerto Ricans into the monster, one by one. Sparks singed their hair, burning pinholes on their skin. The monster's jaws crushed slabs of stone, swallowing the rocks before spitting them down the chute. Inside the belly of the stone crusher, Raulito and the other men stuck out their bare hands to catch the hot rocks and toss them aside. Raulito screamed, but no one could hear him over the din, not even himself.

His hands stank like charred meat.

"You survived," Abraham said.

"Bet you wish you hadn't." Miguel's hands hung from his wrists like trowels.

Someone placed a tin bowl of slop in Raulito's hands. The bowl fell. The prisoner cook yelled at Raulito.

Raulito stared down at the unfamiliar things that dangled at his sides.

Abraham picked up the bowl and the prisoner cook spooned in some more slop.

"Don't try to guess what it is," Chico said. "It's better not to know."

"You! Porto Rican!" The guard pointed his rifle at Raulito. "Eat!"

"You're no good to them dead." Luis shoved brown mush into his mouth. "They'll make you eat even if you don't want to."

Raulito scooped up some slop with the thing that was once his hand.

Raulito slept on the floor with his hands on his chest like the dearly departed; he was dreaming.

The guards clanged their iron rods against the machine. Rocks tumbled down the chute faster than they could catch them.

"Stop the machine!"

"Too many rocks!"

"Stop the machine!"

"¡Ayuda! Help!"

The stones hailed down on the Puerto Ricans; they couldn't move, the stones trapped them up to the waist and still they didn't stop. The Puerto Ricans stretched out their arms toward the Hot Box opening, where they could see the guard's uniformed legs.

"Vicente! Marco! Save me!" Raulito shouted.

"Shut up, you bastard! *Shut up!*" Someone shook him.

Raulito opened his eyes.

"Sleep is the only time I can forget this hellhole, so shut the fuck up." Miguel's huge hand gripped Raulito's shoulder.

Raulito closed his eyes.

Marco, wait for me.

On Sundays, the prisoners didn't work the stone quarry because it was the Sabbath and the missionaries didn't think it godly. Instead, Raulito and his fellow portorros attended a religious service in the prison yard. He gave thanks for religion, because it allowed him to get out of his prison cell and sit in the sun. He knew nothing about religion; his mother had never spoken about God, only about los espíritus and dead relatives. He had never gone to church or opened a Bible. He knew the fog of Cerro Morales that crept in during the night, and the sun that warmed the mountain after the fog had left for the day. He knew the birds that twirled in the sky above the creatures that made la tierra their home. Raulito knew his mother's rare smiles and the sweetness of his brother's love, a sweetness he savored like the taste of sugar in his coffee. He knew that he hoped more than anything to make it out alive so one day he would see Marco again. Was that God? If so, his heart ached for God, ached like a hot stone buried inside him.

"These white people want to save our souls," Abraham said.

"What's a soul?"

"Your mother or father never talked to you about your alma?"

"I never really had a father," Raulito said. "Is it important?"

"Only as long as they keep talking," Abraham said.

The prisoners set up wooden benches around a massive banyan tree; its blooms perfumed the yard where six days a week, rain or shine, they sat on the cold, wet ground and ate their wind-dusted meals. During the Sunday service, the sun shone on the prison yard as if it were the plaza of Any Town, Puerto Rico. Men in black suits and ladies in hats and long gowns sat opposite the prisoners. Armed guards watched from sentry towers. The missionary waved a black book and talked on and on. Raulito didn't understand a single word, but he hoped the man in black talked all day long.

CHAPTER FIFTY-NINE

HEAVEN

The butterfly landed on her open palm and she made a house for it with her cupped hands. It was gold with iridescent blue stripes; the flutter of its wings tickled. She brought her hands to her lips and whispered the words she wished she could say to her little girl. *I hope what they say about heaven is true and that you are in a happy place with your brother. I hope that you know Sonia and that she can be a mother to you both. I love you. I miss you.*

Valentina opened her hands and set the butterfly free. She watched it fly away up in the sky until the yellow disappeared into the blue.

CHAPTER SIXTY

FUCK SHERIFF HENRY

Fuck the rain that turned dirt roads to mud and made people want roads paved with pieces of coral. Fuck the fucking inventor of the rock crusher! Fuck Judge Wilcox! Fuck Sheriff Henry! Yes, fuck Sheriff Henry, Captain Henry. High Sheriff Henry of Oahu, maldito Satan Henry! Fuck him for feeding Puerto Ricans into the Hot Box! Fuck Oahu! Fuck!

CHAPTER SIXTY-ONE

PAU HANA

They were back in Puerto Rico in their little wood house with the corrugated-iron roof. The rooster crowed in the batey and the birds sang. He lifted a strand of his wife's hair and pressed a kiss on her naked shoulder. Valentina could sleep until midmorning if he or the children didn't wake her. He decided to brew the coffee and bring her a cup before he went to the finca to check on his coffee trees. He stopped in the children's room to peek at his trio of little angels, tiptoeing so as not to wake them. In the kitchen, he took the lid off the large tin filled with his own coffee. He brought the tin to his nose and breathed in the greens of the mountain.

The morning siren shrieked over the plantation and into the hovels and broke into Vicente's dream.

Valentina wrapped the rice in tí leaves. She placed the rice and pasteles, also wrapped in tí leaves, on an enamel plate, draping a dishcloth over it. They walked with the children and Paco, who had come by for something to eat. It was a Sunday and the weather was fine. At the Japanese camp, they stopped to ask directions of a japonesa in a sky blue kimono.

"Con permiso, señora," Valentina said. "¿Dónde vive la señora Mikioki?"

La japonesa shook her head.

"This won't be easy," Vicente said.

They heard someone playing a ukulele.

"It's pretty, not the cuatro guitar, but pretty."

"Maybe I should learn to play el cuatro since you love it so much," Vicente said.

"Maybe you should," Valentina said.

They walked down the row of shanties.

"I'm sure we'll find her." Valentina walked on ahead.

"Can we play with them?" Lourdes pointed to a group of children who had gathered.

"I don't—" She stopped to consider.

"Let them," Vicente said.

"Paco, stay with las niñas," Valentina said.

"Maybe this wasn't such a good idea," Vicente said.

"Tú verás," Valentina said. "Everyone will come out."

Vicente smiled. "Are you saying that the Japanese are nosy like the Puerto Ricans?"

Together, they went down the row of shanties. Men and women came out and watched them without speaking; some bowed. Vicente and Valentina returned their bows.

"We'll never find your friend this way," Vicente said.

A man in a kimono walked toward them. He bowed, and behind him, Mikioki bowed, as did Valentina and Vicente.

"All this bowing," Vicente said in an aside. "Can't we just shake hands?"

"Buenos días, I would like to present my husband, Vicente." Valentina pointed to Vicente.

More bows.

"Akihiko." Mikioki pointed to her husband.

They held out their gifts of food. More bows. Akihiko pointed to a shanty. They sat down on bamboo mats and drank tea in tin cups and ate pasteles and rice in silence and smiles. Valentina wondered where she could get bamboo mats. Only after they were finished did Vicente and Valentina utter the word they had come to discuss, a word that contained their hope to make a better life.

"Huelga," Vicente said.

"Huelga," Valentina said.

Mikioki and her husband stared at them.

"Somehow we must overcome the problem of language," Valentina said.

Vicente took a piece of charcoal and a scrap of paper out of his pocket.

"You're brilliant!" Valentina smiled at him.

"I've been giving it some thought," Vicente said.

He drew stick figures in a row of cane; a large stick man on a horse loomed over them.

"Luna." He pointed to the man on the horse.

"Luna," Akihiko said.

"Trabajadores de la caña." Vicente pointed to the stick men. He wrote *Puerto Rican* and pointed to himself; he wrote *Japanese* and pointed to Mikioki's husband.

Akihiko bowed.

Vicente returned his bow, satisfied.

On the back of the paper, Vicente drew a new picture. Stick men walked away from the luna on horseback.

"Huelga," Vicente said.

"Huelga," Akihiko said.

A machete hung on the wattle wall. Vicente pointed to it, then shook his head.

"Huelga," Vicente said.

"Huelga," Akihiko said.

"No work," Valentina said. "Pau hana."

"Pau hana," Vicente said.

"Pau hana," Mikioki said.

"Pau hana," Akihiko said.

Akihiko said something to his wife, and she returned with a bottle and tiny porcelain cups.

"Saké." Akihiko offered Vicente a cup.

"Saké." Mikioki offered Valentina a cup.

They drank.

"It's alcohol." Vicente looked in the tiny cup.

"It's delicious." Valentina took another sip. "Ono."

Mikioki smiled and refilled her cup.

"I wish we had more paper." Vicente held up the drawing.

Akihiko spoke to his wife and she returned with parcel paper smoothed into a neat pile and tied with string. Akihiko began to draw dozens of figures clearly recognizable as Puerto Rican and Japanese men walking off a sugarcane field. He wrote words over the men in Japanese characters.

"Huelga." Akihiko pointed to the men, then to Vicente and himself.

"Pau hana," Vicente said.

They bowed.

"Now the hard part," Vicente said. "How to agree on demands."

"Draw the luna hitting a cane worker and then cross an X over it," Valentina said. "I'm sure they beat the Japanese, too."

Vicente drew a stick-figure luna hitting another stick figure and then he drew an X.

"Huelga," he said.

"Pau hana," Akihiko said.

Akihiko drew a little schoolhouse filled with children; some wore pava hats, and others kimonos.

"This might work," Vicente said.

They hurried to the Puerto Rican camp; the children had run on home to their hut. It was almost time for the 8 p.m. siren. But Vicente and Valentina didn't want to return to their hovel after their visit with Akihiko and Mikioki; they wanted to stop and enjoy the night. They wanted to walk to the pond and skinny-dip in the moonlight, to look up at the stars, which were as brilliant as on any night in Puerto Rico.

"Can you smell that?"

"What is it?"

"Plumeria." Valentina stopped at a bush covered with flowers. She plucked a bloom and held it up.

"They're so many different colors. This one is yellow with a pink center. Isn't it beautiful?" She tucked it in her hair.

"Beautiful." Vicente looked at her.

"Do you really think striking together will do any good, Vicente?"

"We have to try," Vicente said. "Pa'lante."

"Pa'lante." Valentina put her arms around his waist.

"Siguemos la lucha, pa'lante as we say. We keep going forward as we always have, am I right?" Vicente looked at his wife, still as pretty as the girl he'd met in Ponce.

The siren blared a warning.

"We'd better run." Valentina moved away.

"No."

"But the police—"

He took her hand. "We walk."

CHAPTER SIXTY-TWO

DREAMS

Lourdes and Mirta played hide-and-seek among the trees, their giggles rising to greet the moon. It was Saturday night, and the Puerto Ricans could stay up as long as they wanted without dreading the blare of the siren and the nightsticks of the police. They could choose to wake on Sunday when they pleased, just like in Puerto Rico—though that now seemed like a dream from long ago.

The strains of a ukulele came from the Japanese camp.

After a few minutes, Valentina said, "It's a strange sound, isn't it?"

"Nothing like the cuatro," Vicente said, smiling.

"But still nice," she said.

They called the girls and walked to the pond. It was their special place because it was their place—a little too far from the Puerto Rican camp, where there were streams closer by, and the Japanese had their own communal baths and their own favorite streams and rivers. Music and laughter were coming from the direction of the hut belonging to Dolores and Eugenio, whose turn it was to host the party. They'd join their friends later.

He remembered how on a night like this in Puerto Rico, on another island half a world away, he'd been talking to the bride, his cousin, and there she'd been, Valentina.

Now, they leaned against the trunk of a palm tree.

"I'll grow coffee again," Vicente said. "One day I'll have my own coffee farm again."

Vicente recalled the last time he had gone to his farm, how he'd sat on a tree stump taking in what once had been and was no more, how he'd promised himself that he'd return to his mountain and plant more trees and build another house for Valentina. His children would grow up on the mountain with Raulito's children and their children's children. Back then, he'd thought that would be possible.

Lourdes began to teach Mirta a song Valentina liked to sing to her when she was younger. "A la rorro niña, a la rorro ya, duérmase mi niña, duérmaseme ya—"

Valentina joined in. "Que los angelitos tu sueños velarán."

She covered her eyes with her hand. "Esa canción de cuna—"

"Querida." Vicente put his arm around her.

"Why do you think it happened to us? Twice?" Valentina leaned her head on his shoulder.

"I don't know," he said.

Vicente and Valentina settled on the ground, their backs against the tree trunk. They listened to their girls sing. He drew her into his lap, he reached under her dress.

Valentina protested, "The children—"

He removed his hand.

Valentina's hair brushed his cheek. "Vicente, what if we're cursed?"

"Querida, we're not cursed, we're blessed."

"You think so?" She wasn't sure.

Valentina rubbed her stomach. She wasn't ready to tell him. Not yet. Vicente would be so happy. He'd wanted another baby. And she thought she did, too, but she couldn't forget the ones she'd lost. The months after Evita died—and then Javiercito—she wasn't yet able to think about Javiercito, she had to be strong for Lourdes. And now there was Mirta, who needed her, too.

Valentina recalled one night in the little wood house Vicente had built—when los tiznados had surprised them. She had huddled with the sleeping children as she listened to Vicente shooting at the bandits, defending their home, their family. She'd bitten back her screams. But he'd come back to her and he'd taken her to bed. They'd made love, and afterward, she'd fallen asleep.

"Seguir la lucha," Vicente said. "That's all we can do."

"Pa'lante," Valentina said.

They listened to the little girls sing.

THE END

ACKNOWLEDGMENTS

As the daughter of Puerto Ricans who were taught little of their own country's history, I've been obsessed with learning about my heritage for years. One day, I stumbled upon the fact that over five thousand Puerto Ricans had gone to work on the sugar plantations of Hawaii after the US invasion and the San Ciriaco hurricane and never returned. It made me think of my father, who died in Chicago without ever achieving his dream of owning that little finca back on the island—the dream of so many who leave. What about the Puerto Ricans who had gone to Hawaii in the early 1900s? Did they have the same dreams to return? And so began my own journey to *The Taste of Sugar*.

I couldn't have written this novel without the work of the great Puerto Rican historians Fernando Picó and Carmelo Rosario Natal. Nor would I have known where to start without Norma Carr's *The Puerto Ricans in Hawaii, 1900–1958*. Years ago, I was fortunate to meet Norma in Honolulu while on a family vacation. She told me, "Write the story like a movie." And then there was Joan Hori, curator of the Hawaiian and Pacific Collection at the University of Hawai'i at Mānoa, who photocopied every single Hawaiian newspaper from 1900 to 1902 that had a mention of Puerto Rico or Puerto Ricans. Joan kindly mailed me all these copies for less than I should have paid. (This was before the newspapers were digitalized.) My research led me to anthropologist Iris López, who had interviewed the descendants of the Puerto Rican migrants. Iris, now mi comadre, inspired Raulito. "Give Vicente a brother," Iris said to me. "The plantations often separated families." I'm grateful to El Centro de Estudios Puertorriqueños in NYC, where I viewed nineteenth-century articles from Puerto Rican newspapers on microfilm.

I'm grateful also to the Eduardo Lozano Latin American Collection, Hillman Library, University of Pittsburgh, for allowing me to borrow books in both Spanish and English that I never thought I'd be able to hold in my hands.

My agent Betsy Amster encouraged me by her willingness to read draft after draft after draft even on planes when she couldn't look up Spanish words. She's always had my back. Un abrazote to the brilliant Cristina García. I attended Cristina's Las Dos Brujas Writers' Workshop in San Francisco thinking I had a finished novel and came out with her words guiding me to be braver, "We're not in this business to be loved, we're here to make a difference." Gina Iaquinta, my gifted editor at Liveright, helped me to keep my title of Revision Queen and to fulfill the vision I had for the novel. It wouldn't be what it is without Gina. I'll always be grateful to Gina and the Liveright team for their enthusiasm for my story.

Thank you to my first readers: my cheerleaders Larry Starzec, Lauren Jiles-Johnson, Jane Cavolina, and my children, Alyssa Vera Ramos and Wilfredo Ramos Jr. You make your mami very proud. Mi prima Elena Casaretto was my muse for Valentina's Elena. Gracias, prima. Gracias to Mercedes Suazo for helping me con español. All my love to my husband and partner, Wilfredo (Fred) Ramos, who was on this journey with me from the beginning, always encouraging me, paying the bills, never complaining about all the books I bought for research, believing as I did that Puerto Rico's past is relevant to its present and to its future. Pa'lante.

BIBLIOGRAPHY

In addition to the many newspaper articles about the time period, especially in Puerto Rican and Hawaiian newspapers and the *New York Times*, the following books and articles were helpful in the writing of *The Taste of Sugar*.

Aráez y Ferrando, Román. *Historia del ciclón del día de San Ciriaco.* San Juan, Puerto Rico: Imprenta Heraldo Española, 1905.

Schwartz, Stuart B. "The Hurricane of San Ciriaco: Disaster, Politics, and Society in Puerto Rico, 1899–1901." *Hispanic American Historical Review* 72, no. 3 (1992): 303–34.

Sources for the Study of Puerto Rican Migration, 1879–1930. History Task Force, Centro de Estudios Puertorriqueños, Hunter College, City University of New York, 1982.

The following books by Fernando Picó:

Amargo Café. Río Piedras, Puerto Rico: Ediciones Huracán, 1981.

Los irrespectuosos. Río Piedras, Puerto Rico: Ediciones Huracán, 2000.

Libertad y servidumbre en Puerto Rico del siglo XIX. Río Piedras, Puerto Rico: Ediciones Huracán, 1983.

Puerto Rico 1898: The War After the War. Princeton, NJ: Markus Wiener Publishers, 2014.

Puerto Rico, tierra adentro y mar afuera: Historia y cultura de los puertorruqeños. With Carmen Rivera Izcoa. Río Piedras, Puerto Rico: Ediciones Huracán, 1991.

The following books by Carmelo Rosarío Natal:

Éxodo puertorriqueño: Las emigraciones al Caribe y Hawaii, 1900–1915. San Juan, Puerto Rico: Carmelo Rosarío Natal, 1983.

Los pobres del 98 puertorriqueño: Lo que le pasó a la gente. San Juan, Puerto Rico: Producciones Históricas, 1998.

Puerto Rico y la crisis de la Guerra Hispanoamerica, 1895–1898. Hato Rey, Puerto Rico: Ramallo Brothers Printing, 1975.

El puertorriqueño dócil: Historia, pasión, y muerte de un mito. San Juan, Puerto Rico: 1987.

Carr, Norma. *The Puerto Ricans in Hawaii, 1900–1958.* PhD dissertation, University of Hawaii, 1989.

Carroll, Henry K. *Report on the Island of Porto Rico.* Washington, DC: Government Printing Office, 1899.

Davis, George W. *Report of the Military Governor of Porto Rico on Civil Affairs, 1899–1900.* Washington, DC: Government Printing Office, 1902.

Dinwiddie, William. *Puerto Rico: Its Conditions and Possibilities.* New York: Harper & Brothers, 1899.

Souza, Blase Camacho. Papers, 1989–2003. Archives of the Puerto Rican Diaspora, Centro de Estudios Puertorriqueños, Hunter College, City University of New York.

Takaki, Ronald. *Pau Hana: Plantation Life and Labor in Hawaii, 1835–1920.* Honolulu: University of Hawaii Press, 1983.

Wagenheim, Kal, and Olga Jiménez de Wagenheim, eds. *The Puerto Ricans: A Documentary History.* Princeton, NJ: Markus Wiener Publishers, 1999.